TEN SPOT

TEN SPOT

DENIS HAMILL

ATRIA BOOKS

New York • London • Toronto • Sydney

ATRIA BOOKS

1230 Avenue of the Americas
New York, NY 10020

ISBN: 0-671-02616-X

First Atria Books hardcover edition June 2005

10   9   8   7   6   5   4   3   2   1

ATRIA BOOKS is a trademark of Simon & Schuster, Inc.

Manufactured in the United States of America

For information regarding special discounts for bulk purchases,
please contact Simon & Schuster Special Sales at 1-800-456-6798
or business@simonandschuster.com.

With love to my brother Joe, last but certainly not least

BACK IN THE DAY . . .

June 24, Nine Years, Eleven Months, and Three Weeks Ago

Cookie Calhoun would've laughed at being late for her own murder.

She always joked that she wanted her epitaph to read, "A dollar short, an hour late, but I had a friggin' ball."

She had to be at the Music Box restaurant near the Brill Building in Manhattan to set up for the lunch rush by 11:30 a.m. And it was already 10:35. And she still had to put on her makeup. And get her six-year-old son Brian's bag packed for the babysitter.

She rushed from the kitchen after packing juice boxes and cereal bars and Hulk and Batman action figures into a bag and passed through the living room toward the one bathroom in the crowded, three-bedroom Bay Ridge tenement apartment.

"Where's my gahdamned lucky tie," asked Cookie's second husband, Rodney Calhoun, who stormed out of the master bedroom. "Can't go to the track without my gahdamned lucky Twin Towers tie."

"How the hell could it be lucky?" Cookie asked. "You wore it the last four times to the track and came home with a wallet flatter than Twiggy."

"Who's Twiggy?" asked Brian, who was named after Brian Jones of the Rolling Stones. His big blue eyes were a constant nagging sore spot in Cookie's marriage to a fifty-three-year-old black man who always questioned whether the child was even his.

"Twiggy was a famous model in the sixties," said Cookie.

"She must be old as the hills now," said Brian.

"Thanks," Cookie said. "She's only a few years older than me."

1

Rodney glared at Janis and said, "Someone's got it, I swear I'll strangle her with my gahdamned tie."

"Who you think you're threatening?" Cookie asked.

Rodney said, "Your brats'll be mooching here till they collect Sosh S'curity?"

"While you run from the bookies, my kids're chasin' a dream, Rodney."

"They tryin' to pass for black in the hip-hop world," said Rodney. "News flash: I was down with the hip-hop world since Kool DJ Herc boogied up from Kingston and Grandmaster Flash scratched his first side. I was there when hip-hop was shittin' yellow in the Bronx River projects, and I tell you these cracker kids wastin' they motherjumpin' time today in this battle with Iglew, who's gon' make them wish they was born slaves."

"Thanks for your support there, sport," said nineteen-year-old Janis, stepping out of the bathroom holding her mascara and applicator. Janis was named after Janis Joplin and was from Cookie's first marriage to Ray "Nails" McNulty, whom Cookie'd never really stopped loving, even after she'd busted him cheating, and the divorce, and her remarriage to Rodney, who'd had his act together back in the day.

"No black rappers still be living with they mama when they nineteen," said Rodney. "Or seventeen like that there." He nodded at Cookie's son Jimi Jim, named after Hendrix and Morrison, who paced the living-room floor rapping along with "Broke in Brooklyn," the demo tape he and his sister had made and that had gotten them the audition at Lethal Injection Records. "How you gon' keep it real in the music when you got it made in the shade like a house nigga at home?"

"Main reason I work this ass off is for my kids, *all* my kids, so I'll decide who lives here. And if anyone goes out that door on their ass, it might just be you, Rodney, because as long as this ass is paying the rent, my kids live with me. Word up."

All three kids broke up laughing.

"Who you think you're talking to, bitch?" Rodney said, moving toward Cookie.

Cookie stood her ground. "I warned you, Rodney, never again—"

"Leave Mom alone!" shouted Brian.

"Shut your trap, boy," Rodney said.

"Don't talk to my little brother like that," said Janis.

Rodney pushed Brian aside and bumped Cookie, raising his hand over his head. "Say one more word. Go ahead say something, bitch."

"Touch my moms and I'll crack your fuckin' skull, old man," said Jimi Jim, grabbing a plaster lamp off the end table.

Brian covered his ears and shouted, "Please stop! Please stop! Please stop!"

"You wouldn't *dare*, would you, Rodney," Cookie said. "Unless you want the whole world to know what I know about who and what you really are."

Rodney glared at her. "Don't be talking foolish—"

"I'll say whatever the hell I want, when I want, and—"

Rodney said, "Do yourself a favor. Stay home today. Do some motherin'. Take the day off, Cookie. Take the gahdamned day off."

"Since when do you give a damn?" she asked.

He opened his mouth to speak, but no words came out. Rodney snatched two twenty-dollar bills out of Cookie's handbag as he stormed out the door, sans tie.

"Take my advice: Stay home today. Mind the kid yourself!"

Rodney slammed the door behind him.

Two years before, Janis and Jimi had formed a rap act called Bigga Wiggaz, and this morning they were finalists pitted against a gangsta rapper name Iglew, real name Ignatius Lewis, from the Richmond projects in a rap battle to see who got to go on a worldwide tour to open for Baru, a Celtic hip-hop band that had a huge crossover white and black following and Lethal Injection's first top-ten rap album on *Billboard*.

"Hurry up, Janis, yo," screamed Jimi Jim, hiking his baggy Hilfiger jeans. He paced the living room, rapping, his body jerking, firing imaginary pistols at the floor, and bursting into a skillful break-dance. Brian rapped along with him, gyrating on the floor, trying to match his big brother's terrier-quick moves.

Cookie watched her two sons from two different men dance and rap in harmony:

Bin broke in da Bronx / Down with my last token / in Queens /
lost in Hoboken 'n' lean 'n' flat in Ma'ha'en /
But you don't know / how low / you can go / till you go
Broke in Brooklyn / no jokin' / not enuf for a smoke or a pig in a
poke . . .

Janis danced out of the bathroom, gold hoop earrings swaying, using a sizzling curling iron as a microphone, and rapping along with her recorded voice on the demo tape. Cookie beamed, her forty-one-year-old body moving to the music.

> While three blocks away / on eviction day / the landlord vents
> when we can't pay the last three months' rent / here in Bay Ridge /
> with no food in the fridge / ain't that a switch / ain't that a bitch . . .

Cookie sang into her hairbrush, boogying to her children's music.

> Makes you wanna pull the trigger / 'cause no matter how you figure /
> Maybe we ain't black, yellow, or zebra, / but we f'sho po' white wiggaz /
> in double-trouble / every day a struggle / Tryin' to juggle / the books /
> 'n' / broke in Brooklyn, yo . . .

And now the whole family joined in the final verse.

> But when the landlord say / you got to go / we always know /
> we always got each other / brothers / sistahs and muthuh /
> Can't take that away / come paydays or eviction day / or any day /
> and long's we got one another / even living in the gutter / no bread 'n'
> buttuh / We got more than most others / 'cause we might be broke
> but we'll never be broken in Brooklyn, yo.

Mrs. Donatella, the old lady from downstairs, banged on the ceiling of the Bay Ridge tenement apartment, as she did every day and night.

"Sorry I can't watch the kids for ya, Mama," said Janis.

"You crazy, Jan, I'm a nervous wreck worryin' about yuse," Cookie said, bumping her daughter sideways at the sink and grabbing Janis's mascara. "Just be *you*. And make sure Jimi Jim follows your lead, because you're better with ad-libs."

"Iglew, that nigga be good, Mama."

"Don't be using that word," Cookie said, looking at Janis in the mirror. "Your little brother is half-black."

"I didn't say *nigger*. I said *nigga*. Difference. I'm a wigga. Iglew's a nigga."

"But you're a betta rappa. I wish I could be there today, baby, but I'd be too damned nervous. And I'd give you guys the jimjams. Besides, I have to work. The phone gets turned off Tuesday if I don't make a partial payment by tomorrow."

"You're the best, Mama," Janis said, sharing Cookie's lipstick. "When we win this thing, and we go on tour and we get us a record deal, I'm gonna buy you a house. In *your* name. Paid in full. So no crazy lady downstairs can bang on the ceiling."

"She thinks she's God," Cookie said.

"And no more eviction notices, turn-off threats, or noise complaints."

"Buy the house for yourself, baby. I'll live in the basement. All I want is to see my kids happy. All I ever wanted."

Janis kissed her cheek and said, "What did you mean when you told Rodney that you knew something he didn't want the world to know? What's that noise?"

Cookie looked at Janis, biting her lower lip, as if she wanted to confide in her.

"It's better you don't know, baby doll. Just remember, every man you ever meet will never really be who you think he is. That's all you need to know."

"I hear that."

Cookie hurried into the living room. She wrapped her arms around Jimi Jim.

"Follow your sister's lead," she said, tapping Jimi Jim's temple. "Listen to the music in your head. Remember who you are and where you come from and be that person and empty your heart and soul. This is a once-in-a-lifetime chance, JJ."

"You made us chase the dream, Mom. So we're gonna win it for you."

"No, win it for *you*. Do that and I win, too."

Brian said, "And when I get big, I'll be in Bigga Wiggaz, right, Jimi Jim?"

"F'sho, squirt."

Janis strutted out of the bathroom, in skintight yellow pants, her hair tied up in Rodney's Twin Towers tie. Gorgeous.

Cookie gathered her kids for a silent Hail Mary, as they often did on days of major family matters. Then Cookie said, "Okay, go kick ass and take names."

Cookie grabbed her handbag and her work apron and nodded for Brian to follow and scrambled out the door. She hurried down two flights into the street with Brian and double-timed up Fort Hamilton Parkway from the rent-controlled tenement, the Bigga Wiggaz music pounding out the open windows into the humid early-summer street.

"I'm gonna call the cops on you marble-cake bastards," shouted Mrs. Donatella from the window. Cookie looked at the gray-haired woman and tapped her temple with her index finger, then upturned her middle finger and kept walking.

Cookie waited for a green walk sign at the corner and crossed busy four-lane, two-way Fort Hamilton Parkway toward the babysitter's tenement on the opposite side of the street. Halfway across the street, she heard a half-dollar coin that Janis had given Brian tinkle to the gutter.

"Damn," Brian said, turning to run after it.

"No," Cookie shouted. "Run to the other curb. I'll get it."

Brian dashed to the far curb as Cookie chased the rolling fifty-cent piece back into the middle of Fort Hamilton Parkway.

Then Cookie caught something yellow out of the corner of her left eye.

Coming at her.

Fast!

A streaking yellow blur. Rocketing her way.

Cookie screamed, "Brian!"

She saw that her son was safe on the sidewalk. Then the yellow blur grew into a mustard monster, building larger and more ferocious by the nanosecond, bearing down on her, the chrome grill of the van like a row of giant steel teeth, the headlights two savage silver eyes. The engine roared louder as the yellow blur became the sun itself barreling at her, and she did not hear a horn or a skid or the squeal of a brake and only heard the desperate scream of her son Brian: "Mommmmeeeeeyyyy!"

The pain of impact was ferocious, and then all she saw was a swatch of jagged blue sky, a mighty pylon of the Verrazano Bridge rising to the whipped-cream clouds, a little crimson river of her own blood rushing away from her on the hot, tarry gutter, and Brian rushing toward her and the disappearing yellow blur that sped even faster in departure, and then all Cookie heard was the final soft kicked-puppy's yelping of her son and the fading Bigga Wiggaz music and the muffled screams of neighbors and strangers, and then Cookie Calhoun did not see anything or hear anything else.

ONE

Monday, June 20, Nine Years, Eleven Months, and Three Weeks Later

Bobby Emmet stood on the deck of the *Fifth Amendment* moored in slip
99A at the Seventy-ninth Street Boat Basin in the Hudson River on Manhattan's Upper West Side, painting the rusting anchor chain with a fresh
coat of gray enamel. His younger brother Patrick, a lieutenant in the NYPD
Intelligence Division, was painting the railings, dressed in paint pants and
a PAL T-shirt. Both of then listened to Izzy Gleason give details of his latest adventure in his search for true love.

Plus, the rap music on Hot 97.1 FM played so loud from inside the
forty-two-foot fiberglass Silverton that Bobby was certain the bass line was
making the boat rock.

"So I'm at the courthouse this morning, waiting for Tu Bitz to be transferred in from Rikers for the trial, but there was an escape attempt by some
wacko last night so the whole place is in lockdown," Izzy said. "Everybody's in the courtroom—press, Iglew and his posse, cops, the Feds—
everybody waiting for the defendant. So I'm standing there in the
courtroom killing time till the judge declares a scratch on the morning pro-
ceedings. Then the whole courtroom comes to a screeching silence when
in walks this possible client for *you,* Bobby, which means she's half mine,
because she emailed me about hiring you. All the homeys recognized her
off the bat. But who the hell knows what the real skinny is when a broad
comes at ya over the Web, because personally I got worse luck with internet broads than Helen Keller had with fuckin' eye charts."

Izzy screwed the cap off a fresh Bud and Frisbeed the cap overboard

7

into the river, the suds from the beer dotting his gray, $2,000 Brooks Brothers suit.

Patrick walked into the salon laughing, grabbed a suit hanging in a dry-cleaner wrapper, and looked downriver where he saw an NYPD harbor patrol chugging into view.

"Come on, I might be married eight years, but I'm not dead," Patrick said. "What about this broad who contacted you online? Hurry. I need a few laughs and thrills before I go save what's left of Western civilization."

"Matter fact," Izzy said, "my last broad, Francisca Diaz, contacts me through that website Maggie set up for me, and she shows up and says she has a few minor legal details she might need some help with down the road, but the real reason she wants to meet me is because she seen me on TV in the Chinaman case and thinks I'm cute."

"You sure it wasn't Helen Keller?" Patrick asked.

Bobby said, "Tell me about this client who wants to hire me. Who and what and—"

"First, I gotta tell ya about this Francisca broad, who I arranged to come to meet me," Izzy said. "I'm a real swell guy like that with broads who say I'm cute. But I'm gettin' slick in my old age. I tell her to meet me at the outdoor café up the block from here, at Northwest—"

"The one on Columbus and Seventy-ninth, across the street from the Museum of Natural History?" Bobby asked. "Love the food."

"Great joint, but the best thing on the menu is the poonie parade that marches by the outdoor café every day," Izzy said, grimacing down his first gulp of beer of the day. It was 10:46 a.m. "So, I call the owner, Matthew, a real sweetheart, and I tell him to make me a reso at the table closest to Seventy-ninth. I tell this Francisca to arrive at noon."

Izzy slurped more beer and pulled a small pair of binoculars from his jacket pocket.

"This here way I can stand across the street with these binocs I got from a Peeping Tom I defended," Izzy said. "And eye-tap this broad when the hostess leads her to the table. To make sure she ain't a bison with an ass you can see from the front like the last website honey I met. That one emailed me a hot thong-bikini shot, but when she showed up in my room at the Chelsea Hotel, I needed a fuckin' piano mover with a dolly to get her back out the door. But when this Francisca Diaz shows up at Northwest, she's a sizzlin' hot Rican, ass like a Greek statue. We ordered drinks, she went to the ladies' room, came back, handed me her panties under the table, told me I was the kind of man a woman would want to marry on first sight. She asked me to take her to my place. This only happens in porno movies. But once we get back to the Chelsea, all she wants to do is dunk for apples. Capice?"

A rap song ended and a broadcaster gave a news update, focusing on a big hip-hop promoter and owner of Lethal Injection Records named Ignatius "Iglew" Lewis who was lobbying the governor to repeal the infamous Rockefeller drug laws under which some people were doing twenty-five years of hard time for possession of as little as an ounce of cocaine. This was a hot-button issue in the gubernatorial race between the incumbent governor, Luke Patterson, and his Republican opponent, Agnes Hardy, a billionairess widow.

An interview with Iglew blared from the radio. "These laws are draconian and from another century," said Iglew, who many law enforcement people believed had made his seed money from drugs and was now the CEO of Lethal Injection Records. "Seventy-five percent of the inmates doing time in New York penitentiaries under these laws are black brothers and sistahs . . ."

Bobby half listened. He didn't like this guy Iglew, but he agreed with a lot of what he had to say about the Rockefeller laws. They were outdated and cruel and unusually harsh, oftentimes making low-level users and dealers pay for a lifetime for the sins of their reckless youth. When he'd worked as a detective for the Manhattan District Attorney's Office, Bobby was often conflicted about busting young black kids who would be sent to jail until their lives were half over under those mandatory sentences.

The sound bite ended, the announcer gave some ball scores, and a new rap song exploded from the speakers.

"Are you fucking listening to me about this broad?" Izzy asked.

"I know the music is louder than an air raid, but talk lower," Bobby said. "My daughter's downstairs and one of your stories could land her in therapy. And, I'm not interested in your sex life, Izzy. In fact, I can't think of anything I'm less interested in. So keep your voice down and tell me about the new client."

"No, c'mon, tell me about this *Francisca* babe," Patrick said.

"So, anyways, every time over the next three days I tried to get in Francisca's pants, she either had her period or some kinda women's problem and—"

"Stop! Way too much information, Izzy," Bobby shouted.

"Skip to the good parts," Patrick said as the police boat chugged close to the *Fifth Amendment*.

"No, tell me about the goddamned client," Bobby said.

"I mean, Francisca was gorgeous, but she never let me get to second base," Izzy said to Patrick. "I finally found out why when she got pulled over doing ninety by a state trooper on the Taconic."

"Caught in the act?" Patrick asked, a smile splitting his Irish boyish face.

"Best I ever had," Izzy said, emptying three Sweet'n Lows into his beer bottle.

"The hell you doing?" Bobby asked, watching the foam rush up.

Izzy put his mouth over the bottle and the foam puffed his cheeks until his lips exploded. He choked, did a little puppet's dance, the beer sloshing all over the deck and his expensive suit. Bobby jumped back three feet as Izzy gulped the beer.

"You ruined the suit, asshole," Bobby said.

Patrick laughed. "He does a regular floor show."

"Fuck it, it'll keep the chinks who run all the French dry cleaners busy in the economic recovery," Izzy said. "It's the patriotic thing to do, spreadin' the hip-hop cash around. Speaking of French dry cleaners, you ever see anyone but a Yid or a Chinaman run a New York French dry cleaner in your whole life? Never once, not one fuckin' time, did I ever find an off-the-boat frog runnin' French dry cleaners."

Bobby looked at him, blinked, and said, "Okay, I know why you don't work for the ACLU. But all this has *what* to do with *my* potential client?"

"Francisca, first," Patrick said. "Tell me about Francisca!"

"And what's with the three Sweet'n Lows you just used to poison a perfectly good bottle of Bud?" Bobby asked.

"Oh, that, well, my doctor told me to slow down on the sweets."

The rap music blared louder from below. Bobby shouted inside, "Maggie, for God's sake, can you turn that knucklehead music down?"

"Yo, that's Slim Shady, old man," Maggie yelled back, appearing at the door, wearing shorts, sneakers, and rubber gloves, holding a sponge and a bucket, her hair in a babushka, smiling at Bobby with a perfect row of front teeth since the teenage braces had been removed. She would be sixteen in two months and she was already a young woman and starting to look the way her mother had when Bobby and half the world had fallen in love with Connie Matthews. *God, already divorced eight years . . .*

Eminem was rapping about owning the music, and how it was time to seize the moment, because it was a chance of a lifetime. Bobby didn't want to admit that the lyrics were actually pretty damned good. *Christ,* Bobby thought, *writers like National Book Award winner Stephen King sang his praises. Nobel Prize–winning Irish poet Seamus Heaney said there was no gainsaying Eminem's raw energy.*

But the steady thump of the bass was pounding Bobby Emmet's late-thirties head like a Roy Jones Jr. ass-kicking.

"It sounds like jail when they suspend visits," Bobby said, referring to the eighteen months he'd spent in the penitentiary several years ago, before this pain-in-the-ass lawyer named Izzy Gleason came along, sprung him, and as repayment placed Bobby into a kind of indentured servitude. Izzy had been suspended from the bar for three years for a host of reasons, most having to do with his outrageous behavior in the courtroom. On his come-back trail, Izzy who was 39-0 in murder trials, had visited Bobby in jail and told the penniless ex-cop who was doing life for a murder he didn't commit that he could win him a new trial. That would give Izzy a ton of badly needed publicity and Bobby a chance to investigate his own case and exonerate himself of the charge of killing his girlfriend.

In exchange, Bobby had agreed to do the investigative work on any of Izzy Gleason's cases for three years. Along the way, the time frame became extended because of new legal favors for old friends. None of it was legally ironclad, of course, but Bobby Emmet prided himself as a man of his word.

These days, Izzy had been defending clients from the hip-hop world, especially since a column that Bobby's old pal Max Roth from the New York *Daily News* had written about him was reprinted without permission as a cover story on a hip-hop monthly called *Felony Magazine.* Roth had no doubt that Izzy had been behind that little scam.

Bobby had sleuthed a couple of those cases for Izzy, helping to get some big-name guys from Queensbridge and the Marcy projects off attempted-murder charges and various garden-variety gun, assault, and drug raps. Bobby detested helping some of them, but ever since he'd been falsely arrested for murder, he always gave everyone the presumption of innocence. Turned out that three of the seven cases he'd worked in the hip-hop world had had something dirty about the arrests.

Bobby'd had minor run-ins with a special NYPD/FBI task force that had been set up to monitor crime in the hip-hop world. The FBI guy was a ruthless white man named Tom Noonan, whom some of the rappers had even written verses about. He'd worked on all the big cases, Tupac, Biggie, Jam Master J, and aided in the arrests or investigations of Supreme McGriff, Puffy Combs, Lil' Kim, 50 Cent, Eminem. Noonan's FBI underling on the task force was a short, natty agent named Lou Scarano, and their NYPD liaison was Detective Sergeant Samantha Savage, whom Bobby had never met. But he'd got a few terse phone calls from her on some of the Izzy Gleason cases, warning him that he was being closely monitored and that his private-detective license could be in jeopardy if he compromised any of the task force's delicate investigations.

Bobby hung up and went about his business, motivated now while investigating the cases for Izzy in the Howard, Marcy, Red Hook, and Richmond projects. He stepped on as many toes as he could find in the hip-hop scene, ganstas, promoters, singers, agents, club owners, bodyguards, bimbos, posse members, record-label moguls, and cops.

Bobby hated rap and the hip-hop world, hated the glorification of violence and materialism, and subliterates who misspelled their own names in jailhouse tattoos walking around calling themselves "writers." He also hated that his daughter loved the music and the fashion and the purpose-fully subliterate lingo and misogynist videos and the mindless hard-R movies. Hated the moguls who managed by fear and lived by the gun. Hated the whole scene. But a deal was a deal, and so he worked for Izzy to repay him for his freedom, and in the end he helped protect a few hardly innocent but not-guilty rappers from doing time. That gave him some inner peace. And almost made his pact with Izzy bearable. He also knew he was giving this snobby, nasty bitch named Samantha Savage fits, messing up her cases. That gave him some payback satisfaction.

Max Roth from the *Daily News* wrote about a few of the cases, because they were good stories, and because he wanted to help get Bobby some other gigs so that he could eventually get away from the reprehensible Izzy Gleason.

In general, Bobby and Izzy had nothing in common except for a mutual need for oxygen and water to sustain life, but somewhere deep inside, Bobby liked Izzy. Izzy was a self-destructive guy who pined for his kids, who still resented him for screwing up his family and his life, getting suspended from the bar for a long time, and who really was searching for love as he spent half his life trying to con women into bed only to have the tables turned on him.

Izzy said, "So, where was I?"

"Three Sweet'n Lows into a Bud," Bobby said. "On your long voyage around the horn to tell me about our potential paying client. Which I could use."

"Francisca!" Patrick said as the police boat cut its engine.

"Oh, yeah," Izzy said. "So, anyways, here I am on the Taconic, Francisca's driving the Lexus, which is an automatic, and playing with *my* gearshift as she floors the car on that highway that has more twists and turns than two snakes fucking, and the trooper pulls us over. I'm trying to get my zipper up when the cop walks up, wearing the big Smokey the Asshole hat, askin' for the license and reg-o. Francisca gives them to him. He looks at it, gapes at Francisca, then glares in at me like I'm some kind of flesh-eating Nicaraguan fungus. He goose-steps back to the trooper car, runs the license. Ten minutes later he walks back, hand on his gun, and says to Francisca, 'Would you please step out of the car for a sobriety test *Mister* Diaz.' Right away, when he calls her *mister,* my balls retract so far I'm gaggin' on three fuckin' Adam's apples."

"She was a guy?" Patrick said, war-whooping.

"When Francisca gets outta the car, the trooper handcuffs her," Izzy said. "Turns out, Francisca's real name is Francisco, and this little fagarican has warrants out for bigamy and nonsupport on four kids from three wives as *Francisco.* He also married three rich old *guys,* as *Francisca.* And the Lexus is stolen from one of the husbands. He's a bilingual, bisexual, bigamist car thief with four screamers. And then Francisco has the balls, and I do mean *balls,* to ask *me* to defend him! 'For old times' sake!' Old times! I know this switch-hittin' bone smuggler three dirty days and he's asking me to do a pro boner. Meanwhile, I just had the best knobjob I ever had from a broad named Francisco, not knowing if I'm a home wrecker or a ho-mo."

Patrick laughed as a cop tossed him a rope, and he pulled the police boat alongside. "What I love about Izzy stories is how glad I am to be married and living a boring family life," Patrick said.

"And your point is *what,* Izzy?" Bobby said.

Izzy pulled three carob bars from his inside jacket pocket, tore off the wrappers and tossed them into the river, and stuffed one bar into his mouth.

"Hey, slobbo, it took twenty years to clean the Hudson," Bobby said.

"And the boat's in my name, so if I wanna litter from my boat, it's my ticket," Izzy said. "Besides, maybe it'll wash up in Jersey where my license is still suspended."

The boat was the only thing the judge had let Izzy keep in his divorce settlement. Bobby paid the city's Department of Parks just $438 a month to moor it in the boat basin, and with rents on two-bedroom apartments in Manhattan starting at $3,500 a month, and the PI business suffering like most others since 9/11, he was in no position to bicker with Izzy. Bobby also had access to Izzy's office in the basement of the Empire State Building and the six-year-old Jeep Cherokee that he had parked up in the garage. It wasn't really a bad deal, especially since Izzy gave him 10 percent of his fees. Besides, Bobby had grown kind of fond of living on the *Fifth Amendment*. Maggie loved it when she visited him every other weekend, especially in the summer months.

"I'm atta here," Patrick said, shaking Bobby's hand and boarding the police launch. "Let me know if you need help on any of your new cases, Bobby."

Bobby turned to Izzy and said, "So, what about this client?"

"What client?"

"The one you've been threatening to tell me about," Bobby said.

Maggie climbed up on deck, waved good-bye to her uncle Patrick.

"Oh, right, broad's name is McNulty," Izzy said. "When she walked into the courtroom, every rapper in the place knew who she was."

"McNulty?" Bobby said with a twinge in his chest and a rumble in his gut. He remembered one of the most indelible interludes of his life with an older woman named Cookie McNulty right after he'd first separated from Maggie's mother, Connie, about ten years ago. Just a onetime fling with a woman who, like him, was in the middle of a painful separation from a spouse, searching for companionship on a rainy school day after they'd both dropped their kids, who had puppy-love crushes on each other, at school. Bobby had offered to share his umbrella with Cookie, which led him to walk her home, where she invited him up for coffee. They laughed about their kids being sweet on each other while they were both suffering from marital wars. Two coffees led to a pair of beers, one laugh found another, a pat on his hand led to a kiss on her lips and then another, until they landed in bed where they did everything they could think of all day long as rain nibbled the windows and Bob Dylan played on the stereo, until it was time to go back and pick up their kids.

They didn't make a second date.

Bobby'd got back together with Connie after a few months. Then it ended in divorce a year after that. He'd heard Cookie had got back together with her second husband, even though she'd suspected he was cheating with groupies in the hip-hop music world. She wanted a father in her son's life. It was the penance a middle-aged woman paid for the sin of choosing the wrong guy.

Izzy said, "Yeah, McNulty. She contacted me because she read about me in the *News* and then in *Felony* magazine. But it was your name she was most interested in."

Dread filled him. But he tried to mask it. *"My* name? She know *me?"*

"I knew some McNultys when I was a kid going to school in Bay Ridge," Maggie said.

"You did?" Bobby was playing dumb.

"You remember, the gorgeous kid I had the crush on was named Brian Calhoun. His sister and brother's name was McNulty from the first marriage."

"Brian Calhoun? The one Mom freaked out about?"

"Yeah, because he was half black. Brian Calhoun, mmmmm . . ."

Izzy said, "Growing up, my hero was Algonquin J. Calhoun, the attorney on *Amos 'n' Andy,* no relation to Haystacks Calhoun, who once wrestled four midgets at once."

"I vaguely remember, Mag," Bobby said, knowing exactly whom she was talking about. Guilt rose in him like rusty steam.

"C'mon, daddio, you getting AARP moments already?" Maggie said. "The mother was remarried. Her first husband was named McNulty, nicknamed Nails. She had two kids with him. Janis and Jimi Jim were white rappers. Then she remarried, this time to a black guy named Calhoun, who was in the rap business. You've hated rap music that long, old white man. She had a kid with him, Brian."

He couldn't fake it anymore. "The hit-and-run? That McNulty? The one where the mother was killed in front of her son on Fort Hamilton Parkway and Ninety-second Street?"

"That's the one," said Izzy, waving to a woman and a teenage boy waiting on the rotunda overlooking the boat basin. "Ten years ago next week. And she wants to talk to you about that case that's as cold as an Eskimo's balls by now but—"

"Izzy, don't talk like that in front of my daughter."

"Chill, Pop, I'll survive," Maggie said, swiping the binoculars from Izzy and spying the woman and the teenage boy walking down the steps. They passed through the gate held open by Doug, the dockmaster who managed the marina for the City Department of Parks, and walked down the floating walkway toward slip 99A.

"Oh, my frigging God!" Maggie shouted. "Izzy, you creep, you didn't tell me Brian *Gorgeous* Calhoun was coming here! I look like the Wicked Witch of the West! And you have my first heartthrob hottie from back in the day coming on board!"

Maggie raced down into the cabin to fix herself up as Bobby eyed Janis McNulty walking toward the *Fifth Amendment* in cutoff, low-rise jeans, flip-flops, and a belly shirt revealing a rippling egg carton of tanned muscles flexing around a diamond-pierced navel that ignited in the morning sun.

Brian Calhoun, her younger stepbrother, strode a step behind, with an awkward hitch in his step. His short, nappy hair, chiseled features, and blue eyes in the handsome mocha face making him look like a teenage Derek Jeter.

Bobby was blinded by another reflection, this one twinkling from the rotunda. Like a mirror stunning his eyes. He shielded his eyes and peered up at a black SUV, a Navigator, brand-new and gleaming, windows as dark as the soul of a hit man. The driver's window was opened about four inches. A long lens jabbed out and the sun reflected off it like the SOS light of a ship at sea. Bobby couldn't tell what the driver looked like. And the car was parked broadside, so he couldn't see a plate number.

By reflex he took out his Sanyo 8100 cell phone/digital camera that had taken Maggie a full day to teach Bobby to use. He flipped it open, pretended to dial a number, but instead pressed the camera icon on the tiny keyboard, selected "Camera" on the menu stack, and clicked the camera icon again. A recorded voice said, "Say cheeeese!" An image of the Navigator freeze-framed on Bobby's little screen. He then selected "share" on the menu and sent the photo directly to his daughter Maggie's phone, where she could download the digital image later on her computer and clarify it with the same digital enhancement software NASA used on images from space. Maggie had bought the software for him for Christmas from his buddy Leonard, who ran the Snoop Shop surveillance-gadgetry store on Twenty-third Street.

The little camera was a great piece of technology, but it didn't have a zoom function.

"Izzy, where're those binoculars?"

"Maggie swiped 'em. I know I wanna closer look at the wrinkles around her zipper myself."

Bobby's eyes shifted to Janis, who paused on the floating walkway and turned to her kid brother Brian. Izzy walked up to Bobby and whispered in his ear, "That ass makes J. Lo's look like mine, don't it? Think: Goldie Hawn, at twenty-nine, bent over an ottoman, searching for a contact lens in a silver shag rug. Bobby, I don't care what she can afford, you gotta take this case just on her heroic heinie alone."

"Izzy, if you don't shut up, we're talking about you going overboard with your front teeth rattling out of *your* ass."

Bobby also remembered Janis McNulty now. Most times Cookie took little Brian to and from school. But sometimes, when Cookie couldn't make it, Janis picked up her kid brother from PS 231 in Bay Ridge in those days when Bobby was still married to Connie Matthews and living in a brownstone. Bobby had insisted that Maggie go to a public school so she would get a real education, in a multicultural setting that reflected the real New York. It was one of the first chasms in the marriage. Connie wanted to limo her to Dalton in Manhattan every day.

Bobby recalled that the hit-and-run made headline news for one day, moved back to page sixteen for the funeral, then disappeared into the yellowed clip file like the vague "yellow van" after a week. He was still a Manhattan DA detective then. The killing was in Brooklyn so he never worked the case. But it bothered Bobby because he'd spent that one glorious rainy school day with Cookie Calhoun, when they both just needed someone to hold on to, to tell each other that they were still desirable and full of life and hope. One encounter, but the sweet memory lasted a lifetime. He'd never told anyone about it. She'd told him her lips would always be sealed, too. And when Cookie died, Bobby felt as if he'd swallowed a slow-acting poison, because it made him sick for days, weeks, and months afterward. But after a few years, he chose to forget the death and remember the rainy day of guiltless indulgence with a beautiful older woman who exploded with life, rather than the day Cookie Calhoun met such a senseless end.

Cookie was a hit-and-run vic, nothing more sinister than that. Probably just a reckless drunk who'd crossed her path at the wrong bleary time. One of those motiveless killings that was essentially unsolvable unless some new piece of information arose from the anonymous murk.

Bobby remembered Maggie crying her eyes out at the time because the victim was the mother of the boy she had her first crush on at school. Bobby chose not to go to the wake, but stood in the back of St. Patrick's Church at the requiem Mass.

Bobby also recalled the mother from a couple of PTA meetings, a beautiful, sassy, funny, smart, age-defying hippie chick who was in every aspect of her kids' lives. She always bragged about her two oldest kids, who rapped in the tradition of House of Pain and Baru, a brother/sister act who dazzled the Bay Ridge club scene and looked as if they might catch a break in the big time before the accident smashed the family.

He especially remembered the daughter, because she was the image of her mother, but twenty years younger and even prettier. Gorgeous.

Bobby was married then, but he remembered doing a few double takes when Janis McNulty showed up in her tight jeans.

And now here she was, almost ten years older, not an ounce heavier, and if anything, even prettier on the verge of thirty, all-girl and all-woman at the same time in those low-rise shorts and small, oval shades, her long blond hair billowing in the river wind. She looked so much like her mother that an eerie involuntary shiver ran through him. He rubbed the graveled skin of his muscular arms. Janis walked up the plank to the *Fifth Amendment* with a small brown paper bag clenched in her left hand. The glint from the rotunda continued, but he could not take his eyes off Janis. He looked for a wedding ring on her left ring finger, but it was the only one of her fingers that was bare, like an open invitation.

Brian followed a few steps behind, his hands jammed into his back pockets.

"C'mon B, bend a knee," she said, head-locking him with her toned right arm.

Izzy leaned to Bobby's ear and said, "In Macy's window, in front of my dying mother."

Bobby elbowed him in the ribs. Izzy howled.

Janis paid no attention, walked up to Bobby, removed her shades, and looked him in the eyes. She smelled like scented soap and girlie creams and herbal shampoo, and heat radiated off her like an engine. But she didn't sweat. She hung her shades on the rim of her low-cut blouse, dangling them in the cleavage of her braless breasts.

"Hi, I'm Bobby Emmet," he said, extending his hand.

Janis placed the paper bag in Bobby's hand and gripped her other hand over it, still staring into Bobby's eyes. Her hands were small and soft and strong as C-clamps.

"I remember you, Bobby. Remember you well. I'm Janis McNulty."

"I remember you, too," Bobby said.

Brian stood back near the entrance to the boat, gazing out at the river in a shy and detached way, as gulls pedaled the wind downtown like late commuters. Janis kept her hands on Bobby's hands with the paper bag in between. Then she leaned in and spoke closer to his ear, close enough for him to feel her hot breath on his skin and to smell her subtle perfume. He was certain it was the same perfume her mother had worn when she'd worn nothing else that rainy afternoon. . . .

"That's twenty-five thousand dollars," Janis said. "Cash. I want to hire you to find out who killed my mother almost ten years ago. And I need you to do it fast."

T W O

When Maggie stepped out onto the deck of the *Fifth Amendment,* she'd put on fresh makeup, lipstick, and hoop earrings, her long blond hair now hung down to her shoulders, and she'd changed into a Brooklyn Cyclones T-shirt that was two sizes too small and knotted at the sternum to reveal her tanned, flat belly. She looked Brian Calhoun in his pale blue eyes and said, "Yo, Bri . . ."

" 'Sup, Mag?"

"Long time."

"Yeah."

"Lookin' good."

"Ditto."

She nodded toward the door to the cabin. Brian shrugged, nodded shyly, and with his hands still in his back pockets followed Maggie inside the *Fifth Amendment,* where Jay Z rapped trash, boasting that he'd slept with rival rapper Ja Rule's child's mother.

"Real sweet modern love song," Bobby said, watching his daughter disappear inside with the grim-faced kid he hadn't seen in a decade.

"Jay Z's slammin', but we're gonna bury him, too," Janis said, doing a little wiggle of the hips and shoulders.

"Hey, will you do that on my back," Izzy asked. "In stiletto heels?"

Janis pointed at him, looked at Bobby in mock shock, and broke up laughing.

"He talk like that in court?"

"Worse," Bobby said, pulling up a deck chair for Janis as Izzy yanked a pair of cold, wet Buds out of the cooler. Janis grabbed one and Izzy popped the other. He took out his Sweet'n Lows and Bobby waved a finger, telling him no. Izzy shrugged, grabbed a paper cup, and mixed the beer with diet Coke and took a deep gulp.

"First of all," Bobby said. "I can't take twenty-five thousand up front—"

"Don't mind him, he's just an asshole," Izzy said, grabbing the paper bag. "What he means is, I'll take it and give him his cut."

Bobby glared at Izzy and pointed to the bag and then Janis. No words.

"Half now?" Izzy said. "Half on results?"

Bobby shook his head. Izzy tossed Janis the bag.

"Like I said, an asshole," Izzy said.

"You don't want the gig?" she said. "The yellow pages are filled with PIs."

"Yeah, and they all stand for 'pathetic imbeciles,' " Izzy said. "Bobby's the best."

"That's why I'm here," Janis said. "I know some of those people you both helped walk out of court. I want you to help me. And it has to be fast. In five days."

"No problem," Izzy said. "Half down, if we don't get results by then, I'll show you how you can write most of it off on your taxes by saying you rented this boat."

Janis laughed as she watched Izzy open a bag of sugarless peanut butter cookies and eat one after the other and wash them down with his Bud/diet Coke, his body jerking left and right, always in motion, as if he'd swallowed a roller coaster.

"I'd like to use you in a video," she said. "Love to see you rappin' . . ."

"Why do you need results so fast?" Bobby asked. "You can't expect to solve a ten-year-old cold case in less than a week."

"Well, main reason is because the anniversary of my mother's death comes up in less than a week, on the twenty-fourth."

"It would be nice to solve it by then, but . . ."

She reached into her shoulder handbag and pulled out a bunch of diaries, chose the one she was looking for, then turned to a specific page.

"My brother Brian hasn't been the same since that day," she said. "I raised him after that. His old man fell apart after Mom died. He's an Alzheimer's basket case now. He was a loser anyway, would've only screwed the kid's head up more than it was already. We never could afford to leave that rent-controlled apartment in Bay Ridge, and he was in school out there. So that's where I raised him. He's been in and out of therapy ever since. School counselors, shrinks, Ritalin, Prozac, orphans groups, the whole bit. He's had more doctors than friends. He's a terrific kid. Never in trouble. But since that day of the hit-and-run, he's suffered from ferocious survivor's guilt, compounded by what they say is acute obsessive-compulsive disorder. He still has the JFK half-dollar I gave him that day. But he believes that if my mom hadn't chased after it after he dropped it, she would never have gotten hit by the yellow van. It's crazy, I know. But people bent on suicide are generally a little crazed."

"Sad story," Bobby said. "Heartbreaking. But what does it have to do with solving the case before the tenth anniversary of your mother's hit-and-run?"

Janis held up the diary, glanced at the cabin door, leaned in closer to Bobby, and said, "The shrink told me I should monitor his diary. To see what he's thinking privately. He has multiple passages in the last month saying that if it's still unsolved by then, he's gonna off himself on the tenth anniversary of Mama's death." She opened the diary, turned to a specific page, and read a passage aloud. " 'If we cannot bring you justice by your tenth anniversary, I'll admit that whoever did this has won. If I can't beat them, I'll join you. You are where you are because of me anyway.' "

Izzy said, "Jesus, lady, maybe you better just give us a twenty-five percent down payment and lay the rest on a gang of shrinks and a padded room."

"Shut the hell up, Izzy," Bobby said.

"No, it's cool," Janis said. "He's half-right. I do need to keep him under watch. But I refuse to put him back in a nuthouse. Tried that once; he came home beat-up and worse. Never again. But these days all he does is read heavy stuff like *The Lovely Bones* or the *Virgin Suicides*. He even read Camus's *Myth of Sisyphus*. Spends hours downloading tons of stuff from the internet on teen suicides. Goes on and on about Dr. Kevorkian until I wanna kill myself! Look, I can chain him to a radiator, put him in a padded cell, and keep him with me every minute of every day. But it only takes one minute, one razor on the wrists in a warm bath, one leap out the window, or a handful of goofballs and I could lose him. I can't let that happen. The only way to save my little brother from himself is letting him know he isn't responsible for my mother's death."

Janis explained that she and her brother Jimi Jim hadn't been able to go to the rap battle that June morning ten years ago. And that changed everything. The other rapper, Iglew, got the gig opening for Baru, and by the end of the world tour Defz Do' was a huge hit in its own right, with a three-record contract for Lethal Injection, and a sold-out concert tour of its own after the first album went platinum. Today, Iglew was a solo act and had his own label, a three-hundred-million-dollar-a-year hip-hop clothing line, movie deals, and a string of clubs in all the big East Coast cities.

Meanwhile, Janis and Jimi Jim went into debt paying to bury their mother, watched the stepfather have a nervous breakdown, suffer a stroke, and then be hospitalized for early-onset Alzheimer's and placed in a nursing home. Brian received about $800 a month from Social Security until he reached eighteen.

Bigga Wiggaz became defunct. To survive, Janis opened a hip-hop memorabilia shop and Jimi Jim designed album covers. They struggled to keep their noses above water. But they remained together, as a family.

Janis became a surrogate mom for Brian; and they fought to keep him out of the foster system. Then they had to raise him through the difficult years of trauma, puberty, high school.

Then last year, Brian started writing some songs, and that inspired his older brother, Jimi Jim, and together they encouraged Janis to start writing some rhymes, too. Soon they had a combination of six old songs and ten new ones, and they scraped together the dough to cut a new demo. They brought it to a new low-budget label called Brooklyn Born, where they got the $25,000 advance.

"Jimi Jim was against spending money on a PI," Janis said. "That's why he's not here today. He thinks I'm chasing ghosts. I told him, no, I'm trying to prevent another family funeral. And I really, really wanna catch the son of a bitch who took away my mama and make him pay for what he did."

Bobby looked at her, in all her long, sexy elegance, sitting on the deck chair of his boat, sipping a Budweiser. The diamond on her muscle-ripped belly seemed to wink at him. She was so hot that Bobby half expected steam to rise up out of her taut, shimmering skin. But when he looked in her blue eyes when she talked about her mother and kid brother, there was a deep, cold void that no one could ever reach the bottom of until some justice was done in her shattered life. Here was a young woman who had given up everything, her youth and probably a multimillion-dollar socko career to dedicate herself to raising her little half brother. A mixed-up, suicidal kid. A kid who was downstairs now probably putting the make on Bobby's only daughter—who'd had a mad crush on the kid as a child.

"Jesus Christ," Bobby said. "Ya know, Janis, I hate cases where I feel emotionally involved. You're from the old hood. I knew your mom a little.

I remember you. I remember your kid brother. I'd feel funny taking your money. I'm also afraid that if I take the case, and I let you down, I'll be writing gloomy stuff in my own diary."

"Oh, man, stop being a fuckin' pussy," Izzy Gleason said.

Janis laughed at Izzy. "Yo, this dude is epic-level hot shit."

"Yeah, that's what the last broad I met said," Izzy said. "Lemme tell you about—"

"Spare us, Izzy," Bobby said. "This is serious here."

"Yes, it is," Janis said. "So maybe Izzy's right. Maybe you are too much of a herb for the job, Bobby. I'd heard different, but if you don't have the onions . . ."

She stuffed the brown paper bag in her pocketbook and stood up to leave. Bobby felt as if she'd just put his manhood in her purse, too.

"Hey, lady, I didn't say *no*," Bobby said.

"Look, lemme make this easy for ya, okay?" she said. "I can go to a million other PIs and they'd probably go through the motions, like the cop assigned to this case, make believe they really tried, and let the meter run. I don't expect miracles. I don't expect you to even succeed in a week. But here's the deal: because you're from Brooklyn, the old neighborhood, I figured you'd give me the best bang for my buck."

"Whoa! If he don't take you up on *that* offer, honey, I'll do it in court in front of the judge and jury," Izzy said, eating his sugarless peanut butter cookies. "And gladly take whatever sentence they give me. And you don't even have to give me the buck."

Janis turned to him and laughed. "He might be an asshole, but just daring to say that to me you gotta love him. Old-fashioned Brooklyn balls."

"Be careful, he takes everything literally," Bobby said.

"Here's all I want, Bobby," Janis said. "I want that kid inside to know I did every damned thing in my power to get to the bottom of what happened to Mama. I want him to know that's he's not alone in that deep dark hole he lives in. I want him to know that even though the cops, the DA, and the press and his father stopped giving a shit a long time ago, some people still care. Brian has a big brother, but he never had a grown *man,* a real father figure go to bat for him, fight for him. So, *fuck* political correctness, okay? I'm not looking for a guy who's in touch with his feminine side, here."

"I'll show you mine if you show me either one of yours," Izzy said.

She made an imaginary pistol of her fingers and shot Izzy dead. Then she looked back at Bobby and put the barrel of the same finger-pistol to his thumping heart.

"I'm looking for a real guy," she said. "I thought after reading about Bobby Emmet from the old hood in Max Roth's column that you might be that guy. If I can get Brian to believe that someone like you is really fighting for him, for us, for Mama, maybe I can get him to believe that life's worth living, and he'll let me and his brother help him climb out of the hole, understand? If I can do that, then that's the best twenty-five grand I ever spent. And who knows, maybe you'll never find the scumbag who did it. But maybe you'll learn enough details to make Brian stop believing that he's the one who's responsible. I want him to know that ten years later, the spirit of our mama still lives. If you can pull just a small piece of that off, Bobby Emmet, you'll be my hero until the end of time."

"Now that's what I call a great fuckin' rap," Izzy said. "Put that into rhyme and even Hasids'll spend their last shekel on the CD."

Bobby stared into Janis's eyes, knowing he'd never felt so manipulated by a woman in his whole life. There was no way, if a man grew up in the macho streets of Brooklyn, that he could ever turn down that spiel. Especially from a woman who looked like Janis McNulty.

But he was still on the fence.

He sat on it for ten seconds, until Maggie stepped on deck with her arm looped through Brian's, whose face was as ashen as a pallbearer's, his eyes waxy with despair.

"Is it really true you're gonna try to find out who killed Brian's mother, Dad?"

"Well . . ."

"Cool, I can't wait to help you," Maggie said. "In fact, Brian and me are gonna work on it together. Aren't we, Brian?"

Brian shrugged. "Whatever . . ."

Bobby looked at Janis McNulty, their eyes locking, a sly smile slashing across her gorgeous face. He'd seen that same smile once before, in post-coital silence as rain beat against a Brooklyn window on an unforgettable school day.

"I'll need twenty-five hundred to get started," Bobby said, standing, locking his hands behind his head, letting all the muscles in his body jumble and dance.

"No problem," Janis said.

"Maybe for you," Izzy said.

"For expenses," Bobby said. "Otherwise, Izzy and I thought it over—"

"We did? When? Where was I?"

"—and we decided to do it pro bono."

"Oh, yeah?" Izzy said. "Then she better have some girlfriends to do some volunteer office work. Older and a little softer's okay. Typing optional. Meanwhile, I gotta get to court."

"And then I need you to tell me everything you know," Bobby told Janis. "No matter how insignificant you think the details are."

Izzy motioned Bobby to the side, handed him a small Panasonic microcassette. "Be in the police row behind the defense table at two p.m. sharp and hand this to me."

"What is it?"

"My whole case, don't lose it. Be there on time. Give it to me when I ask for it."

"That's all I have to do?"

"That's all," Izzy said. "I gotta go."

Izzy said good-bye as Janis counted out the cash, flattened it in Bobby's right palm, and gripped his middle and index fingers in her strong little hand.

"Thanks," Janis said. "My man."

Those two words sent the white blood corpuscles racing through Bobby's blood throwing up a panicky defense against all the dangerous things he was thinking.

"I need you to talk to someone who can make this public again," Bobby said. "I need to let people know you haven't forgotten about this case. I want you to offer ten thousand of that money as a reward for information leading to the arrest and conviction of the person or persons responsible for your mother's death. Stir up a hornet's nest. I want people to start making phone calls. I want rats to start scurrying. I want to bring your dead mom back to life in people's minds. I want people to search their consciences. Time changes people. Monsters that people once feared have died or are in jail. Loyal spouses are now jilted ex-spouses. People with terminal illnesses sometimes want to unload a cargo of guilt. I need you to go public."

Bobby took out his cell phone and dialed a familiar number.

THREE

Max Roth stood on the corner of Ninety-second Street and Fort Hamilton Parkway in Bay Ridge, Brooklyn, scribbling notes into his reporter's notebook imprinted with the name of the *Daily News* as a photographer snapped a photo of Janis and Brian and Jimi Jim.

Bobby watched, pacing the sidewalk, looking up at the various restaurants, video stores, bodegas, appliance shops, pizza joints, and cafés, searching for security cameras. When the photographer was finished, Brian and Maggie walked to Lou's Pizzeria, which occupied one of the two storefronts of the tenement. The second storefront had blackened windows with a simple inscription: Twoboro Social Club. A few men wearing short-sleeve knit shirts, creased pants, and polished shoes stood outside, chatting. They all kissed a short, stocky, immaculately groomed and dressed man in his midfifties on the cheek. Bobby knew his name was Georgie "Gorgeous" Caridi. He was the heir apparent to Vito "Sleighride" Santa, who was doing fifty years on a RICO pinch.

Last Bobby heard, Sleighride had lung cancer in a federal pen in Texas, probably preferring a coffin to one more jailhouse burrito. The club was now being run by Gorgeous Caridi, a ruthless little capo who loved money.

All the tabloids said that the day they pulled a sheet over Sleighride, Georgie Gorgeous took over the club, the turf in this part of Brooklyn and part of Staten Island, and all its holdings. Out of respect he wouldn't make a move until Sleighride drew his last breath. Which was imminent.

Still, Bobby made them all for small-time wiseguys, so small that they had survived the RICO indictments that had sent most of the big-shot mobsters to jail. Most of the surviving mafioso wiseguys in post-Giuliani

New York scratched for one final big score and then a retreat from "the life" to grow tomatoes and watch ball games in Jersey or Florida before their own inevitable RICO indictments came down. It was a dying trade. Like the dot-com craze, the Italian mob in New York was now a bursting bubble. The RICO law had created more rats than a garbage dump. Tough street guys facing life missed good Italian food, wine, their goomatas, and their kids—in that order—so much that they ate the cheese and started to squeal to get placed in the Witness program.

All the high-profile mobsters were in cages for life. The soldiers and new capos were incompetent or frightened and looked for fast money and a soft place to land. The Russian, Asian, and Hispanic mobs had taken a big chunk of the drug, prostitution, and gambling rackets. Most of these second- and third-generation Italian guys outside Twoboro Social Club looked like "associates" or "connected guys" rather than "made men."

Wiseguys always saw things, Bobby thought. The job of a wiseguy was to stand outside social clubs "to see what I could see" and scratch his balls, shifting his overweight frame from one polished Italian loafer to the other, and to whisper things in each other's ears. The Feds liked to think they talked about big mob hits and hijackings and drug deals, but Bobby knew from wiretaps and directional microphones that 95 percent of the time these mooks discussed which deli made the best ham-and-provolone-with-peppers hero, where to get discounts on knit pullovers, and who was banging whose goomar. They were small-minded people who made small-talk about nonsense. Asking any of them about a ten-year-old hit-and-run would be next to useless.

". . . so who else could have seen this yellow van?" Roth asked Jimi Jim and Janis.

"Mrs. Donatella is one of those old Brooklyn ladies who always sits at the window, leaning on a pillow, watching everything that happens on her street," Janis said, pointing to Mrs. Donatella, who was sitting at the window, leaning on her pillow, watching them talk about her.

"She don't know air-conditioning's been invented yet, this old bag," said Jimi Jim, who was six foot one and about 160 pounds of fidgety, unbridled energy. "She's two hundred and eighty-six years old. Same as her weight."

"She's in her late fifties," Janis said.

"Look at her, though," Jimi Jim said. "She looks like she watched George Washington retreat across the fuckin' harbor from that window.

She watches, she snoops, she sees everything, she calls nine one one like she's programming her fuckin' pacemaker, busting everyone's balls. Ever since Mom married Rodney, she went haywire. Soon's a nigga moves into her building, she freaked. She yells at dog walkers, kids playing ball, kids hanging out and makin' out. Everyone around here called her Malocchio, guido for 'evil eye.' "

"He means Italian," Janis said, smacking Jimi Jim on the back of the head. "What's wrong with you? That's a reporter you're talking to, not a glue-head."

Roth raised his eyebrows and looked at Bobby.

"What can I tell you, the PC police don't patrol certain precincts of Brooklyn," Bobby said, noticing a black Navigator squeal a fast right onto Ninety-sixth Street. He noticed but remembered that there were tens of thousands of black Navigators in New York. And he wasn't even sure the SUV he'd seen at the marina earlier was a Navigator.

"The regular cops don't do shit either," said Janis. "The first responder at the scene that day was an ambulance driver, also a woman, named Dianne Rattigan, but she couldn't have seen anything. They never let us talk to her. She only talked to the DT who caught the case, an NYPD highway-homicide detective named James Ford. He's retired now. He went through the motions, like a guy taking batting practice, but I don't think he ever really worked the case. After six months he stopped calling. When we called him he'd take two, three days to respond. Then he'd say there wasn't much to go on. Just a yellow van and a few blind leads. I spend all my days haunted by yellow vans. I can be having a wonderful day, a great day, filled with hope and promise, but then if I see a yellow van pass me on the street, my day is ruined. I stop, I wonder, did that guy, that woman, did that son of a bitch kill my mother?"

Max scribbled furiously in his notebook, clearly touched, and asked, "What did this Mrs. Donatella see?"

"Old snatch said she didn't see nothin'," Jimi Jim said. "She's a fuck-ing racist Guinea twat who hated my mother for marrying a nigga, heah'm sayin'?"

"Oh, I hear you all right," Roth said, glancing at Bobby again.

"In the hip-hop world, sometimes that's a term of endearment," Bobby said, rolling his eyes and running his fingers through his hair.

"Guinea, twat, or nigger?" Roth asked.

"C'mon, Max . . ."

"Endearment my McDonkey ass," said Jimi Jim. "When my moms was murdered, that nigga Calhoun flew the coop like a rat pigeon. They say he had a stroke. Then they put him in some nursing home over Shaolin."

"Sha-olin?" Roth said.

"*Shaolin* is what Wu-Tang Clan from the Stapleton projects calls Staten Island," Bobby said. "Hip-hop talk."

"Ebonics?" Roth asked.

"It's just what niggas call it, yo," said Jimi Jim. "But you'll see. Rodney'll show up when the album hits with a bullet, lookin' for a handout like it's check day."

"Shut up," Janis said. "He's been in the nursing home since right after mom died. They said the stroke was from diabetes and smoking and bad diet. And then the trauma of the hit-and-run. Then they say he developed symptoms of early-onset Alzheimer's. He's at the Narrows View Nursing Home not far from the other side of the Bridge, just off Hylan Boulevard."

"You visit him?"

"We took Brian a couple of times, but you need to make an appointment," Janis said. "They say he needs to be segregated from other patients because he's younger and stronger than most and sometimes has fits of violence. So they segregate him. The few times we took Brian, he just sat there like . . . I dunno, like . . ."

"Like a sack of shit," Jimi Jim said. "I had better conversations with tackle dummies."

"What about other neighbors, motorists, storekeepers," Roth said, holding a yellowed clip from the *Daily News* library that quoted local shopkeepers and neighbors after the hit-and-run, none of whom saw anything but a yellow streak race from the scene.

Janis regurgitated the same stories from the time. All the witnesses said it happened so fast that no one ever had a chance to get a plate number or make or a better identification of the van. As Bobby scanned the local shops, he also studied the rooftops, knowing that since the 1990s many of the local buildings had been vacancy decontrolled by landlords who had paid rent-controlled tenants to move so they could renovate the apartments and sell them as condos for up to $600,000, with doormen and other security systems such as exterior cameras that scanned the street.

Many of the cameras were concealed by little pigeon-hawk statuettes that served a double purpose as urban scarecrows to warn off wary pigeons, who lived in mortal fear of their predators. Bobby doubted that ten years ago there was even a tenth the number of cameras as there were in today's Big-Brother-is-watching New York. He'd recently read that an estimated twenty thousand security cameras now scanned the more than six thousand miles of city streets.

Bobby continued to scan the rooftops until his eye collided with the massive towers of the Verrazano Bridge, from which the thousands of miles of cable were suspended across the 4,260-foot-long span. The armature and roadways of the bridge were built upon those cables, a marvel of modern engineering, and a colossus where seven hard hats had died during construction in the early 1960s. Bobby used to be able to see that twinkling bridge from his bedroom window when he'd still lived with Connie, when Maggie was a wailing, hungry infant in her crib. He'd learned that the bridge that was the night-light of their lives was so long that the towers had been constructed a few inches out of parallel to accommodate the curvature of the earth.

Bobby waited at the crosswalk for the light to turn green and walked to the middle of the street, to the spot where the hit-and-run had taken place. He squatted. He shielded his eyes from the afternoon sun and did a 360-degree spin on the balls of his feet, realizing that one of the last things Cookie Calhoun might've seen before she died that day was the Brooklyn-side tower of the Verrazano climbing into the baby blue heavens. He knew from being a cop that even back then the bridges and tunnels of the city had special high-performance security cameras mounted on the structures in case of the then far-fetched possibility of terrorist strikes. But also to scan for lone-nut saboteurs, snipers, teenage hooligans, suicide leapers, graffiti taggers, and low-flying aircraft. Mounted cameras also kept track of weather and traffic conditions on the bridge and the on-ramps and access streets on both sides of the span.

Bobby took out his cell phone, flipped it open, clicked to the camera mode, and saw the image of the bridge towers come into perfect view. Which meant a camera mounted anywhere on the bridge could have had a clear shot of this intersection.

Bobby had gone through the police academy with a cop named Kevin Burns, who later became a lieutenant in the Staten Island Highway Unit. He was a good guy, a real hustler but an honest cop. He'd heard he got out on three-quarters disability pension and moved West. But he knew he had a nephew whom he'd finessed into the Staten Island Highway Unit, which consisted of just about 250 men and women who cruised the highways and bridges of the city in one-man cars. These days, most of them worked twelve-hour shifts, racking up the overtime under the five-million-dollar-a-week antiterrorism initiative called Operation Atlas.

Bobby made a quick call to his younger brother Patrick, at the NYPD Intelligence Division.

"I'm swamped, Bobby; what can I do for you?"

Bobby said he needed to find out if the younger Burns was working today. He also needed to know whatever he could learn about a retired highway detective named James Ford. Patrick told him he'd make a few calls and get back to him.

The light began to blink *Don't Walk.* Bobby folded his phone and approached Janis and Jimi Jim and asked, "Did this Detective Ford ever get the security tapes from the Verrazano?"

Janis and Jimi Jim looked at each other, shrugging. "Never mentioned it to us," said Janis. "It never even came up. Why, could the cameras see this far?"

"Maybe," Bobby said.

Max Roth walked Bobby off to the side, folded his notebook, shoved it into his back pocket, and said, "I have plenty. Good update, with a twist. I like that they're using the money from their music to chase the driver who killed their mother. I'll quote the sister. The older brother is a half a flake."

"Didn't have an easy life, Max," Bobby said.

Roth nodded. "I hear ya. I'm gonna try to talk to the Mrs. Donatella woman. It'll be a good read. But don't expect miracles. What's sleazy Izzy Gleason got to do with this?"

"He's going to oversee the reward process and basically represent the family, pro bono, filing papers and writs on old evidence and for freedom-of-information files," Bobby said. "Plus, he knows the hip-hop world since he defended some of the wack-jobs you already wrote about. The people in that world respect him."

"They would," Roth said. "They have the same moral base. None. When're you gonna rid yourself of this scuzzball?"

"Soon," Bobby said. "In the meantime, I wanna have a talk with this Iglew guy. And the people at Lethal Injection Records. Long shot, but people have killed each other for less than a chance at a world tour and a record deal. When Cookie Calhoun died that day, so did any chance of Bigga Wiggaz getting a big break. Coincidence? Probably. But maybe not. No one in that world likes to talk to white ex-cops like me. Unless I have

Izzy running interference. They talk to him. He can open doors for me. That rapper Tu Bitz—"

"Not to be confused with 50 Cent."

"—right, Tu Bitz personally paid Izzy to represent five different guys on drug and gun charges. All of them are part of his posse. I'd say all that money came from Lethal Injection Records."

"From what I know, Lethal Injection got its seed money from drug sales in the Richmond projects in Staten Island," Roth said.

"That would be RIP projects in *Shaolin*," Bobby said. "But it's become one of the five top rap labels since the mideighties. Untold millions."

"I better go file," Roth said. "But let me ask you a question. Why you involving yourself in all this? I know you still owe Gleason for getting you out of the joint. But you seem more personally involved in this one."

"I sort of knew the mother. And I sort of know this world now. Kids from the old neighborhood. Like I said, it could be a random drunk."

"Sort of knew the mother? With you that usually means—"

"Plus," Bobby said, cutting Max off, "my daughter went to school with the youngest kid, Brian."

"He wouldn't even talk to me."

"Could you do an interview about watching your mother get run over by a truck? Especially if you felt responsible for it?"

Max Roth nodded. "I can't tell you how many people from the Trade Center I interviewed felt guilty that they made it out and coworkers didn't. Let me go talk to this old woman, Donatella. See ya in the funny papers."

Bobby shook Max Roth's hand and watched his old Brooklyn college buddy walk toward the McNulty tenement. He called up to Mrs. Donatella.

"Ma'am, I'm Max Roth, from the *Daily News*," he said, holding up his press card. "Would you mind if I came up and asked you a few questions?"

Mrs. Donatella spit at him, a big silver dollar of saliva spiraling from her second-story window-ledge pillow perch. Max Roth lurched out of the way of the spit.

"Bah, fongola, you moolinyan lovin' hebe," Mrs. Donatella said.

"Excuse me," Max Roth said.

Bobby laughed and then spotted the black Navigator again. He didn't know if it was the same one and had just circled the block. But it sure looked the same. Still, people often circled the block in legal-parking-space-starved Bay Ridge, searching for a treasured place to leave their $40,000 vehicles. Bobby watched the Navigator this time, hoping to get a peek at the driver or a plate number that Maggie knew how to trace by accessing the database of the State Department of Motor Vehicles with pirated software.

Bobby took out his cell phone again and hit the camera icon and snapped a few frames of the Navigator.

The Navigator slinked along Fort Hamilton Parkway, windows tinted like the mask of a bandit. It slowed, stopped on the very spot where Cookie had perished a decade earlier, as if waiting for the green light to turn red. Bobby clicked a second photo of the Navigator's profile. He waited with the phone/camera pointed at the Navigator to see the plate number when it passed. As the green light turned yellow, a city bus, with *Staten Island* showing in the destination window, roared past in the traffic lane closest to Bobby, obscuring his view of the black SUV. The bus stole the yellow light. Sped across Ninety-second Street. And accelerated up the on-ramp to the Verrazano Bridge. The black Navigator hugged the left lane parallel to the bus, which ran interference until the bus disappeared around the winding on-ramp to the longest suspension bridge in the world. From his angle, Bobby couldn't get the plate number on his camera screen.

Slick, he thought as he snapped an image.

Bobby looked up to the massive blue-gray tower of the bridge and thought again of the security cameras. He checked his watch: 11:23 a.m.

FOUR

Bobby walked alone with Janis along the esplanade of Shore Road, under the Verrazano, beside the Narrows, which was patrolled since 9/11 by Coast Guard and NYPD harbor patrol boats, escorting the tugs that pushed the tankers out past Nortons Point and Coney Island and into the open sea. He'd already put Maggie in charge of hacking into the Metropolitan Transit Authority's database, into the subdivision of the MTA Bridges and Tunnel Authority that oversaw seven bridges and two tunnels that were vital arteries in the city's circulatory system. He knew from working old cases for the Manhattan DA's Office that there was a chief security officer for the whole system and a chief of technology. He told Maggie to bypass those guys and hack deeper into the system to find out who was the individual head of the security on the Verrazano Bridge at that time, on the date that Cookie Calhoun died. Maggie said she could find that from old payroll records, which also listed job classifications.

"I can do that on my notebook from the Jeep, using the satellite phone," she said.

Bobby left Maggie and Brian alone in the Jeep as he took Janis on a walk and talk along Shore Road, where he could be certain no one was following them.

Strolling, Janis told Bobby about the argument Cookie had had with her husband, Rodney Calhoun, on that morning right before she'd died. Bobby would definitely want to visit Rodney, Alzheimer's or no.

He'd also want to talk to the first husband, Ray "Nails" McNulty, who was Janis's and Jimi Jim's father, who had been only a peripheral figure in their lives since Cookie's death. If anything, he had gone into deeper

35

decline, wailing uncontrollably at the funeral. Bobby recalled the commotion at the funeral Mass when several men had had to carry a distraught Nails out of the packed church. He'd looked like a legless straw man.

Janis said Nails had remarried, moved to Staten Island, and had a kid by another domineering woman who was so racist she didn't want her precious white daughter to associate with her "half-nigger half brother Brian."

Janis and Jimi Jim said that if Brian wasn't good enough for their father's new kid, they wanted nothing to do with her either.

"We were gonna rename the band Dyzphunk Phamily," she said, spelling it out, laughing in a dark way that wasn't so much a laugh as it was a masked sob. "But we stuck with Bigga Wiggaz because we still have a Brooklyn fan base from the old days. Look, my stepfather was an asshole, but no way do I think he killed my mom in front of his own son. And my father is basically an Ozzie Osbourne, sixties burnout type, harmless, lovable, with a few die-hard brain cells attached to a dry-cell battery, but hitched to the lowest kind of Staten Island shanty-Irish, my-shit-don't-stink racist bitch you could imagine. I mean she still hates Puerto Ricans, Italians, and Asians. She calls Russians white sambos. But my father, he's a little shot. He works, does his handyman stuff, hands over the pay to the wife, and has his six-pack. We see him now and then. Never misses birthdays. He always looks ashamed. He should be. He has to sneak over to see us, waiting on line to pay cash on the bridge toll in case Brenda, my step-bitch, checks the E-ZPass statements at the end of the month. I mean, I love him, I love Nails—that's what we call my father—love the old man, we all do, even Brian, but he's kind of a sad sack. He loved my mother till the day she died. Adored, no, *worshiped* her. He took it worse than anybody."

"You said your mother loved him, too."

"Yeah, but it was over. My mom was a sixties chick, too. But free love stopped when they got married and had me. My old man got weak, had a stoned fling with another chick while working on a rehab job over in Staten Island . . ." Janis nodded to the forgotten fifth borough of Staten Island, which was like the stepchild of the city, lying in a lumpy sprawl on the other side of the great bridge like a gargantuan, comatose walrus. "And she told him she was using birth control. She lied. She got knocked up—"

"This is his current wife?"

"Yeah. And she wouldn't have an abortion. Used the Catholic excuse. My mother freaked. Threw Nails out. With nowhere to go. No steady job. No pad. All his friends were married. So he moved in with the bitch over in Staten Island where he could hide from his shame. And just never left because he never had anywhere else to go. I know he never loved Brenda. She was side ass that bit him on the ass. Then she became the mother of his new kid. And she became a habit more than a wife. A roommate with an attitude. I know a lot of people like that, people who never loved their spouses. Fucking nuts, no? I mean living the only life you're ever gonna have with someone you don't love? Or even like? Shit, my moms did that with Rodney."

Bobby looked at Janis, at her sun-splashed face that any man could learn to love, and couldn't believe she'd shouldered ten years of sagging emotional luggage without any worry lines or a stoop in the shoulders. Men might be physically stronger than women, he thought. But when it came down to what's important in life, to dealing with real pain, problem solving for troubled kids, and fighting to hold together a fractured family, women were tougher. And some women were tougher than others. Janis McNulty was one of them. It was going to take a strong guy to ever capture and hold on to her heart.

"What about this Iglew guy?" Bobby asked, watching a Little Leaguer launch a baseball into the near-noon sky on a sandlot field across six lanes of hurtling highway on the watery rim of Brooklyn. A black Navigator passed. Doing forty in a 50 mph zone. Bobby's skin graveled.

"What about him?"

"Think hard, but think ruthlessly honest," Bobby said. "He raps hard-core, but did he have it in him back in the day to kill a woman to bury Bigga Wiggaz?"

"Listen to *you*, yo," Janis said. *"Back in the day, hard-core."*

"I been working in The World."

"I hear ya."

"Plus I have a kid, sixteen."

"I noticed," she said. "I don't know if men know how sexy it is to a woman to see him be so cool with his kid."

Bobby was caught off guard. "Yeah? Oh . . . well, thanks . . ."

"No, don't get me wrong. Even when I see a husband pushing his new-born in a carriage, or a toddler in a stroller, or tossing a football with his son, or standing on line with his daughter to see *Harry Potter,* it stirs me up, makes my heart pump. Knowing there's still men out there like that. Which brings me to your question. It makes my heart sing to see good loving guys because I believe there's no shortage of evil suckers out there. Yes,

I think some of them could kill a woman in cold blood. They do it all the time. They kill their own, over drug deals and because the dinner's cold or because there's no money when daddy's kicking his jones. Do I think Iglew is capable of killing my mother? I know your lawyer friend represents some of his boys, but, yeah, I do."

Bobby stopped, looked at Lady Liberty still holding her torch for a traumatized city, the way Janis McNulty had kept the home fires burning for her shattered family, and said, "Why?"

"He started as a dope dealer. Crack. He probably wrecked five thousand families, one red cap, one glass stem, one butane lighter, at a time. Back in the day Iglew worked in the Richmond projects for a major dealer that cops only knew by the nickname Deity. Some messianic Five Percenter loony from the eighties."

"I know who they are," Bobby said. "It's a jailhouse cult. I had run-ins with them in the joint. I never heard of Deity. But then I worked the Manhattan DA's Office. We rarely had overlapping with Staten Island. Their stuff used to overlap into Brooklyn. But these days they do most of their own prosecutions in the Staten Island courthouse. But I remember the Fives."

"You do know your shit," Janis said.

"When someone's trying to kill you inside, you wanna know who they are."

"Well, this Deity, whoever the hell he is, supposedly went into jail as a crack-dealing monster," said Janis. "He came out as Deity. Iglew kept tryin' to get to meet Dee, but he was like some Wizard of Oz behind a curtain. Iglew wanted Dee to let him rap for Lethal Injection, which Dee built with the crack money from the projects. But Dee kept sending down word, never meeting with him, testing him. Making him prove himself. I heard he used him to settle beefs with guys who dissed him when he was in jail. Then to amuse himself, Deity said he would have to have a rap battle with us. With Bigga Wiggaz, to get the tour with Baru, and maybe a record deal. For Deity it was a goof. Make Iglew battle some white rappers. Like a spectator sport. I was down for it. Jimi Jim was down. I don't know if Iglew was down for it. He was good, but I think we were better. He would have been so humiliated if we beat him in a rap battle, in front of his homeys, in front of this Deity wack-job."

"So humiliated that you think he was willing to kill somebody?"

"I dunno. That's why I came to you. Maybe."

"But why the hell would Iglew kill your mother instead of you or your brother?"

"Killing us would have been obvious. Would have made him the prime suspect. He had direct motive. But he knew that if someone killed our mother, no way would we be able to show up at a rap battle. Or go on a world tour. And if he made it look like a hit-and-run, well, no one would really pursue it. If that's true, he was right."

"He that slick?"

"Put it this way," Janis said. "After Mama's hit-and-run, Iglew had hit after hit, and some friggin' run. The people who were running the label got jammed up in a drug beef, and Deity, who was really slick, made Iglew the head front man of Lethal Injection. Put the talent out front. Like P. Diddy at Bad Boy. Rumor has it that Dee still silently and secretly owns it, and Iglew is just a front. They say Dee maybe lives out of the country, just sits around waiting for money to reach his offshore account. Meanwhile, Iglew runs the show. Hey, you can't be too stupid to run a three-hundred-million-dollar-a-year record company, and a clothing line."

Bobby thought it all over. Thought about some of the carnage he'd seen in the joint committed by Five Percenters who thought they were doing the righteous work of Allah. He thought about the bodies left in the city's projects in the crack wars, starting back in the late 1980s—murdered cops, infants, and entire families. One rookie police officer named Byrne was shot at point-blank range while dozing in his patrol car in Queens when he was supposed to be guarding a witness against a crack crew. The witness was never found.

As they passed under the Verrazano Bridge, Bobby saw a black Navigator ramp off the Fort Hamilton Parkway exit.

"You really ready to peel the scab off this old wound?" Bobby asked. "You ready for the backlash? If Iglew and maybe this phantom Deity are somehow involved in the killing of your mother, these crazy people could come after you and what's left of your family. Murder has no statute of limitations. You'll be threatening their freedom. Their empire. This isn't about winning a rap battle. There could be hundreds of millions of dollars at stake. You prepared for that?"

Janis put her hands on her hips and looked Bobby square in the eyes as joggers and bicyclists and dog walkers passed them. A siren of high noon sang across the blue-green Narrows. Fighter jets thundered overhead, airborne centurions in terror-age New York, ready to blow skyjacked passenger jets zooming for skyscrapers out of the heavens. Over Janis's shoulder, Bobby watched the black Navigator speed out of sight.

"I got a kid brother who's tried twice and is ready to try to kill himself again," she said. "If he succeeds, I don't wanna live. This family has suffered for ten years. I can't handcuff myself to my kid brother to make sure he doesn't put himself to sleep or try to jump off that goddamned bridge." She looked up at the mammoth span, Bobby studying her jawline, so similar to her mother's when it had lain across his belly. "But I can try to save him from himself by finding out who did this and why. And, hey, maybe this was just a drunk who did an accidental hit-and-run. If that's it, at least we *tried*. But maybe someone murdered her, Bobby. I need to know. My kid brother needs to know. I might not be ready for Deity and Iglew coming to the door, busting caps in my ass. But I certainly am not ready to see another undertaker coming to take Brian away. So, yeah, let's just do it."

Bobby met Maggie at Lou's Pizzeria on Fort Hamilton Parkway, where she was sitting with Brian Calhoun. As they left the store, Maggie told Bobby that a man named Stephen Greco was the security chief on the Verrazano Bridge on the day Cookie Calhoun was killed. He was still working there. Maggie said she'd called the Verrazano Bridge control center pretending to be Greco's daughter, and someone had told her he wouldn't be off duty until 4 p.m. "This isn't exactly atomic secrets," she said.

Bobby did know that recent information obtained from Al Qaeda prisoners indicated that the Brooklyn Bridge had been targeted. He believed the Verrazano would be an easier and more strategic target because if it collapsed into the Narrows, it could block New York harbor's access to the open sea. And yet a teenager with a few key strokes could learn from simple city health, pension, and retirement and payroll databases where the people in charge of the security worked and lived and how many kids they had on the health plan, in case they ever wanted to take a hostage to exchange for classified security data.

Maggie also learned that Dianne Rattigan, the first paramedic on the scene at the old hit-and-run, was still working the Brooklyn ambulance circuit.

"I ran her name through a Lexis search and I saw that she had to testify at several medical malpractice trials," Maggie said. "On two separate occasions, when lawyers were trying to establish time lines, Rattigan testified that she eats lunch in the Lutheran Medical Center employee's lunchroom almost every day from two-thirty to three-fifteen."

"Nothing is private anymore," Bobby said.

"Actually, her testimony even says when she went to the ladies' room. And she said she vividly remembered one crash victim because the woman was carrying a bouquet of daisies—which Dianne Rattigan testified are her favorite flowers—when she was hit by a city bus."

Bobby said good-bye to Janis and watched Maggie and Brian stand off on their own as a car from Bay Ridge Car Service pulled up to the curb to take Maggie home to her mother's new pad in the Trump International Hotel and Tower overlooking Columbus Circle, a forty-five-million-dollar, ninetieth-floor piece of the sky over New York with a 360-degree wrap-around view of the city. Her husband, Trevor Sawyer, owned the biggest cosmetics fortune in America. Connie Matthews was the heir to the second-largest cosmetics fortune in America. When they married, it was as if they took deed to every woman's face in America.

It also meant that the old ten-bedroom, single-floor condo in Trump Tower was too small after a few years of marriage. As soon as Trump finished the International, Connie insisted they buy the triplex from the heiress of one of the biggest pharmaceutical companies in America.

Some people played Monopoly for real, Bobby thought.

Billionaires like Trevor bought airlines, buildings, newspapers, casinos, hotels, cable companies, ball teams, until they got bored. And then they rolled the dice and hopped around the board and bought and sold new possessions that made the gossip pages. And they played with those "properties" for a while until they were bored. And then they rolled the dice again from places like the ninetieth-floor triplex of Trump International. In the end the most expensive crypt in the boneyard didn't make you any less dead.

But before she went home to the fifteen-bedroom, seventeen-bathroom pad with three kitchens, indoor swimming pool, and gymnasium, Maggie stood in a graffiti-scarred tenement doorway of Bay Ridge whispering to Brian Calhoun. Bobby had no idea what they were saying to each other. But Brian, who kept staring at the tips of his untied sneakers, simply nodded, shrugged, licked his lips, and rocked back and forth like someone ready to fall off a ledge and out of this desperate thing called life.

"Mag, the car's waiting, and I gotta get to court," Bobby shouted.

"They're cute together," Janis said. "Girls dig him, but he's usually so withdrawn that he doesn't go out with them much. The only time he expresses himself is with music."

"Maggie spends half her life in cyberspace," Bobby said. "What the hell ever happened to stickball and hopscotch?"

"And fu—"

"Jesus, don't say that!"

"What? 'Fun on the beach'?"

"Oh, that's okay."

"You're worried about your daughter losing her virginity?"

"Stop!"

Janis smiled and whispered in his ear, "Relax, that's probably already a done dealio, Pops."

"Shut up!"

Then Bobby watched his daughter lift Brian's chin with her hand and look him in the eyes. She said something to him and then leaned in and kissed him. An openmouthed kiss.

Bobby turned away as if he'd just been shot. "Oh, man, I can't watch this."

Janis chuckled, a deep, dark guttural laugh. "Hey, it could be Madonna," she said. He looked at her. Their eyes met. She looked so much like her mother that he wanted to kiss Janis. She looked so much like her that he couldn't.

Instead he put Maggie into the back of the car service, kissed her on the cheek, and sent her home. The car pulled away. When he turned, Janis McNulty was still staring him in the eyes. She grabbed his face in her hands and kissed him on the lips. A kiss from the grave. As if Cookie Calhoun herself were asking for his help to save her son from himself.

"Thanks for helping me save my kid brother's life," Janis said.

A chill quaked through Bobby Emmet. Then Janis hurried to her brother Brian and threw her arm over his shoulder and walked him back into the tenement. Mrs. Donatella leaned at the windowsill, watching them with contempt, and spat out her window on the sidewalk where they had walked.

"Bah, fongola, moolinyan," she said.

FIVE

Thirty-eight minutes later, Bobby walked into a packed courtroom at Staten Island State Supreme Court on Richmond Terrace as an assistant district attorney named Billy Queenan walked away from a stunning-looking black woman sitting in the witness chair, nodded to Izzy Gleason, and said, "Your witness."

Bobby searched for a seat in the front row reserved for cops and lawyers. He flashed a replica of his old shield to a court officer, who nodded, and then Bobby searched the courtroom for familiar faces. In the rear he saw a bunch of guys in Lethalwear clothes occupying two full rows. All of them had shaved heads, and in the middle of them sat Iglew, wearing dark, tiny oval shades and a light-colored suit with a dark T-shirt underneath. He was surrounded by his posse and bodyguards so that the press could not get near him when he entered and left the courtroom.

Bobby couldn't figure whether he came to the trial every day to show his support for Charles "Tu Bitz" McCoy—a six-foot-five, 260-pound black man with a shiny bald dome and hoop earrings in both lobes—or to intimidate him. Izzy and Bobby suspected it might be to let Tu Bitz know that his immediate family, and distant relatives—brothers, sisters, wife, kids, mother, father, uncles, aunts, in-laws, mistresses, ho-girls, and homeys—would never be safe if he ever flipped on them and decided to turn state's evidence against Iglew. Or this hoodoo specter named Deity, whose identity was a mystery. "They'd kill his fucking Korean dry cleaner to get even for dimin'," Izzy told Bobby. "In the hip-hop world they fumigate anyone remotely connected to a rat."

Bobby looked around the courtroom and saw many of Tu Bitz's relatives, fans, supporters, and posse in attendance. Except for press, the ADA, six jurors, the judge, Izzy, and himself, almost everyone was black. But seated in the back row he spotted two middle-aged white guys, positioned across the aisle from each other. One he recognized right away as Joe Brightman. He was Governor Patterson's closest pal since high school. Patterson never made a serious political move without getting Brightman's advice on how it would play in the polls. Bobby knew the governor was in a close primary and that the Rockefeller drug laws were one of the biggest issues in the campaign, especially among the minority vote. Brightman was probably here to see how it was playing with the press and the public, taking the political temperature.

Seated across from him was a man in his early forties, stocky, chest like an oil drum, his thick, wavy hair still yellow and charged with adolescent highlights. He wore a blond mustache and a beige linen suit with white shirt and beige tie. Bobby didn't recognize him. He didn't dress like a pol. Too bright for a lawyer. Too well dressed for a cop. Bobby shrugged. Trials attracted all walks of life.

On his way back to the prosecution table Queenan snapped the fingers of both hands and then made a little bongo sound when he banged his open palm against the top of his loose right fist, smiling in triumph.

Izzy must be in deep shit, Bobby thought, then found himself frozen in the act of sitting when he looked at the breathtaking black woman in the witness seat. Detective Samantha Savage had a magnetic, almost hypnotic presence, seated in relaxed cross-legged poise, elegant hands folded on her lap, shoulders ramrod straight, head held high accentuating the sharp, pronounced jawline and long neck and straight-ruled clavicle bones visible above the scoop-necked blouse—a living, breathing Botticelli portrait. As he took his seat, Savage stared straight at Bobby for a long, challenging moment, as if daring him to make an untoward suggestion, and then her large, intelligent eyes closed like theater curtains. When she slowly opened them, she ignored Bobby, as if he had already been committed to history, and watched Izzy Gleason whisper in the ear of his client.

From working his case for Izzy, Bobby knew that Tu Bitz didn't get his moniker from twenty-five bullets taken from his body over the years, as the street myth had it. He got it because of the two "bits," or jail sentences, he'd already served in his criminal career as a drug dealer, gangbanger, and rap-music-industry enforcer, causing him to serve one-third of his thirty-four years in a cage.

Tu Bitz shrugged at whatever it was Izzy whispered in his ear.

Bobby looked to his left in the cop row and saw two other members of the Hip-Hop Joint Task Force, of which Savage was an NYPD member. The two guys were those notorious Feds, Special Agent in Charge Tom Noonan and Special Agent Lou Scarano. Bobby knew of them, but every attempt he'd made at contacting them had been rebuffed. Noonan and Scarano leaned forward, looked at Bobby, and whispered to each other. Scarano waved over a court officer and whispered in his ear.

The court officer walked to Bobby. "You still on the job?"

"Retired," Bobby said, knowing Scarano was trying to get him ejected from the reserved police row. "But I'm working for the defense."

"Sorry, but I gotta ask you to find another—"

"He's with me, Judge," Izzy shouted, turning and pointing at Bobby. "I need my investigator to sit there to confer with me or else it'll hold up the trial every time I have to go looking for him out in the hallway."

The judge nodded to the court officer to let Bobby sit where he was. Bobby winked at Noonan and Scarano. With his back to the judge, Izzy thumbed his nose at the Feds. The courtroom burst into laughter, a few of the jurors guffawing. The Feds looked away, staring at Savage. Iglew and his posse remained silent, composed, as if drilled in their emotionless behavior.

Judge Irving Glass sighed and said, "Mr. Gleason, please restrain yourself from your legendary junior-high-school antics in my courtroom."

"Sorry, but my nose always gets itchy when I smell baloney, Your Honor," Izzy said.

"Proceed with cross, Mr. Gleason," the judge said, leaning back in his swivel chair.

Izzy stood, removed his jacket and draped it over the back of his chair, loosened his tie, rolled up his sleeves, and walked to the jury box. He looked at everyone's face, smiling, his red hair offsetting his squinty blue eyes. He leaned over the jury box, put on his glasses, and peered down at the jurors' shoes as if searching for something.

"Nope," he said. "Not there. . . ."

A few of the jurors giggled, looked at each other, and exchanged whispers.

Judge Glass said, "Mr. Gleason, are you ready to cross-examine?"

Izzy raised a finger and hurried to the court reporter, wheeled the startled little bespectacled man's chair away from his desk, and looked under it. Bobby watched the wacky defense lawyer rummage around in the waste-basket, then push the court reporter back to the desk. Then Izzy peeked behind the American flag that stood in a stand by the wood-paneled wall. Izzy exhaled in frustration, then glanced behind the two amused court officers.

"No, not there either," Izzy mumbled, scratching his head. Bobby thought, *He's stalling for time because he has no case.*

Bobby glanced at the black woman on the stand, but she didn't smile, frown, sigh, or squirm. She sat as poised as a sculpture.

The judge frowned, looked over his bifocals, and said, "Mr. Gleason . . ."

"One moment, Your Honor, please." Izzy walked to the defense table and took his binoculars from his inside jacket pocket.

"Fuck you doin', nigga?" Tu Bitz whispered, loud enough for the whole courtroom to hear. "Three strikes I'm outta heah till the fat bitch sing at my funeral, yo."

The jurors stifled laughs.

The judge said, "Mr. Gleason, can you please tell me what you think you are . . ."

Izzy dragged his chair to the window and jumped up on it, adjusted the binoculars, and peered out at the vast low-rise urban sprawl of Staten Island, spanning across Curtis and McKinley high schools, past the railroad yards, and the ferry terminal, and the old abandoned navy homeport that Danny Aiello the actor had tried to resurrect as a movie studio, but which was ground down by the self-interests of the city government. Izzy panned across the harbor to Brooklyn, sweeping over the church spires, mosque domes, and marble synagogues, panning the emerald parks and concrete playgrounds, the condo-converted dirty-brick factories and overpriced brownstones and austere municipal buildings and dirty-green Lady Liberty and the majestic spans of the downtown bridges leading to the wounded but undefeated skyline of Manhattan.

"Nowhere in sight, ladies and gents," Izzy said, mopping his face, and scratching his head.

The ADA stood, flapped his arms, and said, "Your Honor, I object to this . . . this outrageous behavior."

"Mr. Gleason," the flabbergasted judge said. "Please explain this."

"I wish I could, Your Honor," Izzy said. "But I gotta find it first."

He's finally lost the last of all his marbles, Bobby thought, watching Izzy jump down off the chair and drag it back to the defense table. The jurors and the spectators and the defendant and the court officers giggled. Iglew and the Five Percenter posse sat in composed silence. Bobby saw Iglew wrestling his face muscles against a smile. The judge wasn't anywhere near laughing.

Detective Samantha Savage never so much as shifted in her seat as she watched Izzy's antics with an almost out-of-body stoicism. Bobby wondered what kind of man it took to make her come to life in bed. He wouldn't even want to try. Not because she wasn't beautiful. But because he was afraid of striking out, or her making him feel inadequate.

Izzy dropped to all fours and scampered across the tile floor, looking under the defense table, then duckwalked to the prosecution table, pulling a magnifying glass from his back pocket and snooping like Sherlock Holmes. The jurors roared laughter.

ADA Queenan leapt to his feet, pointing at Izzy, shouting, "Your Honor, I object!"

The judge stood, leaned over the bench, and shouted, "Mr. Gleason, what the hell do you think you're doing?"

Izzy looked up at him from all fours, scratched his head, and said, "Me? Oh, I'm just looking for the prosecution's *evidence,* Your Honor. He keeps talking about it. But I haven't seen it yet. So I figured the prosecutor must have hidden it somewhere. Because I sure haven't seen a trace of it and neither has the jury. Have we, guys?"

The jurors looked like the audience in a comedy club interacting with the stand-up comic as Izzy stood and approached the bench.

"Mr. Gleason," the judge shouted, pointing his gavel. "I'm warning you, any more theatrics, any more histrionic stunts, and I will hold you in contempt."

"Sorry, Your Honor, but I thought I heard the prosecutor say in his opening that this was a search for truth. Okay, so I thought I'd do a thorough search. Because he certainly hasn't done one."

"You've made your point, Mr. Gleason! Now move on with your cross-examination! Or I will dismiss the witness. And you'll *find* yourself in a jail cell!"

"Sorry, Your Honor, no disrespect meant for the court."

"Move on," the judge said.

Bobby studied the smiling jury. Izzy owned them now. He watched Izzy walk back to the defense table, rolling down and buttoning his cuffs, straightening his tie, and winking at juror number nine, an attractive ash-blond woman in her middle forties, a tad wide in the hips, who seemed to give him goo-goo eyes right back.

He's flirting with a juror, Bobby thought. *He wants to get suspended again.*

Izzy pulled on his jacket. He ripped open a small towelette and wiped his hands as he approached the witness box, where the beautiful black, female detective sat with the authority of a queen on her throne. Bobby knew who she was although he'd never met her before. He'd spoken to her many times on the phone and had seen her photo in all the hip-hop magazines, exposed as the top NYPD detective on the NYPD/FBI Hip-Hop Joint Task Force, which everyone tried to deny existed, but which was as real as the crimes they investigated in the shoot-'em-up, drug- and gun-riddled hip-hop netherworld.

None of her pictures came close to the charisma that steamed off her in person, the kind of energy that radiates from certain pop icons, powerful politicians, and messianic clerics.

Bobby stared at her. She had short-cropped hair and her supple skin was as creamy as Godiva chocolate. She had a regal, almost aristocratic bearing and oozed an impregnable confidence so standoffish that it was sexy. It was as if someone had hung a No Tresspassing sign around her neck the year she'd blossomed to womanhood. Bobby thought that if she were a mountain, she'd be Everest; if she were a bank, she'd be Fort Knox. As a woman, she made you want to conquer her at first sight, instead of falling in love.

"Good morning, Detective Savage," Izzy said.

"Good *afternoon,* Mr. Gleason."

"Oh! Good! You can tell time!"

"Yes. And I rarely waste it."

"Know the big hand from the little hand?" Izzy said, wiping each finger individually with the towelette, lingering on his middle finger. Then he made a clock of his arms, indicating four-thirty. "So this would be four thirty, like the time in the morning you arrested my client."

"Correct."

"And speaking of hands," Izzy said, still stroking his middle finger, "you wouldn't want to be accused of having dirty hands in your profession, as part of the FBI/NYPD Hip-Hop Joint Task Force . . ."

"It's a gang task force, Mr. Gleason, not a hip-hop task force."

"You can call it what you want. But the press and the people you arrest all call it the hip-hop task force, is that not true?"

"I suppose that's the street name for it, the tabloid name for it. I'm not a fan of the tabloids. They make my hands dirty."

Izzy laughed. "And the people you arrest, most of them have something to do with the rap music, or hip-hop industry, correct?"

"Many do."

"So you do know that the people in that industry often use tape-recording devices, right?"

"That would be affirmative, Mr. Gleason. They are so-called recording artists, so, yes, I guess it's true that that they would often use recording devices."

"My client, the defendant, Mr. Charles McCoy, aka Tu Bitz, is a recording artist. You do know that, don't you?"

"Yes, I do."

"Have you been investigating him long."

"Depends on what you consider long."

"By that, I mean long before the night, or early morning, that you arrested him for possession of the two kilos of marijuana and the loaded handgun in his car as he drove down Bay Street."

"He's been a POI, or person of interest, to us for some time, yes."

"Why? You a fan of his music?"

"Hardly. He has a long record of weapons and narcotics charges. Which are also the topics he often sings about."

"Yeah, but he did his time for those crimes, did he not?"

"Yes."

"And after his last incarceration did he not come out and launch a highly successful recording career?"

"Yes, that's affirmative."

"He made his money legitimately."

"Technically, yes, but I've always suspected his record label was founded on his drug money."

"Objection, Your Honor," Izzy said. "Speculation, unfounded."

"Sustained," the judge said. "Stick to the questions, Detective, please."

"Okay," Izzy said. "So your testimony to the prosecutor today was that on the night of December twenty-third of last year, you had Mr. McCoy under surveillance and saw his car swerving erratically on Bay Street in

Staten Island, and although you were off duty, and in plain clothes, you felt a need to pull over his car, on suspicion that he was driving while intoxicated?"

"I was afraid he might hurt someone or himself, and so as a police officer I felt an obligation to protect the public first and him second."

"That was a great yuletide gesture. So you're saying you put your cherry light on your car roof, hit the siren, and pulled him over on Bay Street before he ramped onto the Verrazano Bridge?"

"Affirmative."

"And your testimony earlier to the prosecutor was that you then approached his car and asked if he had been drinking?"

"Affirmative."

"And he said he'd had several glasses of champagne?"

"Affirmative."

"You're saying that this man, this man who has a long and unpleasant history with the police, a man who wrote songs about defying and fighting the cops, volunteered this information to you?"

"Affirmative," Detective Savage said.

Bobby knew Izzy had some kind of ace up his sleeve, because he was leading Savage around like a poodle on a leash. An elegant poodle. Bobby looked at Tu Bitz, sitting at the table like a black granite memorial to malevolence, and then at the skeptical, racially diverse Staten Island jury, and Bobby knew they weren't buying it.

"And then you asked him to voluntarily submit to a physical walk-the-line, touch-your-nose, and count-from-ten-backwards sobriety test?"

"Affirmative."

"But he refused a Breathalyzer?"

"Affirmative."

"And he failed the walk-the-line test?"

"Affirmative. He lost his balance and poked himself in the eye instead of touching his nose."

"Bool sheeeee-it," Tu Bitz said from the defense table.

"Be quiet, Mr. McCoy," the judge said.

"And you asked my client, Charles McCoy, permission to search his car?"

"Affirmative."

"And you're gonna sit there and tell me he gave you permission?"

"Affirmative."

Tu Bitz chuckled in a deep echoey way and mumbled, "Oh, man, what boolshee-it."

"Mr. Gleason, instruct your client to refrain from commenting."

Izzy turned to Tu Bitz and said, "Dummy up, bro."

Bobby saw the judge widen his eyes, lean back, and exhale as the jury broke into laughter. Izzy shrugged, walked closer to Detective Savage, sprayed Binaca in his mouth, and said, "And you swear under oath, under fear of perjury, that this is true?"

Savage hesitated, gazed at the sweaty prosecutor, and then to FBI agents Noonan and Scarano and said, "Affirmative."

"And that at that time, he was standing in the gutter, no cuffs on him, and you left him standing out there," Izzy said, walking to the exhibit table and lifting a bagged 9mm Glock automatic and two kilos of marijuana in a large plastic evidence bag. "And he didn't attack you from behind, run away, or hail a gypsy cab or a dollar van while you searched the car where you came up with this handgun and the marijuana, marked exhibits A and B?"

Several black jurors laughed; a few smirked and frowned in disbelief.

"Affirmative."

"Great," Izzy said, walking across the courtroom, toward the jury box, where some jurors were still trying to contain smiles, especially juror number nine, who smiled at him. Izzy poured himself a glass of water, dropped two lemon-flavored Alka-Seltzers into the glass, and added four Sweet'n Lows and stood with the fizzing concoction. The jury erupted again. "Don'tcha think he woulda needed to smoke two kilos to go along with that?"

"Objection," shouted the ADA.

"Mr. Gleason," the judge said. "You're testing my patience."

"Sorry, Judge, it's just that I'm having a real hard time swallowing Detective Savage's testimony," Gleason said, swirling the fizzing glass.

"Move on," the judge said.

"Detective Savage, remember when I told you that my client was a recording artist and often used recording devices in his line of work?" Izzy asked, watching the bubbles fizz in his glass.

"Affirmative, I recall."

"Well, what if I were to tell you that in a recent interview my client was quoted as saying he always carries a small RadioShack, voice-activated tape recorder with him when he's driving?"

Bobby saw Savage uncross her legs, planting both feet on the ground, like a flight passenger preparing for takeoff.

Izzy said, "He can't spell too well, thanks to the wonderful public schools in East New York, so he was quoted as saying he uses a tape recorder to get down rhymes that come to him as he drives his ride from the East Side to the West Side, when he's down with a sporty shorty on the side, heah'm sayin', yo?"

The jury broke into laughter. The court reporter said, "Can you repeat the question, please, if it was one? Slowly."

"Withdrawn," Izzy said, staring into the Alka-Seltzer bubbles.

"Is there a point to all of this," the ADA asked.

"Yes, please get to the point, Mr. Gleason," the judge said.

"The point is that that's how many rappers write. By rappin' into a tape recorder. Did you happen to read that interview, Detective Savage?"

Detective Savage squirmed in her seat, the first chink in her armor making her uncomfortable. "No, I can't say that I read that interview."

"Pity because maybe you should have looked for a tape recorder in my client's car when you searched for the handgun."

Izzy walked to Bobby and asked him to give him the tape he'd given him aboard the *Fifth Amendment*. Bobby handed Izzy the small microcassette. Izzy cinched it between his thumb and forefinger, so that the jury could see it. He held it up to the light, rotated it through his fingers like a lucky coin, then snapped it on the bare defense desk with a loud click.

All by itself.

Nothing else was on the desk—no yellow legal pads, no mounds of transcripts, no motions. Just the microcassette, sitting dead center.

Like a little ticking bomb.

The judge, the ADA, the jurors, the bailiffs, Iglew, and Tu Bitz all stared at the tiny tape. Detective Samantha Savage couldn't take her eyes off it. She swallowed hard, her hands fidgety now, a sheen of sweat misting her brow. Then she looked up at Bobby, drawing a deep breath. The oxygen didn't make the tape go away. She looked to Noonan and Scarano. They squirmed, Noonan's expensive suit pants squeaking on the wooden pew. Noonan licked his lips, glanced from Savage to Bobby, who looked him in the eyes and winked. Then Bobby's eyes met Savage's again. She was staring at him. He winked at her, too. She looked away. Worried.

She's mortal, Bobby thought. *Izzy dragged her down from Olympus, blew the doors off Fort Knox. Lies always leave you naked.*

Funny thing was, caught in her lies, Samantha Savage was even sexier in Bobby's eyes. The little girl within revealing herself. Vulnerable. A damsel in distress. In need of a knight on a steed. A knight named Bobby Emmet.

"Is that a question, Mr. Gleason?" the judge asked.

"Sorry, Judge. No, but I would like to ask Detective Savage if she knows the penalty for perjury in a class A felony case in this state?"

"Affirmative," Savage said, her voice as soft as prayer.

"Hah? Can you please say that louder! Maybe I'm going deaf from all the hip-hop music my client plays all the time, Your Honor, but I couldn't hear the defendant's response!"

"Yes!" Detective Savage said. "I am aware of the penalty for perjury."

"Oh, good," Izzy whispered in the courtroom that was now so silent everyone could hear his Alka-Seltzer's final fizz. "Because I'd like to know, Detective Savage, if you would like to amend or recant your earlier testimony in any way before you leave the stand today?"

The ADA jumped to his feet. "Your Honor, may I have a moment with the witness."

"Excuse me, pally, but she's *my* witness right now, right, Your Honor?" Izzy said, walking to the defense table, and tapping his index fingernail on the little tape with the *da da-da-da-da da* beats from the *Dragnet* theme.

He's a legal terrorist, Bobby thought, watching Detective Savage lick her lips, the muscles in her jaw bunching like an infant's fists, widening her eyes and drying her palms on her pants legs.

The judge said, "The witness will answer."

"Is the defense offering that tape in evidence, Your Honor?" the ADA asked.

"Mr. Gleason?" the judge asked.

"Tape? What tape would that be?" Izzy said. "My client's latest hit, 'Stuck in the Zipper of Love'?"

Everyone in the courtroom, including the judge, laughed. Even the ADA turned away and snickered. Detective Savage did not even smile. Bobby turned and Iglew smiled for the first time. Bobby shifted in his seat and watched Joe Brightman adjust his tie. He saw the blond man across from him take a deep breath and exhale in a slow, controlled stream.

"The tape on the defense table," the ADA said.

"Oh, that," Izzy said, a big smile spreading on his face as he passed the jury box, Groucho-ing his eyebrows at juror number nine. "Well, that depends on the witness's response to my question."

All eyes shifted to Detective Savage, who squirmed on the witness stand, taking a deep drink of water, the long, pronounced tendons in her elegant neck jumping as she swallowed. She tried to compose herself and cleared her throat and pulled taut her lips.

She said, "Well . . . perhaps . . ."

"This is New York, lady, where *perhaps* don't fly. Do you or don't you want to amend your testi-*phony* . . . er, um, I mean you've been testi-*lying*, um, testifying all morning, pardon my Brooklynese, and I'm having a hard time keeping it down."

Izzy stirred the Sweet'n Lows with his Bic pen and guzzled the Alka-Seltzer as the jury laughed. Some shook their heads; others leaned back in their seats, belly laughing; others hung their heads and giggled. But Bobby knew Izzy had them all in his inside jacket pocket. No matter what the beautiful cop said, Izzy's client was going to break-dance out the door.

"Maybe some of my remarks were paraphrased. . . ."

"*Perhaps. Maybe. Paraphrased,*" Izzy said, belching into his fist. "Hey, the jury never says *maybe* he's guilty, or *perhaps* he's not. They don't *paraphrase* three strikes you're out, life without parole. It's one way or the other, lady. C'mon, Defective, I mean, um, *Detective,* enough with the bubble-wrapped words. How about a few concrete answers. Okay, lemme make this easy for ya, okay, babe—"

"Objection," the ADA said with a defeated wave of his hand.

"Please address the witness in a more dignified manner than *babe,* Counselor," the judge said.

"Sorry, hon . . . withdrawn . . . *Detective.* Okay, so, let's start from the beginning. And this time, I'll stop calling you babe if you stop giving me *affirmative*s or *negative*s instead of simple *yes* or *no* answers, okay? Did you ask the defendant if he had been drinking?"

"No."

"Did he say he had been drinking?"

"No."

"Did you ask my client to voluntarily step out of the car?"

"No."

"Did you demand that he do so, at gunpoint?"

"Yes."

"Did you pull him over in the first place because he was driving erratically?"

"No."

"Did you give him a sobriety test?'"

"No."

"Did he give you permission to search his car?"

"No."

"So you pulled him over, made him get out at gunpoint, then you hand-cuffed him, behind his back, so he couldn't get away, didn't you?"

"Yes. I was alone, in my own car, I had no radio, and I had no choice."

"Oh, yes, you did. And then after he was handcuffed, you searched his car without permission, isn't that correct?"

"Yes."

"Your Honor, I move to dismiss on false arrest, failure to Mirandize my client, violation of the Fourth Amendment, and about two or three dozen other things."

The judge looked at the exasperated ADA, who just threw his hands in the air and waved.

"Motion granted. Case dismissed. The defendant is free to go. And I will be contacting your superiors, Detective Savage, and discussing this case with the Internal Affairs and the District Attorney's Office."

SIX

Tu Bitz threw his arms around Izzy, lifted him in the air like a throw pillow, mussed up his hair, and said, "You my nigga!"

"I could lose my license for saying 'likewise,' bro," Izzy said.

Bobby stood as Noonan and Scarano inched down the row to pass, making their way toward the courtroom exit.

"Step aside," Scarano said.

"Your mother never taught you *please?*" Bobby said.

"I know all about you, Emmet," Noonan said. "And I'm going to know more. And more. And more. Until you're sending jail mail home to your daughter again."

"You fucked with the wrong people this time," Scarano said.

"Sore losers," Bobby said, and turned sideways to let them pass. As Scarano squeezed by, Bobby ground the heel of his thick-soled Skechers shoes onto the smaller Fed's thin loafer, crushing his big toe with all 210 pounds. Scarano howled and jerked backward, slamming into Noonan, knocking the special agent in charge onto the floor between the benches.

"Jeez, sorry, guys," Bobby said, offering his hand to Noonan to help him up. Noonan took his hand and Bobby crushed his fingers in his powerful hand until he could feel his bones crunch, air bubbles popping in the joint fluid of his knuckles. Bobby yanked Noonan two feet off the floor to a dangling position as Scarano flipped off his loafer and massaged his pulsing toe. Bobby leaned close and whispered into Noonan's ear, "You ever fucking mention my daughter again, G-boy, and you'll be competing in the Wheelchair Olympics."

Bobby kept smiling and looked deep into Noonan's eyes. The head

Fed looked astounded that anyone would dare speak to him like that. Bobby crushed his fingers harder and curled him upward like a dumbbell.

"I want this man arrested," Noonan shouted, wobbling, but the court officers just saw Bobby helping Noonan to his feet.

"For what?" the baffled court officer asked.

Noonan shouted, "He threatened me."

"I didn't hear anything," the court officer said.

Bobby crunched Noonan's hand one last time, then clapped him on the shoulder and squeezed soft tissue.

"Tough day," Bobby said. "Your partner lost his footing. He knocked you down. I helped you up. Don't let's make a *federal* case out of it."

"I'll be seeing you around," Noonan said, rubbing his pained hand and shoving Scarano in the mean little pecking order of life. "Move it!"

The Feds left the courtroom and Bobby watched an amused Iglew staring at Bobby as the Feds passed his aisle. Then Iglew left inside a flying wedge, surrounded by his bald-headed posse.

Through the open doors Bobby saw Brightman leave the courtroom.

The blond-haired man with mustache left amid a knot of spectators and headed for the men's room. In the commotion, Izzy introduced Bobby to Tu Bitz, telling him that Bobby had done some of the initial investigative work on the case.

"Yo, any friend of Izzy Gleason is aye-ite with me, heah'm sayin', even if you used to be Five-O," Tu Bitz said, as he was surrounded by his mother and brothers and sisters and fans and friends.

Tu Bitz held out his hand for Bobby to shake. Bobby didn't like the guy or his music or his history or his street rep. But he thought he might be someone whose help he could use on the Cookie Calhoun case. He thought about crime between the hip-hop gangstas the same way he thought about Italian and Russian mob intramurals. If they wanted to kill each other off in a Darwinian opera, fine. Make the undertakers and the florists happy. When they killed innocent civilians, especially a mother in front of her kid, Bobby hated them.

Bobby had never heard of Tu Bitz going after anyone but rival dope dealers, gunslingers, and hip-hop gangbangers.

Bobby had done fundamental work on the case, verifying for Izzy from a bartender and two cocktail waitresses, one of whom Tu Bitz had had sex with in the "chill room" of The Do or Die Club, that on the night of his arrest the infamous rapper had not been drinking because he had been taking Cipro antibiotics for a kidney infection. Which had made Izzy certain that Detective Samantha Savage was a liar. This made him believe that at least some of Tu Bitz's version of events might be true. Which made Detective Savage easy to manipulate on the stand. Because, just as you can't cheat an honest man, even a great lawyer can't expose a truthful witness as a liar.

Lying cops had once framed Bobby for murder, so he had a lower opinion of bad cops than he did of hoodlum rappers. Did Tu Bitz have an illegal gun? Yeah. But did Savage bust him clean? No. She tried to frame him.

So, even though he'd never exchange holiday cards with him, or ask him to babysit, Bobby shook the big man's hand. The rapper tried to put the atomic vise grip on Bobby, a silly old macho street tactic to intimidate him. But Bobby was better at it than Tu Bitz, after turning his hands into C-clamps in the joint by squeezing a handball for eighteen straight innocent months until he was certain he could strangle any man with a single free hand in order to stay alive as a cop in the can. He still gripped the ball daily. And so Bobby squeezed Tu Bitz's hand until he felt his knuckles crush together like kindling. He saw surprise light up the big man's eyes like a pinball game on tilt. Tu Bitz leaned sideways from the pain, fighting not to show it.

"Thanks for your help," he said, his deep voice an octave higher. "Ever need anything from me, say yo."

A half dozen jurors approached Izzy, saying they were going to find his client innocent even without the cop recanting her earlier testimony. A few asked for business cards. Juror number nine approached in a sly glide and asked if Izzy handled divorces.

"Depends. Kids?" Izzy asked.

"Two, away in Harvard and Princeton."

"Property?"

"House in Manhattan Beach, one in Miami Beach."

"Call me for lunch tomorrow," he whispered, handing her his card. "Wear the white pants you wore the first day, the skintight ones, with the red thong I could see through the pants. And those matching red shoes. Bring a toothbrush."

She bit the edge of Izzy's business card, smiled, and sashayed for the door. Izzy growled as he watched her strut in her tight, navy blue pants. "I got two clients inside who'll add ten grand to my fee when I smuggle them in her unwashed thongs," he whispered. "Red and black pay best. They cut 'em up in little one-inch squares and keep them moist in cellophane off cigarette packs. Whenever they get their horns up, they take out the one inch square, put it to their nose, and they're off to Viagra Falls."

Bobby knew it was only a matter of time before Izzy got in trouble with the bar again. Which would end his obligation to him. But it would mean he'd probably have to sell the boat, and then Bobby would be looking for new digs. Besides, he didn't want to see Izzy go down, for the sake of his kids.

Bobby turned back to Tu Bitz and said, "I might take you up on that offer."

"Be my pleasure, yo."

Bobby gave him a final jolt of pressure that made the big man groan. Just then Bobby saw Detective Samantha Savage trying to shove through the crowd, clearly abashed after her disastrous performance on the stand. Bobby let go of Tu Bitz's hand, and the big man clapped him on the shoulder with his other hand. It felt like an anvil dropped from a roof.

"I need to talk to Ignatius Lewis, one-on-one," Bobby said.

"Iglew? He don't like talking to nobody, usually. Specially crackers. But I see what I can do. He owe me a few, heah'm sayin'?"

"I hear ya," Bobby said. "And maybe Deity, too."

"That shit never happen. Dee a witchman, a prophet, talk to the gods."

Bobby watched Izzy approach Savage and offer her the small microcassette. "Thought you might want this, babes," Izzy said.

"Excuse me," she said, trying to brush past him.

"Go on, toots, take it," Izzy said. "It's blank."

Samantha Savage stood in the courtroom well, astonished, looking down at the little cassette. Then Bobby watched her look up at Izzy, her large eyes glittery with rage, and hold her head high.

"Your day will come," she said.

She looked at Bobby and they held the stare for a long moment.

"Some people sure sell themselves cheap," she said, and clicked out the door on her medium heels. As the door closed, she took one final long look back at Bobby Emmet, who stared her right in the eye.

Although Izzy had left her like a wet spot on the floor of the witness stand, there was still some uncommon quality about her, something deeper and more primal than her obvious beauty that made Bobby weak in the knees. Maybe it was the way she looked through his eyes, into his brain, and out the other side of his head. Maybe it was the way she got off the floor and promised to come back another day, an unwillingness to accept lasting defeat, which was always the sign of true champion stock. Maybe it was the way she walked, like a woman who blazed her own trails, like the one she made through the courthouse crowd, ignoring a blaze of TV news camera lights and a herd of print reporters, and right into an elevator a nanosecond before the doors closed.

Whatever it was, Samantha Savage intrigued him.

He walked into the hallway to wait for Izzy Gleason. Bobby saw Tu Bitz and his entourage mob Izzy. He came out into an iceberg of flashbulbs and klieg lights as the press surrounded the victorious rapper and his lawyer.

Bobby stood by a window looking down two stories into the street and saw Samantha Savage traipse down the wide granite steps, where she had an animated conversation with Noonan and Scarano. She pointed a finger in Noonan's face as Scarano tried walking off his sore toe. Noonan wagged a finger at Savage, shaking and clenching and opening his other hand, which Bobby had crushed. They looked as if they were both assigning blame for the courtroom fiasco.

Then they went still and silent.

They all watched as Iglew's posse whooshed out and trotted past press and a big crowd surrounding a woman who looked like Agnes Hardy, who was staging an impromptu press conference. Iglew's flying wedge cleaved through the press and the fans straight to three waiting Lexus SUVs, the hip-hoppers and the three cops exchanging long, eerie looks.

Bodyguards surrounded them and guys with their hands inside their jackets stood outside of each SUV. Iglew approached his Lexus, followed by his bodyguards. Then Bobby could have sworn he saw Noonan flash three fingers downward at Iglew, the way a catcher signals a pitcher for a curveball. Iglew seemed to nod in an almost imperceptible way as he climbed into the second Lexus. A bodyguard who kept his hand inside his jacket looked both ways, then climbed in behind Iglew.

Savage and the two Feds watched the rappers spin away.

Noonan and Savage exchanged some final unaffectionate words. Then all three walked to a parking zone reserved for police vehicles. Noonan and Scarano climbed into a Crown Victoria.

Then from his window perch above the scene, Bobby felt the hairy legs of a spider scaling his spine as he watched Detective Samantha Savage climb into a gleaming black Navigator and speed off down Bay Street.

Bobby felt someone tap him on the shoulder. He turned. Izzy stood with juror number nine and pointed to the stocky, yellow-haired man in the beige linen suit who'd sat alone in the courtroom.

Izzy said, "That's James Ford, the cop who was assigned to the McNulty hit-and-run. I have absolutely no fucking idea what he's doing here. I defended guys he busted a half dozen times here on the island. DWIs, pot, a high-speed chase after a deli stickup. Nonsense. He had gray hair back in the day. Before he became fucking Custer."

Bobby watched Ford walk to the elevator rank and press the down button.

Bobby said, "I thought he was retired."

Several other people gathered at the elevator, including Joe Brightman, the governor's right-hand man, who dried his hands on a brown, industrial paper towel and pushed it into the wastebasket. Bobby figured they'd both been in the men's room at the same time. It might mean nothing. It might mean something.

"Guess what?" Izzy said.

"What?"

"You're the investigator. Go ask him, Sherlock."

Juror number nine laughed louder than the lame joke deserved. She would have laughed if he asked why the moron threw the clock out the window.

She said, "*Sherlock*. In addition to being a genius you're a real scream, Izzy."

"You have no idea, lady," Bobby said, and hurried onto the elevator after James Ford boarded with the crowd. Bobby watched Ford stare up at the floor indicator as the elevator descended.

Bobby turned to Joe Brightman and said, "How ya doin', Joe?"

The pol looked at Bobby, startled, and said, "Do I know y—"

"Bobby Emmet. You came to me a few times when I worked on Hogan Place when the governor was doing clemency reviews."

"Oh, right, the investigator. You were good. Very good . . ."

"You didn't take any of my calls when I needed your help. Your boss's help."

The elevator stopped at the next floor to pick up more passengers. Brightman looked at Bobby, uncomfortable, and said, "That was beyond my pay scale at the time."

Bobby glanced at Ford for a reaction. The too well-dressed ex-cop was still looking at the overhead floor indicator. But Bobby sensed he was listening.

"So, what's your interest in this one, Joe?"

"Ya know, high-profile case about a hot-button issue," Brightman said. "Wanted to have a personal look-see. What's yours?"

"Legwork for the defense. Working another case, too. About an old hit-and-run."

He looked from Brightman to Ford again. Ford didn't react. Which this time Bobby knew had to be intentional because that kind of talk should have ignited interest in a veteran highway cop.

Brightman said, "Oh."

"You might remember, name was Carla 'Cookie' Calhoun, a six-year-old boy watched his mother die, Bay Ridge, ten years ago."

The doors opened at the lobby and the passengers moved out. Bobby watched Ford move through the crowd, planting his beige panama on his head.

"Sorry, doesn't ring a bell."

"It will soon," Bobby said.

Brightman looked at him and said, "I gotta go."

Bobby watched Ford move through the revolving door. Brightman pulled open another door and left the building fast, Bobby following.

On the steps of the courthouse a large crowd of press and citizens had gathered to listen to Agnes Hardy, dressed in snug jeans, sneakers, a baseball cap with both the Yankees and Mets logos, and a tight *Hardy for Governor* T-shirt, holding an "impromptu" rally. She spoke through a bullhorn to the afternoon crowd of Staten Islanders. She looked gorgeous in the bright sun.

"I came here today to learn that justice again was not served," Hardy said. "Another drug dealer walks because of faulty police work, technicalities in the law. And my opponent, the man who calls himself your governor, refuses to debate me, refuses to come clean and get off the fence and tell us if he is going to continue to support the Rockefeller drug laws or if he is going to cave to special interests and help repeal them. Listen, when my beloved husband, Lance, lay dying, I rode with him in the ambulance to the hospital. He held my hand and made me promise that I would use our resources that he worked a lifetime to build to fight to keep the kinds of ghouls that killed his daughter with their poison in jail cells. I promised him on his deathbed that I would dedicate my life to that end. And when I threw my hat in the race for governor, I made that same promise to you the voters and citizens of this state. Yeah, no secret, I'm rich. I've heard the rags: 'Rich Bitch,' 'Wealthy Widow,' 'Party Hardy,' and all the others. Guess what? Yep, I'm rich. And I will be a real bitch on the drug peddlers in this state."

Big applause thundered across the steps, which Bobby knew would be the evening-news sound bite that would play on a news-cycle loop all night long.

"I'm rich but my stepdaughter is dead. From a drug OD. All our money couldn't save her from this plague. Like tens of thousands of other kids from every gender, socioeconomic, racial, ethnic, and religious walk of life, the dealers got the poison into her body and took her from us. Rich or poor, our kids are dying. So, yes, I'm rich, that's right, too rich to ever be bought off by special interests. Rich enough to vote my conscience. Rich enough to keep my promises. I say unequivocally here today, as I have been saying all along, that when I'm elected, I will veto any attempt to repeal these vital Rockefeller laws that protect our children from these drug cartel predators who deal in weapons of mass destruction. If anything I will support harsher, more stringent drug laws, I will appoint or support tougher prosecutors and judges, to make sure that no more predicate felons walk through the revolving door of justice like we are seeing here today."

She was interrupted by more applause. Bobby didn't agree with her, but he was impressed with her campaign skills. She was a great communicator. She was a candidate who had otherwise middle-of-the-road positions that would fly in New York—no new taxes, pro-choice on abortion, pro–death penalty, pro-immigration, pro-environment. But she had made the drug laws the centerpiece of her campaign, and she knew how to personalize it, sell it to the mothers who had lost kids to drugs and those who lived in terror of it happening to them. And she looked great in dungarees and sneakers.

Bobby watched Brightman hurry down the courthouse steps and head toward Richmond Terrace. He saw James Ford rush toward a waiting Lincoln Town Car.

"Excuse me, Mr. Ford," Bobby called.

Ford pretended not to hear, kept walking for the Lincoln Town Car.

"Detective James Ford," Bobby shouted, louder this time.

Ford stopped, turned, adjusted his lemon-tinted shades, and peered from under the brim of the panama at Bobby, a half-smile on the tanned, supple face.

"Yes?"

Bobby introduced himself, told him he was a PI working the McNulty case.

"I remember it, sure," Ford said. "Very sad. But one of those motiveless crimes that are essentially unsolvable if the guilty party doesn't incriminate himself."

"Really? So you worked the case pretty thoroughly?"

"I worked myself to the bone on that one. All I ever got was misinformation, blind alleys, dead ends."

"One of them lead here today?"

Ford blinked several times. "No . . . Actually I'm retired."

"I know."

"I was just curious. High-profile case. Every once in a while I miss the job and I like to see what's going on. Izzy Gleason was always an entertaining lawyer."

"Miss the action, huh?"

"Sometimes."

"You mind me looking at the Calhoun case file?"

"That would be up to the PD. Probably in some dusty cold-case drawer."

"You talk to the ex-husbands at the time?"

"Oh, sure. Nothing there. Not much there when she was alive, either, I'm afraid. You know, the usual, skells, one white, one black, but not killers."

"Uh-huh. Talk to neighbors?"

"They never saw a thing. Happened so fast."

"Security tapes?"

Ford looked at Bobby and frowned. His muscular driver walked around the car in short sleeves, showing off arms that looked like legs.

"I covered *everything*," Ford said. "Listen, Emmet, I don't mind being second-guessed. I understand a young woman being distraught over the death of her mother. But as one ex-cop to another, please don't insult me."

"Sorry, I didn't mean to be insulting."

"It was ten years ago. The security-camera craze has multiplied out of control since. Today insurance companies insist that lemonade stands have security cameras. But in that part of Brooklyn that long ago, you were lucky if all the banks had proper video surveillance. Never mind nearby tenements and mom-and-pop shops."

Bobby didn't mention the possibility of Verrazano Bridge security tapes. Just in case Ford tried to make it difficult for him to track them down. If they even existed.

"I'm just trying to do my job."

"Times are tough. I understand that you take what you can get. It's hard for cops after we leave the job."

"Did I say I was an ex-cop?"

Ford just stared Bobby in the eyes, then turned toward the Town Car. The muscle-bound driver pulled open the back door for Ford.

"What about the gangster social club on the block?" Bobby asked. "Twoboro?"

"The little bookie joint? What about it?"

"Think maybe someone meant to run down a wiseguy, say like Vito 'Sleighride' Santa, or Georgie Gorgeous, and killed Cookie Calhoun by mistake instead?"

The driver stood waiting for Ford to climb into the backseat so that he could close the door. Ford laughed at Bobby, the kind of mechanical chuckle that came more from heartburn than the heart. "Now you're being ridiculous," he said. "In one day you've elevated an old hit-and-run into a mob hit?"

"Who said I'd only been working one day?"

"Well, the way you spoke to Joe Brightman in the elevator, I assumed . . ."

Bobby watched a black Navigator with tinted windows cruise along Richmond Terrace, moving in a traffic cluster.

"That the way you worked the Calhoun investigation? Assuming it was a piece of shit and leaving it at that?"

Ford cocked his head, grinned, and said, "I think we're finished."

"I'm not."

"Don't tempt me to prove you wrong, Mr. Emmet," Ford said, climbing into the backseat of the Town Car. Bobby moved toward him. The driver blocked his way, flattening his palm on Bobby's chest.

The driver said, "Mr. Ford says he's finished, here, ace."

Bobby nodded, dropped his car keys, bent to retrieve them, and on the way up head-butted the thick driver in the balls. The driver yowled, cupped his groin, and did a little staggering dance away from the car.

"Sorry, Peewee, that was clumsy of me."

"That was uncalled for," Ford said.

"I have no scientific proof," Bobby said, "but I've been doing a survey about a theory I have that guys who hire other guys to open doors for them are the same ones who answer penile-enlargement ads. Any truth to that?"

Ford just glared at him as the muscle-bound guy duckwalked off his pain.

"Okay, so that question was optional. But here's a ten-point question: How did you know the guy I was speaking to was Joe Brightman?"

"You mentioned his name."

"I called him Joe."

Ford nodded, paused, and said, "Maybe I saw him on the news."

Bobby leaned in to Ford in the air-conditioned car. "You mind showing me your logbook from the day of the hit-and-run?"

Ford looked at him and laughed, the sun mirroring off his glasses. "Piece of free advice, Mr. Emmet. You're barking up the wrong tree. The truth is the hit-and-run *was* a piece of shit. Sad. But shit. Nothing there. Probably just some illegal, drunken Mexican who ran a light. It's as beneath your dignity as it was of mine. I had no choice but to work it. You do. My advice is look for other work. . . . Eric, hurry up, I'm late for my three o'clock."

Eric the driver hobbled to the driver's door, like a fighter recovering from a low blow, pointing at Bobby. "You, I'm gonna remember."

"I bet you say that to all the fellas," Bobby said. He turned to Ford. "What about Deity? Think he might've had something to do with it?"

For the first time, Ford flinched. "I have no idea what you're talking about." He powered up his tinted window. Eric put the car in drive and pulled away.

Behind him the Agnes Hardy news conference had broken up and her handlers hurried her to a waiting Jeep Cherokee.

Bobby watched both cars head for Bay Street, toward the Verrazano.

SEVEN

At 3:05 p.m. Bobby found Dianne Rattigan eating a cheese sandwich on white bread, and a bag of Deli potato chips, in the cramped employee cafeteria in the windowless basement of Lutheran Medical Center in Brooklyn. She wore bifocals and held a *New York Times* at arm's length, folded to Paul Krugman's column about the coming economic collapse of Bushanomics.

He saw her scribble something on a sheet of paper in a small memo book and then fold the paper into a tiny square and shove it behind the leatherette cover on her portable Bible. She also tore out the long, thin column, folded that, and placed it behind the cover of the Bible.

Bobby had read the same disturbing column with his morning coffee. It was a keeper. He wondered how he'd survive on a cop's pension. He'd be snooping for Court Street shysters for chump change till they pinned his name on his sweater, using his senior-citizen half-fare transit card to tail suspects.

Rattigan looked up and saw Bobby staring down at her. A nervous smile flashed across her face and she returned to her paper with a jerk of her head, fiddling with the stethoscope that dangled around her neck.

"Hi," Bobby said.

She looked around, gazed over her shoulder at other ambulance drivers, hospital workers, security guards, and two uniformed city cops who ate sandwiches and sipped sodas and coffees. Then she looked back up at Bobby, eyeing him from head to toe and smiling. She removed the bifocals and sat up straight at the Formica table, patting her hair.

"Me? You're talking to me, Samson?"

"Dianne Rattigan, right? I heard you often take your lunch break here in Lutheran."

"Listen, Samse, you from DOI, this is my legitimate break. I never steal city time. Not one second. I like what I do; I live for it so . . ."

Bobby laughed and said, "No, I'm not from the Department of Investigation."

"Okay, *Candid Camera,* then? What gives? Only time hunks look like you talk to me these days is when they've been blinded or have a bullet in them. Or if they're process servers sent by some malpractice ambulance chaser. Or my ex-husband's lawyer. So which one are—"

"None of the above. Look, sorry to bother you during lunch but—"

"This isn't lunch, it's death by American cheese, but it's free death, and believe me, with the high cost of dying that's a real break." She hid her mouth with her hand. "Trade secret. The city pays us less than garbagemen, so sometimes an ambulance driver will go out of his way two or three miles and take a non-life-threatening vic here to Lutheran because they give you a free lunch. Works both ways. We only bring 'em patients with health insurance or Medicaid, and in exchange they give us a sandwich and chips. Fridays tuna, ham Wednesdays. Hey, free lunch five days a week, twenty times a month, you save enough to pay the cable bill."

"The world is held together with swindles like that," Bobby said, sitting down at the table, facing her. She pushed her shoulders back, and her chest out, as if remembering what her mother told her to do around a possible suitor.

"Okay, so what's your deal, Samson? Why do I get a Bowflex model ten years younger than me joining me for a cheese-sandwich lunch? I haven't eaten lunch with a guy that looked like you since I picked up the tab for my yuppie divorce lawyer. Before he robbed me blind. Matter fact, I think he was working for my husband. I fired him, got a new lawyer, made sure she was a lesbian so my husband wouldn't try seducing her, and, presto, I should have my final papers any day now. And I'll have the rest of my life free, in case you're interested."

Bobby introduced himself, showed his New York State private investigator's license, and told her he was investigating an old run she'd answered almost ten years before. A tableful of black and Asian nurses and nurses' aides sat glued to *General Hospital,* playing on a TV mounted on a rack on the bile-green cinder-block wall. A woman with a Caribbean accent paged a Dr. Singh on the all-hospital PA system.

"You might not remember," Bobby said.

"Those are people, human beings, not garbage cans that we pick up for a living. Although some people treat us like we're garbage. In my ex-husband's case, worse. But I remember them all. I make official notes in my logbook and then personal ones that I store in my Bible to pray for them in the chapel of whatever hospital I'm in on my last run of the shift. I light a candle and say a prayer, that way I remember them."

She took another bite of her cheese sandwich, crackled a chip into her mouth, took a sip of diet Coke, and checked her Timex watch.

"Okay, how about Carla Calhoun, corner of Ninety-second and Fort Hamilton, a hot day, ten years ago this Friday."

Dianne Rattigan stopped chewing. Dread passed her face like an undertaker's shadow. She put the sandwich on the paper wrapper and riffled the pages of her Bible.

"What about it?"

"Hit-and-run. Her six-year-old son, Brian, watched her die. . . ."

"Okay. What is this?"

"That's what I'm trying to find out."

She checked her watch. "Kinda late on the draw there, aren't you, Samse?"

Bobby smiled. Dianne was probably a real looker once, a big-breasted, garrulous flaming redhead with giant blue eyes and perfect white teeth that had a slight, sexy overbite. In the old days, down Coney, she probably ruled the summer sands, exploding out of a yellow polka-dot bikini, full of life and wisecracks and fighting off the panting boys. She was probably the most whispered-about babe on the ambulance circuit, a hit with fellow paramedics, cops, firemen, and, of course, horn-dog doctors, single and married. But somewhere along the long, frantic lights-flashing, siren-screaming line, between paddling failing hearts, applying tourniquets, injecting poison antidotes, stomach-pumping barbiturates out of OD cases, and pulling sheets over the lost, she'd eaten a few too many free cheese sandwiches with chips, which she wore on her hips like saddlebags filled with fool's gold.

There really was no such thing as a free lunch, Bobby thought. Somehow, you always paid. Dianne Rattigan's cruel payback for a life of saving lives was middle-aged spread and getting dumped by a horny doctor husband and screwed in divorce court where her desirable youth and fierce confidence was officially pronounced DOA at age forty-six.

She checked her watch again. *The clock always ticks louder when you live alone,* Bobby thought.

"You might've been the last person to see Cookie Calhoun alive," Bobby said.

"Listen, I'll never forget her, okay? I brought her back to life with the paddles. Then she died in my arms. She asked me to hold her because she was cold. Never forget her teeth chattering like castanets when she insisted on whispering in my ear . . ."

Dianne took a small bite of her sandwich, crunched a chip against the roof of her mouth, trying to act ladylike. But no matter what she tried, she looked like what she was—a hungry working woman on a fuel stop. She checked her watch. Again. Bobby had met a lot of ambulance workers like Dianne Rattigan in his life as a cop, their paths crossing in the lost hours of the city's night, as they battled to save the lives of bad guys and their victims. She was one of the anonymous, underappreciated heroes of the city, rushing from one damaged stranger to the next, saving as many as she could, treating all as if they were family, and probably going home at night, hound tired, to open a beer, mic some buttered popcorn, and watch *Law & Order.* Alone. The next day she would again be elbow deep in blood and death and despair. Her faith in humankind restored only by the small triumph of salvaging the life of some ingrate she might never meet again. *Thank God for the lonely and the brave,* Bobby thought.

He asked, "What did Cookie Calhoun say?"

"Sorry . . . I was ordered never to repeat it."

"What? By who?"

"The cops. Which is why I figure you came to me."

"Which cops?"

"I'm not so sure I should even be telling you that, Samson. What's this? A beef about the insurance? Trying to recoup the old money? Leave the family alone, will y—"

"I'm working *for* the family."

She looked at Bobby and her watch. She seemed oddly nervous now. "I gotta get back to work. I have a thing about time. If I get back a minute late, and that makes me a minute late for a run, and someone dies because we were a minute late, I see that dead person's head on the empty second pillow in my bed that night and I don't sleep a wink."

Bobby stared at her for a long moment as she jammed the *Times* under her arm and emptied her tray into the trash.

"You're not gonna tell me what she said?" Bobby said, following her. "So that I might bring the Calhoun family some closure and relief?"

She pointed at the Krugman column. "This guy is saying Social Security might not be there by the time I get to collect. I get the city pension, sure, but I can't afford to lose this job, Samse. I got no one to take care of me when I get old. I carry old ladies out of apartments all the time, dead for days with no one knowing. I see myself on one of those gurneys. I need this job, to save, to build my nest egg, to pay someone to be there when I need someone there."

"The family of Cookie Calhoun needs someone to help them make the pain go away," Bobby said. "Her kid who watched her die is a teenager now. With suicidal tendencies. And one of these nights he might wind up in your bus as an OD because he can't find any peace that maybe you could have provided."

She looked at Bobby, her face quaking with tics, muscles shifting like the squares in a Rubik's Cube.

"Listen to me," she whispered, leaning close to Bobby's face, where he smelled the sweat that comes from saving lives. "Ten years ago I was riding high. I met and married a hunky doctor. I was so dizzy in love that I signed a prenup. He'd insisted because his first wife looted him. But I made a bundle on his tips on tech stocks. Then the bubble popped. So did mine. I got *old and—*"

"You're not old."

"And you're not a good liar." She pointed the folded newspaper at him. "I went broke, I got old, and Dr. Hunk lammed with a hot, young paramedic, thirteen years younger than me, that I, like an asshole, introduced him to. I got left with a one-bedroom condo on Bay Ridge Parkway and this civil service j-o-b. I can't afford to lose either one, know what I mean? I'd love to help you, help that family, but they at least got each other, which is more than I have. This is one of those cases I was told never to discuss or I lose the job and the pension, which is all I have. So I don't."

"The cops threatened to have you fired if you told anyone about what you know?"

"I gotta get back to work, okay?" she said, bumping him with her hip. "Nice meeting you. You're a babe. But you're not worth getting fired for. Jesus, I can't believe I just told you my life story. I've been cooking for one too long."

She checked her watch, which Bobby saw was ticking toward 3:30 p.m. "Gotta go, bye."

"Was the cop named Jimmy Ford?"

She froze, as if someone had cocked a pistol and pointed it at her head. She turned. "Did he send you to test me? That's what this is, isn't it?"

"No, I never even met Jimmy Ford before today."

"You think I'm a dunce? He thinks I'm a lonesome sucker for a big, hunky dude? So he sends you and your muscles and your movie-star smile to test me? All these years later? Why? Because of the terrorism thing? What? Listen, tell Jimmy for me, stay out of my way and I'll stay out of his way."

She walked toward the ambulance port, where a black driver stood finishing his free cheese sandwich, talking to other drivers.

" 'Sup, Di, you all right?" the black man asked, eyeing Bobby.

"C'mon, Paul, we better get in the bus," Dianne Rattigan said.

"Something wrong?" Paul asked, still looking at Bobby.

"Nah," Rattigan said, glancing one last time at Bobby, with a face that was a mix of fear and anger. "Nothing I can't handle."

Bobby watched her walk up the long ramp to the ambulance port. She looked back twice more, then climbed into her bus, and Paul sped off into the muggy afternoon.

As Bobby walked down the long corridor to the rear elevators that would take him up to the parking lot, his phone rang. "Hey, big brother," Patrick Emmet said. "I got that info on Burns. He's working eight-to-eight shifts on the bridge. I looked in his jacket. He's clean as a bean. Fact, made a few good collars since nine-eleven. Smart. Attentive. Ballsy. I think they might be putting this guy in for gold soon."

"Thanks," Bobby said, passing a bald black janitor who swabbed the already gleaming floor, his sweaty black face covered in a surgical mask. Someone pushed a squeaky laundry cart behind Bobby.

"You hear from Mom today?" Bobby asked Patrick.

"Yeah, wants to know when we're coming down there to visit."

"Soon," Bobby said, turning and stopping to let the workmen pass. "Maybe I'll take the boat down with Mag. You're welcome to ride along."

A big, muscular white man wearing a surgical mask and a do-rag with his green hospital tunic that looked two sizes too small paused at a soda machine and clunked in some coins. Bobby thought it odd that both of them wore paper face masks. He figured it was the new hospital paranoia in the age of SARS, killer flu, and anthrax. He thought that maybe he recognized the white guy.

"Sounds good," Patrick said over the phone. "Look, gotta go, bro."

"See ya," Bobby said, folding the phone and noticing that the white man wore designer pants and leather loafers. Bobby's ears grew hot, like radar dishes picking up hostile blips. The guy was built like James Ford's driver.

Bobby reached the end of the corridor and made a left to the elevator bank. He pushed the up button. Glancing right, he saw that the janitor had placed yellow caution cones across the corridor so that no one could pass. The janitor pushed the mop and bucket left into the blind L of the elevator rank. Bobby felt the wicked silence of the two men behind him, one black, one white, both surgically masked.

Not good, he thought.

Bobby looked up at the floor indicator panel. In the reflection of the polished steel he saw the dull, distorted images of the men behind him. The white guy reached behind him into his belt.

Then he heard something that didn't belong in a hospital. He knew all too well the metallic, oily click of someone tugging the slide on an automatic handgun. Bobby's heart pounded. He knew from jail that a nanosecond could mean life or death. *Control,* he thought. *Control is the only thing that can save you now. They don't know that you know what they are up to. Control, control, control . . .*

He stood loose-limbed, knees bent. In *control.*

In the wavy reflection of the steel frame he saw the black guy twining a length of wire around his fists, into a garrote.

Control, he thought. He waited. If he reacted too fast, they'd panic. The guy with the gun would shoot. Which the white guy didn't want to do. Or else he would already have shot Bobby. And the other guy wouldn't be tightening the garrote. They wanted a silent kill. Then they'd dump Bobby into the linen hamper, wheel him out. Neat, fast, bloodless—like hitting a human delete button.

Bobby raised his arm to check his watch, and in the reflection of the crystal against the black-and-gold face he saw the garroter approach, wire raised high over his head. He couldn't be sure with the SARS mask on his face, but Bobby thought he might have been in the courtroom earlier.

Control, Bobby thought, watching the second hand tick and tock and tick, and then just as the big man lowered the wire, Bobby swung the raised watch-hand backward with ferocious thrust. The back of his hand crushed the garroter's nose like a plum. Blood burst. The white guy raised his pistol and aimed. Bobby spun the garroter. Yanked his arms backward, making the man loop his wire around his own neck.

The black man said, "Motherfu—"

He didn't have the air to finish the remark as Bobby crisscrossed the garroter's hands. And clutched his wrists.

As the man garroted himself, Bobby clamped his wrists and used him as a human shield. Most of the silencer-muffled bullets perforated the elevator doors. But some of them ripped into the big man, making him dance like a puppet on his own strings, tearing open his arms, legs, and belly. The black man's weight was enormous, but Bobby planted his feet and held him up. It was like holding on to a jackhammer.

The elevator doors popped open. Bobby dragged the garroter in after him, his body jerking, his hands twisting the wire around his own neck. Bobby knew it took just five seconds to fire all thirteen bullets in a 9mm handgun. The shooter had emptied his clip. And he was reloading a clip when Bobby aimed his own .38 police revolver at him from behind the wounded garroter.

Before Bobby could fire, the white guy raced down the wet corridor, slipping, scrambling to his feet, and forearming the panic bar of an emergency exit door and disappearing through it.

Bobby took the elevator from the lower level to the subbasement. He didn't want to have to explain what had happened if he stepped off in the lobby with a half-dead man who looked as if he'd garroted himself in front of a firing squad.

On the way down, Bobby checked the man's pulse. He still had one and was heaving and gulping for air. The man had taken one bullet in the belly. Three more in the limbs. He was big and strong and he was lucky he'd gotten wounded in a hospital. He might live.

Bobby removed a wallet from the man's back pocket and jammed it in his own pocket. The doors opened. Bobby pressed the lobby button on the elevator and stepped into the subbasement. He let the doors close and the elevator rose in the shaft where it would open in front of the ER.

Bobby hadn't fired his own gun, so there would be no ballistics trace to him. And right now he had no time to waste answering a million idiotic questions from the cops. It would not advance his case an inch. It would only slow him down. Word was already out that Bobby was working on something that people didn't want unearthed. Someone had tried to kill him. He needed to know what it was about that old hit-and-run that sanctioned a new killing.

Bobby hurried to the stairs, which he took to the lobby. And out into the parking lot.

As he walked to his car, he pirouetted to be sure no one was following him. As he did his 360-degree turn, he saw an ambulance with a woman with flaming red hair shoot out of the emergency port, siren blaring, lights licking, racing down Fifty-fourth Street.

And then Bobby saw the gleaming black flanks of a Navigator pass on Third Avenue, tinted windows rolled up as tight as the secrets of the past, as it whispered west toward the Verrazano Bridge.

EIGHT

Bobby paid the toll on the Staten Island side of the Verrazano and asked the tollbooth attendant where he could find Stephen Greco.

The tollbooth guy checked his watch and said, "He should be down in about eight minutes. You can pull over to the side there."

Bobby parked his car near the command center of the bridge and surveyed the plaza for black Navigators. He counted three in twenty seconds and was about to check through the garroter's wallet when he was surrounded by three uniformed cops.

"You can't just park here, pal," said one highway cop

"License, registration, please," said a second, fingers summoning the ID.

"Retired from the job," Bobby said, flashing his facsimile shield and NYPD ID card that was also his license to carry his pistol.

The three cops looked at the shield and ID in the badge wallet. Bobby searched their nameplates. One was named Arena, one Sherick, and the third was named Burns. Bobby flashed his PI license and told Burns he was waiting for Greco, the security boss.

"You any relation to Kevin Burns, used to work Highway?" Bobby asked.

"My uncle," the cop named Burns said. "Retired. You know him?"

"We schemed together in the academy."

"That's Uncle Kev, all right," Burns said, signaling to the others that Bobby was okay. "Got out on three-quarters three years ago. Selling insurance out in San Francisco Bay area now. Owns three houses, rents two, lives in one. He got me assigned to Highway right out of the academy. Love it. Especially all the OT on this Operation Atlas gig."

Operation Atlas put a full-court press on the city's top terror targets, one of them clearly being the Verrazano Bridge.

Bobby asked, "You ever work with a cop named Ford?"

"He a pal of yours, too?" Burns asked.

"Nah. Only met him once."

"Lucky you. Not a well-liked guy. Uncle Kev couldn't stand him."

"Why?"

"Loner. Sneaky. Had his own agenda. No one ever wanted to partner with him. Never respected any of the rest of our get-out-of-jail-free cards. He's out to pasture now, too. I don't know how these fucking guys do it. He owns a string of bars and arcades and amusement parks down the Jersey shore. Real estate up the kazoo. On a cop's salary! Uncle Kev was a hustler, made his dough legit after he retired in the real estate boom. But this hump Ford was loaded when he got out. C'mon, how do you get loaded on the PD? Even with the OT. Plus he got out before nine-eleven, so he couldn't have racked up that much time."

Bobby knew from his DA days that the rare dirty highway cop occasionally got in trouble for egregious things like letting women drunken drivers off the hook in exchange for sex in the cop car. Or taking kickbacks from truck hijackers. Or providing unofficial escorts for cigarette and dope smugglers. Or for dealers at truck stops. Or providing cover for illegal toxic dumping. There were a million temptations if you were looking for them in the highway patrol unit.

"Kev thought Ford was dirty?"

"Why else would he be so secretive? Guys who worked with him knew he was into deep shit, and he would risk their jobs, pensions, and fucking freedom by just being with him. But he'd never tell them what it was. Never shared a dime. Never went to a fund-raising racket. I worked a few cases with him but I never trusted Ford. Good riddance. But if you really wanna know more about him, you should ask Uncle Kev, but he's on a safari in Africa for a month."

Bobby asked the cop for a phone number for his uncle Kevin on the left coast. The kid clicked through his cell phone and gave Bobby his number. Bobby entered it into his own cell phone. Burns also gave him his personalized NYPD business card, with his name, Highway Unit, and cell phone number on it. "That's a get-out-of-jail card in case you ever get stopped by anyone in the unit," Burns said. "My cell number's on it. It's a citywide courtesy. Keep it in your car. Ford was the only guy who wouldn't recognize them. Uncle Kev always suspected it was because Ford was afraid of ever getting in trouble for letting a perp slide before he pulled off his big scores. He did everything so by the book it was like you knew he was *really* dirty. Anyone who doesn't take small perks is usually taking something big and is afraid of risking attention on the small shit. That's what Uncle Kev always said. But he could never pin Ford's scam."

"Thanks," Bobby said.

"Any friend of Uncle Kev's. By the way, that's Greco."

Burns pointed to a balding and graying man in his fifties dressed in pressed dark slacks who descended the stone stoop from the command center, unbuttoning his shirt collar, loosening the tie that he let hang unknotted down his sweat-dotted short-sleeve shirt.

"Thanks," Bobby said.

"I gotta go," Burns said. "I just spotted a Mustache Mohammad in a rented panel truck that I don't like the smell of."

Bobby watched Burns signal to a yellow Ryder truck that approached the toll plaza, directing him to pull over beside two National Guardsmen who carried shoulder-slung carbine rifles.

Bobby was glad Burns was working for his city. He approached Greco, who walked toward a black Navigator. It sent the spider scrambling up Bobby's spine again. Bobby quickened his step and called Greco's name.

The little man spun, right hand going behind his back. His tie was navy blue, with an orange print that read *#1 Dad.*

"Yes?"

Bobby told him who he was, showed him his PI license, said he was a retired cop, and that he was an old friend of Kevin Burns's from Highway whom he was sure he knew. Greco seemed to relax and Bobby told him that he was working an old hit-and-run case and gave him some of the details. Greco seemed baffled and foggy.

"Sorry . . . I don't remember. I mean, eighty million cars probably passed over this bridge since then and maybe fifty thousand accidents, more leapers than I wanna count, more road-rage incidents than you wanna recall. I wouldn't remember one incident that happened on Fort Hamilton Parkway on the Brooklyn side ten years ago."

"I didn't think you would," Bobby said. "But I was wondering about something. Do the security cameras on the bridge towers scan the nearby streets? They must, no?"

"You're asking me to divulge security information in post-nine-eleven New York? Either you're crazy or you think I am, guy."

Bobby nodded. "I'm not asking about anything current. I'm asking about almost ten years ago. Before we had an Office of Homeland Security, before Operation Atlas, before we had a perpetual Orange Alert . . ."

"Still, I can't just . . ."

"Look, let me ask you a question. I know you're married, three kids—"

"Whoa, guy, that's personal. How—"

"Youngest is a daughter, Helen, nine years old. She give you that tie for Father's Day?"

Greco grabbed both tails of the tie, looked stunned. "Hey, pal, I think I'm gonna fucking report you."

"The information is on the Web, Steve. Everything you ever wanted to know about me is on the Web, too. I just get paid for doing my homework. But I was you, I'd switch to an unlisted number. Or have the phone put in your wife's maiden name. You are a target."

Greco cocked his head. "The only reason I don't report your ass is because you're a friend of Kevin Burns, who's a good dude. But I don't know you and I don't think I like you knowing what you know about me and using it to get me to tell you stuff I'm not authorized to divulge. So, let's just say, keep your nosy nose outta my affairs and I'll give you a pass for asking me to breach security, okay? I gotta go."

He brushed past Bobby, opened the door of the black Navigator, and tossed his jacket into the front seat.

"Let me ask you something," Bobby said. "How would you feel if some crazy swine ran down your wife and one of your kids had to watch his or her mother die? And he had to live his life with those images in his mixed-up head. And no one ever tried to bring the killer to justice? And if your kid who witnessed it was thinking of leaping off your bridge because he couldn't live with the survivor's guilt? The horror? The despair? How'd that make you feel, Greco? As a father, as a man, as a human being? Or is asking you that another breech of security?"

Greco just looked at him, sweat beading his balding dome, and took a deep breath. He lifted a finger, pointed it at Bobby, and opened his mouth to speak. No words came out. He stood staring at Bobby, as duty, professionalism, anger, guilt, fatherhood, and his humanity all shook together like a killer cocktail under the hot sun. Cars whizzed past. Helicopters beat through the sticky sky. Greco took a deep breath, looked out over the low-rise, endless sprawl of Brooklyn, which was a Dutch name for the Broken Land, strewn with broken people, some of whom would never be put back together again, and sighed.

"If there were tapes, and I'm not saying there were, or are, they might have been reused. Maybe not. What was the fucking date, pal?"

Bobby told him and Greco computed it inside his sweaty head, widened his eyes, and mumbled, "Not long after the first Trade Center bombing so . . ."

"So? So what?"

"So, nothing. So give me a fucking card, and a cell number, and there's a slim *maybe* of a chance that I'll call you back. No promises. But you really piss me off, guy. Really piss me off. I don't like people using my kids as hypotheticals when it comes to death and carnage, know what I mean? And it's hot, and you caught me off guard, but if I think this over and come to my senses, you probably won't hear from me."

"Do what you think is right, Greco," Bobby said, giving him a business card that had his cell number on it. "That's all I'm asking you to do. Just remember that there's a kid's life at stake, that's all. Thanks."

Greco climbed in his seat, slammed the door, banged the heel of his hand off the steering wheel, and lurched from the spot. Bobby turned to walk away. He heard Greco hit the brakes behind him. Bobby turned and Greco powered down the tinted window.

Greco said, "Hey . . . who was the cop assigned to the hit-and-run?"

"Ford," Bobby said. "Jimmy Ford."

Greco stared at Bobby for a long poisoned moment, lashes blinking, his jowls collapsing like a beaten hound's. Worry creased Greco's brow, and then the worry dilated into ice-blue fear in his widened eyes.

Bobby waited for a response. But Greco just stared, lost in the Ford name like a fly in a web. Then the tinted window rose and Greco sped off toward the broken land of Brooklyn.

NINE

While he was in Staten Island, Bobby drove straight to the Narrows View Nursing Home, which sat in the center of a ten-acre grounds with picnic tables, a parking lot, and rolling meadows overlooking the Narrows and the great bridge.

He knew he wouldn't have to drive far to find a florist, and when he entered, he asked the counterman to give him a dozen long-stemmed roses.

"Pick really nice ones, I don't care about the cost," Bobby said.

"They're thirty-nine ninety-nine a dozen," the florist said.

"Forty bucks? No problem."

He knew that would mean the florist would have to walk into the back to get them out of the special chiller where roses were always stored.

The florist disappeared into the back room. Bobby saw a row of gray smocks with the Hylan Florist logo stitched onto the front hanging on a hook just off the workstation where the flowers were cut, arranged, and packaged.

Bobby dropped two $20 bills on the counter, grabbed the largest smock he could find, and left. He threw the smock into the front seat of the Jeep, walked half a block to a Korean grocer, bought a $10 bouquet, and drove up to the nursing home.

"Flowers for room two twelve," Bobby told the security guard at the front door.

"Nobody ever sends that man flowers," the guard said. "Who from?"

Bobby showed him the card, signed, "Love, your son, Brian."

The guard looked at Bobby. "Freight elevator, down the hall on the left."

81

Bobby looked back and saw the guard speaking into his walkie-talkie. He pressed for the elevator and took the stairs to the second floor, carrying the cheap bouquet.

Room 212 was located at the far end of the second floor, closest to the exit door. The door was closed. He opened it without knocking. Rodney Calhoun sat in a wheelchair, his head slumped to his left side, his eyes like black marbles set in custard. He wore a bib and a TV played, but he did not look at it. He didn't look up when Bobby walked in.

He just stared out at the blue sky over the Narrows, the bridge reflecting in both empty eyes. The caged window looked out on a small, pebbled roof of a building annex. Air-conditioner generators whirred. Steam billowed through ductwork from a laundry room below it. Bobby waved the bouquet under Calhoun's nose. No response. He looked at the Velcro restraints on both wrists, which were outlawed in New York State except for patients who were prone to violence to others or themselves.

Bobby walked behind him, picked up the TV remote, then leaned close to his ear. "Why'd you kill Cookie, asshole?"

Calhoun flinched. But Bobby thought it was more from the sudden volume in his ear than the content of the question. Bobby snapped his fingers in front of Calhoun's eyes, then spoke into the other ear.

"You killed your own son's mother in front of him."

"I didn't scratch the record, Daddy," Rodney said.

"What?"

"Tell Daddy I didn't do it, Mama."

Rodney's head began nodding with a mild palsy, one hand trying to undo himself from the restraints that looked as if they were wired to some kind of impulse sensors.

Bobby clicked through the TV channels. He passed baseball games, bowling tournaments, pool games, last season's football highlights, basketball, boxing, horse racing, tennis, hockey, golf.

Calhoun reacted as Bobby flicked the channels. Growing more agitated as each station came and went. Until he was writhing and straining in his chair.

Bobby clicked back to the horse racing, where a live race from Belmont galloped across the screen. Some tremor of focus passed over Calhoun's eyes as he continued to squirm and rattle in his chair. Bobby studied the eyes. He couldn't tell if the response was a conscious reaction or some subconscious trigger.

Bobby bent, grabbed Calhoun's face, looked into his eyes, which were again as flat as poker chips, and whispered, "Your son, Brian, is going to kill himself unless he learns who killed his mother by the end of the week, shitbird."

"What the hell do you think you're doing?" said a voice from behind Bobby.

Startled, Bobby stood and turned and looked at a nurse. "I was just asking him what station he wanted on."

"It doesn't matter what station is on. They're all the same to him. He can't understand you. You delivered your flowers, no?"

"I didn't scratch the record!" Rodney shouted, straining at the Velcro restraints, his muscles bunching in his arms, veins popping in his neck.

"You need to leave," the nurse said.

Bobby found the address on Van Duzer Street in Stapleton where Ray "Nails" McNulty lived with his second wife, Brenda, and his sixteen-year-old daughter, Priscilla, in a rented one-family, wood-frame house with a Yankees pennant flapping from a flagpole and iridescent shingles that Bobby guessed predated Roger Maris's sixty-one-home-run season.

Janis had given him the address and phone number for Nails. But Bobby didn't call ahead. He didn't want Nails or his wife to be prepared for his visit. He parked on the hilly street where smooth, old cobblestones poked through crumbling blacktop. Weed trees sprouted at crazy angles in front yards that were framed with rusting Cyclone fences. The sidewalks were uneven, split with tree roots, and garbage cans with no lids and hand-painted addresses were chained to the fence posts. White boys with dirty T-shirts rode old bikes and small, squeaky scooters, teasing two girls skipping a clothesline rope that was tied to a fence. One teenager tossed a basketball through a portable stand-alone hoop and backboard, eyeing Bobby with that *look* that came from watching cops take away your old man in cuffs. This was white, working-poor New York in the neglected stepchild borough, in shooting range of ritzy Todt Hill, where gangsters who still drove Cadillacs lived in multimillion-dollar mansions to the north and the ominous, austere, bullet-strewn Richmond projects made famous by Iglew were to the south.

Sandwiched in the middle, Nails McNulty lived with a woman who didn't want her white daughter associating with her half brother, Brian, because he was half black. *The whole world is half nuts,* Bobby thought. *The other half is half drunk. We close firehouses in post-9/11 New York as we rebuild the Baghdad zoo, and here in the shanty heart of Staten Island people still hate people because their blood is racially blended. Even when they are blood relatives. Insanity.*

Nails opened the door after the third ring. "Yo."

Bobby told him who he was and why he was there and that he was working for his kids.

"Oh, Jesus Q. Christ," Nails said, running calloused fingers with dirty nails through a graying mop of unkempt hair that had been hip when his hair was still blond like his eyebrows and his lashes. "Please, boss, cop a march, because it'll cause fucking static in the house with the old lady."

"Who the hellllll's thaaaaat, Raaaaaay," singsonged a woman from within, in the same musical key as a smoke alarm.

Bobby thought that the day he heard that voice say "I doooooo" at the altar he would have steered the waiting Just Married limo to one of two places: off a bridge or straight to a divorce lawyer.

Brenda McCabe McNulty appeared at the door, her fortysomething face like a judge's sentence. Not plug-ugly, Bobby thought, and maybe even handsome once in a 4-a.m.-last-call-desperado kind of way, but since worked into a permanent scowl that resembled live Claymation. Her squinty eyes, which popped open after every third word, beamed her low opinion of the world like neon a sign that blinked *Fuck Off!*

"I'll take care a it," Nails said.

"You couldn't care for a corpse even if it was your own."

Sweet, Bobby thought.

Nails fought for control of the threshold. "I sez, I'll handle this."

Brenda shouldered in front of Nails, holding a cooking spoon with a burnt handle in her right hand, tomato sauce steaming off the scoop.

"Yeah?"

"I need to talk to your husband," Bobby said.

"About what?"

"Private. Later I'd like to ask you a few questions."

"Fuck you," she said, trying to close the door.

"He's like a Magnum, PI, Barnaby Jones kinda investigator. It's about Cookie, and the kid, the accident."

"Far's I'm concerned, all the brats you had with her were accidents."

Rage lit Nails's eyes, and he licked his lips and swallowed. He looked as if he'd been swallowing similar comments for so long it was like a jail diet you had no choice but to tolerate.

"What makes you think it was an accident?" Bobby said.

Brenda laughed and waved the spoon. "What, alla sudden Cookie Calcoon is JFK and we're looking at a second gunman over here? We got a conspiracy to kill a waitress from a hip-hop diner who liked riding the big black tar roll? A sambo lover? And her half-breed kid—"

"Why don't you shut the fuck up," Nails said.

"Why don't I stab you in your sleep, talk to me like that."

Bobby said, "Hey, why don't I come in? Everybody calm down. We'll talk, make nice, like that, huh?"

"Nobody comes in my house," Brenda said. "Specially somebody workin' for those white-chocolate brats of his." She paused and shouted to a pretty blond girl of sixteen who was skipping rope with younger kids. "Priscilla, inside, dinner, now, no lip."

Priscilla stamped a foot, said good-bye to her friend, and marched toward the house. Nails gave her a kiss, and she gave him a hug. She brushed past Brenda, and Bobby watched her enter the house—wood-paneled walls, dropped ceilings, cramped with utilitarian Ikea furniture. The place was spotless, with shiny linoleum tiles and area rugs and Berber carpeting on the stairs to the upstairs bedrooms. *Lot cleaner than the space between Brenda's ears,* Bobby thought.

"I'll take a walk with ya," Nails said.

"Then you better eat out," Brenda said. "Leave now, you ain't eatin' here tonight, numb nuts. I'll eat mine, feed Priscilla, and dump the rest down the shithouse bowl."

Bobby ordered two beers at a place called The Wooden Leg on Targee Street, a little corner tavern where people dissected the world using the daily *Staten Island Advance* as their guide. Six men sat on stools watching ESPN updates on the TV. New York had changed since the last time Bobby was in a corner tavern. A smoking ban was in effect now. The place did not reek of nicotine and ashes. People saw each other through a clear-aired barroom, which only italicized how ugly a daytime drinking crowd could be. Bobby had never smoked, hated the smell of cigarettes, but the libertarian in him hated any restriction on personal freedom, and he missed the foggy-saloon atmospherics and the traditions that went with them. It was like drinking in a library. It bothered Bobby that no half-lit divorcée sipping a manhattan would ever again turn on her midnight barstool, unlit cigarette clasped in her ringless fingers, smile at a widower as Sinatra lamented on the juke, and say, "Hey, handsome, got a light?"

" . . . Cookie was the love of my life, ya know."

"Really?" Bobby said, not wondering why. He felt kind of morally corrupt drinking with a guy whose wife he'd bedded one rainy afternoon when all of them were separated. She'd divorced Nails and remarried and separated from Rodney Calhoun by then. Still, he had no intention of telling him. It would only make Nails's regret deeper.

"Loved that woman. Loved my kids . . ."

"The wife I can understand you referring to in the past tense. But your kids, you still don't love them?"

"Course I do. I just don't get a chance to see 'em much. You see what the warden is like."

"She's tough."

"She's fuckin' *sick*. But where'm I gonna go? Less I hit Mega Millions I can't leave. Trapped. Rents even here on the Island are a grand a month for one bedroom. Court says if you got a daughter, weekend visits she gotta have her own bedroom. So I need two bedrooms. Fuck am I gonna come up with twelve-fifty for two bedrooms? Plus the child support. And the two gases, two Con Eds, two phoneses, two cableses. I'm fifty-friggin'-six, my back's ruint. I can swing a hammer but I can't carry sheetrock. Means I gotta work with a helper, he's ten beans an hour, even a Guadarican, and without Brenda, I got no health insurance. She gets it from her job workin' as a civilian receptionist for the One Hundred Twentieth Precinct. Where she got all kindsa contacts so that even if she beats the shit atta me in my sleep, which she does now and then when she drinks Hennessy, the cops come and arrest me 'cause they side with her. I'm fucked pi squared. But I love my daughter, Priscilla, and that's the only thing that keeps me from leavin'. Brenda knows she got the upper hand. Brenda got two assholes, the one she shits with and the one she sends out to work every morning. It's like doin' time. Way I look at it, it's the penance I do for cheatin' on Cookie, the love of my life."

He took a long, slow swallow of beer, his gray, stubbly Adam's apple rising and falling in his neck like the surges of his aching heart. His veiny red eyes blinked, as he placed the glass onto a soft coaster, blond, girlish lashes batting.

"Know anybody who wanted to kill her?"

"Brenda."

"You serious?"

"I don't think she did, but I think she would have if she thought she'd get away with it. She hated me sending them support checks. It boiled her fucking brains every month."

"But you don't think she did it?"

"I know she didn't. She was with me like a fly on shit."

"You might consider a different metaphor."

"Who's he?"

Bobby nodded and said, "You think she might've planned it? Got someone else to do it?"

"Nah. At heart Brenda's a coward. She'd be afraid of doing the time. If she had to go to jail, she'd have to live with the people she hates."

"Blacks."

"All non-Caucasians. She ain't big on your average Chinks or your Portos or even your basic American ginzos, either."

"She teaches that poison to your daughter?"

"Priscilla is an angel," Nails said. "She don't have a bad word for nobody."

"Did Detective Ford ever interview Brenda?"

"He interviewed me. The once. That's it."

"Did he check your alibi?"

"Yeah, he asked Brenda if I was home at the time of the hit-and-run."

"That's it? He ask for any other proof you weren't at the crime scene?"

"Nah. He asked if I drove a yellow van."

"That's it?"

Nails nodded and shrugged and lifted his beer glass again.

"You didn't kill her, did you, Nails?"

Nails looked at him, his eyes lost in eternal grief, and said, "I would have died for her. I'd gladly die killing the fuck who killed Cookie. No problem. Matter fact, my dream is someday that I can die that way, one-on-one with the fuck who killed my Cookie. Right to the end, we were still close, we'd meet on the sly."

It was like Bobby hearing a door to a secret room creak open.

"Oh, yeah?"

"Yeah, ya know, we were childhood sweethearts. We had beautiful kids together. I loved her. I think she still loved me a little, too. It took her years to start talking to me again. But when she did, we'd compare notes and talk about dumping our spouses and getting back together again, like the old days, when we met, up on Hippie Hill in Prospect Park, smoking weed through a water pipe with rose wine in the bowl. We'd laugh. We'd dream. But it was just talk. We had a good goof talkin' about trying to fix up Rodney and Brenda. But it was never serious. That would have meant lawyers, mayhem, upheaval, killings . . ."

"Killings?"

"You know, figure a speech. I had a new kid, she had a new kid, it woulda been a real mess. So we'd just meet, in Prospect Park, Owls Head Park, or walk along Shore Road, have coffee, talk. The other kids never even knew. Brenda sure didn't know."

"You sure about that? Sure that Rodney didn't know, maybe?"

"Nah," he said, drawing a deep breath. "Oh my God, I wish I had one more day, one more morning, to just sit and talk to her."

"Did you two, ya know . . . I hate to be personal, get busy?"

He squirmed on his barstool. "I wish. But Cookie wasn't like that."

He looked at Bobby, drained his beer, and stared up at a bubbling beer sign behind the bar as if it were a window into the next dimension. The bartender came and reached for Nails's mug. He reached for Bobby's but Bobby put his hand on top of the glass and shook his head. All he needed was a DWI in the new .08 alcohol-level intoxication law. Bobby stared at Nails, long and hard, reading the tics and the eyes and the body language that spoke volumes about the ravages of lost love. And human regret.

Bobby had a cop's sixth sense, a built-in bullshit-o-graph that always worked better in conjunction with a glass of beer in a gin mill than with a rubber hose in an interrogation room. Nails oozed truth in his answers, in his eyes, in his broken heart that he wore on his soiled sleeve. But Bobby felt that he was still hiding something.

"Tell me the rest, Nails."

"Rest a what?" He looked at Bobby, then looked away, back up at the beer sign.

"You're carrying something around inside. I'm working for your children, Cookie's children, for your family. Tell me the rest, for Cookie's sake."

The bartender pushed the fresh beer toward Nails. He waited for him to walk away and lifted the beer, dipped his upper lip into the suds, took a belt, and wiped.

"Until now I never spoke about this, about Cookie, to nobody, like that cop made me swear not to."

"Ford?"

Nails nodded.

"He told you not to discuss Cookie's case with anyone?"

"That's right. Said I could get in a lot of trouble if I talked about this case to the press. Or other law enforcement people. Or anyone else. But since you were hired by my kids, you ain't official. I feel good talking to you."

"Did you tell Ford anything else? Something about motive? About why someone might want to kill Cookie?"

"I told him she was a waitress at the Music Box in the city, near the Brill Building, where all the music honchos used to eat lunch. And that she'd mentioned to me in private, sworn to secrecy, that she'd overheard a lunch conversation between a couple of big shots about a big crime. They thought she went into the kitchen. But she was behind the counter, bending down, tying her shoes. She always had sore, tired feet. She walked about eight miles a day. Doctor ordered her special new shoes she liked. But the laces always opened on them. She was bending down, tying the shoes, and she overheard one guy say someone who took a fall for someone. Major time, too."

"Who?"

"Don't know. She wouldn't say. But she said she learned the identity of someone really big. A secret owner of the record company that was supposed to be a secret. She had a name for him . . ."

"Deity?"

"That's it, yeah. Fuck kinda name's Dee Iti? Ginzo? Ends in a vowel, no? Like your Frank Nitti, there?"

"No, Deity means 'godlike.' "

"Like a priest? Nah, I don't think so . . ."

"Tell me what else she said."

"She said she duckwalked through the swingin' doors into the kitchen and one a them shouted, 'Who's that?' But she didn't turn. She got lost with the rest of the help in the kitchen. Made like she never heard nothin'. She didn't tell me who the guys were or nothin'. Just that she knew something about this Dee Iti character and she was terrified someone maybe knew that she knew. Ya know?"

"That's all?"

"That's all she told me. She asked what she should do. I told her dummy the fuck up and make like she was a priest who heard a confession. Say nothin', do nothin', and nothin' would happen to her. But I know she was afraid. My guess is she probably blurted it at Rodney when they was fighting. They fought more than me and her did. I think she was afraid that he knew what she knew what she wasn't oppose to know, ya know?"

"You told all this to Ford?"

"Yeah, but he said I should just keep quiet or else it could maybe hurt Janis and Jimi Jim and little Brian. Or me. Get me sucked into a big headline story and that could put my new kid in danger, too. Cookie didn't say so, but I had the feeling the people she overheard talking in the restaurant were hip-hop big shots, and those crazy fucks go around killing each other like cowboys and Indians, ya know. Ford, he scared the shit atta me. I mean someone'd just killed Cookie in fronna her kid, right?"

Bobby could still see the fear in Nails's eyes as he finished his second beer, and so he bought him a third round with a $20 bill and left the change on the bar.

"Get yourself some dinner," he said.

TEN

Bobby climbed back into his Jeep and drove the Staten Island Expressway toward the Outerbridge Crossing, a gruesome-looking cantilevered span that was actually named for a guy named Eugenus Outerbridge, the first chairman of the Port Authority of New York, who'd lived in Staten Island, and that's why they called it a crossing instead of the Outerbridge Bridge. *I'd rather have a shit plant named after me,* Bobby thought.

He called Maggie and asked her if she'd had time to look at the photos of the parked black Navigator that he'd snapped at the Seventy-ninth Street Boat Basin and the one that had cruised past him in Bay Ridge at the spot where Cookie Calhoun was killed.

"They're the same car," Maggie said.

Bobby checked his rear and side mirrors, sifting the clogging traffic for Navigators, and exited the expressway, taking the service road for two exits before ramping back on, to be sure he wasn't being followed. He wasn't.

"How can you be so sure?" Bobby asked.

"I used the NASA digital enhancer and it came up with the same rusty little ding on the left rear fender, shaped like a pair of puckered lips, near the taillight," she said. "But, sorry, no plate number."

Bobby had gotten James Ford's Social Security number and a mailing address in Surfside Heights from his brother Patrick at the NYPD Intelligence Division. Using that basic information, Maggie said she'd done an Accurint.com search on James Ford. Accurint was a database that stored 20 billion records from four hundred databases dating back thirty years and gave lawyers, skip-tracers, and PIs a complete background check into a person's criminal, civil, banking, collections, insurance, landlord/management-company, marital, and child-support status and endless other information.

"James Ford lives in a thirteen-bedroom, twenty-four-thousand-square-foot mansion in Rumson, New Jersey," Maggie said, adding that she was sending Bobby a long text message with the details. "This guy must be doing all right, Pop. Bruce Springsteen and Bon Jovi live in Rumson. The 2000 Census tells us Rumson has a total population of 7,137 of which 6,978 are white, 17 are black, 36 are Hispanic, and 106 are Asian and Other, all living in 2,394 households, of which only 69 consist of two to four units."

"What Ron Kuby calls Whitelandia," Bobby said.

"Honkadelphia is more like it," Maggie said. "No one is writing hit songs about the boyz in the Rumson hood, tell you that, old man."

Maggie emailed an old NYPD ID photo of James Ford to Bobby's phone, which he would click on after he hung up with Maggie. And using the Accurint corporate holding database search engine, Maggie also gave Bobby a list of Jimmy Ford's varied businesses in Surfside Heights, which included the Wavecrest Motel, an upscale hundred-room complex with pool and diner. In town he also owned two nightclubs, called Surge and Urge, a high-end beachfront restaurant called Starfish, which the *Newark-Star Ledger* and the *Asbury Times* had both given four stars, an amusement park on Neptune's Pier, and a string of boardwalk arcades all owned under a corporation called Exit 82C Inc.

Bobby also knew that the Garden State Parkway exit for Surfside Heights was 82C, and the veteran highway cop had decided that this exit was the pot of gold at the end of his NYPD rainbow.

Bobby also knew that it was only an hour's drive from Staten Island without traffic, so he took the ugliest bridge in New York across the Arthur Kill to Perth Amboy, New Jersey, and sped south on the Garden State toward Exit 82C on the famed shimmering Jersey Shore to get a quick look at Jimmy Ford's retirement world.

"Maggie, find out whatever you can about who owns the Narrows View Nursing Home in Staten Island," Bobby said. She said she would.

Bobby got off the highway, looped through the sandy streets, where young people walked in shorts and sandals through the bustling seaside community. Bare-chested and tank-topped college guys strutted, flexing their overdeveloped steroidal muscles, gleaming with baby oil, hair streaked with platinum highlights, coming on to broiled-brown and surgically augmented babes, passing dozens of honky-tonk saloons, cheap-eats joints, summer bungalows, rickety motels, and the barking carnies of the tourist traps. The weather was warm and the sinking sun was still shining and a soft zephyr blew in from the noisy blue Atlantic as Bobby parked in the crowded lot of the Wavecrest Motel.

He popped into the motel diner, ordered a glass of iced tea, and saw that the kidney-shaped pool was jammed with families and couples catching the final rays of the early evening.

"Jimmy Ford come around much?" Bobby asked the waitress, midforties and weary, walking as if she had sore feet and wearing a sad, gray face that suggested she would be going home to fat cyber-swine kids who didn't appreciate her endless toil in the real world.

"Mr. Ford's around whenever he has friends staying in the motel," she said. "That's about it. You a friend?"

"I was a cop in New York."

She smiled and nodded. "Yeah, his police buddies stay here. At least I think they're cops. They act like cops. Who else wears suits in Surfside Heights?"

"No kidding?" Bobby said, finding it odd since he didn't think Ford had many NYPD pals.

"Matter fact, two checked in this afternoon. Same guys have been here many times. They eat breakfast here together. But they eat the big dinner with Mr. Ford over at Starfish. The suits. I remember the suits. You staying here? If you're hoping for a special rate, there isn't one. Everybody pays the same, no exceptions."

"Nah, just passing through," Bobby said.

"Want me to say to Mr. Ford you sez hello?"

"Yeah, tell him Rodney Calhoun dropped by."

Bobby left a $5 tip and left.

"Thanks, Rodney . . ."

Bobby walked down to the boardwalk, watching the endless looping chairlift that sailed people above the beach parallel to the boardwalk, moving slower than a New York City bus in rush hour. He strolled north passing the arcades and Italian-sausage-and-pepper joints and young girls in string bikinis and short-haired boys who shadowed them, buying them pizza and ice creams, and lighting their cigarettes. He moseyed out onto Neptune's

Pier, two football fields wide and four hundred yards long, and according to Maggie's text-message information, owned by Exit 82C Inc., where long lines formed for the scores of rides. One daredevil contraption called the Bungee Bonzai launched people 230 feet into the sun-setting sky over south Jersey and dropped them in screaming, screeching, heart-thumping free fall, only to bounce upward again on elasticized cables. Bobby figured you could die on that from shaken-adult syndrome after your brain ricocheted off the inside of your skull like a game of four-wall paddleball. That ride alone cost fifty-five bucks a pop.

"Wanna take a shot, pal?" asked a carnie with oversize false teeth that looked as if he'd won them in Ford's arcade.

"Rather take a shot in the head," Bobby said as a young couple climbed aboard, the girl clutching the guy's arm for dear life. The guy had that look in his eyes he'd seen in Golden Gloves fighters just before getting KO'd in round one. Bobby thought you'd have to be high on drugs to get on the ride and sell drugs to afford it.

He watched a gorgeous blonde, blue-eyed woman hand the barker her money and climb into one of the swinging gondolas.

"You gonna let the lady ride alone, pal?" the barker asked.

Bobby looked at the blonde, all brilliant white teeth, golden-toned arms, and blue in the eyes.

"Don't embarrass him," she said, nodding to Bobby. "I'm used to riding solo."

Some opportunities come once in a lifetime, and here was a stunner sitting alone on a death ride who could sure use a man at her side. Bobby took a deep breath, handed the barker his cash, his contribution to Ford's old age, and climbed in next to the blonde.

"You've done this before?" Bobby said.

"Every night before I go to work I get a reduced rate. Gets my juices flowing."

"How long is your outpatient pass good for?"

She hit him in the ribs with her elbow. "What's life without a little danger."

"I wouldn't know."

"Fireman?"

"No."

"Too bad."

"Sorry."

"Don't be. You're not a lawyer, are you?"

"No."

"Well then, you have nothing to apologize for."

And then the motor kicked and the ride started, slowly at first, and raised them into the Jersey sky, up above the glittering arcades and the miles of blue and tan shoreline, above the boardwalk and Ford's amusement park, and the glittering nightclubs and the restaurants and the flatlands and the highways. Bobby saw a small oasis of twinkling lights at the end of the boardwalk that he guessed was Ford's four-star Starfish restaurant.

Then the ride peaked until they were upside down, looking at the world the way astronauts probably saw it in the early days of the space program, and the blonde grasped Bobby's big bulging biceps and screamed, "Ahhhhhhhhhhhhhhhhhhhh!"

And Bobby yelled, "Hooooollllleeeeey shiiiiiit."

And then went soaring off to the other side, a free fall into heartstopping lunacy, whipping them back up and over again and again and again and again until Bobby felt as if he were inside the eye of a hurricane.

And then it was over. They came to a breathless rest.

The blonde was as composed as a gymnast, but still held on to Bobby's bulging arm.

"Great arms. You work out, huh?"

"A little."

They dismounted the ride but she held on to his arm.

"I want an invite to the wedding," the barker said, laughing.

"I didn't get your name."

"I didn't give you one."

"I'm Bobby."

"*Hey,* Bobby," she said, giving his right biceps a final squeeze.

"*Hey?*"

She checked her watch and said, "Gotta go."

"*Hey,* you still didn't tell me your name."

"I know."

"Can I buy you dinner?"

"I have to go to work."

"Where?"

"I'd rather not say."

"Can I call you or something?"

She looked at Bobby, cocked her head, thought it over, and said, "Tempting but, I don't think it's such a good idea. If I did, I'd be a sucker for those arms, and if I fell for you, I could never live with myself for ending up with feelings for a guy I met in an amusement park."

She checked her watch again and said, "Bye."

And then she hurried off through the crowd and up the street to a parking lot until he couldn't see her anymore.

Chase her, he thought. Don't let this one get away . . .

He didn't.

The spellbinding sunset ended, night fell in soft, shaded stages, leaving wisps of dotted clouds that resembled Satan's face stenciled in the warm heavens. People oohed and aahed and then the face disappeared into the vapors as a cackle blared from the spook house called Dante's Inferno. Bobby walked down from the boardwalk and up to Esplanade, Surfside's main street, and passed by Urge and Surge, where lines wrapped around the block to get in, young people dressed to the skintight nines, the guys all pumped up in muscle shirts, solid gold-rope chokers collaring their bull necks, and sporting barbed-wire tattoos around their vein-popping biceps.

Bobby would never understand why any free American man would wear a permanent symbol of enslavement on his body. He chalked it up to the blissful stupidity of youth, which Oscar Wilde had lamented was wasted on the young.

The chicks were vacuum-packed into low-rise jeans and microminis, strutting in spaghetti-strap high-heel sandals, thinner and more feminine barbed-wire tattoos around their ankles, boiling with hormones, weed, and Ecstasy and lite beer, sucking on mentholated cigarettes as if they were life-support hoses. The youngest chicks, the under-twenty-ones who were old enough to drive, screw all night, and vote but too young to drink, flirted hardest with the swaggering macho bouncers with phone numbers scribbled on chewing-gum wrappers and matchbook covers, hoping to cocktease their way past the velvet ropes into the packed clubs. Two babes, one in white hot pants, the other in a sheer fishnet micromini that revealed the black thong beneath, strutted past the line.

The bouncer waved the two hot babes right into the club, taking their $20 bills and phone numbers as they passed.

Punishing hip-hop music pounded out of the doors of the clubs,

Eminem and Iglew and Tu Bitz and Jay Z. Bobby was amazed that he could now tell one from the other.

A shiver shot through Bobby, thinking of Maggie soon going in search of fake proof to get into similar clubs back in New York. He dreaded the day she first told him she was going to go "down the Shore" for the weekend with some girlfriends. Where predatory ghouls prowled the bars, looking for untended drinks to spike with Liquid X and Rohypnol, for a little bit of date-rape summer fun.

Bobby watched each kid pay $20 at the door for the privilege of getting inside, where they'd spend $10 a pop for watered-down drinks at the bar.

All cash. All night. All summer.

All Ford's.

Bobby strolled east on Esplanade until it ended at Starfish, an oasis of tiny silver Christmas lights dotting the lush trees and hedges sculpted into the shapes of fish set against the inky sea, where the three-quarters moon spilled a golden catwalk to the stars. Thirtysomething and older adults, mostly couples, dressed in summer chic designer clothes, waited at the outdoor patio where beautiful twentysomething waitresses served $10 piña coladas, margaritas, and mai tais from a tiki bar, waiting for their individual little beepers the gorgeous hostess gave out to ring, indicating that their impossible-to-get-without-a-reservation table was ready, so that they could sit down to order their $16 appetizers, $32 entrées, and $100 bottles of wine.

A big sign on the hostess station read *Sorry, No Credit Cards Accepted.* Bobby thought there should have been another sign: *Abuse Me, Please!*

Cash-and-carry Ford was doing all right, for a guy who retired making $68,000 a year after twenty-two years on the NYPD. Bobby figured Ford was worth millions. Balzac had said that behind every fortune there was a crime. But Bobby knew that unless he hit Lotto, married right, or scored in Hollywood, behind every cop's fortune there was a career criminal.

Bobby walked through the cocktail crowd, so many waiting for tables that they stood in knots, shooting the breeze and twirling their drinks. It was *the* Surfside night scene for those too old for the clubs. No one was in a rush. No panhandlers worked the edges of the crowd. No one here sweated the mortgage.

Bobby made his way to the tiki bar and shouldered a spot near the wait station and couldn't help gazing at the behind of the barmaid as she bent over to get a handful of beers from a cooler behind the bar. When she stood back up, she placed a cocktail napkin in front of Bobby, and he was surprised. She took a step backward. It was the chick from the amusement ride, her hair now pinned up with seashell combs, wearing a scoop-necked, skintight Starfish T-shirt. A little nameplate that she hadn't worn before read *Suzy.*

"Cranberry and soda," Bobby said. "And I swear, I didn't follow you."

"It would be okay if you did," she said. "Sure you don't want a little Grey Goose in that?"

"I wish, but I'm driving."

"Where to?" she asked, mixing the cranberry juice and soda into a pint glass and rimming it with a wedge of lime and spearing a red straw into the cubes.

"Back to New York."

"Have the wife drive."

"Don't have one anymore."

"Oh, *man,* take me with ya," she said with a soft, sexy growl.

"Need a ride?"

"Wish I could," she said, grabbing a slip from a waitress and mixing drinks with blinding speed, bottles pouring, soda gun squirting, beer caps popping, wedges of lime, slices of orange, and twists of lemon jabbed, added, and rimmed with professional dispatch, all mounted on trays and sent off into the throng, where gab and laughter got lost in the tireless roll of the waves.

"If everybody in the New York bureaucracy worked half as fast as you, we'd have a balanced budget in two weeks," Bobby said.

"Boss here is a slave driver." She leaned close and whispered, "I *hate* this job. But Princeton Law isn't cheap."

"Pretty impressive."

"Well, I had to take off two years after community college to work when my mom got sick. Then I went back to school. It's like I'm doomed to the Garden State. So I work here summers to pay my way through."

"The boss can't be that bad if you keep coming back."

She squinted, mixing a Long Island Ice Tea. "You a friend of Jimmy Ford's?"

Bobby shook his head.

She glanced into the restaurant, which was decorated in a nautical motif of old beams, fishnets, rusty anchors, and mounted marlins. "Ford Knox—that's what we call him—still has his baptismal money. Buried somewhere in that Rumson mansion of his."

"Real sport, huh?"

"His favorite *sport* is dwarf tossing. Loves pushing little people around. But look, when you grow up like I did in a place like Paramus, you take what you can get. He pays zilch but the tips are good. And at least I have a plan. After her divorce my mother worked all her life as a crossing guard. I promised myself that wouldn't be me."

"Good for you."

"I worked from the day I could get working papers in a little pizza shop near the Paramus courthouse. Bald, fat, married asshole lawyers— and even a few judges—coming on to me like I was something on the menu. A topping. I was a *kid*. A *teenager*. Still reading Archie comics, chrissakes . . ."

She was going to say more, but bit her lower lip and raised her eyebrows as she jammed four glasses with ice cubes and built four screwdrivers with fresh-squeezed orange juice, rimmed with orange slices, and rattled them onto a waitress's tray with five piña coladas that came premixed out of a machine, like Slurpees.

Bobby took a gulp of his club soda and cranberry.

"Get to New York often, Suzy?"

"No time," she said. "Plus prices of hotels are insane. I take my mom once a year to a Broadway musical. Day trips. In that little pizza shop, my dream was someday to be a lawyer in New York. Better than any of the assholes in Paramus. I'm waiting to hear from a big Park Avenue law firm for an internship. Later, maybe work my way up to junior partner. Or a nice little practice, where I could do pro bono for working people getting screwed by big-shot lawyers."

"Well, if you're ever up in New York, I'd love to show you around. I love a good play, but I don't do musicals."

"Oh, man, I'm with *you*. I go to those shows for my mom. But give me Tennessee Williams or Sean O'Casey or Neil Simon or Woody Allen any day of the week. You sure you're not a lawyer? I promised myself I'd never date a lawyer."

"Retired cop. Live on a boat. I'm a weekend father."

"Sounds good to me. I'm Scarlett, by the way. Scarlett Butler. My mom said I looked like the baby Clark Gable and Vivien Leigh would have had if Rhett had stuck with her instead of walking away and frankly not giving a damn."

"Not Suzy?"

She fingered the nameplate. "Oh, I just wear this for people who I don't want to know my real name."

"Another hangover from the pizzeria?"

"You got it. I also never date guys I meet working here. It's a rule of mine."

"I guess that leaves me out."

"I didn't meet you here. Besides, you have those great arms."

"You have great legs. And . . . well, never mind."

She smiled that smile again and made a bunch of drinks for two waitresses, then came back and replenished Bobby's drink.

"One good thing about this job is that you don't have the boss around, huh?" He didn't want her thinking he was snooping.

"He's inside now, eating with friends. Usually he's out here, greeting people, playing the big shot. Mr. Surfside. If he was out here now, he'd never let me have a conversation with anyone. He'd be too afraid it would cost him an extra quarter."

Bobby wrote his phone number on a cocktail napkin and handed it to her. "Call me if you ever want to come up. I'll come down and pick you up in my boat. Beat the traffic. The boat has two sleeping compartments. With locks on the doors. Docked on the Hudson River, at the Seventy-ninth Street Boat Basin on the Upper West Side of Manhattan."

She kept looking at him as she shook a martini, her toned arms tight with little muscles, her small breasts moving under the tight Starfish T-shirt, trying to read Bobby.

"I don't even know you."

"Let's see: I don't bowl or ballroom dance, I'm too old for rock concerts, too square for hip-hop, and I'm a Mets fan. If you're into opera, ballet, or classical music or the Yankees, I'll tag along and pretend I'm having a blast. I don't eat sushi and I think French food is overrated. On the other hand I never met a bowl of pasta I didn't like unless it came out of a can. I haven't worn a tie since divorce court and I hate ten-digit local dialing, anonymous-call rejection, bad breath, dirty nails, bosses who exploit their workers, especially when they look like Scarlett O'Hara, and guys who hit on barmaids, but in your case I can't help myself."

She poured the martini, dropped in an olive, gave it to a waitress, took another order from a different waitress, and said, "I need to sleep on it."

"If you wake up with a yes, what do you like to eat?"

"Anything but pizza."

Three waitresses came with drink orders and Scarlett became swamped with work. Bobby walked to the end of the bar and peered into the restaurant. He saw Ford seated at a corner, dressed in a fresh white linen suit wearing a different white panama hat and open-necked Hawaiian shirt and white loafers with no socks, seated with two men whose backs were to Bobby. Eric, Ford's driver, sat at a table for two across the aisle from them eating a burger. The yellow-tinted glasses hid Ford's eyes. The two guys he spoke with in an animated, gesticulating way just seemed to slump forward, as if being lectured.

They each had bowls of pasta in front of them, but as they both seemed to talk at once, only Ford paused long enough to eat a forkful, then sucked baby clams off tiny shells. He drained a glass of white wine. A waiter rushed to refill the glass. And only his glass. He gulped some of the wine, wiped his mouth, balled the napkin, threw it on the table, and karate-chopped his open palm and pointed a manicured, lacquered-nailed finger at both men, lingering on the taller, heavier man.

Bobby thought he recognized the two men who had their backs to him. Afraid of being noticed, he hesitated and returned to the bar.

"One for the road?" Scarlett asked.

"No thanks."

"What time does the boss hang around till?"

"He usually leaves after he eats. He's single but I've never seen him in here with a woman."

"Ever, ya know, bother you?"

"No, thank God. Far as I know he has a woman in New York. Don't ask me who. Ford's just a guy I work for. Like half of everybody else in Surfside."

"Gotta run. Hope you decide to call."

"I hope I do, too."

Bobby left her a $20 tip. Less would have been cheap for a chick he wanted to date. More would have made him look as if he were trying to buy her affections.

He didn't miss the irony that money he left for Scarlett came from Janis McNulty, whose mother he'd once bedded. He was attracted to her daughter, too.

I'm no different than the guys outside Urge and Surge, he thought. *Just an older dog that hasn't learned any new tricks. I'm what Maggie has to look forward to in the love sweepstakes of life.*

He hurried back to the Wavecrest Motel, had an eerie feeling that he was being tailed or watched or monitored. Surfside was like James Ford's personal little kingdom.

He jumped in his Jeep and drove straight to the Avis rental place down the road, took a pair of nightscope glasses from his glove compartment with him, and rented a small, black Taurus for one night for $89. He saved the receipt for Janis.

The whole transaction took less than ten minutes. Then he drove back down to the end of Esplanade and almost collided with a big black SUV that roared out of the parking lot. Bobby couldn't see it clearly in the cloud of dust that rose from the gravel. It might have been a Navigator. He was tempted to follow it, but ahead of him he saw James Ford standing at the front of the restaurant. He'd finished dinner and appeared ready to leave.

Bobby didn't even know if it was a Navigator that had just left. But he did want to know more about James Ford.

So he parked across the darkened road from the Starfish parking lot. He sat with his lights off, the radio playing the Mets game, low. They were losing. Again.

He watched diners leave the restaurant, some half-stewed, most raving about the food. One couple argued.

"Don't tell me you tipped that bimbo thirty percent because you *didn't* like her tight young ass."

"Margie, shut the fuck up," he said.

"I had an ass like that, too, when I was in my twenties."

"I know, but you've been sitting on it ever since," her husband said, handing his ticket to the valet kid with the red vest. The argument continued, driven by wine and gravity and menopause and the underlying desperation of getting old. By the time the valet kid brought the Benz, the couple was silent and went home pissed off after a $300 dinner. *Probably to sleep in separate beds,* Bobby thought.

After thirty-four minutes Bobby saw James Ford in his unmistakable white suit and panama hat crunch up the gravel walkway from his restaurant and into the lot. The two men in the dark suits walked with him, the smaller one favoring his right foot. Eric walked a few steps ahead of them and signaled to the red-vested valet-parker to get his car. The valet trotted to a special spot near the mouth of the lot.

Ford stood with the two men across the darkened roadway from Bobby's parked Taurus, where he sat slouched, the transistor turned down, the window opened.

". . . no more fucking around," Ford said. "Everything we ever built could unwind. Understand?"

The taller one said, "Understood."

"How the fuck could they fuck it up that bad?"

"I have no idea," said the larger man.

"I'm going to meet you-know-who right now," Ford said. "I'm gonna say everything's smooth sailing. I'm not gonna say there's been a bump in the road. Because I expect that this bump will be smoothed out. I want what's been buried to stay buried, and I don't give a hairy rat's ass who else you have to bury to keep it buried. Understand?"

"Understood," said the larger man as Ford's Town Car swept through the lot, its headlights illuminating the three men. Bobby peered out from his rented Taurus, using the nightscope glasses, and saw the two men James Ford was addressing. The taller man was Special Agent in Charge Tom Noonan, and the short guy, who walked with a mild limp, was Special Agent Lou Scarano, of the so-called Hip-Hop Joint Task Force. The same two Feds Bobby had encountered in the courtroom earlier in the day at the Tu Bitz trial. The ones who'd had an animated encounter with Samantha Savage in the street outside the courthouse afterward.

The valet took Scarano's ticket and went to fetch his car.

Eric opened the passenger door of the Town Car, and James Ford climbed in without saying good-bye. Eric swept out of the driveway. Bobby watched the black Town Car pass in the moonlit night.

Bobby counted to ten-Mississippi and followed in his dark Taurus.

ELEVEN

Bobby tailed Ford's Town Car back onto the Garden State and cruised in the middle lane as Ford raced in the left lane.

Eric never signaled as he crossed three lanes of traffic to get off at Exit 109. Bobby slowed down, grabbed the exit, and followed the Town Car into the town of Rumson.

Bobby followed Ford at a discreet distance through a few leafy back roads of ostentatious minimansions and then onto congested Rumson Road, where he didn't find anyone driving American-made cars. Ford's car made a left onto Oak Drive. Bobby slowed, pulled over for thirty seconds, then followed for a little less than a mile into a realm of crickets and marked estates, loamy with the smell of hibiscus, Kentucky bluegrass, and new money. Using the nightscope glasses, up ahead Bobby saw a pair of twelve-foot-high electronic gates part, and the Town Car rolled through them and up a long, circular gravel drive to an immense three-story, white mansion on a hill overlooking a sprawling fifty-acre estate, with two tennis courts, an Olympic-size pool, Jacuzzi, guesthouse, and gazebo on the bank of a private duck pond. A collection of cars, including a Bentley, a Rolls, two Mercedeses, a Jaguar, and a black Navigator were parked in a carport at the end of the driveway. The Navigator was sandwiched between two other cars and Bobby could not get a look at the fender, where he was looking for a rusted, kiss-shaped dent near the taillight.

Two barking rottweilers ran toward the Town Car, tails wagging, built like minilocomotives with teeth. Bobby checked the address Maggie had given him for James Ford. This was the right one. He'd moved eighty-five miles and several million dollars south of his old Staten Island attached home in Rosebank where he'd lived while earning $68,000 a year as a Highway detective for the NYPD.

Bobby raised the nightscope glasses, and through the green-hued, low-light lenses he could see that all the cars had New Jersey plates. Bobby dictated the plate numbers into the recording chip on his cell phone for later reference.

Bobby lowered the glasses and called Maggie. His ex-wife, Connie, answered. "Who the hell is calling my fifteen-, I repeat *fif-teen*-year-old daughter at ten o'clock at night?"

"Hi, Connie."

"Oh, Bobby. Sorry. Are you pretending to be her father tonight?"

"Take a Midol, Con."

"Who the hell did you introduce her to from Brooklyn? Some son of a bitch keeps calling her and she keeps calling him, and all I hear when I try to listen is Ebonics. 'Sup, yo, boo, bling-bling, slammin', chill pill.' You can't even eavesdrop on kids today unless you hire a goddamned high school dropout to translate."

"How's Trevor?" Bobby asked.

He watched James Ford step out of his Town Car and checked his watch and waited.

"France. Something to do with a new fragrance. Personally I hope he's cheating on me. He so friggin' straight it's depressing. He wouldn't cheat if I dropped Heidi Klum belly-down on the bed asking to have her temperature taken."

"Well, you never trusted me, so I guess you got what you wanted."

"You cheated," she said. "I know you cheated. I just never caught you."

"Never when we were together. Not even once."

"Lies go hand in hand with cheating."

"You know this from experience, do you?"

"Trevor will be away for three more days. Wanna have lunch?"

"Sure, with Maggie, the three of us like?"

"No, alone. We need to talk. About Maggie."

"You pick the place, I'll be there. But give me notice, I'm working a case."

"Why don't you take the job as the head of security for our company?"

"I'd feel funny paying you child support from money I earned from you?"

"For the thousandth time, I don't want your measly twelve hundred a month!"

"But I wanna pay it."

"Send it to those starving kids in Somalia."

"I do that, too. Whatever I can afford."

"No wonder you live like one. When are you gonna grow up and get an *apartment,* where the downstairs neighbor isn't a striped bass?"

"You rented the one I had my eye on, Con. I couldn't live in anything smaller. So I'll stay where I am until I can top yours."

"What the hell is going on with our daughter? She's walking around singing, giddy. She on drugs? That monkey-poxed dog of a lawyer of yours getting our kid all hopped up on something? Who the hell is she on the phone with? I tried to have it tapped, but she has all kinds of scramblers and gadgets."

"Mom," Maggie shouted in the background, "for God's sake, get off my phone!"

Then he spotted another set of headlights piercing up Oak Drive, slowing as they neared Ford's estate. Bobby drove farther up the road, with no lights, and made a U-turn and sat on the shoulder of the pitch-black road. He raised the nightscope glasses and saw a sleek black Chrysler New Yorker bearing a blue-and-white New York Empire State plate with the word *OFFICIAL* spelled out in blue letters along the bottom. The blue plate number was NYS1.

There was a commotion in the background on the cell phone, and as Bobby watched the gates open electronically again, Maggie came on the line.

"Dad?"

"Maggie, I have a bunch of plate numbers I want you to run. But right now I need you to run plate number NYS1 through the New York DMV database."

"I don't have to," she whispered.

"Why not?"

"Because I know what it is from playing around on the state database. It's the license plate for the governor of New York."

Bobby held his breath, didn't exhale for several seconds, too stunned to let go of it. "Thanks, Mag," he said, exhaling. "Be careful what you say in front of your mother."

"Don't worry."

"I'll call you in the morning."

Bobby hung up and took his foot off the brake and let the car roll down the hill until he could peer through the gates with the night glasses. The New Yorker parked. Then Agnes Hardy, Republican candidate for governor of the state of New York, stepped out of the back of the New Yorker and shook James Ford's hand. The driver stepped out of the front seat. Bobby focused his glasses and saw that it was Joe Brightman, who'd sat across the aisle from James Ford in the courtroom at Tu Bitz's trial earlier in the day.

Brightman, the governor's right-hand man and lifelong pal, with the woman who wanted Patterson's job? Meeting with James Ford? In New Jersey?

Now the silhouette of a woman appeared in the window of an upstairs bedroom, peeling back the window curtain a few inches. Bobby clicked some photos with his phone/camera, hoping something would come out of the murk.

Bobby watched Agnes Hardy take James Ford's arm as they climbed the wide marble steps of his mansion, passing under the Corinthian columns, followed by Brightman. The silhouette of the woman disappeared from the window.

Bobby wanted a closer look at that parked black Navigator, but the rottweilers sat on the stoop, panting, and he needed some sleep in order to think.

Hail, hail, the gang's all here, Bobby thought. *But what the hell is going on? And what does it all have to do with a hit-and-run in Bay Ridge ten years ago?*

TWELVE

Bobby drove the Taurus back to Surfside, turned it in, retrieved his Jeep, and after seeing that the West Side Highway was mobbed, he took the streets uptown from the Lincoln Tunnel. Tenth Avenue was alive with cops and robbers and tourists and hookers and lovers and strangers and the homeless and the insane. The lights of Manhattan blazed like a zillion little miracles, which was something no one who'd lived through the Blackout of 2003 would ever take for granted again.

In New York light was life.

He'd stopped looking for black Navigators in his mirrors. He was sure now that the black Navigator he worried about was parked in a driveway in Rumson. *Something is rotten in Jersey,* he thought.

After Tenth Avenue became Amsterdam Avenue, Bobby swung a left onto Seventy-ninth Street. He purred down the darkened street toward the boat basin, one of the best-kept secrets in New York, yawning, his brain sloshing with new, raw, unprocessed information. He couldn't wait to climb aboard and dump himself into his bunk and let the river rock him to sleep.

He yawned again and shook his head, and then by instinct, as he always did before going home, he glanced one last time in his rearview. And through the prism of yawn-induced tears he saw it. Again.

A black Navigator.

"Shit!"

Bobby stomped the brakes. Pulled out his gun with his right hand. Yanked up the door handle with his left. Jumped out. And ran toward the Navigator.

The Navigator's high beams switched on. It lurched into reverse, squealing a crazy K-turn past Bobby, who held his revolver in the palm of his right hand. Half-blinded, he used his hand as a visor over his eyes, spotting the kiss-shaped dent near the rear taillight as it sped back up toward Broadway. But his eyes were still too stunned to get a license plate number.

"Asshole," Bobby shouted.

He climbed back into his Jeep, thought about doing a chase, but he was too damned tired. He coasted down to the boatyard and into the lot under the rotunda, keeping the gun on the seat next to him.

He parked and locked the car, walked cautiously through the cavernous garage, waiting for predators to leap from behind parked cars or cement girders. He scanned pools of shadow and the interiors of the parked vans and cars, the pistol cocked.

Bobby made it out of the garage and unlocked the chain-link gate to the Boat Basin, passed Doug the dockmaster's station, which was empty for the night. He walked up the floating walkway to slip 99A as a Circle Line passed downtown on the last slosh of its final cruise of the night, a carnival of lights dancing on the black river. A faraway tug moaned. A police harbor-patrol boat with searchlight splaying chugged upriver, toward the George Washington Bridge—another American icon fixed in the crosshairs of Al Qaeda.

Bobby waved to the guys in the harbor patrol, most of whom he knew and who occasionally stopped for a turkey burger or a brew on the *Fifth Amendment*.

The boat was darkened and Bobby's calico cat, Outlaw, pranced on the deck, yapping for grub.

"Go eat a rat," Bobby said.

Outlaw meowed and Bobby unlocked the door to the main compartment at 11:30 p.m., deprogrammed the alarm that was set to Maggie's birthday, went inside, flicked on the lights of the main salon, and turned on the TV to New York 1, the all-news station, which was just starting its thirty-minute news-cycle update. Outlaw meowed louder, prancing back and forth across the salon, agitated and annoying. Bobby turned the volume louder to hear the top story about an as-of-yet-unidentified shooting victim in Lutheran Medical Center who was discovered by hospital workers on an elevator that afternoon. The victim was in serious but stable condition in the hospital.

"On another note, the gubernatorial race is heating up," the broadcaster said. "Republican challenger Hardy said again today that she lost a stepdaughter and indirectly a husband to drugs, and so if she is elected, she would never sign any repeal of the controversial Rockefeller drug laws. She demanded that Patterson meet her in person to debate the issue."

They showed footage of Hardy giving a sound bite claiming that Governor Patterson was wishy-washy on the issue, imploring him to accept her debate challenge and to take a firm stand on the Rockefeller drug laws. "Through a spokesman Patterson said he would soon be issuing a statement concerning her debate challenge and had a panel reviewing the laws and would await the outcome of their findings before making up his mind on how they might be amended if not repealed," the newscaster said. "Meanwhile, Ignatius 'Iglew' Lewis of Lethal Injection Records, and a self-styled black spokesman, was again appealing to both candidates to repeal these laws."

The polls were showing Hardy making substantial gains on the incumbent, spending tens of millions of dollars on TV ads, attacking Patterson for being soft on crime and fiscally incompetent.

Outlaw meowed louder, more guttural now, and the news show cut to canned footage of the same Iglew speech Bobby had heard on the radio news earlier in the day. He thought how odd it was that he'd seen Iglew in the courtroom this afternoon, where Joe Brightman, the governor's aide, also attended the Tu Bitz trial. And had seen Brightman with the governor's opponent a little over an hour earlier at the home of James Ford, who was the original cop in charge of the Cookie Calhoun hit-and-run investigation.

Bobby couldn't take the screaming cat anymore, turned the volume louder, and walked to the kitchenette, opened the fridge, took out half a can of 9-Lives tuna, banged it into Outlaw's double-bowl tray, and filled up the second half of the tray with Meow Mix, as Outlaw ignored the food and continued to squawk.

Then Bobby smelled the perfume.

"You take sugar in your tea, baby?" Bobby said.

Samantha Savage slid open the door as Bobby plopped a Barry's Irish tea bag in a mug, filled it with water, and banged it into the microwave, pressing 212 on the timer, the area code for Manhattan. It was a quirk but it made a perfect cup of tea.

"Negative. How'd you know it was me?"

"You wore that perfume in court."

He told Savage to have a seat on his leather sectional couch.

"How long you been following me?" Bobby asked.

"Since I followed Janis McNulty and Izzy Gleason from the courtroom this morning up here," Savage said.

"Why?"

"I wanted to know what she was up to."

"Why?"

"What did she say? Why'd she come to Gleason, and then to you? Why?"

"That's privileged."

"That's baloney," Savage said. "Throw me a bone."

Bobby looked at her, the perfect skin, the swan's neck, the tailored dark suit with the long, elegant body, the smart dark eyes.

"I'll pretend you didn't mean that."

"Don't be a *pig*," she said. "I hate a man who treats a woman like a *pig*. Or a bitch or a ho. Understand?"

"Yes, teacher," Bobby said. "So you showed up to testify. The morning session was postponed because Tu Bitz was delayed."

"Affirmative."

The microwave beeped, and without asking, Bobby poured milk in the tea and handed her the mug and put one on for himself.

"I usually take tea with lemon."

"Not Irish tea, not in my house. My mother would never forgive me."

"While in Rome . . ."

"Belfast, actually, but anyway, when you saw Janis McNulty in the courtroom this morning, you got hyped up?" he asked.

"Affirmative. Correction, let's just say curious."

"Then you followed them in Izzy's car to here?"

"Affirmative."

"Why?"

"I'm here to ask you questions, Mr. Emmet. Please don't attempt reverse psychology on—"

"Okay, so then you tailed me to Brooklyn, to the place."

"Aff—"

"What place?"

"You tell me, Mr. Emmet."

"Okay, look, you can call me Bobby, I'll call you Sam, okay?"

"You may *not* call me Sam, Mr. Emmet."

Bobby laughed. "Okay, Samantha."

"Detective Savage would be preferable."

"You go through the police academy or West Point, Sammy, babe?"

"Don't you dare call me that."

"Look, toots, it doesn't take Columbo to know me and Janis McNulty went to look at the spot where her mother was killed in a hit-and-run almost ten years ago."

"Is that why the tabloid columnist was there? Roth?"

Bobby checked his watch: 11:40 p.m. "Should be rolling through the presses around now."

"Mistake."

"Why?"

"I don't think either of you are equipped or prepared to deal with the people you might encounter."

"You weren't exactly prepared for that ass-kicking you got on the stand today, honey," Bobby said.

Rage flushed her face. "No one has ever called me *honey*."

"Jesus Christ, take a chill pill, girl! What did your daddy call you? *Vinegar?*"

She banged the tea on the coffee table and stood, pointed a finger at Bobby. "Don't you dare bring my family into this."

"Take the stick out of your . . . never mind. Since Abner Louima that expression really doesn't suit anyone from NYPD."

Bobby wanted to break through that officious outer shell, trying to find the woman who lived inside. She took a deep breath, picked up the mug of tea, walked to the porthole over the kitchenette sink. She sipped, staring out at New Jersey.

"My apologies for losing my composure," she said. "It was inappropriate."

"No problem. I like a chick with balls. Metaphorically speaking, of course."

"That was inappropriate of you. We're even. Gosh, this is splendid tea."

"Irish penicillin. I gave up coffee last year when I learned that black tea had as many medicinal properties as green tea, helps fight off infections, diseases, and doesn't give me the afternoon crash that coffee did. It's great for your sex life, too. Sorry, was that inappropriate, too?"

"Interesting," she said, smiling for the first time.

"So, you followed me all day, all night?"

"Actually, I lost you for a while. I had to go see my delegate because the Brooklyn DA wants to question me in the morning about my testimony today."

"Good luck with that."

"I'll probably get suspended. Or put on modified until IAB investigates and it goes to the PD trial room. But they haven't asked for my gun and badge. Yet."

Bobby walked from the couch to the kitchenette. "Why'd you really come here?"

She looked at him through the steam, her face softening for the first time.

"I was going to ask you to back off this case. I'm afraid someone will get hurt."

He didn't know if she'd followed him as far as Lutheran Medical Center, where he spoke with Dianne Rattigan. Or Staten Island, where he spoke with Steve Greco or Nails McNulty.

"Like who?"

She took a deep breath, sipped some tea, and looked up at him.

"There are bad people involved here. They'd do anything to protect what they've built. That record company is worth hundreds of millions of dollars. There are political ramifications involved. This is bigger than a one-man snoop job. But you could upset enough things to get people you don't even know hurt."

"Like who?"

"I can't really say. Then I'd really be in deep doo-doo."

"Doo-doo? If you're gonna talk shit, talk *shit*, honey."

"Please don't call me hon . . . I feel funny being here."

"Why?"

"I'm probably going to get suspended because of you and Izzy Gleason and—"

"Hold it right there. If you get suspended, it'll be because you lied. Izzy just caught you in the lie."

"Touché."

"And stop with the affected, look-at-me-I-went-to-finishing-school speech patterns."

"My apologies, that's just me. It's how I was raised."

"Really? By who? Sir John Gielgud?"

"Negat—nah."

"Progress. She said 'nah.' And like any good Irishman, here we are hanging out in the kitchen, even on a boat."

She laughed and sipped her tea. Bobby took a bottle of Jameson out of a kitchen cabinet and splashed some into his cup. He attempted to pour some in hers. She covered the top. He looked in her eyes, which were mesmerizing, and highlighted with green, like his cat's. She took her hand off the top of her mug, still looking Bobby in the eyes, and shrugged and said, "Oh, what the heck."

"Heck?" Bobby said, holding her stare, filling her mug to the rim with Irish. "Two gulps of that and you'll graduate from *heck* to *hell*. I mean, who the hell says heck in the twenty-first century?"

"If I get suspended, the whole case I've been working on for two years will go straight to hell. People I care about will be doomed. I feel like I've been set up."

Bobby thought about Noonan and Scarano meeting with James Ford in Jersey, and then him meeting with Hardy.

"By who?"

She looked at Bobby, blinked a few times, took a deep gulp of the whiskey-tea, her eyes opening wide as it banged her breast plate.

"Wow-wee," she said, breathing in and out.

"Answer me."

"I better go."

"Who's setting you up, Sammy?"

She didn't answer.

"You talk to Rodney Calhoun lately?" Bobby asked, coming right out of the upper deck of left field.

Her eyes fluttered; she looked at the ground, took a breath, and wiped the palm of her right hand on her pants and switched hands with the tea mug and wiped the other hand. She looked as if she were back on the stand with Izzy shredding her to jerky.

"I can't tell you anything while I'm carrying a badge," she said. "You're supposed to be telling *me* things. In fact there's a pretty big conflict here. Izzy Gleason defends the people I try to put in jail. You work for Izzy Gleason . . ."

"I work for a lot of different people, not Izzy exclusively."

"Like Janis McNulty," she said, taking another sip of the whiskey-tea, enjoying it now, making her looser in the limb and the shoulders.

"Yeah. Why, you trying to put her in jail, too?"

"Negative, Mr. Emmet. Her mother was a victim. Which makes her and her siblings victims."

"It sure does." He gulped some of his tea, the whiskey soothing a long day.

"You care about her, don't you?"

Bobby shifted his weight, rolled his shoulders, swirled his tea. "I care enough to want to get answers for her. Like any client. I can't tell you everything she told me. You know that. But she has a kid brother who's taken the loss of his mother pretty damn hard. She wants to bring some peace and justice into that kid's life."

Savage clinked her mug against his mug and sipped some more, stared into his eyes. "She's very pretty."

"So are you," Bobby said.

"Please, don't say that."

"So was her mother."

"Oh, so you knew the mother?"

"I never said that. There are lots of pictures."

Savage drained her mug and washed it out and put it into the drying rack on the sink.

"Thank you for the tea."

"Thanks for dropping by. Come again."

She walked to the door, slid it open, and Bobby followed her on deck. The night was still warm but the river breeze mixed with the whiskey and the moonlight, and it felt like paradise on the Hudson.

Samantha Savage paused at the exit. "You might be meddling in something bigger than you think."

"Like how?"

"Okay. I'll say this much. My sources tell me there's a sudden rush to liquidate Lethal Injection Records. There have been offers on the table. All rejected. Today, suddenly I hear certain people want to sell, sell, sell."

"Who would that be?"

"This Deity phantom. My sources tell me Iglew is resisting. In the hip-hop world, with hundreds of millions at stake, people often die. Violently. Be careful."

"Thanks. Good luck tomorrow with the DA."

They stood inches apart, looking each other in the eyes, and she said, "Thanks, Bobby."

"Thank you, Sammy."

And he watched her walk down the walkway, a small dip in her step as the Irish whiskey reached her knees. She climbed the stairs to the rotunda, looked back and saw him watching her, and climbed into her black Navigator and took off into the night, another jammed-up cop in the big city.

THIRTEEN

The Next Day, Tuesday, June 21

He grabbed his gun when he heard the pop. It sounded like a .22 caliber being fired on the deck of the *Fifth Amendment* just outside his salon door. The clock on his night table read 10:11.

He pulled on shorts and Top-Siders and lowered himself into a coiled crouch and burst through the bottom of the door with the gun outstretched.

"You want a mimosa or plain Moët?" asked Scarlett Butler, pouring bubbly into two plastic champagne glasses as she sat at a table on the aft deck, wearing a neat pin-striped skirt suit, white dress blouse, and sensible heels. She didn't look like a cocktail-slinging daredevil who rode death-defying rides to get her heart pumping every night. She scratched Bobby's yapping cat with her free hand.

"Plain."

"Me, too."

She handed him a glass as he lowered his 9mm automatic.

"You always say hello with a nine-millimeter?"

"I wasn't expecting you. I thought the popped cork was a shot."

"When I got home last night, there was a call on the machine about an interview today for an internship at a Park Avenue law firm. I drove up to Hoboken, parked the car, caught the tube in, and by the time I got into Manhattan there was a message on my voice mail saying that the meeting was postponed till one p.m. I was in Manhattan, so I thought I'd buy a bottle and drop in on you. I left your number home but I remembered slip 99A

117

at the Seventy-ninth Street Boat Basin. I was intrigued. I never met a boat bum before."

"I look like one right now."

"That's not such a bad thing," she said, taking a sip of champagne, leaving a rose-colored ridge on the glass.

"You a cop?"

"Retired. I do investigative work for a lawyer."

"That's right. You told me that. Anything interesting?"

"Not as interesting as you. Time for brunch?"

"Sure. I'll buy."

"No, you won't."

"Does that mean I'll owe you?"

"I hope so."

"Good. I like compromising positions."

Bobby gulped his champagne, jumped in the shower, and dressed. Scarlett left her briefcase on board and Bobby led her up to Northwest, and they ordered brunch at an outdoor table as the city bustled with life. He ate French toast and Canadian bacon with two large glasses of orange juice. She had an egg-white omelet and a Virgin Mary, watching him wolf his food.

She said, "You eat like an escaped POW."

"Long day, yesterday. Need fuel."

"I needed two champagnes to take the edge off."

"Edge off what?"

"Meeting you again. And the interview."

"I'm a pussycat. And how can someone who looks like you, as smart as you, who rides that killer contraption every night, and who works for James Ford be nervous about anything?"

She looked at him as she sipped her Virgin Mary, a small smile lighting her face. Bobby noticed men who passed gawking at her, her face radiant in the morning light in this part of Manhattan where the buildings, like the Museum of Natural History across the street, were low and the sky was big and blue, a part of town that felt more like a neighborhood than a business center.

"That ride's for kids," she said. "The Park Avenue law firm is for grown-ups. Scary. And Ford, he's just a figment of his own imagination."

"You think so?"

"He's a businessman."

"How do you think he made all his money?"

He felt like a crud trying to pick her brains about Ford and the god-damned case instead of getting to know a real woman.

"Ford's fortune is held together with smoke and mirrors," she said. "Loans and notes and stretched credit."

"He doesn't accept credit cards in any of his places."

"No. Strictly cash."

"Funny, no? A guy who lives on credit, not giving any?"

"Why are you so interested in James Ford? He part of your investigation?"

She's onto me, he thought. "Nah. It's just part of my old skeptical flat-foot personality. I'm a retired cop and I live on a boat. He's a retired cop who lives like a sultan. It always makes my antennas rise."

"He got lucky. Invested in a tank town at the right time and watched it blossom in the Clinton economy."

"Yeah, maybe . . ."

"So, tell me about what you're working on."

"I can't really."

"Oh, Christ, what are you Father Flynn who can't reveal confessional secrets?"

"It's just an old hit-and-run."

"And what, you think Ford is involved?"

"I didn't say that. And if he were, I couldn't tell you. Tell me about you and this interview? What firm?"

She smiled. "Why, you know from law firms?"

"I used to work for the DA's office. We dealt with all the best and worst law firms in the city."

She widened her eyes, paused, shrugged. "Kormel, Childs and Mercer."

"Great firm. Mostly white-collar stuff. Some white-collar criminal stuff. Accounting fraud, mergers, unfriendly takeovers."

"Boring, I know. Forget me. I know too much about me. I wanna know more about you." She checked her watch, raised her eyebrows. "I have two hours and ten minutes. So far I know you woke up alone. That's a good sign for a single girl like me."

"I went to bed alone, too. Which isn't good for a single guy like me."

"That can be remedied."

"Oh, yeah? How?"

"Seduce me, dummy. Throw a make on me. Try charming the Victoria's Secrets off me."

"You're wearing underwear?"

"Wouldn't you like to know?"

"Sure."

"Try to find out. Give me your best rap."

"I'm almost afraid to try."

"Why?"

"With you, I thought I'd be a gentleman, a Charlie good guy. Interested in your personality, your life, your future. Your *mind.* I liked you the minute I met you. I'm afraid of screwing it up."

"You can't screw up what you haven't tried to screw."

He laughed, slapped two twenties on a $26 tab, grabbed her hand, and yanked her out of her chair. She laughed as he dragged her across Columbus Avenue, rushing straight to the Museum of Natural History. He bought two tickets and marched her straight up to the T. rex exhibit, clutched her by the back of her hair and kissed her on her mouth.

"You think going caveman will work with me?"

"Worth a shot."

She kissed him back with enthusiasm, and they made out like a pair of teenagers. Bobby heard the snickering and goofing of a bunch of kids, and then a security guard tapped him on the shoulder and said, "Yo, man, schoolkids."

Bobby separated himself from Scarlett and they looked at the grammar school class laughing at them.

"Tarzan and Jane, man," said one boy.

"Flintstones," said a girl.

"Fred and Wilma," said another girl. "Where Pebbles, yo?"

All the kids laughed. Bobby grinned in a bashful way and growled. The abashed teacher shepherded the giggling kids to the next exhibit. Bobby watched them go. Then Scarlett grabbed him by the back of his hair and pulled his face to hers and kissed him, deeper this time. Primal urges rose in him.

By the time they returned to *Fifth Amendment,* Bobby had his arm draped over Scarlett's shoulder and she had an arm looped around his waist. Doug the dockmaster gave him a knowing nod, as if he approved of his latest companion.

"You bring a new chick aboard the SS *Fling* every day?"

"Been a while."

"You mean to tell me all you do is run around trying to solve some ten-year-old hit-and-run, all work and no play?"

He looked her in the eyes, saw the half-naughty smile, head tilted down, eyes gazing up, her teeth so sparkly white that it looked as if she'd never missed three brushings a day since she'd got her first buck under her pillow from the fairy godmother.

"This is play."

"Give me time, it could be serious. That scare you?"

"Of course."

"Honest, too? You keep getting better."

"If you take the internship, you'll dump the job at Ford's place?"

"Maybe. Maybe I'll just work weekends. The dough is good down there."

"C'mon, there's gotta be some guy, too."

"Not interested in some guy. I need a *man*."

"Like James Ford."

"*God*, you're obsessed with him, aren't you?"

"Just interested. Sorry."

"He's not that interesting. He's just about business. That's all. He keeps his private life private. That's not so unusual. He could be gay for all I know."

Bobby shrugged.

"Is he in trouble?" she asked. "Let me know, in case I'm gonna lose that job."

"I'm not a cop or a prosecutor. I just dig up information."

"Does this information look bad for him?"

"I don't kiss and tell."

She stopped on the floating walkway and kissed Bobby as they walked down to the *Fifth Amendment*. "I like that," she said.

They climbed aboard, entered the salon, and Scarlett punched him in his muscled chest, then pulled him down on top of her on the sofa.

"Thanks for brunch."

"Thanks for dropping by."

"Can I come back?"

"Anytime."

They kissed and made out there for several minutes until she wrestled her way on top of Bobby—rumpled, riled, breathless. Straddling him, she blew her hair up out of her face, sighing. She checked her watch.

"Jesus Christ, what am I doing?" she said, jumping to her feet and straightening her blouse. "It's twelve-thirty."

"You'll never come back."

"Sure I will."

"Prove it."

She reached under her skirt and pulled off her pink thong panties and tossed them at him. He caught them, tracing the hand-embroidered stitching on the front.

"You talked the Victoria's Secrets off me. I'll be back to collect them."

On the way up to the rotunda Bobby carried her briefcase as he whistled for a taxi. "Next time, can we watch that Mets game together?"

"Absolutely."

"Butter on the popcorn?"

"Sure."

"Can you do me one big favor?"

"Name it."

"Can we not talk about James Ford?"

"Promise."

"So if there's anything else you want to know about him, ask now, okay?"

"Okay. How close is he to Agnes Hardy?"

"The one who's running for governor of New York?"

"Yeah."

"She's been in the restaurant a few times. But a lot of celebrities have been. You mean do I think he's boinking her?"

"Or whatever."

"Don't know. I'll ask the girls what they know and let you know. But then I don't want to talk about my boss anymore. You can understand that, can't you?"

"Yeah."

"That it?"

"Yep."

"Grab my hair and kiss me good-bye."

He did. She darted her tongue in his mouth. And then she hopped in the backseat of the taxi. Bobby handed her the briefcase. For the first time he saw the initials emblazoned on the handle: *SB*. She winked, flashed open her legs, and pulled the door closed. Then the taxi sped off in a yellow streak as he fingered her pink panties.

FOURTEEN

Tu Bitz told Izzy to meet him at his five-bedroom apartment at the Richmond projects in Staten Island and that he'd escort them to meet Iglew as promised.

"It's like trying to get an audience with the pope's mistress," Izzy said.

After meeting Tu Bitz, Bobby and Izzy left the graffiti-marred projects that were nicknamed RIP with Tu Bitz and two bodyguards and walked for their cars parked on the street.

"Walking with Tu Bitz in RIP is like strolling through Bethlehem with Jesus," Izzy said.

"Wasn't he crucified?" Bobby said, crossing the quadrangle of the projects, housing some ten thousand people in sixteen hundred apartments in six square blocks of southern Staten Island, with a clear view of the harbor and the disfigured Manhattan skyline.

"Yeah, but I just resurrected Tu Bitz from the dead," Izzy said, watching the bodyguards hand out autographed photos to the crowd.

Bobby's cell phone rang at 12:03 as the temperature hit ninety-six with a humidity factor making the real feel 105 degrees. Bobby's feet composted in his steel-toed Timberland boots. But with bad guys back in his life he wouldn't leave home without those two portable lethal weapons.

Bobby answered the phone. Steve Greco, the Verrazano security chief, said he wanted to meet him. Bobby asked where. Greco said in ninety minutes at the Lovers' Lanes bowling alley in Bay Ridge. "I can't bowl but I'll be there," Bobby said.

Ahead of them, young kids rushed to Tu Bitz, who was flanked by the bodyguards. The crowd asked for autographs and collected handfuls of quarters—two-bits pieces—that Tu Bitz tossed out from a big bucket like chicken feed to the poor kids, 90 percent of whom came from single-parent, mothers-only families in a part of the world where murder was still the number one cause of death for young black males.

RIP was like an urban asteroid that spun in its own orbit. Home of such rap legends as Iglew and Tu Bitz, this was also the place where street lore had it that the mysterious Deity had made his rep, and his fortune, selling Red Cap crack in the 1980s, arming his two hundred dealers and his mules with Uzis and Glock 9s. He was a cipher, an enigma, never ID'd. RIP natives considered him a "witchman." Some thought he didn't even exist, that Iglew invented him to add mystique to the label.

Tu Bitz tossed out hundreds of dollars' worth of quarters to the kids who ran from the nearby playground, some of them dripping wet from the summer sprinklers, some rapping their own rhymes for him, or break-dancing or showing off their graffiti prowess with big colored chalks on the blacktop walkways.

Two uniformed cops stood watching, fingers looped in their gun belts, gabbing to each other.

Bobby and Izzy followed Tu Bitz, who climbed into a Lexus SUV with his bodyguards.

"Follow us," he said.

Bobby followed the Lexus SUV through Staten Island, down Hylan Boulevard, a jumbled suburban sprawl of low-rise gas stations, fast-food joints, and auto-parts stores that reminded Bobby of Los Angeles without the palm trees.

Bobby's cell phone rang again. He answered. It was Janis McNulty.

"Phone's been ringing off the hook all morning over the Max Roth column," she said. "Everyone wants to blame the next-door neighbor. A dozen guys wanted to take me out. Two people blamed their husbands. One woman with a Jersey number said it might be connected to some old palimony suit involving Governor Luke Patterson. That call probably came from the Hardy campaign office. Crackpots. But there was one call that intrigued me. I need to see you about one call in particular."

"Rear parking lot of Lovers' Lanes, two o'clock," Bobby said, and flapped closed the phone as he shadowed the Lexus SUV to the bucolic outer rim of Tottenville, a neighborhood that was like a small, sleepy coastal New England town with a 718 area code. A scattering of designer cafés, boutiques, and new-wave fusion restaurants told Bobby that inevitable Manhattan yuppies had arrived to live in the old stately homes and brand-new mansions that dotted the unspoiled shore.

Bobby tailed Tu Bitz's Lexus SUV up a twisty blacktop road that passed under a canopy of leafy elms, and through twelve-foot-high electronic gates and up the circular path toward the twenty-five-thousand-square-foot mansion that sat on the hillock overlooking a private beach on Princes Bay. An American flag snapped like a locker-room towel in the sea wind. The nearest neighbor was hidden around the crescent-shaped bay a quarter mile away. Iglew's fifty-acre compound where he threw his famed Gatsbyesque parties was circled by twelve-foot-high corrugated-steel fences where posted Warning signs cautioned that they were electrified.

The Lexus drove past the gazebo and a six-car garage housing a Porsche, Cadillac, Lexus, Jaguar, and Ferrari—and a black Navigator.

Two yachts named *Iglew Too* and *TBII* and several smaller pleasure craft were moored at a two-hundred-foot dock. A bigger mooring field bobbed with buoys a hundred yards off the roiled shore. The Lexus SUV circled past two tennis courts and a full-court basketball court, and a large aviary squawking with falcons and hawks, and pulled up in front of the three-story, broad-shouldered gray-stone mansion that faced the sea and the shimmering Jersey Highlands. From this angle Bobby could see a small corner of an Olympic-size swimming pool and a portion of a white pool house at the rear of the house.

Bobby's cell phone rang again. He answered. It was Max Roth. "My voice mail is full," Roth said. "One woman's called five times. Won't give a name. Says she has info. She has the ring of truth in her voice."

"Okay, let's talk later, Max," Bobby said. "Listen, quick one: Was Luke Patterson ever involved in a palimony suit? Back in the day, maybe?"

"News to me. But I'll check it out."

"Thanks, later."

Bobby folded and put away his phone as he parked behind the Lexus SUV in front of the mansion.

"From South Hell to East Egg," Bobby said. "On the same little island."

"Staten Island used to be a one-horse town," Izzy said. "Until the horse ran away. Couldn't take the stink of the fucking garbage dump."

Tu Bitz and his bodyguards climbed out of the Lexus SUV and waited for Bobby and Izzy to join them. Then they all climbed the wide circular stairs, passing between the two Corinthian columns to the front door, where a bald bodyguard wearing a Lethalwear tracksuit patted Izzy and Bobby down.

"Drop your pants, frosty," he said to Bobby.

Bobby said, "Actually, curly, I was hoping for a little more foreplay first, maybe flowers and some chocolates."

"You dissin' me, motherfucker?"

Tu Bitz said, "Open the door before I put you through the motherfucker."

The bald bodyguard unlocked the door and opened it.

Bobby's work boots echoed off the floor of the all-Italian marble as he entered. From deep in the house came a muffled roar, like a stereo with too much bass.

"Talk about jungle music," Izzy whispered.

"To match your shrunken head," Bobby said.

"Ungawa."

Tu Bitz led a puffing Izzy and a fascinated Bobby through the professionally decorated house. Bobby admired the designer couches, gleaming teak dining-room tables, dark wooden shades on the broad windows overlooking the ocean. The expensive modern art hanging on the walls reminded him of his ex-wife's condo in the Trump International. His Timberland boot sank so deep into the Persian rug on the parquet floors that it was like walking in sand. They passed through the living room, where a beautiful, twentysomething, teary-eyed black woman bounced a baby girl with pink ribbons in her hair on her lap.

"Sorry, Janel," Tu Bitz said. "Everything gawn be all right."

She glared at him, then gazed away, out the window at the storm clouds that moved across the hot summer sky.

Bobby followed Tu Bitz and the bodyguard past the twenty-by-thirty-foot kitchen outfitted with stainless-steel industrial appliances and gleaming copper-bottom pots hanging over a horseshoe-shaped, butcher-block-topped island that was surrounded by barstools with gleaming high backs.

"Kitchen like Le Cirque, but I betcha they still bring home suitcases from White Castle after last call on Friday nights," Izzy said.

"Why don't you swallow your tongue," Bobby said.

Tu Bitz led them through a music room crowded with oversize armchairs and overstuffed furniture. Three big-screen plasma TVs played different hip-hop videos. The walls were covered with platinum and gold albums, and dozens of music awards and photos of Iglew at various stages of his career, many of the photos—including ones at high school graduation, college graduation, and the Grammys—posed with a woman Bobby figured was his proud mother.

"The top floor is Iglew's executive offices where he runs the label," Tu Bitz said. "Down the basement we got three recording studios, full mix rooms. Da works, yo. You don't need to leave here to lay tracks. We shoot videos here, too."

"Impressive," Bobby said.

Bobby noticed clusters of small snapshots in silver frames on the top of an ivory-colored grand piano, on end tables, and on a mantel. Some of the pictures were of Iglew as a boy. Some as a successful adult. A lot of them were candid snaps taken at glitzy parties here at the mansion, famous men posing with gorgeous girls in string bikinis. Some were taken with politicians, Governor Luke Patterson, Mayor Mike Bloomberg, and Hilary Clinton. Some were of Tu Bitz and various women. Then Bobby spotted one on a knickknack table of a familiar-looking man holding a newborn infant in a hospital room.

Tu Bitz opened a swinging door off the kitchen leading to the Florida room. The heavy smell of animal urine stung the air.

"Jesus Christ, asparagus musta been on sale," Izzy said.

Bobby pretended to sneeze, groped for a tissue in a box on the end table, palmed the small framed picture, and slid it into his back pocket.

Then Bobby heard the low, thundering growl of an animal. He turned and looked through the swinging door and saw two raging orange eyes. The gorgeous Bengal tiger bared teeth the size of railroad spikes. Bobby froze.

"Smells like Rikers on Paddy's Day," Izzy said.

Then Izzy saw the tiger. And grabbed his crotch and crossed his legs. "Okay, ignore my last bill," Izzy said, turning toward the exit.

Bobby grabbed him. "Stand still."

The tiger roared.

"Shut the fuck up, Tony," Tu Bitz screamed at the tiger. "Siddown."

The tiger sat.

Bobby said, "Tiger's name is *Tony?*"

"You got a fucking problem with that?"

"No, it's a *great* name."

"That supposed to be a dumb-ass Frosted Flakes joke?"

"No, but come to think of it . . ."

Two bald black men flanked the tiger as they steered Bobby and Izzy through the Florida room, where a glass-topped, eighteen-foot-long bamboo dining table surrounded by rattan chairs dominated the room. Through the large window overlooking Princes Bay, Bobby saw Iglew sitting in a lounge chair–float in a twenty-by-twenty-foot hot tub with two twentysomething women in string bikinis. Iglew was reading the *Wall Street Journal* as one babe replenished his champagne glass.

Tu Bitz led Bobby out onto the patio that led to an Olympic-size, inground pool.

"Okay, please say, 'Everybody into the pool,'" Izzy said, undoing his tie.

"You have no time for a swim," Iglew said, glancing over his bifocals. "I can give you five minutes. That's all. Care for some Cristal, Tu?"

"Nah, gotta go downstairs, lay some track."

"Need some backup chicks?"

Iglew nodded to the two girls. They climbed out and walked past Bobby and Izzy toward the door to the Florida room.

"Maybe the video," Tu Bitz said.

Izzy whipped out his wallet, handing each girl his business card. "Free consultations, ladies. Ever need legal help . . . or any other kind of help . . . call me. Collect if you want from Rikers."

The two silent women smiled and padded into the house with Tu Bitz. Izzy watched them pass the tiger, which pranced and growled on a leash held by one of two bodyguards at the door.

The guy who'd frisked Bobby walked to the swimming pool with a basket of fresh-killed pigeons and handed one bird to Iglew.

"Tony, c'mere, boy," Iglew said, jamming the newspaper into a rack on the arm of the chair float.

The tiger bounded across the room as Iglew tossed him the bird, which the tiger caught in his cavernous mouth. Iglew spun on his chair-float, sipping champagne, as Izzy and Bobby watched the tiger devour the bird in a bloody blizzard of feathers.

As the tiger ate, Iglew sipped his Roederer Cristal Champagne and looked at Bobby and said, "Okay, Mr. Emmet, what you want to talk to me about?"

Bobby took a folded copy of the *Daily News* from his back pocket, opened it to Max Roth's column about Janis McNulty, and handed it to Iglew. He glanced at it as he floated in the pool.

"So?"

"You familiar with the date that woman was killed?" Bobby asked.

"Am I supposed to be?"

"You were supposed to have a rap battle that day against Bigga Wiggaz."

Iglew looked at him and frowned. Then he exploded in laughter and spun himself around in the bubbling tub, doing a belly-laughing figure eight. "Oh, man, you are a comical dude. Let me explain something to you, my man. See, I bought my mama a house in Beverly Hills. One in Boca. A condo in White Plains, to be near her sister. And I bought her that beachfront house over there." He pointed to another modern home with wrap-around balconies and an in-ground pool a few hundred yards down the beach.

"Nice," Bobby said.

"I even had my attorneys purchase the plantation in South Carolina where my maternal great-grandmother was a slave. I wanted my mama to see her name on that deed."

"Yeah, and you have a piece of a clothing line, gorgeous subservient women, cars, jewelry, houses. You make noise about buying a ball team. This is all very interesting, but I'm here about a murder."

"Let me finish." Iglew spun his chair to the edge of the pool. "This is germane to your inquiry. I'm trying to explain that even though she has all those resources and opportunities at her disposal, all my mama ever cares to do is go back to that shithole RIP housing project. She wants to hang with her gray-hair homeys. So, I say, okay, you still wanna hang in RIP, I'll make it a resort. I sent my interior decorators to turn her five-bedroom pad into a *House Beautiful* cover. Stickly furniture, an industrial fridge, four-poster bed, big-screen plasma TV, better carpets than Saddam Hussein's grandest palace, drapes from a Broadway stage, whatever you want, Mama, because you are *everything* to me."

"Congratulations, you're a mama's boy," Bobby said. "But I'm here about a different mother, Janis McNulty's mother, who was killed ten years ago and—"

"I'm very much aware of that, Mr. Emmet. And you're obviously here because in your eyes I'm a suspect in her death. And that's why I'm trying to establish a baseline for you. So that you know a little more about who I am and not what the gossips and the police would have you believe. See, in marginalized places like RIP, they get a woman like my mama, a projects single mother, into a mind-set where oftentimes you can take the Negro out of the project, but you can't take the project out of the Negro."

"I can sympathize with the plight of the underclass, but I'm here about Cookie Calhoun, who has been six feet under for ten years because—"

"I can make all my mama's dreams come true because I am *The Shit;* I am the top dawg in the record world. And I got here because my mother told me early that I had *The Gift.* Mama encouraged me with books and music and dreams and precious quiet time at home, at an old broken-down piano. As the gunshots exploded outside in the crack wars of the 1980s, she told me I could create a whole other world beyond that pile of dirty, bloodstained brick called RIP with a pen and paper and a song in my heart."

"That's a lovely ode to your mom but—"

The tiger pranced up to Bobby, sniffing, a ticking sound coming from its throat, its bloody upper lip rising. Bobby froze. The hairs on his flesh stood erect. Sweat burst from his pores. Izzy tried to stand still but his knees buckled.

Iglew snapped his fingers at the tiger and it turned and slouched into the Florida room and lay in a corner, watching, panting. Iglew hopped out of the hot tub in a fluid motion, all shredded muscle and wearing Lethalwear trunks. He grabbed a towel and dried off.

"My mama gave me the gift of cultivating my own born gift. She was the mother of my invention. And because of her, as you have already observed, I have a particular fondness for the institution of motherhood. Mother's Day is the holiest and most joyous day on my calendar. The reason why black folk use the word *motherfucker* so frequently is because of the lasting scars of white slave owners fucking our mothers. That's why we called slave owners *motherfuckers.* Or *crackers,* which comes from the motherfuckers cracking their whips at those of us who fought for the dignity of our mothers. Or *ofay,* which, when decoded from pig latin means 'foe.' The worst part of slavery was not just the owning of us, Mr. Emmet. It was the repeated raping of our mothers. Often in front of us when we were children."

"Is there a point to this fascinating history lesson?" Bobby asked.

"Yes, simply put, I love my mama. I love mothers all over the world. All mothers, of all colors. I worship mothers, Mr. Emmet. I could never kill anyone's mother or associate with anyone who did."

"You and Cody Jarrett," Bobby said.

"Touché, yo, *White Heat* is one of my favorite white flicks."

"Maybe what you're saying is true. *Now*. Now that you have so much to lose. But people change. What about ten years ago? When you had nothing. Nothing to lose?"

"You're right, ten years ago I was a little wannabe rapper nobody," Iglew said, pulling on a silk Gucci robe. "And the powers that be told me back then that if I wanted my shot, I had to battle some wigga girl and her little skinny brother from Brooklyn, from Bay-fucking-John-Travolta-*Saturday-Night-Fever*-Ridge. That was *played* enough. But still I said okay. It was demoralizing to have to battle a wigga group from Bay Ridge, but it was part of the process, paying dues. But that day Janis McNulty didn't show up. I thought she'd punked out. But then I learned that her mother was killed in a hit-and-run. The truth is, I felt terrible for her. I truly did at the time. I ache for anyone who loses a mother."

"You won the battle by default."

"Yes. But, at the risk of sounding like a blowhard, it saved her from having her sorrow compounded by public humiliation."

"Janis thinks it would have gone the other way," Bobby said.

Iglew laughed, checked his watch, and sipped more of his champagne. The tiger finally calmed down, and Bobby could hear its hair-trigger panting and loud chuffing as it licked its bloody paws. Bobby had read somewhere, probably in the prison library, that tigers were the only cats that did not purr.

"Then how come no one has heard of her since?" Iglew said. "Except as a club act? Or this new album that'll never get airtime on a fledgling label?"

"Sometimes you get one shot at being lucky," Bobby said. "You had yours. Look what happened. You toured with Baru. You got a record deal on what was then a fledgling label—"

"I made it a powerhouse."

"—you became a star. Yes, and now that label is one of the top labels in hip-hop. You don't own it, really. Deity, whoever he is, does. And now he wants to sell it out from under your nose."

"Who is spoon-feeding you this high-octane fiction?"

"On the grapevine, Ignatius," Bobby said. "Funny, I start asking about this old hit-and-run and already people are trying to liquidate me. And Lethal Injection. Why?"

Iglew waved his hand in a dismissive way. "Nonsense. This is my label.

As for someone trying to hurt you, that certainly has nothing to do with me. You matter not in my life, Mr. Emmet."

"I will."

"Are we finished?"

"You mind telling me exactly where you were that morning that Cookie Calhoun was killed? Just for the record."

"Iglew was at Lethal Injection in Manhattan, before I moved the operation here. Waiting for that McNulty girl and her brother to arrive for the rap battle."

"Who's your alibi?"

"The two guys from my defunct group."

"Where are they?"

"Alas, they're defunct, too. One OD'd, one perished from AIDS."

Bobby nodded and said, "Did James Ford ever ask you about Cookie Calhoun?"

Iglew's hips swiveled, tics rippling in his face like trapped worms. He tied the robe belt tighter, gulped some champagne as if his throat had gone dry.

"James Ford?" he said, tapping his forehead. "No data. Lotta water under the Verrazano Bridge since then, podna. Iglew packed four lifetimes into ten years."

Iglew was a good actor, but he couldn't hide that Ford's name had pierced him like a bullet. He walked across the patio, nodding for Bobby and Izzy to follow, and passing the tiger, who gazed up with those killer eyes. Iglew grabbed the tiger by a loose choke collar and led him through the swinging doors toward the kitchen. He opened a heavy door to the basement.

"Go on, Tony."

The tiger bounded down the stairs with a soft roar.

Iglew slammed the door and strolled through the house and led Bobby and Izzy out onto the stoop. The bodyguards slouched at their posts. Izzy handed out business cards to the various bodyguards as he walked down the corridor. All of them took them and gave clenched-fist salutes, meeting his fist with theirs.

"Free consultations if you mention Iglew's name," Izzy said. "Discounts for up-front cash payments."

Iglew led Bobby and Izzy to the Jeep.

"James Ford's name doesn't ring a bell?" Bobby asked.

Bobby waited for Iglew's answer.

"Iglew doesn't store Five-O names in his head."

"Five-O? I didn't say James Ford was a cop."

Iglew nodded, squished his mouth, and bared his teeth. "Most crackers who question Iglew are."

"I didn't say he was white, either."

Anger igniting in his eyes for the first time, Iglew stared at Bobby.

"That's it. I gave you more time than I give my mama. Later."

"Think you can arrange for me to talk to Deity?"

"Sorry, no way."

"Then how about Rodney Calhoun?"

Silence fell on the stoop like in that moment before a jury foreman gives a verdict. "Haven't seen or heard from him in ten years."

Izzy started the engine and tried pulling Bobby into the Jeep. Bobby paused before climbing in and said, "Then how about Clarence Mathers?"

Iglew turned.

Bobby waved the wallet he'd taken from the garroter who was shot at the Lutheran Medical Center the day before. He opened it and looked at the name and address on the New York State driver's license.

"Clarence Mathers lives at this address," Bobby said, tossing Iglew the wallet as the doors started to close.

"Yeah, a lot of the guys use this as a mailing address, so? Insurance."

"He dropped it yesterday at Lutheran Medical Center. Tell him I hope he gets well soon. Oh, and, Ignatius, old chum, next time you try to kill me, send somebody good. Somebody like you."

Iglew looked at Bobby as he climbed in the Jeep, and Izzy peeled down the circular drive and out the security gates.

FIFTEEN

Bobby bowled a gutter ball, turned to Steve Greco, and asked, "Someone did request those tapes that day?"

"Yes."

"The same day?"

"Two hours afterward," Greco said, hefting his personal red-speckled bowling ball.

"How do you know?"

Greco looked around Lovers' Lanes, which he'd selected because he said the noise was too loud to be overheard or recorded. Organized teams of male seniors, middle-aged wives, and loud teenagers clogged the alleys, rolling skilled strikes and spares, competing in a fierce frenzy in a game Bobby was never any good at. Like darts, pool, and golf, Bobby didn't consider bowling a sport. It was a game. There was a difference.

A few families also bowled together. The bar was half-full with middle-aged men and pensioners sipping cold beers and watching ESPN on one TV and MSN on the other. A jolly-faced black man pushed a four-foot-wide dust mop up and down the alleys, collecting potato chips, pretzels, beer nuts, and any other debris off the gleaming wood floors. His cell phone rang and he answered, leaning on his mop and saying, "Hey, babes."

The whole world lived on cell phones, and Bobby thought that someday an extraterrestrial Svengali would find a way to hypnotize every human being alive through a cell phone signal and turn them all into an army of slaves.

Greco eyeballed everyone. A man who works security for a living takes certain precautions. Bobby had watched his car mirrors the entire trip from

135

Tottenville to Brooklyn, making a few U-turns and running two red lights to be sure he wasn't followed. He wasn't.

Greco said, "I told you I really don't want to get involved in this."

"Who was it?"

"You didn't get it from me. Right? I don't need the hassles. I got nineteen years in. Vested. Five more I can put in my papers."

"No problem. Was it Ford?"

Greco hefted his ball, held it in both hands as he eyed the pins. He glanced over both shoulders, like a deadbeat gambler who owed big money to badass wiseguys. Bowlers bowled, drinkers drank, the waitress served drinks, and the porter gabbed on his cell phone. Then Greco glanced sideways at Bobby and nodded as he slid into his left-handed ball release with the grace of a seasoned bowler. The ball hooked right and Greco left two pins standing. It didn't seem to faze him. Bobby grinned at the conspiratorial precautions. But then he thought about being attacked himself the day before.

"He signed for them?" Bobby asked.

Greco nodded again as he sat and entered his score on the sheet at their table, took a sip of beer with his right hand, and waited for his ball to return. A waitress came and brought another diet Coke and another beer for Greco. It was his third beer in twenty minutes. He had been finishing one at the bar when Bobby entered. He'd ordered another one at the table, drunk that in two long, nervous gulps. And here was the third one.

"Did Ford return them?" Bobby asked as the waitress took away the empties and Bobby paid her with a $10 bill and told her to keep the change.

"Funny thing is, I was out the day he took them out," Greco said. "My daughter was born that week, and Clinton had signed the family leave law and my wife busted my balls to take two weeks off and I did, and that's why I don't remember the accident. You have a new baby, for two weeks nothing else happens in the world, know what I mean?"

Bobby remembered that special time when Maggie came kicking and screaming into his life and changed it forever, all his priorities rearranged, with the kid who was the pride of his life on top. "I know the feeling."

"But I remember Ford. When I got back, I saw that some highway cop had taken the security tapes out when I was out on leave. Something that never would've happened if I was working. I would have made them review them at my security office and would have demanded an official request from police brass, a letter with a seal from the commissioner's office at One Police Plaza to release copies. Never the originals. Gotta remember it was a hairy time. Especially right after the first Trade Center bombing. Security was on high alert. We wanted to preserve security tapes on all potential terrorist targets instead of reusing them because you just never know, do you, when one of those trucks is the one that takes out a bridge or a tunnel or a government building or a skyscraper. You want to have it on tape in case you can highlight and enhance a license plate or a face. You keep them marked Do Not Erase. In a vault."

"So when you got back from family leave, you saw that Ford had taken out some security tapes?"

"That's right," Greco said, then took a gulp, looking around.

"But he hadn't returned them?"

"Yeah, and it could have caused a real pain in the goddamned ass if anyone at the bridge authority found out. I got my wife's kid brother into the job, rabbied him, figured he worked here long enough maybe he could take over the Marine Parkway Bridge or maybe the Throgs Neck someday. But the kid has one of them personalities, do anything for you. Loves to be loved. Eager to please. And intimidated by authority. So when a slick homicide detective like Ford comes along, flashing his gold shield, asking for tapes, razzle-dazzling him, he gives them to him like he's helping to save the republic."

"Sounds like a good kid."

"Great kid. But an asshole. And since the buck stops with me, because I'm his boss and I put him in charge in my absence and no one really knows he's my brother-in-law . . ."

He shrugged, took a belt of beer, dried his hand over the air blower, rolled his bowling ball, and made the spare.

Bobby said, "The old nepotism sweepstakes. Human nature."

"My wife busted my balls like prison rocks. So I shuffled some paper. All legal, all legit, he passed all the tests, but it coulda caused favoritism-resentment on the job if it came out, so I had to chase this Ford asshole around, busting his balls for these tapes. That's life. You get your balls crushed, you gotta crush someone else's. Then Ford starts crushing mine right back. Kept asking why the tapes were so important to me. Said they might be part of a very important case he was working. I say, I don't give a shit, they might be part of a federal terrorist investigation someday, and if they're missing, my ass is in the sling. My job, my pension, my new baby's future was on the line."

"You get them back?"

"Took me two weeks to get them back from this asshole. Said they were being analyzed. Trying to bulldoze me. Grilling me like I'm some kind of skell, perp. Ford wants to know why I need these particular tapes."

"But he gave them back?"

"He gave me back fucking *copies!* I could tell because I'm good at what I do and knew they were degraded. They were twelve-hour, stop-action videotapes, pretty good quality, but a little blurry. But they have ways of enhancing stuff these days you can't believe."

No one was better at it than Bobby's daughter, Maggie, on some special computer called an Avid, which could digitize Pleistocene hieroglyphics and transform them into a Jerry Bruckheimer epic.

Bobby thought of an email Maggie had sent him recently where an image from 10 million light-years away is enhanced ten times with each subsequent image until it zooms through space, illuminating stars, moving through the galaxy, the solar system, passing planets, until it singles out what astronomer Carl Sagan called the pale blue dot known as planet Earth. Then, continuing in magnifications of ten, the image highlighted the United States, then Florida, and finally an oak tree outside the National High Magnetic Field Laboratory in Tallahassee, from which the hypothetical photo originated, and then continuing to magnify by tens, it focused on a leaf on the oak tree, exposing its eerie cells, the mighty nucleus, mysterious chromatin, the miracle of DNA, and finally the mind-blowing subatomic universe of electrons and protons.

Everything could be reduced to a common denominator, Bobby thought. *I need to magnify everything here in multiples of ten.*

"So I never watched the tapes start to finish," Greco said. "Personally, I never cared what was on them, tell you the truth. Like a cop, you can't take this job home with you or you'll live in constant despair. But I could see the tapes weren't the originals and that they were copies, and that really pissed me off. I contacted Ford again. Told him I wanted the originals. He told me they were the originals. Bald-face lie. And he knew that I knew. But I couldn't report him because I didn't want to send up a red flag and get my brother-in-law in trouble and ergo, myself, for not reporting it right away. So after a few months of back and forth with this shitbag Ford, I finally gave up. But it led to a strained relationship with Ford over the years."

"I can imagine."

"He'd stop at the plaza sometimes, mooch coffee. Awkward. Every time I'd see him, he'd smirk, knowing I knew he burned me. But he didn't give a shit. He lived on Staten Island so I'd see him when he crossed the bridge time to time, always dressed nice, good cars, alone. The shit-eater on his face. Like a guy who's fucking your wife. And the truth is, he did fuck me."

"What did you do with the copies?"

"I put them into the vault, marked Do Not Erase, in case anyone ever came around looking for them. Good thing, too."

Bobby walked back from knocking down three pins, dried his hand, took a swig of diet Coke, ate some popcorn, and asked, "Why?"

"Because the Feds asked for them."

"Who?"

"According to my records, two agents, named Noonan and Scarano."

Bobby reached past his diet Coke for Greco's beer.

"Hey, that's mine."

"I know," Bobby said, gulping half the bottle, trying to make sense of the news. "So what happened?"

"The Feds were part of some organized-crime task force back then. A lot of gangsters went back and forth over the Verrazano, ya know. Castellano, Sammy the Bull, the Persicos, all those goombahs. That's why the Verrazano's called the Guinea gangplank. I call it the RICO Raceway. I figured they must have someone on that tape who wasn't supposed to be there. Or something."

"And then you gave them the tapes?"

"They insisted that they hadda take them with them. But I refused. It got fucking testy and chesty, tell you that. I already got burned once. I let them sit in my office and view them. They got all kinds of excited. And they went ape shit when they realized that they were *copies*. They wanted to know who the hell got the originals. I told them Ford."

"How'd they react to that?"

"They started threatening me. The same way Ford did. I said, okay, that's it, I'm stuck in the middle of a cross-jurisdictional turf war between NYPD and the FBI, my balls're in a juicerator, and I said I'm going to my boss to come clean."

"What did they do?"

"They did a Chernobyl meltdown. Said that as a matter of national security—fucking *national security*—I couldn't tell another soul about these tapes. I figure they must have the blind sheikh on these tapes lighting a fuse or something. So I didn't say shit to anybody. They demanded the tapes. I refused. It got fucking hairy. This Scarano, he even took out his gun! My heart was like one of them alarm clocks with the little hammer hitting the bells. I had to ask them to leave. Noonan made Scarano put the gun away. They said they'd be back with a paper. Which they came with two days later."

Greco took a swig of his beer, dried his sweaty hands over the hand blower, and remained silent as the jolly porter with the dust mop came by, mopping up droplets of condensation that had dripped off the beer bottle.

" 'Scuse me, gents," he said. "Rainin' cats and dogs out there now."

Bobby checked his watch: 1:43 p.m. He had some time before he met Janis McNulty in the lot.

Bobby waited for the porter to pass and said, "Then you gave them the copies?"

"Yeah," Greco said, draining his beer and signaling to the waitress. She nodded.

"Shit."

"But this time I wasn't gonna get burned again. I made another copy in case anyone else ever came busting my balls. I kept the first degraded copy in the vault. And gave the Feds the copy off the copy, a second-degradation copy. They never asked if there were any others. I think they thought I was a stooge. A pencil pusher." Greco mounted his beer bottle on his crotch. "They can push *this*."

Bobby laughed and Greco took a gulp of beer.

"And they knew Ford had the original?" Bobby said.

"Yeah. Then I never really heard from them again. I saw Ford plenty of times. Not the Feds. I didn't forget about it, but I had bigger things to worry about, like raising my kid. And since September eleventh, well, that whole episode seems like old news from another century. Same bridge, different world."

"You ain't kidding."

"But when you busted my balls about it the other day, it bubbled up. You're a PI so I wasn't exactly frank. I don't have to tell you squat. But you hit me between the eyes with the comment about my Father's Day tie. Then mentioning the McNulty kid who watched his mother die. And who was thinking of maybe doing a swan dive off my bridge. It just killed me inside. Couldn't sleep. It ripped my guts out. Then I read that Max Roth's column this morning, read the quotes from the kids."

"Break your heart," Bobby said.

"Oh, *man,* Roth has a way with the words that makes you feel *dirty* as a cock-a-roach if you can help and don't do something about it. So I called you. But you can't let an inkling of this trace back to me. Please, I got a wife, kid . . ."

"Promise. I appreciate it."

"I'm not doing it for *you.*"

"The McNultys will appreciate it."

"I wish I could say I'm doing it for them. And I will feel better if they get some peace and some justice. But I'm doing it for *me.* I thought about my own kid. That could be *her.* I also thought about this fucking Ford. You tell me he never did anything about the case? But yet he wanted this tape so bad that he basically stole it? Leaving me holding the bag. And the Feds wanted it so bad they threatened me? So then I check the logs and I see that this tape isn't even classified anymore. After seven years it was supposed to be destroyed or reused. But we went to a new system. And then came nine-eleven and who the hell had time to clean out the vault and . . ."

"You still have the tape?" Bobby asked, holding his bowling ball in both hands, the little holes too small for his thick fingers.

Greco nodded toward his bowling bag, which sat under the bench where they were stationed. Then he spoke out of the corner of his mouth, "Along with copies of the paperwork Ford and the Feds both signed. But remember, it's for deep background only, and you didn't get this shit from me. I gotta piss."

Bobby heaved the ball down the alley with the force of a cannonball and knocked all seven remaining pins down.

"Yes!" he said.

Bobby waited nervously for Greco to return. The waitress came, brought another round of drinks, and took away the empties. Bobby paid her and tipped five bucks. She smiled in a tired way, and Bobby wondered what she took for headaches after working all day in a bowling alley. He needed something after less than an hour.

Bobby returned his bowling shoes, carrying the bowling bag with him. He got his Timberland steel-toed boots back, carried them to his table, sat down, and tied them and waited for Greco to return. He was in the john for almost ten minutes. *Long leak,* Bobby thought. *Maybe he ate something here. Anyone who eats in a bowling alley deserves to sit for ten frames on the bowl.*

He checked his watch: 1:56. He couldn't wait any longer. He took a sip of Greco's beer and reached into the bowling bag and took a manila envelope. He looked around the way Greco had, certain no one was watching. But of course he couldn't be.

But he felt safe in the crowded bowling alley in the middle of the summer day. He riffled through the documents; saw the requisition forms signed by Ford for the original tapes. Then other forms on FBI letterhead signed by Noonan and Scarano.

He noticed something odd about the signature at the bottom of the document signed by Ford and was trying to process it when he heard a scream from behind him.

"Call nine one one!" shouted the black porter, who rushed out of the men's room. "There's a dead man in the gah-damned men's room! Blood every which where! Call the po-lice! Man killed himself!"

Instinct made Bobby fold and shove the manila envelope into his back pocket. In the pandemonium, as bowlers stampeded toward the men's room and the bar, Bobby loosened his belt two notches, unbuttoned the top button of his jeans, and without standing reached into the bag, opened the two videocassette cases, and grabbed the two VHS tapes. He pushed one tape down the back of his jeans, one down the front. His shirttails draped over his pants. He snapped the tape boxes closed, wiped them clean with a paper napkin. He elbowed Greco's copy of the *Daily News,* opened to Max Roth's column, into the bag and plopped Greco's ball on top. He zippered it, wrapped a napkin around the handle, and carried it toward the commotion, eyes darting to the porter, the bartender, the waitress, and the guy who'd exchanged his shoes.

It all took less than ten seconds.

He shoved through the crowd and peered into the men's room.

Stephen Greco sat on the bowl in the last toilet stall, a pistol with a silencer in his right hand, the back of his head blown off from a bullet in the mouth. His head was twisted at a grotesque angle so that his chin rested on his left shoulder, blood drooling down the ceramic-tile wall. His pants were pulled down around his ankles, pockets pulled out. Bobby knew this was no suicide. Steve Greco bowled and wrote left-handed and the gun was in his right hand. From outside the bathroom door bowling pins scattered and rock music played in Lovers' Lanes.

The bathroom window leading to an alley was wide open to the torrential rain.

Bobby carried the bowling bag into the crowd, looking into the faces.

"Weren't you bowling with him?" asked one bowler from the Bay Ridge Spares.

"I served them," said the waitress. "They was together. But this guy never followed him inside. I waited on him, I should know."

Bobby kept walking for the side exit to the parking lot, carrying the bowling bag in one hand. Palming a .25 in his left hand, not much bigger than a cell phone.

He hit the panic bar on the side door and stepped out into the midafternoon thunderstorm. Gulls flapped inland from the Narrows into Fort Hamilton Park, yapping in the place from which Washington's bedraggled Brooklyn brigade once hurled cannonballs at the British armada.

A police car yelped to the curb at the front of Lovers' Lanes, lights flashing, followed by a whooping ambulance. Bobby sloshed toward his Jeep in the lot in the rear of the bowling alley as rain shelled the sticky city, lightning illuminating the towers of the Verrazano.

"Up with the bag, motherfucker," said a man who stood between two parked cars.

Bobby turned and looked at the porter, hood pulled low over his face that didn't look so jolly with a TEC 9 in his hand.

"You gonna kill me, too?" Bobby asked, extending the bag outward with his right hand. And with his lowered left hand he fired a bullet through the porter's left foot, a little pop lost in the storm.

The porter screamed, tottered, and bent sideways to grab his foot. Bobby kicked him in the face with the steel-toed boot, his broad nose splitting.

"Who the fuck sent you?" Bobby said, mashing his .25 into the ruined nose. "Why'd you kill that poor son of a bitch? He had a beautiful little girl. Who? Tell me before I fucking kill you."

The man moaned, blood pulsing though his sneaker, also leaking down his face, his eyes bobbing in his head like lottery balls as he mumbled prayers.

Then lightning sizzled and thunder clapped again, a one-two punch of visual and aural disorientation in the already disconcerting downpour.

Bobby saw the meat of a baseball bat at that last second. He ducked and it hit him high on the skull, which would have been a foul back if his head were a ball. A flock of silver steel birds exploded in front of his face, amid a cacophony of honking horns, two-tone sirens. Bobby bent low at the knees, brain slushy, and swung the ten-pound bowling bag upward. It detonated off a face with an awful *thwunk* and he heard someone say, "Uhnnnn." Bobby raised his .25, staggering through the rain, lightning arcing and thunder rolling like drunken gods brawling in the heavens.

Control, he thought. *Don't go down. Stay on your feet. You need one of them.*

Someone swung the club down on Bobby's wrist. His .25 fell with a splash, and a second guy grabbed the bowling bag and dove into the rear of a black Navigator. The bleeding porter dragged the guy whose face was smashed toward the same car.

More police cars whooped to the front of the bowling alley, lights flicking above the low rooftops and splaying on the wet brick wall of the rear parking lot and mixing with the lightning in a psychedelic light show. Bobby's head pounded, as if Lilliputians were trying to kick their way out.

Bobby scrambled through the puddles for his handgun, the videotapes jammed into his pants digging into his tight flesh.

Then he looked into the muzzle of a TEC 9. The porter's bloodied face was needled with rain, smiling the way he had in the bowling alley. He dragged his crimson hoof, his brown face runny with blood.

"Fuck him, we got the bag, lez book," someone shouted from the Navigator.

Even with the cops pouring through the front doors, the porter lifted his bad foot and said, *"This* for *that* motherfu—"

And then the steel pipe came down on top of his head. Already balancing on one foot, the porter toppled left to one knee. Trying to train the automatic pistol. Bobby glanced up. Janis McNulty swung her anti-auto-theft device called The Club down on the porter's head. He wouldn't go all the way down. She hit him again. Harder. Then Jimi Jim hit him with a second piece of The Club, the thinner steel inner rod. Both beat the porter, who waved the gun in the rain as the black Navigator squealed out of the lot toward the rear exit.

Bobby grabbed his .25. Aimed it at the porter. The dazed porter tried to point his gun at Bobby. "Don't be an asshole," Bobby said.

And then Bobby heard a woman scream, "Scarano, nooooo!"

Followed by a gunshot.

The bullet entered the middle of the porter's forehead like a last red cent to end his murderous little life. This time the porter went all the way down.

Bobby turned and Lou Scarano stood in a frozen histrionic firing stance in the pouring rain. Tom Noonan stood next to him, his gun at his side. Noonan pushed Scarano's gun in a downward motion, facing the ground. Behind them stood several uniformed cops. Samantha Savage approached them from the side, dressed in a black trench coat tied around her thin waist, rain drooling off a floppy brimmed hat that made her look as if she'd just stepped out of a 1940s movie.

"You didn't have to shoot him!" she shouted at Scarano. "We needed him alive!"

Janis helped Bobby to his feet, still holding The Club in her hand. Even though they were a dozen feet away, Bobby heard Noonan turn to her in the rain and say, "We? There's no *we* anymore, Miss Savage. You've been suspended, you're no longer a part of this task force, and you shouldn't even be here."

"I followed Emmet from Staten Island," she said. "He was meeting with Tu Bitz and Iglew. My guess is you were tailing Steve Greco. Why?"

Bobby was shocked she addressed them in such an open and critical manner. *Had to be part of an act,* he thought. *For my benefit.*

"That's no longer any of your business," Noonan said. "And this is certainly no time or place to discuss it."

"You didn't have to shoot—"

"This was a perfectly good shooting," Scarano said. "Civilians were in danger. A crazed gunman was trying to kill them."

Bobby was still groggy. He'd asked Janis to meet him here. That was no coincidence. He also wasn't surprised to see Savage, Noonan, and Scarano here. They probably had been tailing Greco. But he wasn't buying the dissension in their ranks. Even in his head-throbbing haze he figured that for a public display of misdirection.

But then through the crowd of ghoulish citizens, wet bowlers, agitated uniformed police, and Lovers' Lanes staff, he saw Dianne Rattigan appear from the rain. Her second ambulance crew raced to the porter with a gurney. *Was this just a coincidence?* He remembered that this was the sector where she worked. Just blocks from where she had heard Cookie Calhoun utter her last words. There might be nothing out of the ordinary for Dianne Rattigan to answer a call in her own sector. But he wasn't buying it. *Too pat,* he thought.

Rattigan checked the porter for life signs. There weren't any. Paul the ambulance driver covered the porter with a sheet and threw a shifty sideways glance at Bobby. Noonan walked over, bent into a catcher's crouch next to Rattigan. His face was a controlled, menacing emblem of authority, staring at the rain percolating in the puddles as he spoke. Rattigan looked at him, nervous. She glanced at Bobby and lowered her head. Nodding. Noonan patted her shoulder. And she took a deep breath, closed her eyes, and nodded again.

Is she neck-deep in this with them? Bobby wondered

Noonan glared at Bobby as he stood. "You and me are gonna have a nice long chat," Noonan said.

Bobby did a quick assessment of the situation. He might have been a half step off his game, like a wobbly fighter on his stool between rounds after a knockdown, but he tried to focus. *A black porter kills Greco,* he thought. *For the tapes. He figures I have them so he comes after me. Then Noonan and Scarano just so happen to arrive on the scene. Scarano kills the porter so that he can never flip on them. I know Noonan and Scarano are in cahoots with Ford, and using black heavies to do their dirty work. Then Dianne Rattigan arrives. Probably to whisk away their wounded. I need to isolate her.*

"I want transport," Bobby said to Rattigan, blood trickling from his head. "To a hospital. Now."

"First, I want you alone with me in a room, Emmet," said Scarano.

"Not until I get medical attention," Bobby said.

Dianne Rattigan looked at Noonan, skittish. Noonan looked around at the crowd.

"What the hell are you waiting for, lady," Janis McNulty shouted in front of dozens of witnesses. "He's bleeding for chrissakes! From the head!"

Janis ushered Bobby into the back of Rattigan's ambulance.

"I want a CAT scan, stitches, twenty-four-hour observation to be sure there's no bleeding in my brain."

Rattigan looked at Noonan, frightened, confused. The crowd watched.

Noonan nodded. Scarano smirked and looked sideways at Noonan before gazing away.

Inside the ambulance Bobby beckoned Janis McNulty closer. Rattigan irrigated his wound, staring at Janis as if she were an apparition, and said, "Have we met . . .?"

Rattigan turned and told Paul to take Bobby to Victory Memorial Hospital.

"I wanna go to Lutheran," Bobby said.

"Victory's closer."

"I insist. Besides, the lunch is free."

Rattigan smiled and turned again to the driver, and when her back was turned, Bobby shoved the videocassettes into Janis's pocketbook. He whispered in her ear where he'd meet her in three hours.

Janis nodded and slipped off into the rain.

Rattigan slammed the doors and the ambulance raced Bobby toward Lutheran Medical Center. Bobby was now alone in the back of the bus with Dianne Rattigan.

"Beautiful lady."

Bobby said, "Yeah."

"She looks so damned familiar. She your gal?"

"I don't have a gal."

"I don't believe you. Guy looks like you, he's got a—"

"She's my client."

"Client?"

Dianne Rattigan slathered bacitracin ointment on Bobby's scalp to prevent infection and held folded gauze tightly to the wound.

"Her mother died in your arms."

He felt the pressure on his head wound ease off. He looked up at her, her eyes growing frightened and blinky.

"Lots of people die in my arms."

"Not all of them leave you with secrets."

She pushed the gauze so tight against his wound he jumped. "Don't go there, Mr. Emmet, please."

"*Bobby.* And she could be less than a week away from another family funeral."

"Please, Bobby . . ."

"I want you to read Max Roth's column in the *Daily News*."

"I only read the *Times*."

"I already know that someone is in jail doing someone else's time and Cookie Calhoun knew about it and—"

She pushed harder on the wound.

"Owww . . . Why do you let them threaten you, Dianne?"

She looked at Bobby, widened her eyes, then shifted them toward Paul the driver, who kept looking in his mirror.

"You've had blunt force trauma to the head," Rattigan said. "Try not to talk. Let your brain rest."

Bobby rode in silence for a while. He didn't know if Dianne Rattigan was just scared. Or in cahoots with Ford and the Feds. Either way, he didn't trust her. He needed information. A decent man had just died, leaving a woman a widow, and a kid without a father, and Bobby was tired of Dianne Rattigan holding out on information. That information might be a clue to who'd killed Cookie Calhoun. What Greco knew about Cookie Calhoun had gotten him killed. Bobby wasn't going to slap information out of Dianne Rattigan. But he was going to do whatever the hell he could to get her to talk.

When Paul turned on the siren, Bobby looked into Dianne Rattigan's face. He'd known a few attractive women detectives over the years who'd used their sex appeal to get lonely guys to spill information. Or even confess to crimes. He was always amazed at how powerful a truth serum a little perfume and a lot of cleavage could be. But guys were basically dogs and could be led around by the dick.

He didn't know if he had what it took to make lonely Dianne Rattigan talk. But he was going to give it his best shot. Out of duty. For Cookie Calhoun. And her suicidal son, Brian. And for Steve Greco, whom he'd led to his own murder.

"Can I take you to dinner?"

She laughed, smirked, and said, "You're delirious." She shone a flashlight in his eyes to check for pupil dilation. "You nauseous?"

"Nah. So is that a no?"

"Is what a no?"

"My offer to take you to dinner."

She laughed, incredulous. "You hitting on me, Samse?"

"I'm asking you to dinner. Not the altar or the Adultery Arms Motel."

She laughed. "No . . . I mean, no, it's not a *no*. *Yes,* I think you're delirious. But if you're not, and if the offer still holds after the C-scan says you're all right, the answer is sure. Yes. But I'm not supposed to date vics."

Of course she'd say yes, he thought. *So she can pick my brains about what I know. To win brownie points with Ford and Noonan and Scarano.*

"Name the place," he said. "Embers. Peter Luger's. Ponte Vecchio . . ."

The driver blared his horn and whooped the siren, giving them the cover she needed to talk freely.

"Ya know, I haven't cooked for a man in a long time . . ."

Of course, he thought. *She wants to control the environment. Hidden cameras. Microphones. Maybe even a trap. But I can't say no.*

"Deal. Anything but liver. Tonight?"

"Sorry, working."

"Playing hard to get?" *Yes, she was,* he thought, *to keep it from being obvious.*

"I'm doing double the next two days for the OT to build up my IRAs, but I'm off Wednesday night. You like salmon?"

He told her to write her address on a piece of paper, shove it in his pocket, and he'd be there at eight.

"I'll bring the wine," Bobby said.

"Chardonnay?"

"Deal."

"Everything okay back there," Paul the driver shouted.

"Couldn't be better," Dianne Rattigan said, scribbling her name on a sheet of paper and stuffing it into Bobby's pocket. Then she wrote a note to herself: *Wednesday, 8 p.m., dinner with Bobby. Home. Salmon.*

She folded the note into a little square and shoved it behind the leather book cover of her Bible.

Does she know that I know she's trying to use me? he wondered as the ambulance rumbled into the emergency room port of Lutheran Medical Center.

SIXTEEN

While waiting to be triaged in Lutheran Medical Center, Bobby saw Dianne Rattigan blot a tear from her eyes as she read Max Roth's column in the *Daily News*. She blew her nose and took a deep breath.

Was it an act? he wondered, his head pounding.

She wrote a little note to herself, folded it, and shoved it into the back cover of her pocket-size Bible.

"I always make notes of what I gotta do and who and what I should light candles for," she said.

"I know, you already told me that."

"Oh. Right. Tonight I'll light a candle and say a prayer for the McNultys and Calhouns."

Bobby saw her check her watch.

"Clock's on the wall," Bobby said.

"I was checking the date," she said, and kept reading.

Bobby hoped that was because she was trying to calculate the days until the ten-year anniversary of Cookie Calhoun's killing. Which Bobby now believed was a murder.

Maybe she was concerned. As she read the column, Bobby casually said, "You're gonna miss your free lunch."

"I started a new diet."

"When?"

"Fifteen minutes ago."

"Hey, what happened to that guy who got shot here in the hospital yesterday?"

Without looking up from the column Rattigan said she'd heard he was out of intensive care and in a trauma care unit on the fifth floor and was expected to make a complete recovery.

"Did you know him?" she asked.

"No, just curious. Must've just missed all that commotion."

She nodded as she finished the column. She thumbed a tear from one eye again. Sighed.

"Oh, sweet Baby *Je-sus*. You really think this boy will hurt himself?"

"Put it this way, I hope you don't get the call. Especially if you could have prevented it."

She looked at Bobby in a jumble of fear and professionalism. "That's just not fair, Bobby."

"Neither is keeping a secret that could save his life."

"You don't understand. That cop . . . and the others—"

The radio mounted on her shoulder crackled with news of another run, a domestic stabbing in Sunset Park.

"Gotta run," she said.

He grabbed her hand. Squeezed it, looked in her eyes. "Tell me, Dianne . . ."

"See you Wednesday," she said, running toward the ambulance port.

"Might be too late," Bobby shouted, but then she was gone in a swirl of lights.

Bobby finished triage, received a few butterfly stitches in the ER, and was rushed to radiology, where he was strapped to a table and sent into the CAT scan tube, where a computer took a three-dimensional image of his brain.

He was afraid of taking a look at that mystical gray lump that gave him so many bad thoughts. Like the ones he was having right now. Bad thoughts about bad people who did bad things to good people, like ending the life of a good man who had been a loving father and dedicated husband and hard worker with a good heart that told him he must do something about the plight of another family.

Bobby was convinced that the same people who had left a hole in the McNulty/Calhoun family had also blown one through Greco's head and his family's heart and soul.

Somewhere right now a nine-year-old girl was being told she would never see her daddy again. No CAT scan would ever pick up the lifelong three-dimensional damage that traumatic blow would do to her.

When they wheeled Bobby into the waiting room to await results on the CAT scan, he watched a doctor walk to a closet and take out and dress in a fresh green linen smock, green linen pants, a face mask, shower-cap-style head covering, formfitting, elasticized crepe shoe coverings. He snapped on a pair of latex gloves.

When the doctor left, Bobby got up, put on his steel-toed boots, pulled on hospital green pants over his jeans, a green smock over his summer shirt, a pair of green foot coverings over the big construction boots, and a pair of latex gloves. He pulled a second pair of latex gloves over the first because he knew fingerprints could be left through one pair.

He left a note on the gurney telling the doctors to call him on his cell phone with the results of his CAT scan.

Then he took the paper bag in which Dianne Rattigan had stored his personal belongings—belt, wallet, cell phone, money, keys, and .25 automatic and a second clip. The only other thing he'd had in his pocket was the small family photo he'd swiped off the dresser in the Tottenville mansion.

He pulled on the face mask and elasticized head covering and walked to the stairwell to climb the five flights of stairs to the posttrauma unit. He stopped after three flights, his head light and his breathing short. Then he continued, his strength coming back in installments, the liver pumping unnatural amounts of glucose to match his rising fury.

He stepped through the fifth-floor stairwell door, and right in front of him a uniformed hospital guard sat reading *El Diario* outside the southernmost room on the floor. As Bobby came through the stairwell, the guard looked up, nodded, went back to the sports pages, where he was reading about the Mets losing another one, living in the subbasement with one of the highest payrolls in the major leagues.

Bobby walked by the room and saw the patient's name in the plastic slot on the wall-mount outside: Mathers, Clarence. Inside, he saw a guy propped up in a bed, oxygen and other tubes in his nose, plasma, glucose, and meds dripping from an IV pole.

He tried to kill me, Bobby thought. *The people who sent him killed Greco. It isn't fair that he lived.*

Bobby figured they had the notorious patient who had been shot in the hospital basically quarantined from the rest of the floor in case he attracted unwanted press or hostile visitors. Bobby walked to the end of the corridor, saw just two nurses on duty at the station, a mostly drowsy afternoon. The nurses looked at him, baffled by his presence, and they whispered to each other as he passed.

Bobby scoped his territory. He saw a maintenance room with a door ajar. He walked in, searched the shelves, found two large containers of industrial detergent. Bobby unscrewed the caps, and as he walked to the northern end of the hallway, he emptied the two gallons of detergent onto the floor. He also spun wheelchairs, gurneys, food carts, and laundry carts that were flattened against walls to the center of the corridor.

At the end of the corridor Bobby unspooled the flattened high-intensity fire hose, opened the northernmost window five inches, looped the nozzle through the window guards so that the snout faced in toward the hospital corridor like a cannon barrel. Then he slammed the window down, bracing the nozzle between the heavy window and the metal frame.

He gazed down at the distant guard reading the Spanish language newspaper at the far end of the corridor. The nurses talked on phones at the station. A food service worker collected lunch trays.

Bobby spun the water-pressure wheel all the way to the left, yanking it with all his might into a locked position.

Then he burst through the exit door just as the water swelled and raced through the flattened hose. Bobby descended one flight, stepped through the fourth-floor door, hurried along to the southern end, and took the steps two at a time back up to the fifth floor. When Bobby stepped onto the fifth floor, pandemonium had been loosed. Two feet of soap suds covered the floor. Nurses screamed. Patients wailed. Everyone slipped and flopped. One old patient with no teeth spun his wheelchair in circles through the suds, cackling dementedly. The food service woman splashed around on the floor, her cart overturned, chicken legs, bread, butter patties, dinner rolls, string beans, coffee cups, apples, milk containers, and dishes and silverware and plastic tray covers all sloshing into the mix like a big soup in the mounting suds. Alarms rang.

The copy of *El Diario* lay on the guard's empty chair outside Clarence Mathers's room. Bobby saw the dutiful guard trying to make his way across the wet floor, through the mayhem, to the water source. But the blast of the water knocked him down and slid him backward on the sudsy tiles. Two orderlies picked him up, and they tried advancing to the water source on their hands and knees.

Bobby entered the hospital room. Clarence Mathers lay in the bed, swathed in bandages. His neck was bandaged from the garrote. Both arms and a leg were wrapped in gauze from bullet wounds. A big bandage covered the belly wound.

"Fuck goin' down, Doc?" Clarence Mathers said, his voice a faint wheeze, his eyes dreamy with morphine. Stoned.

"You, motherfucker," Bobby said, opening his Swiss Army knife blade and cutting the first tube on the IV pole.

"Doin', yo?"

Bobby smacked Clarence Mathers across the face. His eyes popped open.

"Fuck you doin', Doc?"

Bobby lifted his face mask and put his mouth to Clarence Mathers's ear and said, "The question, asshole, is *who* the fuck sent you to kill me? And why? Was it Iglew or Deity? Or Ford? Who?"

"Fuck you," Mathers said, slurry with opiates.

Bobby dumped the bucket of ice water onto Clarence Mathers's face. He shook his head like a hound, tried to sit up, lit with rage and scowling in pain.

"I do you for that there."

"No, shit for brains, I *do you,*" Bobby said, cutting the glucose tube.

"Don't be doin' that, yo."

"You are going to fucking *die,* asshole."

Bobby had been in trauma units enough times to know exactly what tube was what. Nothing he'd touched yet was life threatening.

"The fuck are you?"

Bobby removed his face mask. "The guy who's gonna end your worthless life."

"Oh, shit, you're the snoop."

"Who sent you?"

"Suck my dick."

"Speaking of which, I've seen your woman and your baby."

"You lie . . . where the fuck my old lady and my boo?"

"Next time they see you, it'll be in a coffin unless you tell me who sent you."

"I tell you that I go inna grave without a coffin. So fuck you."

"Janel's gonna be fucking more than me to support your baby."

"Don't be talking 'bout my woman and my little girl, asshole."

"That little girl of yours will be growing up with no father, a little chickenhead in RIP."

"Don't be talkin 'bout my baby-boo like that."

Bobby cut the oxygen line and Mathers's eyes popped open.

"You lie," Mathers said. "You don't know nothing about me."

Bobby held up the photo he'd swiped from Iglew's house, of Mathers with his woman in a hospital maternity ward, cradling his infant daughter.

"They want you dead because word is you're dropping dimes left, right, and center. They'll feed you to Tony the Tiger."

"You know about the tiger?"

"And his honey-dip bimbos."

"I still say you lyin'."

Bobby covered Mathers's face with a pillow, threw a short right hand into his belly wound. Mathers howled in muffled pain. Bobby lifted the pillow.

"Your fucking boys just killed a decent man, a very good man, who is never gonna see his kid again," Bobby said. "Now I'm making sure you never see your woman or your kid again."

Bobby placed the pillow over Mathers's face.

"Wait," he heard him shout, muffled by the pillow. "Please don't do that shit."

Bobby lifted the pillow. "You gonna tell me?"

"You really seen my woman? And my little Darla?"

"Yes. Iglew was trying to get Janel in the pool with him."

Mathers's eyes popped wide, anger snarling his face. "Say the fuck what?"

"Darla will be calling Iglew Dada in a few months after they bury you."

Mathers gasped for breath. Bobby lowered the pillow again.

"Please, don't be puttin' that shit on my face no more."

"I got thirty seconds. Who sent you to kill me? And why?"

"Came from Tu. Wasn't spozed to kill you. Just choke you up good, make you talk to see what you knew. Some cop Tu deals with wanted to know."

"Ford?"

"I don't know names. I deal with Tu. Chain of command."

"This cop was afraid I'd find out what?"

"Man . . . Iggy really hittin' on Janel?"

"Fuck it, you blew your chance."

Bobby pushed the pillow into his face. Mathers flapped like a fish on a boat. Bobby lifted the pillow. Mathers started talking in gasps.

"Okay, it's all about the hit-and-run," Mathers said. "Some shit about the governor. Rodney Calhoun . . . Iggy . . . Dee . . . Five-O . . . You lookin' into that old hit-and-run could fuck up everything. You know how much money we talkin at LI? Hun'ids of millions, most of it cash and carry, yo. Now Dee gotta liquidate, fast, and Iggy don't wanna go there. He say he has unfinished biniz. Family biniz. But Iggy don't really own it. Dee does. Iggy always take care of me, but the man already got so much ass he'd need a boxful of dicks. And still I always knew he wanted to hit Janel's. And steal my baby."

"Iggy told Tu to have you scare me off the case?"

"I don't know how it came down. I deal with Tu, who mentioned the cop."

Bobby was running out of time. He needed answers to basic questions. Fast.

"Where can I find Rodney Calhoun?"

"Boston Market, he a side order."

"I don't believe he's a vegetable. What about Deity?"

"Find a cure for cancer before him."

"What's with the governor?"

"C'mon, man, my rap sheet, I can't even fuckin' vote. But they need to get somebody out of the joint. That I know."

"Who's doing whose time?"

Bobby heard feet squish behind him. He pulled down his surgical mask to cover his face. He took the .25 out of his belt.

"Hey," a voice said behind him.

Bobby turned, the Hispanic guard stood soaking wet, gaping at Bobby. "Everything okay, Doc?"

Mathers shouted, "He's trying to fuckin' kill me, yo."

"He's delirious," Bobby said. "Too much morphine. Get a nurse in—"

"Where's your name tag, Doc?" the guard said, suspicious, reaching for his gun. "Why you wearing work boots? Why are those tubes cut and—"

Bobby pointed his .25. The guard placed his gun on the floor and said, "Man, I ain't 'bout to die for no thirteen fifty-three an hour, okay, boss?"

Bobby picked up the gun, emptied it, walked the guard into the bathroom, and dropped the gun in the toilet bowl. He took the guard's handcuffs, chained him to the invalid-friendly guardrail next to the toilet bowl.

"Sorry, pal," Bobby said.

"I'm cool, boss."

Bobby closed the heavy bathroom door. He walked to Mathers in the bed, took out his tape recorder, rewound some of it, and played it for him. "Tell your homeys about what you told me," Bobby said, "and I'll play the whole tape for them."

Two nurses appeared at the door, sopping wet, covered in suds.

"That man needs new dressings and check his IV feeds," Bobby said.

"More morphine, man," Mathers shouted.

Bobby brushed past them and banged through the exit door and descended the steps, taking off the hospital gear as he did.

He called Max Roth as he jumped on a Fifth Avenue bus back toward Lovers' Lanes, where he needed to collect his Jeep.

"Most of the calls were from horn dogs who wanted to meet Janis," Max said. "But one caller, using a voice scrambler, keeps calling. Leaves messages but won't leave a number. The number comes up as private, has caller ID block. Caller says he knows stuff but he's scared. Says he'll call back at six p.m."

"Max, you have call forwarding?"

"Sure."

"I'm gonna give you a number to call-forward the call to."

Max said, "Who?"

"Better you don't know right now, that okay?"

"But I want whatever the caller says."

"Our usual deal. You get it before any other reporter in town."

"Exclusive," Max said.

"True to that."

"What?"

"Sorry, 'word is bond,' " Bobby said, and hung up. Then he called his brother Patrick at the Intelligence Division of NYPD, where no calls ever come in marked private or anonymous, where everything is descrambled.

"Patrick," Bobby said. "There will be a call forwarded to your line at six o'clock. I need the descrambled name, address, and phone number. Just say you're Max Roth."

Bobby told him what it was about and Patrick said, "I want the official collar."

"Of course," Bobby said. "And somewhere along the way I might need you and your very legal gun and your backup."

"You're my brother, tell me where and when."

"Not until I finish breaking some more laws."

"I didn't hear that," Patrick said, and hung up.

As the bus rocked through Bay Ridge, Bobby was still feeling light-headed. He couldn't afford to take another shot in the head.

He needed help. All these goons coming at him with a promise of more to come.

He opened his phone, dialed Izzy Gleason, and said, "Tell your cousin Herbie to meet me at the *Fifth Amendment*. Tell him to pack his usual luggage."

Izzy said, "About fucking time! When you ask for Herbie Rabinowitz, I know it means you're gonna stop acting like a pussy and get serious."

SEVENTEEN

At five p.m. they gathered to watch Cookie Calhoun die on tape.

Maggie finished digitizing the video footage on her Avid Express video-editing system. Bobby stood with Izzy behind and to the left of Maggie. Janis and Jimi Jim stood directly behind Maggie. Brian Calhoun stood just to Maggie's right.

Maggie sat in front of three monitors at her fifteen-foot-wide computer station in her "homework room" in her mother's ninetieth-floor condo in the Trump International. The room had six workstations, each with a different computer setup—laptops, desktops, color printers, copying machines, faxes.

Bookcases overflowed with reference books, computer guides, dummies' books, CD-ROMs, boxes of diskettes, printing paper, photo-copy paper, and boxes of water, pretzels, and Raisinets in case of an emergency. A small generator was stored in a wall closet, in case of a blackout or power failure, with a built-in exhaust system, so that Maggie's computers would never go down. She used a cable modem, but in case that also failed, she had hookups to a portable satellite-phone system.

The rain had stopped and the sun was shining and traffic helicopters buzzed in the baby blue sky past the big windows flying south along the West Side Highway and the eternal Hudson. U.S. Air Force jets roared by as the city went on Orange Alert after some vague new terrorist threat. Bobby knew he was standing at about exactly the same height as those poor morning workers when the first plane had hit the South Tower on 9/11 when New York had become the Pearl Harbor of the twenty-first century.

Trevor was still in Europe, and Bobby's ex-wife, Connie, was at a

Friends of Central Park luncheon in the Boat House Café in the park that glistened to the left like an enormous emerald after the earlier rain.

She was expected home anytime now.

"Herbie's late," Bobby said. "Not a good sign."

"I told him five; it's three minutes after," Izzy said.

"A lot can happen in less time than that," Brian said.

No one had a reply to that. Janis and Jimi Jim had spent most of the early afternoon arguing with Brian that maybe it wouldn't be good for him to view the hit-and-run tapes.

"I'm sixteen years old, and if you don't let me see the tape, I promise you, you'll never see me again," Brian had told Janis and Jimi Jim, in a flat, earnest tone. It was more a mature statement than an adolescent threat, a declaration from a kid who had made a decision in life. It spooked Janis and Jimi Jim.

Janis called Brian's shrink, asking his advice. The shrink told her to view the tape first. To be sure Brian could handle it. And said that if wasn't too gory, it might actually be a good thing for him to watch, a kind of cathartic shock therapy so that he could actually see that the death of his mother was not his fault. Reality was always better than a guilt-distorted memory.

Janis watched the blurry, grainy high-angle video footage first. Alone. And while it was appalling—showing six-year-old Brian drop his coin, turn to retrieve it, but being shooed to the far curb by Cookie, who then chased his dropped coin toward the other curb just as the yellow van turned off Ninety-first Street, increased speed, and knocked over Cookie—it was plain to see that the only thing Brian was guilty of that morning was dropping a half-dollar.

After having a good, private ten-minute cry, Janis had decided to let Brian watch the footage. Bobby was eager to see it, too.

He checked his watch again and said, "Let's get started, Maggie."

Then a knock came upon the door and a British butler in waistcoat with pearl buttons and bow tie named Maurice poked his head in. Bobby crushed Connie's shoes about actually hiring a British butler to run a staff of twelve, but with an apartment this size you could invite the Third Infantry Division for a sleepover.

"Maggie, you have another *gentleman* caller," Maurice said.

Herbie Rabinowitz stepped past Maurice wearing a flannel shirt with the sleeves hacked off, his rumpled jeans bunched at his muddied size-fourteen boot tops, his thirty-two-year-old, six-foot-six, 260-pound, broad-shouldered, muscle-rippling body filling most of the doorway as he entered. His orange-and-blue yarmulke boasted a Mets logo, bobby-pinned to a deep pile of dark curls that made him look as if he were wearing a toy poodle on his head.

"Hey, buttons," Herbie said to Maurice, washing down two Hydroxy-cut tablets with a slug of diet cream soda. "I'm so hungry I could eat Christ off a plastic cross, so maybe you could tell that wop-import cook I just saw in your not-bad kitchen that I need a gang of kosher burgers, hah?"

Maurice said, "I beg your—"

"Broiled, not fried, with minced red onion and Worcestershire sauce mixed into the meat, and no pork, cheese, or mayo, or I'll break his hairy arm. Tell him dill pickle, and slice up a firm Israeli tomato, nice."

Maurice said, "I'm not sure I'm following—"

"Then have it all blessed by a hat with white socks. There's gotta be at least one rabbi connected to a joint with this much money. Grab any Smith brother you can find. Oh, and, Buttons, make that with shoestring fries."

Herbie thumped into the room, hiking up his pants, carrying a single Waldbaum's shopping bag.

"Okay, so the weather forecast is for a perfect evening for kicking ass," Herbie said. "Gimme a name and cab fare and we're off. Hi, Iz; yo, Bobby, Mag."

Maurice looked at Herbie, blinked, straightened his vest coat, looked at Maggie, and whispered, "Should I call nine one one, Margaret?"

Maggie laughed and told Maurice to order up a double burger platter from the kosher deli on Columbus Avenue.

"You're late, Herbie," Bobby said.

"They made me take the freight elevator like I was common," Herbie said.

"That you're not," Bobby said. "Izzy told you what this is about?"

"Yeah."

Bobby introduced Herbie to the McNulty\Calhoun family. Herbie expressed his condolences, grabbed a box of pretzels from a shelf, and Bobby nodded for Maggie to run the footage.

The same footage Janis had watched earlier ran on the three monitors. Only this time the newly digitized, staggered-action-stills footage was much sharper. The screen to the far left had a lower angle, taken from a camera mounted midway down the Verrazano tower. The one displayed on the middle terminal showed a higher aerial point of view from the top of the tower.

Janis put her hand to her mouth, eyes misting again.

Jimi Jim watched the computer monitors and said, "Oh, Mama . . ."

Janis wrapped her arm around Jimi Jim's shoulder. She tried to put her other arm around Brian. He shrugged it off, twirling the half-dollar he'd dropped on the gutter ten years ago through his fingers, back and forth, as if trying to reverse time.

Janis and Jimi Jim sobbed as they watched the images of their mother dying on the tape. And Brian's silent scream. Bobby looked to Izzy, who took a deep breath and held it. He looked to Janis and Jimi Jim. Then Bobby watched Herbie crush his cream soda can in his big right hand.

"Oh, my God," Herbie said, sorrow and anger screwing up his face.

Bobby wanted Herbie to see the tape so that he could have a tangible point of reference. So that he wouldn't be motivated by a simple payday, going through the motions. So that he would take the job personally. Herbie was the biggest kid Bobby knew. And so Herbie loved kids. And now Herbie watched the monitors, seeing a mother die in front of her six-year-old son, who collapsed on the screen in agonizing grief in the Brooklyn gutter. Herbie looked from the screen to Brian, saw the sixteen-year-old viewing himself react to his mother's death ten years earlier. Veins popped out of Herbie's neck that reminded Bobby of the support cables of the Verrazano.

Now Bobby knew Herbie was in the perfect frame of mind for the job.

"Oy," Herbie said, his eyes jelling as he looked at wide-eyed, stoic Brian. "You okay, kid?"

Brian didn't react. Didn't answer. He just stared at the monitors, his eyes reflecting the images in front of him like a cruel optical effect. Bobby gazed at the man-boy who stood close to Maggie but remained quarantined in his own private grief. He looked like a kid who'd simply run out of tears. And was ready for a different kind of relief.

Herbie squatted next to Brian and said, "We're gonna do something about this."

"Me, too," Brian said.

Maggie pulled Brian closer to her computer station where she sat like an astronaut at the controls, using a state-of-the-art, $24,000 video-enhancement program called dTective from Ocean Systems that her stepfather, Trevor, had bought her for Christmas from the Snoop Shop.

The software would enhance the blurry ten-year-old surveillance images on the screen. Brian continued to roll the same half-dollar through his fingers that he chased on the screen, as the footage reduced to slow motion.

"How does it work?" Brian asked, his voice a whisper.

"First, you saw me take the tapes and transfer them from VHS to digital," Maggie said. "Digital images are made up of thousands of little dots called pixels. Each pixel of each frame of footage contains a mathematical piece of data. dTective uses a process known as image averaging to clean up and clarify the data."

"Mean, makes blurry stuff clear?"

"Right," Maggie said, patting her computer like a pet. "dTective is powered by this baby, the Avid Xpress, the Rolls-Royce of editing tools. Avid captures video at full NTSC resolution—720 by 486—and captures both fields of video, digitizing every single little pixel."

"Cool," Brian said.

"Avid sounds like the name for a cat," Izzy said.

Which reminded Bobby to flap open his cell phone and play a new message from a doctor at Lutheran who said Bobby's CAT scan showed no brain damage but that he should take it very easy. He closed his phone and said, "Mag, we know it's a miracle machine, but can it isolate and enlarge?"

"Yeah, inside the program there are systems called dVeloper and Magnifi and Spotlight, where you can target and output sections with a full screen or to a defined portion of the screen, using the zoom control."

Maggie replayed the fuzzy videotape on the monitor again.

"Even before I enhance it, it's plain it wasn't your fault, Bri," Maggie said.

Brian said nothing, just kept turning the coin over and over in his right hand as Maggie started the tape from the beginning again. Bobby stepped closer, watching it play on the largest center screen. A tape taken from a lower angle played simultaneously on the screen on the right. Maggie had them running in sync.

"Maggie, freeze-frame right there," Bobby said.

Maggie did.

Bobby pointed with a sharpened pencil to a blurry white image. "Enlarge and enhance that area."

Maggie opened the Effect Editor panel, clicked on the target box, and enlarged and enhanced the image on the left-hand monitor. Then she zoomed, added brightness and contrast, until the target area enhanced the image of a woman leaning on a window ledge.

"Holy shit, it's Mrs. Donatella," Janis said.

Jimi Jim said, "Told you that fat ho definitely saw the whole thing."

"She's doing something with her hands," Bobby said, circling a section on the screen with the point of his pencil.

Maggie clicked on the specific area and advanced the spotlighted and enhanced section frame by frame, until the pixels showed that Mrs. Donatella seemed to be making gestures. Hand signals.

"Looks like sign language, maybe," Bobby said.

Janis asked. "Who would she be signing to?"

"Widen the shot again, Mag," Bobby said.

Maggie zoomed out, widening the image, and Bobby traced his pencil point from Mrs. Donatella's point of view diagonally across the screen. He flattened a ruler across the screen to a man sitting on a folding chair outside the Twoboro Social Club.

"Enhance this guy to a full screen, Mag," Bobby said.

Maggie did a point-and-click until that section came into enhanced and spotlighted perspective on the left monitor. The man with a straw summer hat was looking directly up at Mrs. Donatella.

"Advance frame by frame," Bobby said.

Maggie did, and in each frame the man's head turned from Mrs. Donatella until he craned his neck and stood and gazed across the street. And then seemed to turn and walk with alacrity into the social club.

"Back five or six frames, Mag," Bobby said.

Maggie reversed and froze the frame. Bobby walked to the screen and used the ruler again and followed the man with the straw hat's point of view across Fort Hamilton Parkway to a car parked across the street at a meter. Bobby drew an imaginary circle around the car and told Maggie to magnify, spotlight, and enhance.

She did, and after five clicks on various filters and brightness and contrast controls, the images of two men sitting in a car, one holding a clunky, old-fashioned, early 1990s video camera, came into view. The sun visors in the car were down. No matter what Maggie did to enhance it further, the visors cast way too much shadow to make their faces pop out of the murk.

Bobby circled the sun-splashed license plate and told Maggie to enlarge and enhance it. One upgrade at a time the plate number rose up out of the past like an exhumed corpse—US28K1.

"Holy shit," Jimi Jim said.

"Oh, my God," Janis said.

"I'll run that plate," Maggie said, and walked to another computer terminal across the room and entered US28K1 into the national DMV database. "But I think that's a federal database for official government-issue plates. Strictly classified. I don't have the software for that. Especially for a plate from ten years ago. But I'll do a scan. It could take a few minutes."

Maggie clicked all the appropriate boxes and walked back to the Avid Xpress station.

"Now enhance and brighten everything, Mag, and play the overhead shot out in slo-mo," Bobby said.

Maggie rewound and let the old tape play again, and this time as the yellow van turned the corner, it was plain to see that Mrs. Donatella was signing to the man with the straw hat, who was being videotaped by the two men in the Oldsmobile across the street, as Cookie Calhoun crossed the street, Brian dropped his half-dollar, and the van ran Cookie down. And sped away.

The two men in the Oldsmobile did not take chase.

"Freeze, Mag."

The image paused on the screen and Bobby walked to the car with the two men and tapped it with his ruler. "Enlarge and enhance this section again, Mag."

She did.

"The man with the video camera is still taping, turning his camera toward the fleeing van," Bobby said. "He taped the whole thing from his angle. He would definitely have gotten the driver's face or license-plate number on tape."

Bobby tapped his pencil at the rear of the yellow van. "Can we get any of the plate on the van?"

Maggie enlarged and enhanced the rear of the truck. But from the high overhead shot the plate was simply not visible. The most they could make out was the Ford logo.

Bobby tapped on the screen again, to a portion of a legend on the upper-right-hand side of the yellow van. Maggie isolated, enlarged, enhanced, contrasted, and filtered the area. The tops of the letters of one blurry English language word were legible: *Utica.*

"Utica, New York?" Janis asked. "We didn't know anybody from upstate."

"Utica College, maybe," Bobby said.

A larger image above it appeared to be the upper portion of some kind of script, or collection of symbols, but Bobby knew it was not English. Maggie filtered it, gave it gamma and more contrast.

"Chinese characters?" Jimi Jim asked.

"Maybe Greek," Maggie said. "Or Russian? Cyrillic, maybe?"

She clicked it into sharper focus.

"Wait! " Izzy said, putting on his glasses. "I'd bet my bar mitzvah loot that's Hebrew."

Herbie leaned closer, nodded. "It's Hebrew all right. I got my ass kicked for twelve straight years learning that ass-backwards lingo."

"I think the word is *klee*," Izzy said. "Which, if my memory serves, means 'dish.' "

Bobby said, "Dish? Like in plates and saucers? Or satellite? Or gossip? What?"

"Not sure, but I'm half-Yid, half-mick," Izzy said, "and I always said I was better with a cold brew than Hebrew."

Jimi Jim said, "Moms was run down by a van with the word *dish* on the side?"

"Served up on a platter?" Janis said.

Brian just stared at the screens, twiddling the half-dollar. Maggie reached out, grabbed his hand, making him stop. He looked in her eyes. He shrugged, swallowed. Bobby watched the two young lovers. It worried him that one of them was his kid.

"Print that image, Mag," Bobby said. "We'll show it to a rabbi."

"Sorry, that's the best I can make out," Izzy said. "Ask Herbie. He's Orthodox, a very unorthodox Orthodox, but at least he's kosher."

Maggie took the printed image and handed it to Herbie. He looked at it, held it at arm's length, then closer, grabbed Izzy's glasses off his face, choking him with the attached strings that were looped around his neck, and scratched his furry head.

"Hey, Shrek, the neck, hah," Izzy shouted, rubbing a fresh neck welt.

"Sorry, Iz."

Herbie traced his big right index finger over the image and said, "I hate putting my two cents in because you guys are smarter than me."

"What do you see, Herbie?" Bobby asked.

"It's not *dish*, Iz. My guess is a homonyacallit?"

"Homonym?" Bobby asked. "They have homonyms in Hebrew?"

"What are we, the wrong color for homonyms?" Izzy said.

Herbie said, "The Hebrew word *klee* can also mean *tool*."

"Great," Bobby said. "A Hebrew grammar lesson. *Klee*—dish, tool—what's the difference? How does the homonym translate into homicide?"

Izzy said, "Maybe a hardware-store truck?"

Herbie smacked his big hand on the computer table, making everyone but Brian jump, and said, "I'd bet my Mets beanie against Uncle Izzy's bar mitzvah loot that the word is *tool*. Because I can only make out part of the letters, but I think the next word is Hebrew for *die*, as in tool and die."

Bobby said, "Like a tool and die maker? Manufacturer, wholesaler, or retailer? Maggie, check the yellow pages."

Maggie did a search of tool-and-die-related businesses in the state of New York.

"One hundred and twenty-nine statewide, thirteen in the city," Maggie said.

"Any of them in Utica, New York?"

Maggie typed in the name of the upstate city.

"No."

"Any named Utica? Utica Tool and Die? Or on a street named Utica? Or owned by someone named Utica or a corporation with Utica in it?"

Maggie deepened the search.

"Sorry," she said, and looked at Brian, who walked toward the windows looking out over the spires and steel towers of Manhattan, twirling the half-dollar. It fell on the floor. Bobby studied Brian looking down at it. It was on tails.

"I remember growing up there was a tool and die plant in Crown Heights," Herbie said. "One of the last factories in the neighborhood. I applied for a job there once, but with the grand theft auto on my record I couldn't get insured."

"Was it called Utica?"

"Nah, Goldbergs, Goldman's, Goldstein's, something like that. I heard the owner wound up in a pinch, years later."

Izzy poured a bag of carob-coated raisins in his mouth, washed them down with Poland Spring water without chewing. Like pills.

Bobby said, "Don't you even chew?"

"Gotta shovel 'em into the furnace," Izzy said, then looked at Herbie and tapped his temple. "You're not talking Golden's Tool and Die, are ya?"

Herbie shrugged. "Maybe . . ."

"Not the football trophies Golden's?"

"I know the father was a legit businessman, from the other side," Herbie said. "Then the goniff sons took it over. They gambled more than I did. Ran it into the earth. Been gone a long time now."

"The ones I'm talking about were Orthodox," Izzy said. "From Boro Park. But the factory was in Crown Heights—"

"I said that, cuz."

"After the Crown Heights riots they started getting into new shit," Izzy said. "Still made tools, but also made belt buckles, trophies, and knick-knacks."

"Then they got pinched shipping stuff outta the country to the Cayman Islands," Herbie said. "I can't remember all the details."

"The Caymans?" Bobby said.

"But the Feds finally caught on when they sent more football trophies to the Caymans then they got people living there," Izzy said. "But leave it to a pair of milk-phlegmy Boro Park Jews not to know they don't even play football in the Caymans. So some slick Fed wonders why the hell they're shipping thousands of football trophies down there. So they seized a shipment and found out when they scraped the veneers that all the trophies were made out of solid twenty-four-karat gold."

"I remember that case," Bobby said. "That's how they were getting the Rasta and Dominican and Columbian drug cash no one could launder *out* of the country. The druggies bought gold, smelted it, and they made trophies out of it sent it to the islands, where it was resmelted and sold on the open international market for dollars, and where the cash went into the banks without questions asked."

"And which they used to buy more drugs," Izzy said. "To send back up here in a long cycle of drugs to dollars to gold to trophies to gold to dollars to drugs and yadda-yadda-yoo-ha until one of the Golden boys, a gridiron great, was sent for a long one up the river."

"You're telling me this truck might've been owned by the Golden's Tool and Die Company from Crown Heights?" Bobby said.

"A big maybe," Izzy said. "More like a very slim possibility. Which is more than we had five minutes ago."

Maggie gave Bobby the stories she downloaded about the Golden brothers from Golden's Tool and Die on Lexis Nexis.

"One, Herman, died in Otisville," Bobby said, scanning the pages. "The other one, Sidney, is doing time in the Arthur Kill State Correctional

Facility in, where else, Staten Island. They never gave anybody up. I guess they were afraid of reprisals on their families."

"Ya know, I chased that ambulance," Izzy said. "But they went another way. They didn't trust that I was half-mick. They said they had enough problems with the Irish, whatever that meant."

"Maybe it meant James Ford," Bobby said.

Izzy said, "They went with a numb-nuts family lawyer who I wouldn't use to plead guilty. I could've beaten that rap for them. Matter fact, a few years ago Sidney Golden sent out feelers to a bunch of lawyers to handle his appeal. One came to me. But Sidney had no money. I mighta done it for the play, but I was suspended at the time, anyway. But I still could win him an appeal in a heartbeat. Matter fact, I read in the *Law Journal* that Sidney Golden filed his own appeal, requesting a new trial, and it's been sitting almost a year with Judge Cranberry, who I used to clerk for. Now he's a judge you can work with, if he gets rubbed the right way, if you know what I mean."

Bobby connected dots like an ancient astronomer. Was the guy who was doing someone else's time that Cookie had overheard the conversation about in the Music Box restaurant one of the Golden brothers? Did Deity's drug cash get laundered by shipping gold trophies to the Caymans? And then have it loaned to them by the same bank to start Lethal Injection Records? Only to pay themselves back, with interest?

Maggie rushed to the other computer terminal, checked on the results for plate number US28K1. "That plate's marked classified, Dad," she said. "But I know that any car with *US* in the license plate is a federal government car."

Brian drifted from the computer station over to the big windows overlooking the cityscape of New York.

"So you're telling me that maybe, possibly, someone connected to the drug trade might've been behind that wheel?" Janis said.

"He's telling you his guess is as good as ours," Brian said, rolling the coin through his fingers.

"Hey, kid, even when life's a bowl of cherries, it gives you the shits," Izzy said.

Janis said, "Stop looking at the goddamned glass half-empty, Bri. That tape shows me that someone hit Mom on purpose."

"The only thing I know for sure right now is that if I never dropped this half a buck, Mom would be alive today," Brian said.

"Bullshit," Maggie said.

Izzy read the old *Daily News* account of the Golden brothers' bust. "Somehow the Golden brothers got wind of their shipment being busted in the Caymans, and before the Feds could seize their books, the Brooklyn factory got hit with Jewish lightning. The trucks disappeared, reported stolen for the insurance, and probably went to Cohen the Compacter so they couldn't find trace evidence. Nothing was computerized. All the employment records went up in smoke. That's why I knew I coulda walked these two button heads. Without a computer or paper trail the Feds really had no case. I woulda ripped those Feds to confetti. All I woulda needed was one fat, hungry Yid on the jury and a not-guilty verdict would have come in two hours before sundown on a Friday. Instead they used a house-closing lawyer, a Court Street hack named Mel Wax. The Feds ceded jurisdiction to the state because the penalty was worse under the Rockefeller laws, and since they got arrested there, they got convicted in Staten Island on circumstantial evidence, and now they're doing fifteen to twenty-five each under the Rockefeller laws."

"It's more than we had yesterday," Janis said. "Hear me, Brian?"

"I agree," Jimi Jim said. "Stop with the puss, Brian. Chrissakes."

Izzy asked Bobby, "Think it's worth a jailhouse visit to Sidney Golden? I can finagle one tonight."

"Did I turn you down when you came to see me?" Bobby asked.

"Say no more."

EIGHTEEN

Five minutes later, Bobby and Janis stood alone on Columbus Circle.

Maggie took Brian to a Jim Carrey movie.

Izzy said he had to go upstate to visit Francisca in jail before grabbing a bite with juror number nine, in her $2.5 million home in Manhattan Beach, and said he'd make arrangements from the road to visit Sidney Golden in jail that night.

Herbie was getting Bobby's Jeep from the lot and Jimi Jim left to meet an artist about the Bigga Wiggaz album-cover art.

Janis gripped Bobby's hand and said, "I hope you know how much I appreciate everything you're doing."

"You're a client. I'm supposed to do things for you. Within ethics."

"Don't confuse guilt with ethics," she said. "It's like trying to compare Plato and Play-Doh."

Bobby's cell phone rang. The caller ID flashed his brother Patrick's number. The time on his cell was 5:39 p.m. He excused himself to Janis.

She said, "I'm gonna jump down onto the A train, anyway."

She kissed him before he had a chance to resist. He licked her lipstick off his lips. It stirred him in places he didn't want to rouse as he watched her stroll in the tight jeans for the subway entrance.

"Hello?"

Patrick asked, "Bobby, do you know an Angelina Doo-nat-ella?"

Bobby knew his brother often mispronounced foreign names, as had his tin-eared Irish-born parents, getting the syllables out of tune.

"Yeah, what about Angelina Donatella?"

"Ninety-two fourteen-A Fort Hamilton Parkway, apartment two-C?"

171

Bobby's heart jumped. "She's the one who called?"

"Her call to Max Roth at the *News* was call-forwarded to me a few minutes ago. She was talking in circles. Hesitant. Giving clues instead of statements. Like she watched *All the President's Men* one too many times. She even told me to 'follow the money.' Something about the woman named Cookie Calhoun knowing something she wasn't supposed to know about someone in the joint. And about hundreds of millions of dollars. And someone's first marriage. Somehow all tied up to the governor's race. She's terrified of having it come back to her."

"Someone's first marriage?" Bobby said, thinking of Nails McNulty.

"She talked and cried and talked some more, said that no one's left to take care of her. But she knows a lot about that hit-and-run. She's been afraid to talk for ten years. But now some guy she was afraid of is dying, and she sounds like an egg waiting to be cracked. Thinks her phone's tapped. She's paranoid."

"You're the best, little brother. I'll call you back."

Bobby hung up and shouted to Janis, who was descending the subway stairs. She turned, backlit by the evening sun, her blond hair whipping in an updraft of subterranean wind. Stunning.

A *Daily News* front page clung to her left leg. The headline read, "Gov Race ThisClose!"

"Want a ride home?" he asked.

Herbie sat in the backseat, singing along to Eminem on his headphones as Bobby plunged into the white fluorescent glare of the Brooklyn Battery Tunnel. Janis McNulty sat next to him. She smelled like an air freshener.

"How long has Mrs. Donatella lived in her apartment?" Bobby asked.

"Fifty-seven years. Born there. Never lived anywhere else. She's got statutory tenancy under the rent control laws. You'd have to burn her out. She inherited it from her mother, who inherited it from her mother. I think she pays two-hundred and thirty-eight bucks a month and still has original Edison bulbs in the sockets."

"It's right above the Twoboro Social Club storefront, no?"

"Yeah. Her apartment sits on top of two storefronts. The social club and pizzeria."

"One and the same though, right? The mooks in the social club own the pizzeria?"

"Probably."

"Wiseguys?"

"It ain't the Elks."

"Did you recognize the guy in the straw hat in the video?"

"Yeah, sure, he was Vito 'Sleighride' Santa."

"Play on words? He takes people for one-way rides? More like *s-l-a-y* rides?"

"They were friendly to us in the club growing up. Until Mom married Rodney."

"Yeah, wiseguys don't usually donate to the United Negro College Fund," Bobby said, exiting the tunnel and rocking the Gowanus out toward Bay Ridge.

"More like What's a Matta U. The young Turks made remarks, ya know. Especially that Georgie Gorgeous.'Moolie.' 'Marble cake.' 'Vanilla fudge.' Mrs. Donatella called Rodney and my mother 'eggplant parmigiana.' I think Sleighride was bipolar. One day he was jolly, sweet. Next, a quiet, evil-looking torpedo. He had a big fat wife but I always thought maybe him and Mrs. Donatella got busy."

"His goomara?"

"Maybe his goom. She wasn't bad-looking back in the day."

"Yeah?"

"I never seen him go in and out of her apartment or anything. But a few times I thought I heard arguing inside when I passed in the hallway. Her and a man, screaming in Italian. It sounded like him. I saw her a few times with black eyes. But she lived alone. I just think she's fucking nuts from living a life as a spinster."

"Was Sleighride racist enough to hurt your mother over marrying a black guy?"

"Oh, Christ, no. Nah. He had bigger fish to fry. And no way would those guys, especially Sleighride, who dressed as Santa every Christmas Eve and kidded that he was the real Santa, ever kill a mother in front of her *kid*. He had four of his own by my count. Two went legit: one a lawyer, the other owns a string of clothing stores. One followed him into the life, and into life in the can. But one had Down syndrome, which I think he keeps institutionalized. Only took her out now and then. Holidays, birthdays, maybe."

"Really?"

"I saw him with that kid once, in Owls Head Park; he was the most loving father you ever saw. Early in the morning, about six a.m., before the other kids would be around to tease her. Sleighride put her on the swings, on the slides, climbed in the sandbox with her with a pail and shovel. I was jogging around the outside of the playground, and here was this gangster, this killer, this hit man named Sleighride, as gentle as a Saint Francis of Assisi with his handicapped daughter. I'll never forget the image of him. Sad. Poignant. I always wanted to write a song about it."

"Just him and the kid?"

"Yeah. Touching. He might have disapproved of Mama marrying a black dude. But he still sat Brian on his knee when they gave out toys to neighborhood kids at Christmas. It just wasn't his style to ever kill a mother, in front of her *kid*. No way."

"But he's still a killer."

"Oh, sure. That was, ya know, what he did for a job."

Bobby nodded and said, "You keep talking about him in the third person."

"Well, he's still alive. Barely. They finally got him on a RICO two years ago. But he's dying in some federal prison hospital. Lung cancer. Any day could be his last."

Bobby's phone rang. He flapped it open and said, "Hello?"

A woman with a sweet, confident voice said, "Bobby?"

"Yeah?"

Bobby felt uneasy because Janis was watching him and the pheromones coming off her hot skin were making his heart beat faster, making him sweat.

"This is Scarlett."

His heart thumped. "Oh, *hey*. How'd your interview go?"

"Great. I want to see you again. Soon."

"Absolutely. Where? When?"

"Say noon, Saturday? Your boat."

Janis's scent and Scarlett's smoky voice twisted Bobby in his seat. "Perfect. Anything special you want to do?"

"You don't have to be a private eye to figure that out. I'll bring popcorn. Butter. Byyyyee."

Bobby felt Janis's eyes on him.

"Another client?" Janis asked.

He turned to her, and in that moment Janis was her mother again, a bitable smirk on her lips. "Nah."

He took the Ninety-second Street exit and made a right at the light toward Fort Hamilton Parkway and parked on the corner where Cookie Calhoun was killed.

"Thanks for the ride," Janis said.

"My pleasure."

She hesitated as if considering kissing him again. She didn't.

Bobby watched Janice climb out of the car and walk past a gathering of wiseguys outside Twoboro Social Club for the tenement.

Then he gazed up at the shade-covered window of Angelina Donatella.

NINETEEN

At 6:43 p.m. Bobby drove around the block and parked the Jeep. Then he walked back up to her tenement. Georgie Gorgeous and a few wiseguys loitered outside Twoboro Social Club, gabbing. They paid little attention to Bobby as he entered the vestibule of the tenement. He jimmied past the inside door, climbed one flight, and knocked on Angelina Donatella's door. A suspicious voice asked who was there. Bobby said he was Max Roth. She opened the door and Bobby pushed his way in.

"You're not the Jew from the *News*," she said.

Bobby said, "He's my friend. But more important than that, I'm working for the McNultys, trying to find out who killed their mother and why, and I know that you know a whole lot about both."

"I don't know nothin'."

"Yes, you do. If you don't tell me what you know, I'll tell certain people that you did tell me plenty."

Angelina Donatella smoothed her housedress, fluttered her hands, and clunked the dead bolt into the door.

"You prick."

"Yes, I am." He glared in her eyes.

"I need some assurances."

"I need information."

"I'm ascared."

"You should be," Bobby said. "You know scary stuff about scary people."

Bobby moved from the kitchenette where service for two was laid out on the oak table. He moved through the railroad rooms. The windowless

176

room off the kitchen was an ambient-lit study with a heavy, soft sofa and matching armchair with goosenecked reading light and bookcases from floor to ceiling lining the walls. A four-by-six-foot steamer trunk served as a big coffee table, sitting upon an oval Persian rug. The room was secured by heavy four-inch-thick oak doors on each entrance. The room was like a small vault.

The next room was a windowless bedroom with a king-size four-poster bed, one bureau, and an oak armoire to make up for lack of a wall closet. A polished ashtray sat on the night table, next to a gleaming silver tool that Bobby squinted at as he passed.

The living room was furnished with antique settees and overstuffed armchairs that were probably brand-new when Angelina Donatella's grandmother first rented the place when she trundled off the boat from Palermo in the early 1920s. The ceiling swirled with original Celtic designs handcrafted in wet plaster by Irish immigrant masons, and the fine oak cornices, moldings, and parquet floors were probably inlaid by Italian carpenters who'd passed through the same combine of Ellis Island. The heavy velvet drapes matched the predominant royal blue in the Persian area rug.

Angelina Donatella sat in the smaller of the two armchairs, her body bloated inside a long-sleeve, ankle-length housedress.

Religious statues dotted the mantel, surrounding one burning votive candle. Sepia family portraits hung in oval wooden frames on one big wall—cousins and uncles and aunts and grannies at weddings and baptisms and christenings and anniversaries. Missing were photos of Angelina Donatella as a bride, or with children. Or even siblings.

Bobby learned more about Angelina from the photos that were not there than those on display. The pictures that were missing were of kids tearing open Christmas presents, blowing out birthday candles, or receiving diplomas on proud graduation days.

The missing photos were the blessings that were absent from Angelina Donatella's life as "the other woman." Bobby did some fast pop-psychology and figured the missing photos had turned her into the overweight, miserable, foulmouthed bitch on the window cushion, cursing out every happy soul that passed her by.

Loneliness clung to the walls like yellowed wallpaper, accompanied by a pinging, empty silence that made Bobby itch. The room was so immaculate and orderly that it suggested death more than life, more a funeral parlor than a living room. Laughter would have made the blue delft china crack. The whole too tidy apartment begged for a dirty-faced kid set loose with a box of Magic Markers.

Bobby went to sit in the big armchair and Angelina Donatella said, "No, please, not that chair. The couch, please."

"Nah," Bobby said, plopping in the big armchair. "I'm gonna sit in Sleighride's throne. He's a dead man coughing. You can take away the second setting at the kitchen table. You can throw out the ashtrays and the cigar clipper next to the bed. The fat man isn't coming back to his goom anymore."

"You son of a bitch."

"Actually my mother is a sweetheart. You're the bitch. And you're gonna be a dead one soon if you don't talk to me."

"Fongola."

"Oh, yeah, lady. Okay, you stay here. Alone. Let them bury Sleighride. And then they're gonna come to bury you."

"Please don't say—"

"You know and I know that the only reason you were allowed to stay alive with what you know this long is that you were Sleighride's goomar. You saw who killed Cookie Calhoun in front of her son, Brian, and the bad guys know that you know, but the only reason they didn't whack you sooner is because you were Sleighride's side ass."

She looked at him with nervous anger, her eyes glowering and jittery. He could see where she'd been a looker once, great big almond eyes with wrinkly bags under them, and the pronounced Sicilian nose that had so much makeup on it, trying to tone it down, that it called extra attention to it and almost made it look fake. A nose big enough to make a girl self-conscious, wrecking her self-esteem. Bobby guessed that the dark mole on her chin made her more vulnerable and malleable in the hands of a gavone like Sleighride, who must have treated her like a queen in those early cheating days, when she was probably "stacked." Then later, when she got older and heavier, from sitting home alone and eating, she became just another goom.

"You have no idea what it's been like," she said.

"I have an idea."

"I was always second."

"My Stradivarius is in the hock shop, lady, so spare me the home wrecker's lament, okay?"

"Fuck you. I'm no angel but I was never *first*, not once. My Christmas was December twenty-sixth. My New Year's Eve was January second. My Valentine's Day was February fifteenth."

"Your wake is gonna be the day after Sleighride's last breath. Which could be today, tomorrow, a few months tops, if you don't talk to me and let me try to help you."

"Life as a goomata is a curse," she said, walking to an oaken hutch, opening a drawer, and taking out a jewelry box, digging her fingers into strings of diamonds and emeralds and rubies. "He gave me this shit, all real, but nowhere to ever wear it. I'm gonna wear it leaning out the window? Not once, not one time in thirty years with this fat fuck, did he ever take me anywhere but from the kitchen to the bedroom to the living room. Never once spent the whole night. Reason why he's so fat was because he ate two breakfasts, two lunches, and two dinners every day. One with his fat tub a shit of a wife in his Todt Hill mansion over Staten Island, one here. His wife was so fucking fat he used to say that he couldn't do the a-la-zing with her no more. He'd need to roll her in flour to find the wet spots."

Bobby stifled a laugh.

"His words, not mine," she said with a dry laugh. "The son of a bitch, he made me laugh. He made me fucking cry. I hate him for making me love him. He made me everything but a *wife*. And now he's gonna leave me alone. A *giddow,* which is what they call a goomata widow. Alone in this dump and knowing too much. I'm ascared. I need assurances."

Bobby stood and walked to her. "Then talk to me."

"I can't just tell you stuff. You ask, maybe I'll answer. It makes me feel less of a rat. I'll confirm or deny what you wanna know, like that."

"How many times did you watch *All the Presidents Men*?"

"Seven. This is your question?"

"Sleighride and his guys used this as his safe house?"

"Sort of."

"I know he came and went, but no one ever saw him, so there must be a secret entrance."

She nodded for him to follow her into the study. She closed both doors.

"He had his no-neck siggies soundproof this room," she said. "They were brought in blindfolded so they wouldn't know where they were and who they were doing the work for. All the shades drawn on the windows and then taken out blindfolded. He was a paranoid. I think he was more ascared of his wife finding out about me than the Feds finding out he had a secret talk-room."

"This room leads to the social club?" Bobby asked.

"To the pizzeria."

"Okay. First he'd go through a secret side door from the social club to the back room of the pizzeria."

She nodded.

"Then up here. How?"

She nodded at the steamer trunk. Bobby tried to move it. It was bolted to the floor. He lifted a few coffee-table books and a vase of dried flowers from the top and opened the lid of the large trunk. He pulled out a few comforters, a pillow, and then lifted the handle of a false, collapsible bottom. Beneath that was a trapdoor, which when opened, led down to the men's room of the pizzeria.

"That's how Sleigh and his paisans came up and down to talk?" he asked.

"The club and pizzeria were under surveillance. So sometimes people would go in the pizzeria, sit in the back, and then they'd go in the men's room and come up here from the fold-up stairs hidden under the drop ceiling. This room is soundproof and Sleigh had it swept for bugs every week. I was never allowed to let anyone in here. No Con Ed, no telephone, no cable, no plumber. Just his people came in here."

She closed the steamer trunk and replaced the coffee-table books and the vase.

"That's why no one ever saw him come or go from your place," Bobby said.

She nodded.

"And you also did lookout for them from the window."

"He didn't trust cell phones so he made me learn sign language. Not like the deaf and dummies use, which the Feds could decipher. Indian."

"Indian sign language?"

"Not the dot-head kind of Indian. He learned it from some Canadian Indian ironworker he did time with once. Iroquois sign language. You didn't have to have a big vocabulary to say the Feds are taping, or that your dinner is ready, or for him to say to me he had his horns up and that I should go in and shave my legs."

"Too much information," Bobby said, holding up one hand and shaking his head. "Tell me about the hit-and-run."

She waddled from the talk room through the bedroom, into the living room, and pulled aside the curtains and waved Bobby over. Standing outside Twoboro were four guys, all whispering in a deferential manner to Georgie Gorgeous, who checked his gold Rolex.

"Look, he's counting the minutes left in Sleighride's life," Angelina said. "How do you protect me? How do you keep Georgie Gorgeous from making me disappear inside a wall? Make me part of a chop-shop cement floor because I know too much about what he's gonna inherit? It's not like he wants *me*."

"First you have to tell me who you need protection from," Bobby said. "If it's just Georgie Gorgeous, I have people in the police department—"

"Stop there. You gotta be *fuckin'* kidding me. They own cops."

"Feds. The witness program."

"More shit. Where am I gonna go? To Arizona? Nebraska? Wyoming? And do what? I'm old. Who's gonna want me now? I'm fifty-seven years old, over a hundred ninety-two pounds naked. Who do you know is gonna ask me to shave my legs now?"

"Stop talking about that."

"I was gonna be an actress, on Broadway. I could sing. But Sleigh never let me work, so I have no skills, no work record, no pension, no 401(k), my Social Security is gonna be three hundred and change a month. He left me *un gots*. The jewelry, tops sixty grand. A few bucks in the bank. How long's that gonna last?" She raked her fingers off the underside of her chin. "Nada. The goomata retirement plan. How am I gonna get another apartment for a two hunrid and thirty-eight a month in the twenny-first century in Arizona, you tell me?"

"If we jail the right people, no one will bother you. You don't have a lot of moves. You can talk to me, the Feds, or an undertaker. The minute that phone rings saying Sleighride's gone, you won't have to worry about your future. You won't have one."

She sighed, plopped on the sofa, and said, "I wanted to tell them kids upstairs so bad. I always liked Cookie. She had a sassy way about her. Great wife, great mother. Loved her kids. I never gave a shit that she wound up with a colored. That's her business. I wound up with a Guinea gangster, so who am I to judge? But I put on the front, cursing them, to make it look like I would never talk to them."

"You were convincing, even before Cookie was killed. Tell me more."

"No, ask me more."

"Cookie learned something she wasn't supposed to know, didn't she?" She studied Bobby. "Like what?"

"About someone doing someone's time. The identity of a certain person."

"I knew she knew something she wasn't supposed to know."

"About Rodney?"

"She found out Rodney wasn't no broken-down gambler. That was just his front. That was his disguise."

"The way Vinnie 'the Chin' Gigante used to walk around in a bathrobe making like he was du bots, crazy. Rodney Calhoun was no small-potatoes degenerate gambler. Sleighride had him in this room a few times, didn't he?"

"They met here. Matter fact, it was Sleighride that got Cookie her job at the Music Box restaurant in Manhattan to begin with."

"Okay, and . . ."

"Sleighride owned a silent piece of it. That's where Cookie met Calhoun."

"Sleighride did business with Calhoun, obviously."

"But he never thought Cookie would do the dirty with him. Cookie, she was one of them sixties free-love hippie chicks, where color meant nothing. But she was married all them years to that other loser, Nails, who I called Screw, because he had so many loose ones . . . especially when he lost Cookie for some cheap piece of ass."

The irony of a goomata criticizing a guy for cheating on his wife didn't escape Bobby. But he didn't say anything.

"No tangents, Angelina, stay on message," Bobby said.

"The fuck that mean?"

"Focus. I know Rodney Calhoun somehow or the other had a partner, back in the eighties, and together they started a business. A record business. Lethal Injection Records."

"I don't know the name of the goddamned thing. Tarzan music to me. When I was a kid, we listened to the Motown outside, at confraternity, like that. It was great but my father didn't let it in the house."

"Rodney. Tell me about Rodney, not your teenage confraternity."

"Anyway I know they started it with drug money."

"And Sleighride and the boys downstairs gave a piece of that drug money?"

"Don't ask me exactly what, and it had something to do with the governor."

"The governor?"

"Yeah.

"And it was tied to the guy, whoever he is, that's doing time that Rodney should be doing. Which is what I think Cookie overheard about. Who's doing the time? Is it a guy named Sidney Golden?"

Donatella looked at him, a little baffled. *"Who?"*

"Never mind." Bobby leaned closer to Angelina Donatella and whispered, "The *governor?* You're sure it had something to do with him?"

"His name came up a lot."

"As if the governor were involved? Like in Sleighride's pocket?"

"That I'm not sure about. But he was part of the conversation a lot. That's what I mean about not feeling safe. You say you got connections—Feds, cops, DAs. But these people, Sleigh's people, maybe they own the governor. And if they do, why wouldn't they also own Feds and cops and DAs?"

Bobby sat silent for a long pensive moment, trying to fit together the broken pieces of a mirror that had shattered a decade ago, bringing with it more bad luck than anyone could have imagined. With more certain to come.

"What do you think Cookie overheard?"

"I think Cookie learned that back in the early eighties, Rodney had a partner. The partner was driving his car through Staten Island, a burgh which Sleigh and his crew basically owned. It has its own set of rules. Like a small town in the big city. Sleigh and his crew owned judges, assistant DAs, cops from that one-horse-town rock over there. They owned politicians. They made a fortune on contracting jobs, getting permits rubber-stamped, buildings department approvals, zoning variances. They build shit houses with inferior cement, shit materials, nonunion wetback laborers. They cut more corners than a sweatshop. No one questioned them. The borough president was like a coffee boy."

"The governor was an assemblyman from Staten Island," Bobby said, half to himself.

"I didn't even know that. But it fits. Who knows from assemblymen from Staten Island, a burgh the city won in a boat race? The loser must still be laughing."

"Back to Rodney's partner, not boat races, Angelina."

"Anyways, what I heard over the years, the partner got stopped for a traffic violation. Speeding, I think. And wound up getting pinched for a huge dope bust. Headlines. But the dope was really Rodney's dope. The partner was clean. Didn't even know it was in the car."

"Yeah? So . . ."

"So, I think the cop knew it was really Rodney's dope, too. This all traces to Rodney Calhoun."

"But the cop was owned by Sleighride, wasn't he?"

Angelina said, "He owned the cop, for sure. My guess is they were gonna cut the partner loose and bust Rodney."

"Unless he made a deal. In return for his freedom, Rodney had to make Sleigh a silent partner in this new upstart record company."

"That sounds like Sleigh, all right."

Bobby got up from the recliner and sat next to Angelina on the leather sofa.

"So the deal was they would let Rodney's partner go down on the drug bust," Bobby said. "That way Rodney would get controlling interest of this upstart record company. At a time when rap was really starting to take off."

"The company was still small then, just a laundry for Rodney's dope trade," Angelina said. "I think his partner was legit. Really wanted to make it a record company. Didn't know it was a dope-money laundry."

"They couldn't have dreamed the music would be as big as it got," Bobby said. "Videos, clothes line, restaurants. More profitable than the dope. And legit. Sort of."

"That's true. But from the beginning they knew Rodney was too reckless with his gambling and his rap sheet to be out front," Angelina said. "They had controlling interest in the company now. Rodney had other major issues, too, which I don't know much about. So anyway, he was hanging around the Music Box. He met Cookie. And when Nails cheated on her, she had a vengeance fling with Rodney. She got knocked up. But she had become very Catholic again. Divorce was tough for her. But she refused to have an abortion. And so Sleigh made him marry her and he moved in here, upstairs."

"Where he could keep an eye on him."

"Right. Then they got him some kind of bullshit job, with some other company Sleigh was affiliated with, and they put up someone young and hip and black as a front man for the colored record company. You following?"

"Iglew?"

"I'm telling you what I know and you're asking about freakin' igloos?"

"Iglew's a nickname, stage name for the head of Lethal Injection Records."

"Oh. No, I think that guy's name was like a saint's name."

Bobby said, "Ignatius?"

"Him, yeah, Ignatius something or other."

"Lewis?"

"Could be. Sounds right. Not sure. I always heard snippets while I was bringing them in drinks, pasta, cake, coffee. It was funny seeing a colored guy in the same talk room with Sleigh. I could never mention it to anyone. Rodney knew when I called him moolie and marble cake it was just part of the charade. The cover. To make it look like we weren't friendly. Sleigh made me do that from the beginning. Him and his guys did the same. So no one would make the connection between him and Rodney."

Bobby took a deep breath, tried to imagine the Italian gangster and the degenerate black gambler in this room, the silent partners of a record company that now earned over $300 million a year.

"Tell me about the hit-and-run, Ange."

"I was at the window. I seen the van go by."

"Who was driving?"

"The truth? I could not see who was driving. This much I know. I remember it like it was yesterday. I heard Rodney and Cookie and the kids arguing upstairs. They were always arguing. I seen Rodney storm out. I saw him go up to Ninety-second Street, instead of down towards the subway on Fourth Avenue. Then I saw Cookie and her kid come out and leave. Then I saw the yellow van peel ass around the corner."

"What was written on the van?"

"Jew writing. But I can't read two Jew letters."

Bobby bluffed. "All the other witnesses said the address was in English."

"Maybe, yeah."

Bobby saw the chink in her armor. He went for it. "You're playing games, lady. I know there was a Utica Avenue address."

Donatella looked nervous. Frightened. "You only know that because that's what I told the cop, Utica Avenue. The way Cookie died was one of the most horriblest things I ever seen in all my years at the window. I cried my eyes out. I liked Cookie, always did. I told the cop I watched her blood drip down the word *Utica.*"

Bobby had a confirmation on the address, which meant the van was almost certainly from Golden's Tool and Die. "What about the two Feds you were signing Sleighride about? The ones who were taping Twoboro Social Club?"

"Sleigh said not to worry about them."

"Why?"

"Not sure. But it had something to do with Rodney."

"The police questioned you about all this?" Bobby asked.

"I talked to a cop, sure."

"Detective James Ford, right?"

Bobby already knew the answer was James Ford. But he wanted to hear her say it.

"James *who?* No, it was a colored-girl cop named Savage."

Bobby's head jerked left as if caught flush with a sucker punch.

TWENTY

Izzy said, "The deal is simple. Tell us who was driving the fuckin' van that day ten years ago or you can stay in here another ten years."

Sid Golden pulled a loose thread on the sleeve of his orange DOC jumpsuit, looked at Izzy, and said, "I have an appeal I wrote myself sitting on Judge Cranberry's desk for almost a year. I got maybe ten more years on my sentence left, and you're asking me to maybe trade that for a possible life sentence? Or a permanent dirt nap in potter's field?"

Bobby sat mute in his plastic chair in the lawyer's conference room of Arthur Kill Correctional Facility in Staten Island for ten minutes listening to Izzy trying to persuade Sid Golden to take his offer of working for a new trial, just as he'd once done for Bobby, in exchange for the name of the guy who was driving his Golden's Tool and Die van on the day of the Calhoun hit-and-run. The clock on the wall read 8:05 p.m.

A week after the hit-and-run Golden's factory went up in smoke, and he was busted for trying to ship fourteen-karat-gold football trophies out of the country to the Cayman Islands as a way of handling the overspill of Iglew and Deity's drug trade.

Bobby, Izzy, and Herbie had driven to this austere compound consisting of six towers surrounded by razor wire on the southern tip of Staten Island that was built atop a junkyard in 1969 for the incarceration and treatment of heroin addicts. It was then called the Arthur Kill Rehabilitation Center, basically a field camp that was part of Governor Nelson Rockefeller's billion-dollar war on drugs in conjunction with the Rockefeller drug laws. That war was supposed to last ten years and rid New York of drugs and junkies. The plan was the dream of a dope, pure junk. It didn't

187

work. By 1979 Rockefeller had died in the bed of a mistress and the rehab became a medium-security state prison under the jurisdiction of the Department of Corrections. Now it housed just shy of one thousand inmates, most doing time for drug-related crimes, but it also housed a few hardened killers and even one notorious serial killer.

Golden was doing his fifteen-to-twenty-five stretch for those same archaic and cruel Rockefeller laws right here on the other side of the Verrazano. On the same island where James Ford had cut his NYPD teeth, where he'd made a major drug bust that had got him the promotion and the gold shield that made him a highway homicide detective, which made him a dirty, mobbed-up millionaire cop.

The same forgotten borough from where the governor of New York had launched his political career. The same autonomous island that Wu-Tang Clan had nicknamed Shaolin, where Iglew and Deity had made their fortune selling crack through the eighties in the Richmond projects. The same island where Cookie Calhoun's first husband, Nails McNulty, lived with his bigoted wife, who shed no tears over Cookie's grave. The same little piece of Dogpatch, USA, where Vito "Sleighride" Santa called home.

It was all a little too coincidental for Bobby that the jail where the guy who owned the company that owned the van that might have been the one that killed Cookie Calhoun was also located here on the forgotten borough of Staten Island.

"Okay," Bobby said. "I did time and I can see you aren't built for it. That must mean you're still in punk city, in protective custody. Maybe even segregation. You probably have a rabbi somewhere in order for you to do your time here on Staten Island instead of upstate."

"I hate this place," Golden said. "Arthur Kill. They should call it Sidney Kill. It kills you a little more every day. Did you know that *kill* is Dutch for 'creek'? So I am literally up the creek without a paddle here. You think I wouldn't rather be upstate? In Otisville, where the food is better? Where you see the fall leaves turn? Country air instead of the stink from the Staten Island landfill? It hurts more to be so close to home. I watched the smoke from the Twin Towers every day from here, breathed it in. I hear the foghorns of my city. I know the life I lost is right outside and across the bridge. A ferry ride brings me to Delancey Street. It hurts even worse to be in here so close to home especially since my family doesn't visit. They disowned me. They blame me for squandering the family business. For getting my younger brother involved. They blame me he died inside. They blame me for bringing shame and sorrow. So, maybe they send me a few commissary dollars out of guilt or charity now and then. They do that in case God is watching. They do it for themselves, not me. So I don't wanna be here, believe you me. I went through the system, Rikers, upstate, Elmira, Sing Sing, but then after I disappeared from the radar, I was sent here so the people who sandbagged me could keep an eye on me. The monsters who set me up. That cop. The Italians. They run Staten Island. I'm like a prisoner in the dungeon of their castle in their little fiefdom here. My life is like the Count of Monte Cristo."

Bobby looked at him, a small man who had succumbed to greed, but not evil. He was a smuggler. An insurance scammer. A quick-buck artist. He was no big-time dealer like Iglew or Deity. He wasn't as corrupt as Ford. Wasn't a killer mobster like Santa.

Bobby needed Sid Golden on the outside, to help him put the cracked mirror back together. Golden was talking about the same people as Angelina Donatella. He needed him to cooperate.

"Maybe," Bobby said. "But maybe someone in here's watching over you, for that chump change your family still sends."

"I do what I gotta do," Golden said, shrugging his slight shoulders, wheedling his little fingers, the light shining off his bald pate. "So I go without cookies, but no one jumps my buns."

"The other thing that saves you is that you're ugly," Izzy said.

"Thanks, you're a mensch," Sid said. "Any more compliments?"

"Yeah, your breath smells like Jersey," Izzy said.

"And it helps that you're fifty-two years old and the rapists like young Maytags, pretty boys with lipstick, eye makeup, and nylons," Bobby said.

"If you were gay, you couldn't get laid on Fire Island with a fistful of Madonna autographs," Izzy said.

"All of which still makes me a living human being and not a corpse," Golden said. "Which is what I am if I flip on the Italians or the cop."

"But I'm gonna find out who was driving the truck that killed Cookie Calhoun," Bobby said. "And when I do, I am gonna make sure that a new charge is added to your sentence for facilitation to murder after the fact."

"How much more could they give me for that than they already gave me under the Rockefeller laws?" Golden said. "I'm doing twenty-five years, here. I did eight. If my appeal is denied, I'll probably do seven, tops nine more, with good behavior. So you finger me for some bubkes hit-and-run ten years ago. Maybe six years. Even a legal aide could get that to run concurrent. It's nonsense. Have a nice day, excuse me, but I got a sentence to serve."

"Yeah," Bobby said, watching Golden signal for the hack. "But you know and I know that when Max Roth writes a column about all this, and they find out in here that *you* were part of purposely running down a mother in front of her six-year-old son, half white, half black. And that it messed up the kid's head so bad he iced himself."

"The boy killed himself?" Golden asked, his regret genuine.

Bobby told him that Brian promised suicide unless there was proof her death wasn't his fault by the tenth anniversary of her death.

"Oy, that's dreadful," Golden said.

"Yeah, and some big killer con who's doing life without possibility and pining something terrible for his kid is gonna make shit sure you die in the showers with a block of soap in your ass. Anyone who'd do something like that in front of a kid is a moving target in the joint, Sid. You're gonna go just like that pedophile priest bought it up in Boston. And he didn't even kill any of those kids. There is no protection for kid killers inside, Sid."

"If you don't help us help you, you're the exception that proves the rule that our tribe is intelligent," Izzy said.

Bobby stood up and nodded for Izzy to go. Sid Golden swooned, swallowed hard, his fingers fiddling together. He smoothed his orange jumpsuit and cleared his throat and said, "Wait."

Izzy turned and looked at him. "You ready to put your Yid lid on and act schmart instead of like a schmuck?"

"Look," Golden said. "I have no idea who was driving one of my six trucks ten years ago."

"Then you got nothing to horse-trade," Izzy said.

"But no truck ever went out without it being recorded," Golden said. "Because they always had a pretty expensive cargo, if you get my drift. We moved a lot of stuff for people. How am I supposed to know about this one truck out of six off the top of my head? This is the first time I heard of this hit-and-run."

Bobby said, "Didn't you keep records?"

"My tribe always keeps records," Izzy said. "Every dollar every employee ever earned on or off the books is written down. Right, Sid?"

Golden waved his hands in front of him. "All our records went up in smoke."

"Nah, Sid, I can't help ya," Izzy said. "You're bullshittin' me. No way did you send both sets of books up in smoke. Old Yiddish saying, 'Just like lightning never strikes the same place twice, Jewish lightning never strikes the second set of books.' "

"Hand to my heart," Golden said, putting his left hand over his right pectoral.

"There's another set, buried somewhere, part of what's been keeping you alive," Izzy said. "If you die, someone sends the book to the Feds."

Bobby looked at Izzy, impressed. Izzy took out a Joya halvah bar and opened it with a meticulous, slow crinkle of the wrapper, like a striptease for a con deprived simple pleasures like a sweet, especially when he was paying what little commissary he had to some big goon to protect him from jailhouse predators. Golden watched Izzy unfold each corner and peel the wrapper slowly down.

"Like a broad arching her back so you can peel off the panties, no?" Izzy said.

Golden's eyes focused on the candy bar, his lower lip glistening with drool. Izzy lifted the bar, held it between himself and Golden.

"Gorgeous, ain't it?" Izzy said. "A beautiful, naked halvah."

Golden gaped. Then Izzy plunged the whole thing into his mouth and chewed.

"Oh, man, freedom sure don't suck," Izzy said.

Izzy opened his briefcase, pulled out a baggie containing a Carnegie deli bag, and removed a hot pastrami sandwich on seeded rye, two plump dill garlic pickles, and a can of celery soda. Sid Golden gaped, his nose twitching, swallowing a mouthful of saliva.

Izzy bit into one of the crisp pickles, the juice exploding from his mouth. "So, how's the chow in here, Sid?"

Golden said, "So maybe we can talk."

Izzy took out three more halvah bars, placed them on the tabletop, then slathered packets of Hebrew National mustard on the pastrami sandwich and took a giant, greasy bite. The smell of the pastrami and pickles filled the room like a wind blowing from the land of the free. Golden stared at the sandwich, the pickles, the halvah bars, like a teenager at a strip club.

"Where's the ledger, Sid?" Bobby said.

"I want immunity on anything to do with this killing," Golden said. "You can't let the animals rip me apart in here. You have no idea."

"Yes, I do," Bobby said.

"I can get Cranberry to grant you a new trial," Izzy said, taking another huge bite of the sandwich, followed by a bite of pickle, and a sip of soda. "I'll amend your writ and get you out in a day. Your choice."

"This is Staten Island and they own—"

"The appeals court is in Brooklyn, where everybody owns at least one judge," Izzy said. "I can walk you out and win your case with my balls on backward. I can get you immunity on everything."

Golden leaned closer. "What about the Italians? And the Irish cop who locked me up? Ford?"

"Sleighride is ready to die any minute now," Bobby said. "Most of his crew has been RICO'd. Ford's on my radar screen. I'll protect you from the woman cop, too."

"Who, woman cop?"

"Samantha Savage, from the hip-hop task force."

"The who, from the which? Who cares about some woman cop?" Golden said. "Maybe I'll tell you where such a ledger is, but I want a promise you'll take my case, Israel Gleason, and get me out of here."

Izzy held out his hand. "Hebe's honor."

Golden looked at Izzy's greasy, mustard-covered hand. Then looked in Izzy's eyes. "You, I don't trust. You're a ganef and meshuga."

"Good, fuck you, too, then, and have a great life wailing at the yard wall," Izzy said. "Your mother must've sent you to public school with ham on Wonder bread with mayo. No rabbinical student would ever turn this deal down, schmuck!"

Golden nodded to Bobby. "Swear to him and shake his hand."

Izzy said, "Is this an Orchard Street, Sunday-morning, Jew-town haggle here? I'm offering to help you eat lean pastrami in the Carnegie Deli by the day after tomorrow and a lap dance by nightfall in Runway 69 and you need a mick middleman to close the deal? You wound my pride, Sidney Golden. Is this how our mothers taught us? I'm doing for you a mitzvah and you insult me?"

Golden nodded to Bobby and said, "Him, I trust, he has the *look*, even for a goy. You, you remind me of *me*. No way do I trust you."

Izzy held out his hand to Bobby and swore that he'd represent Golden in his appeal and try to get him immunity on the hit-and-run. Bobby shook it. Golden held out his hand to Bobby.

"You swear to make him keep his word?" Golden asked.

Bobby said, "I promise."

"Gentlemen, we have a deal," Golden said, swiping the second half of the pastrami sandwich, ramming it to his mouth with both hands, devouring it. "Now, get me out and I'll show you where to find the ledger."

TWENTY-ONE

At 8:33 p.m. Bobby left the Arthur Kill Correctional Facility on Arthur Kill Road in Staten Island with Izzy Gleason, walking through the center corridor that the cons called Broadway, and hearing the last heavy steel door clanging behind him. For Bobby, even after a brief jail visit, the fresh air and the rosy setting sun were like lottery winnings. He put on his shades, filled his lungs, gazed around the grim slash of Staten Island, and walked toward the parking lot where Herbie sat waiting in the Jeep.

Then Bobby saw her.

Samantha Savage leaned on her black Navigator in the spot next to Bobby's Jeep, this time dressed in jeans and brilliant white sneakers and a belly shirt.

Bobby looked around the lot, saw the microwave video cameras mounted on each of the six manned towers. Knew his name was lodged along with Izzy's as visitors to Sidney Golden. He knew that Ford would learn that he'd been there to visit Golden. He knew he had to get him out. Fast.

Savage walked toward Bobby, smaller in the sneakers than in heels, and sexier in her almost needy demeanor.

"I need to talk to you," Savage said.

Bobby told Izzy to wait for him in the Jeep.

"My advice, run to the bushes and choke the chicken before you negotiate with that chick," Izzy said. "Otherwise, you're gonna think with the little head."

"He always talk behind people's back in front of them like that?" Savage asked.

194

"If you heard what I said behind your back, lady, you'd be calling *me* savage."

"How dare you!"

"In the car, Iz," Bobby said.

"Close your eyes first," Izzy said. "And imagine celling with you know who."

Izzy climbed into the Jeep and Savage stood directly in front of Bobby now, a foot shorter, looking up so that he could see lots of the whites in her eyes.

"I need your help," she said.

"I already have a client in this case."

"I have nowhere else to turn."

"Belly down might be a good start," Izzy yelled from the Jeep.

Bobby walked Savage toward her black Navigator.

"It's a good thing they took my gun away," she said, "or I might kneecap that little asp."

Bobby looked past her at the black Navigator and searched for the kiss-shaped dent near the rear fender. It wasn't there. *She'd had it fixed,* he thought. *To confuse me. She thinks I'm a stooge.*

"Hire a good lawyer, hon."

"Don't call me hon. . . . I can't really afford a good lawyer. I'm afraid to hire a PBA lawyer. I'm afraid of certain influences inside NYPD. I can't investigate myself without a shield and gun."

"Go to the DA."

"That's comical. They're going to indict me."

"The Feds."

"They're part of the setup."

Bobby looked at her and thought, *So are you, baby.*

"How'd you know I was here?" Bobby said.

"I followed you after I staked out the McNultys' house. I figured one way or the other you'd wind up back there. With her."

Bobby thought the real truth was that she'd placed a tail bug on his car. He'd have to sweep it for a tracking device later.

"What made you think that?"

"You're working for her. Plus it's kind of obvious that you're infatuated with her. You were up in her apartment for forty-seven minutes."

She didn't know that he'd been in Angelina Donatella's apartment.

"You know this because you're such a great detective, huh?"

"No, because I'm a woman. If I was such a great detective, I wouldn't be in the predicament I'm in and would not be coming, hat in hand, to you for help. I'm not a great detective. But I'm good enough to know you are."

Bobby figured that if Savage was sent to gain his confidence with cheap flattery, tight pants, and puppy eyes as a plant, to pick his brain, as a double agent, then he could use her. He could feed her misinformation. Misdirect *her*. He could *own* her. He'd test her and see how far she was willing to go. Bobby walked to the Jeep. Izzy said he had to go lay the groundwork for the Sid Golden appeal. "I know exactly how to play Judge Cranberry," Izzy said. "He comes out of the blow-jobs-aren't-real-sex wing of the Democratic Party, so I know exactly how to persuade him to our side without what he'd consider a bribe."

"Tell me no more," Bobby said. "And I didn't hear that."

Bobby asked Izzy to rent a nondescript car so that Herbie could go stake out the Narrows View Nursing Home.

"Who am I looking for?" Herbie asked.

He gave Herbie a picture of Rodney Calhoun and showed him the photo he'd taken of the grounds with his phone camera. He showed Herbie where Calhoun's room was. Told him to see if people came and went from the room. Or if Calhoun himself entered or left the nursing home.

Bobby rummaged in his glove compartment and took out a piece of electronic equipment Maggie had purchased for him in the Snoop Shop and put it in his pants pocket.

"One piece of advice, diamond dick," Izzy said. "This Savage bim came to you. So take; don't give. Let her do the talking. Say nothing incriminating. If you're riding with her, remember it's *her* environment. Unless you got her naked in your own bed, assume you're being taped. And even then I'd check all the usual hidey-holes for bugs. If you want, I'll come do that kind of a thorough sweep for you."

Bobby slammed the Jeep door and walked back to Savage.

"I'll ride with you," Bobby said to Savage. "I'll listen. No promises."

"Thanks," she said, looking up at him, puppy-eyed.

TWENTY-TWO

As Savage ramped onto the Verrazano, Bobby noticed that the flag atop the toll-plaza station house was at half-mast for Stephen Greco. A black wreath adorned the gray door at the top of the stone steps where Bobby had met him. Rage boiled in his arteries. Somewhere a little girl was drowning in anguish over the death of her father. Which Bobby knew was a murder.

As they approached Brooklyn, he listened to Samantha Savage's tale of how she was told by her fellow task-force members Noonan and Scarano that Tu Bitz would be carrying a load of drugs in his car that December twenty-third night. That there was no time to get a warrant. That the tip had just come in from someone at the club, and they knew she was staking him out, on his tail.

"We needed a guy like Tu Bitz," she said. "We needed to compromise a guy like him, have him facing heavy time under the Rockefeller laws, also as a three-time loser, so that if he was looking at the rest of his life, he might flip. Make him turn in Ignatius Lewis and lead us to this Deity character, the secret owner of Lethal Injection Records. He was the conduit. But I should have known that it was too pat. Too neat. Too convenient that they got the tip that late in the night, two days before Christmas, when I was tailing him. When it would be impossible to find a judge."

"You knew there was a chance you'd be busted for illegal search."

"Affirmative . . . I mean, *yes.*"

"You've been after these guys, Iglew and Deity, for how long?"

"Eight years."

"So why didn't you wait? What was one more day?"

She remained silent for a beat longer than Bobby felt comfortable with.

He kept thinking about what Angelina Donatella had told him about Samantha Savage.

"I just couldn't," she said after a long pause. "You don't understand. . . . He had the drugs that night. I might never get the chance again."

"People don't move drugs just once. Why not wait for another day?"

"For some people, even one day can be an *eternity*."

Bobby studied her, a woman lost in a moment of personal turmoil.

"When I was doing time for something I didn't do, every day was an eternity," Bobby said. "But for a cop on a case, it's just another shift. I know. I've done both."

"No, this was different. This was my chance to . . . to get to the others."

Bobby sensed that she was not telling him everything. Some hidden agenda, a different engine, was driving her. It didn't smell like ambition. Or greed. *What the hell is it?* he wondered. *Revenge?* Rather than probe and risk pushing the hidden motivation further in, he'd let her bubble it to the top on her own.

"Okay, so you had Tu Bitz nailed, you wanted him so bad you could taste it."

"Yes."

"But nothing you did made him flip?"

"Affirmative . . . sorry. Yeah."

"Atta girl."

She took her eyes off the road, scowled. *"Atta girl?* Who am I? Lassie?"

"Why do you think he wouldn't flip?"

"Honest?"

"Yeah?"

"I began to doubt that he knew the drugs were in his car," she said.

"Really?"

"I started to suspect they were planted. Then I was tipped. Then I made the illegal search. The flawed arrest . . ."

"When did you first think they might not be his drugs?"

"The look on his face when I found them was one of total astonishment. He accused *me* of planting them. Sometimes you just have a sense when someone is lying . . . and when they're being truthful."

"Bet your pretty little ass."

"I beg your pardon?"

"I'm having one of those built-in polygraph moments right now, and I don't believe you're telling me the whole truth here, Sammy girl."

Her silence was quadraphonic. She sped the Gowanus Expressway toward the Brooklyn Battery Tunnel. Bobby kept looking at her but couldn't get a true read of her. Staten Island loomed behind her like a big brooding pile of old lies and fresh felonies. Something ominous hung over the whole island. Bruise-colored clouds darkened the skies, moving north from Jersey. He looked again at Savage, framed against that forbidding backdrop, still trying to decipher her body language.

Bobby watched as Savage changed lanes twice, avoided just in the nick of time a crazed truck driver who didn't use a blinker, and accelerated past another motorist who was road-raging against the trucker. She handled it all with smooth, confident moves and hair-trigger reflexes. Bobby watched the way she gripped the wheel in her squeaking-tight fists, working the pedals with her small, sneakered feet, big eyes watching six objects at once, and never once getting flustered. Bobby had a theory that, like a good dancer, a woman who really knew how to drive well probably did most physical things well. Especially sex. Watching her drive was like a floor show, a prance down a catwalk, a twirl down a brass pole.

"How'd Tu Bitz react in the box?"

"Like a block of steel," she said. "He said the drugs weren't his. That he wasn't drunk. That he was never Mirandized. That I'd searched the car without permission."

"All of which was true."

She nodded. "But the thing he protested most was the drugs. He said he made so much money as a rapper he didn't need drugs. He said he didn't do drugs anymore either. Both of those things, from my knowledge of him, were true."

"Did you believe then that you were being set up?"

The all-news station warned of a flood watch in New York.

"No," she said. "I was just frustrated. Noonan and Scarano didn't even try cracking him. They said this was my bust. My big collar. The one that would give me the career boost I needed to get promotions."

"Was that what you were after?"

"Negative . . . no. I was most interested in using Tu Bitz as a stepping-stone to the others above him."

"Iglew and Deity?"

"Yes, and whoever else was involved."

"Like who?" Bobby said as she sped out on the Manhattan side of the Brooklyn Battery Tunnel and inched West Street uptown past Ground

Zero, which had become a ghoulish rubbernecking tourist attraction, a mass grave at which tourists snapped family snapshots before visiting the Statue of Liberty and catching a Broadway-musical matinee.

"Whoever," she said, blessing herself as she passed the site where 2,772 people were murdered on September 11, 2001.

The gesture made Bobby fall silent and squirm in his seat as he glanced past her at a ferry gliding across the harbor, toward Staten Island, reminding him of the recent ferry crash where ten people had died and scores were injured, which had only added to the general paranoia of Staten Islanders. Beyond the orange ferry was the dirty rim of cloud-covered New Jersey, another pile of toxic corruption, the place where James Ford had gone to build his empire on the golden shore.

"Denmark was never this rotten," Bobby said, rubbing his temples.

"What's that supposed to mean?"

"Whatever."

"You're making a reference to *Hamlet*. I read all of Shakespeare."

"Me, too. In jail. So spare me the dissertation."

"I am telling you the truth and I need your help."

But Bobby saw her little right fist grip the steering wheel so hard that a long, squiggly vein rose on the back of her hand like the signature of a strangler.

"So why?"

"Why what?"

"Why'd they set you up?"

"I think I was getting too close."

"To who?"

"Deity."

"Is Deity Iglew!"

"No!" She flattened the accelerator, the engine erupting. Bobby flattened his hand against the dash and knew he'd touched a raw nerve. She'd answered too fast. With too much certainty.

"At least I don't think so," she said, moving her foot to the brake, slowing.

The qualification convinced Bobby that something even deeper was going on between her and Iglew. He thought again of Angelina Donatella saying she'd given Savage a fill on the old hit-and-run. But why, then, hadn't Savage done anything about it? Or maybe what she did was help cover it up. And that's why she'd showed up in the parking lot of the

Arthur Kill when he'd gone to visit Sid Golden. To find out what he'd learned from the old smuggler. About Deity. Who might be Iglew.

Bobby said, "Come on, lady, you came to me. You said you wanted to talk. This is like doing a root canal on a hammerhead shark."

"Who do you think is at the top of all this?"

"Top of what? Lethal Injection Records? Or Cookie Calhoun's hit-and-run? Or are they so connected that the future of one depends on the other staying unsolved?"

She glanced at him, hit the gas, and weaved uptown. "Why were you interviewing that inmate Sid Golden at the jail in Staten Island?"

"Hey, I'm asking *you* the questions."

"Was it because he used to run a company called Golden's Tool and Die?"

"Your problems are different than my client's."

She turned her head to Bobby, grabbed his hand, and said, "Oh . . . my . . . gosh . . . Did Golden's company by any chance use a yellow van?"

"Who are you really after? Why were you willing to risk your job, your career, your pension, maybe your *freedom,* for a dirty drug bust?"

"I swear to you I thought I was busting Tu Bitz for drugs that were his. . . . It was a technicality, not immoral. I'd never plant drugs on anybody. Ever, ever, ever . . ."

Bobby studied her as her voice trailed off with a whisper of dread. "Even if that's true, it's hard to see why you crossed the line. I read your folder. Cleaner than a surgeon's hands. So I need to know why you risked it all, Sammy."

"Don't call me that."

"And who?" he asked as they raced past Twenty-third Street. "I need to know *who* you were after. Who was so important that you'd risk everything?"

Unless, he thought, *it was all bullshit. And Ford, Noonan, and Scarano put her out here looking like she was a suspended cop, a dirty maverick, an outcast, asking for Bobby's help, ready to align herself with him. To get him to confide in her. To pick his brains.*

As horns honked and steam rose from sewers and pedestrians jay-walked through the fast traffic to the Chelsea Piers, Bobby looked down at Savage's hand on his, warm and strong and a little damp, her thumb stroking his thumb, trying to find a connection. She took her eyes off the road. Looked him in the eyes. Blinking long lashes. *A cock tease,* he thought.

Then: *BAM!*

The Navigator rear-ended the BMW in front of it that had slam-braked for a blond, athletic female jaywalker in spandex shorts jogging across West Street with a gym bag. The Navigator's hood popped. Bobby whipped front and back in his seat, like a crash dummy, saved by the shoulder strap.

"Goddamn it!" Samantha shouted.

She unbuckled her shoulder strap, threw the Navigator in park, and jumped out, racing to the front of her vehicle to meet the twentysomething, male, yuppie driver of the BMW. The blond jogger trotted off without looking back.

Bobby sat in the Navigator and reached his right hand under the front dash and connected a magnetized, quarter-sized XLF-3 tracker that operated on two 392 silver-oxide batteries. Maggie had bought him all of these little gadgets from the Snoop Shop on Twenty-third Street for his birthday a few years back, and when he activated the Mini-10 tracker receiver that he would mount in his own tail car, Savage's car would blip on his orange computer-tracking screen like a plane on a radar screen. And he could track Samantha Savage at a discreet three-mile distance anywhere she went.

Bobby also used the time to rummage her pocketbook, which sat on the backseat. He riffled a few hundred bucks in cash. He clicked through a half dozen credit cards. He perused receipts from various department stores. He studied her driver's license, with a picture that didn't do her justice, and an address in Bayside, Queens, which he repeated in his head a half dozen times until he had it memorized.

"Your fault, lady," the yuppie said. "You hit me from behind. You have a small dent. I might have a few grand work here!"

"My fault?" Savage yelled. "If you hadn't slammed your brakes to ogle that girl's rear end, I would never have rear-ended you!"

Bobby shuffled through the wallet, glimpsing a photo of a middle-aged black woman who looked like Samantha Savage, and who he assumed was her mother.

"I'm not gonna argue rear ends with you, lady," the motorist said. "I need to see your license."

Bobby was about to close the wallet when in one of those not-so-secret secret compartments he found a snapshot cut to wallet size of Samantha Savage posing with Ignatius "Iglew" Lewis.

Her arm was wrapped around Iglew's waist, head resting on his shoulder. His arm was looped around her shoulder. It was signed, "To Sam, All my love, always, Iggy." Savage had shorter hair than she wore now. Iglew looked a few years younger.

Holy shit, Bobby thought, jamming the wallet in the pocketbook in the backseat and straightening in his front passenger seat.

Savage slammed the hood of the Navigator, yanked open the driver's door, and reached in and grabbed her purse. She hesitated when she saw that it was unsnapped. She looked at Bobby. Blinking.

"You okay?" she asked.

"Been better."

"I'll be finished with this horn dog in a sec. . . . Bobby, me and you, we're after the same people."

"Good," Bobby said, opening his door, climbing out, and talking to her over the roof of the car. "Call me when you're ready to tell me who they are."

"Wait." For the first time her eyes had a desperate little look.

"Nah, I gotta go."

"Please . . . I need your help."

"You need to learn how to tell the truth, *Sam.*"

Bobby dodged horn-honking traffic to the pedestrian path that ran along the Hudson and jogged under the darkening clouds the rest of the way uptown to the Seventy-ninth Street Boat Basin, trying to clear his crowded brain.

Samantha and Iglew, he thought as he ran. *Samantha and Iglew . . .*

TWENTY-THREE

When Bobby arrived back at the *Fifth Amendment,* Janis McNulty sat on the deck, sipping a bottle of Corona with a wedge of lime on top, a six-pack at her feet. Two empties were in the six-pack, and she was working pretty good on her third cerveza in the humid heat.

"Hey," Bobby said. "I thought I took you home already."

"We need to talk."

Bobby looked around. The river was busy with water ferries from Jersey, pleasure craft, Circle Lines, and tugs all heading for port before the coming storm. Neighbors moved around the decks taking in umbrellas, table settings, cleaning, doing repairs.

Then he felt the first drops of rain fall. Another landed on the tip of Janis McNulty's little nose, bursting into her eyes. She laughed, her face igniting with sea-blue eyes and white teeth.

"Fine," Bobby said, opening the cabin door and deprogramming the beeping alarm, which was ready to ring.

Janis stood, picked up the six-pack of Corona bottles, and gazed at one woman in a bikini who looked over her sun reflector that was pattered with rain.

"You must be doing the down-low with that melanoma mama because she keeps eye-tapping you."

"Let's stick to your case," Bobby said. "My personal life isn't relevant here."

Janis followed Bobby inside and slid closed the door. She drained what was left of the beer and placed the six-pack on the countertop. Three of the bottles were now empty. She popped two more and jammed lime wedges in both bottle necks and offered one to Bobby.

"Not when I'm working," he said.

She took a long guzzle, a little buzzed. "You're not working right now."

"Actually, when I'm talking to you, I am working. I don't keep banker's hours. Neither do the bad guys."

She walked closer to Bobby and drank some more of the beer. The top button of her cutoff, low-rise jeans was open, revealing the peach fuzz around her diamond-studded navel set into the tanned washboard belly.

She said, "I need to use the ladies'."

He nodded toward the bathroom door next to the door of the main bedroom. She walked to it, entered, and closed the door.

He remembered that the afternoon he'd spent with her mother they'd also had a few drinks, before and after the first go-round, then before and after rounds two and three. As rain beat on the windows. The way rain peppered the *Fifth Amendment* right now.

When she stepped out of the bathroom, Janis wore the belly shirt and V-string bikini panties, her jeans slung over her shoulder.

"Oh, man," Bobby said.

Janis tilted her head toward him at a sultry angle. She was her mother. From head to toe. Same everything. A clone.

She took a sip of beer, clicked the bottle against the diamond on her belly, and said, "Wanna get busy?"

"Janis, you'd have to be a man to know how hard it is to say no. But I can't because you're a client and . . ."

She looped an arm around his neck and whispered, "You're fired."

"You've been drinking and—"

"I'm a grown woman."

"I noticed."

She handed him the other beer. "Join me."

He pulled the lime out of the mouth of the bottle and took a long, cold gulp.

In that brief instant, she peeled away more than a decade of Bobby's life. He was in his early twenties, pressed against Cookie Calhoun with afternoon rain nibbling the windows and cold beer on the night table.

Janis began unbuttoning Bobby's shirt. The rain fell and the winds rocked the boat. He was still young enough to surrender to such a sweet temptation. But old enough to know that the moment they were finished making love, for those fleeting moments of ecstasy he'd suffer from a lifetime of guilt. No fine wine was worth that hangover. He would not dishonor the memory of Cookie Calhoun by bedding her daughter. Bobby grabbed her wrists.

"Janis, put your pants on."

"Why? I got too much baggage for you?"

"No, I do and—"

His cell phone rang. He was relieved. Even if it was a telemarketer, he'd make believe it was about the case and stay on the line for twenty minutes. Bobby answered the phone as Janis stared at him, abashed in rejection, wiggling into her jeans. He turned away.

"It's awful, Pop," Maggie said. "Brian . . . handful of Mom's sleeping pills . . . bathroom floor . . . frothing at mouth. . . . Nine one one . . . St. Clare's . . ."

By the time Bobby and Janis arrived at St. Clare's Hospital emergency room, Brian's stomach had been pumped. He was in the intensive care unit and on a suicide watch. The doctors were awaiting the results of a CAT scan to see if there had been any brain damage from the overdose, but said his vitals were strong.

"He has youth on his side," said the Indian doctor, who approached them in the frantic hallway where nurses rushed from room to room, checking monitors, giving meds, and answering alarms for a dozen ICU patients. "But this is not just a medical problem, people. Brian is an emotionally disturbed young man. This is a very loud cry for help. This boy is suicidal, and those scars on his wrists tell me this is not his first attempt. Eventually he will succeed. I'm going to check the CAT scan now. And I hate to have to tell you that the administration says that if he is okay, he will be discharged in the morning. If you want him placed in psychiatric observation, he will have to be transferred to a city hospital because his coverage will not pay for a private hospital like ours."

Janis stood in slumped grief, her shoulders hunched, her head bowed. She didn't look a bit like the sultry woman he'd been tempted to make love to twenty minutes earlier.

Maggie sat on a plastic chair, her feet pulled up under her, head on her knees, her eyes puffy and red, mascara streaked like tire skids. Connie sat next to her, holding her hand.

"It's not your fault, baby," Connie told Maggie.

"Yes, it is, because I never should've let Brian use your bathroom. First, because you don't want anyone, not even me, in there. Second, because I know you keep your goofballs in there."

"They're called Seconal and I only use them when I'm completely stressed-out."

"How can anyone with two billion in the bank be stressed-out? About what, Mom?"

"Mag, that's a cheap shot," Bobby said.

"And you're supposed to be Sherlock Holmes," Maggie said. "Maybe if you would have found out who killed his mother . . ."

"Hey, brat girl, that's your father you're talking to," Connie said, pointing a finger at her. "He isn't the cause of Brian's pain. Or his psychiatric issues. Your father's trying to help, for Christ sakes. Grow the hell up and get a grip. You are not going to assign the guilt our way, kiddo."

"*Our* way," Maggie said. "You dumped Pop because he wanted to live like a normal person in Brooklyn. Instead of in a skyscraper ninety stories up from the 'little' people. Or out in the Hamptons and on the Central Park Committee. You ever consider maybe I wanted to stay with him, my friends, like Brian, in Brooklyn? Give me Coney Island over Southhampton any day of the week. Give me a rent-controlled apartment in Bay Ridge tomorrow and I'll skydive out the goddamned International penthouse window and take the subway over there."

"Okay, you wanna live in a slum, go live on the Bowery."

"That's how much you know," Maggie said. "The Bowery's all yuppies now, and million-dollar condos. Skid Row is now Yup Row."

Connie turned to Bobby. "It is?"

Maggie drifted over to Brian's closed room door and peered in through the wired glass where a nurse's aide sat monitoring him. Brian was attached to an IV drip, oxygen, and various monitors gauging his blood pressure and heart rate. Restraints bound his wrists and legs to the bed rails.

Jimi Jim arrived, a jittery commotion of wasted energy, his face in front of Janis's face. "How'd this happen? Who gave him the pills? This is bull-shit!"

"He raided Maggie's medicine cabinet," Janis said.

"You said he'd be better hanging out with her," Jimi Jim said. "What'd him and Bitchy Rich have a lovers' spat? She drive him further over the edge? In her Rolls?"

Maggie looked at him, her eyes bulging with tears.

"That's it," Connie said, storming at Jimi Jim, pointing a finger. "Hey, germ boy, I'm sorry your kid brother tried to kill himself, but nobody talks about my kid like that."

"Mom, please . . ."

A nurse strode up and said, "This isn't helpful. There're other patients . . ."

Bobby held up his hands. "Con . . . Jan . . . please."

Janis approached Connie and said, "Don't talk to my brother like that, moneybags. Our kid brother just OD'd in your pad on your pills. How about we call Page Six on that one?"

"You blaming me for him swiping my medicine, now?" Connie said. "That's like blaming the bank for getting robbed."

"Only someone in your tax bracket would use that analogy," Janis said.

"Everybody, shut the hell up!" Bobby shouted.

Jimi Jim said, "Yeah, Barney Fife wants to talk!"

"Don't you dare talk to him like that," Janis said, putting her finger in Jimi Jim's face.

"You're more interested in him than Mom or Brian," Jimi Jim said.

Connie did a double take, looked from Bobby to Janis, sniffed her, turned her back to the McNultys, and sniffed Bobby. She pushed him backward several steps, his back to a wall. "Smells to me like imitation Chanel No. 5," Connie said. "Brooklyn chic. You banging this Brownie?"

Bobby said, "What's it to you?"

"If you're not, I'm gonna," Connie said. "Right over the freaking head with a Fendi bag."

"Con, c'mon."

"I always suspected maybe you did her mother but . . ."

Bobby looked at her, amazed. Then he looked past her, at Maggie, who stood at the door of the ICU staring in at Brian.

Connie turned from Bobby to Janis to Bobby again. "Please tell me I'm wrong. Please tell me you didn't do the mother and now you're doing the daughter. Isn't that a little like necrophilia, incest, or something?"

"You could make the Immaculate Conception sound like a gang bang, Con."

"Is it true? Did you do both of them?"

Before he answered, the doctor returned, this time with a security guard. Bobby, Connie, Maggie, and the McNultys drifted over to him.

"The CAT scan shows that there is no brain damage," the doctor said.

Maggie took a deep breath and then sobbed with relief. Janis wiped a tear. Jimi Jim shouted, "Yes!"

"Brian will be released in the morning," the doctor said. "I'm afraid just immediate family can stay. I'll have to ask the rest of you to leave."

Janis approached Connie and put out her hand. "I'm sorry, I'm just stressed. It's not your fault."

Connie nodded. "I'm sorry, too. I can be a real bitch sometimes."

"Word is bond on that," Jimi Jim said.

"Chill, Jimi Jim," Janis said.

"Nice name," Connie said, walking toward Maggie. "For a monkey."

Bobby looked at Janis, who steered him off toward the stairwell exit.

"Bobby, please, you have to find out who—"

"You fired me."

"You're rehired."

"I'm no longer for hire."

"Why?"

"Because then I'd have to file a sexual harassment suit against you. But that doesn't mean I won't work it on my own."

"I don't think that would please your ex," Janis said.

"That's why she's an ex."

Janis flashed a soft grin. "Bobby, about earlier, maybe I had one too many."

"Maybe I had one too few."

Janis's smile faded. "Me and the shrink thought that viewing the tapes might help Brian. It backfired."

"Fire the shrink, too."

"I will, if I can ever get the asshole on the phone."

"That's a start."

"Bobby, if we don't find out who killed my mother, I'm gonna lose my kid brother for sure. I'm gonna lose him."

"What makes you so sure that finding your mother's killer will make a difference?"

"You think it was murder?"

"I do, yes."

"Then the reason it matters is this: Brian has already told me that if it was an accident, he believes that dropping the half a buck made Mom's death his fault. As irrational as that might seem to me and you, it's what he believes and it doesn't make it any less real in his mind. But if someone was actually trying to kill my mother on purpose, if there was a murder plan, they would have killed her then. Or some other time. And then it wouldn't carry the same guilt for him. Grief, yes. Guilt, no. I need to be able to prove to Brian that this was murder. And that he was in no way responsible for that. And if he finally comes to peace with that, maybe, just maybe he won't try to kill himself again. *Capice?*"

"Understood. But in the meantime you better keep him under surveillance. Commit him. Do whatever the hell you have to do to keep him from hurting himself until I get a chance to work the case."

"I fully intend to. But I can't let him go into a city loony bin. Kings County or Bellevue. I'll need to put him in a private sanitarium. There's one upstate I read about on the net that specializes in suicidal teens. But it's so expensive it makes the adults who pay for it suicidal. I might have to dip into the reward money. No one has even tried to claim it yet anyway."

Bobby looked at her, the reward reference triggering something in his head, and said, "Good idea. Get him out of the city, under twenty-four/seven watch."

"Bobby . . . thanks."

"I envy the guy who gets you."

"Take it from me, don't."

Janis walked over and draped her arm over Jimi Jim's shoulder as they stared in at their kid brother lying in the bed.

Bobby joined Connie and Maggie at the elevators, where Maggie wiped her eyes with a tissue.

"I'm sorry to both you guys," Maggie said. "I was just . . . I dunno . . ."

"If you say *stressed,* I'll hop you in your fifteen-year-old ass," Connie said.

"Almost sixteen," Maggie said. Maggie and Bobby laughed.

Connie looked at Bobby and gave him the evil eye. "What the hell are you laughing at, dirtbag?" she said.

When the elevator reached the lobby, Connie told Maggie to wait out in the limousine while she spoke to her father. Maggie kissed Bobby, nodded him into the vestibule where they could talk alone.

"I almost forgot," Maggie said. "Remember when you asked me to find out who really owned Narrows View Nursing Home? I did an advanced corporations search on Accurint."

"Yeah?"

"Well, it's owned by Narrows View Inc. Then I did a second advanced search of that and came up with an 800 number. No CEOs listed. So I then did a power search of the 800 area code number to see where the bills go to. And what I came up with is kind of odd. Maybe just a coincidence."

"What's odd? Who owns it, Mag?"

"The bills for Narrows View Inc. go to the same corporation that owns all that stuff down on the Jersey Shore in Surfside Heights. Exit 82C Inc."

"James Ford?"

"Same guy. But the bills are paid electronically from a numbered bank account with no name in some place called Norman's Cay in the Cayman Islands."

He thought immediately of Sid Golden shipping his gold to the Caymans. "Untraceable. Except for the 800 area code number. Off-the-hook work, Mag."

"And guess what else he owns?"

"My boat?"

"No, the building where Brian and Janis live."

Bobby just looked at her, blinking, as the new information searched for a soft place to rest in his overcrowded brain.

"Thanks, Mag."

"No problem, old man. And thanks for coming. And sorry for dissing the job you're doing for Brian. I know you're trying your best."

"Don't give it another thought, kiddo. But do me a favor."

"What?"

"Don't you dare feel a drop of guilt over Brian doing that to himself. The reason he's doing what he's doing is because of what someone did to his mother ten years ago. We clear on that, fly girl?"

She nodded. "Yeah, sort of, Pop. But can you do me a favor?"

"Word is bond."

"Stop trying to talk hip-hop. You sound like a stupid old white man trying to sound young and black. You're better when you talk like a regular old white herb. Like you always do."

"Scram, wiseass."

"That's illier."

She kissed him and trotted through the rain for the limo. Connie walked over to him in the vestibule.

"Finished with the cloak-and-dagger act?"

"She's a special kid."

"Yeah, and so I don't think it's healthy for Maggie for you to be *doing* her loony-tune new boyfriend's big sister, nomean?"

"Connie, do me a favor, will ya?"

"What?"

"Stop trying to micromanage my love life. Besides, it's not true."

"Okay, but did you bang her mother? When we were married?"

Technically he had, but while he was separated, but he wasn't going to tell her anyway. Bobby believed there was a statute of limitations on old lays.

"Cookie Calhoun is dead, Connie. Murdered. Let her rest in peace."

"Why don't you?"

"Because that kid upstairs thinks he's responsible. I have to prove to him he's not."

"It has nothing to do with his sister, though, right? Okay, here's the dealio. I don't want Maggie around that wack-job Brian anymore."

"That's a sure way of making her elope. And do me a favor. Stop trying to talk hip-hop. It makes you sound like a dumb-ass old white broad trying to sound black."

"*Old?* I don't mind *dumb-ass* or *broad.* But *old,* you son of a bitch?"

"To Maggie we're relics, Con."

"I'm afraid of a Romeo-and-Juliet suicide pact, Bobby."

"Just chill out . . . make that *cool it,* Con."

She nodded and looked him up and down. "You're not getting any younger yourself. Even if you still look good."

"You haven't aged a day, Con."

"Yeah?"

"You're as beautiful as back in the day . . . make that *as beautiful as ever.*"

Connie took a deep breath and smiled the smile that had made him first fall in love with her. "What else is money for if not to make doctors rich?"

Which reminded him, he had a dinner date with Dianne Rattigan the next night.

TWENTY-FOUR

Bobby got the Jeep out of the hospital park-and-lock lot.

When he and Janis had run up from the *Fifth Amendment* after receiving the panicked call from Maggie, he'd found the Jeep where Izzy had parked it in Bobby's assigned spot with the keys on the sun visor.

Then he and Janis had raced downtown.

Now he needed to go get some sleep and sort out everything in his head. He needed time alone. To think. To plan. To sleep. And to dream. Dreaming was vital to anyone who was trying to make sense of the conscious hours. The brain needed the fantasy of the dream state in order to function. When it doesn't dream, the brain automatically invents things in the waking hours. That's why insomniacs were often delusional and paranoid. Bobby was becoming paranoid. Feared he was imagining that so many people were all scheming at once, intersecting with each other.

As he pulled out of the lot, he saw a black Navigator slink from a spot on the street a half block down. It tailed four cars behind Bobby in the building rain. He wondered if he was imagining things again. Did Samantha Savage follow him here? He needed to hook up his Mini-10 tracker computer screen to see if a bleep was directly behind him. But he was already behind the wheel and it took ten minutes to install and rev up.

He made a sharp right onto Sixty-fourth Street without signaling to see if the Navigator followed. It did. But the Navigator was still three car lengths behind him and Bobby was swept into the ballet of traffic. Sudden stops in the rain in Manhattan can kill people. At the corner Bobby stole through a red light and made another mad right at the next corner. He parked on Sixty-fifth Street. And waited. But no Navigator appeared in his rearview.

I'm losing it, he thought.

Just the same, he hopped out of the car, walked to the hatchback, opened it, and triggered a hidden lever that released a section of flat metal flooring that concealed a secret compartment where Bobby stored extra guns and various Snoop Shop devices. He chose a long-handled, mechanical electronic-bug sweeping device that resembled an ice scraper called a Boomerang Non-Linear Junction Detector, which could detect tape recorders, radio transmitters, amplifier microphones, and any kind of surveillance device. His pal Leonard, who ran the Snoop Shop, had said, "This baby can find a bug in a jungle. The second and third harmonic sensitivity differentiates between semiconductor junctions and dissimilar metals."

Bobby had no idea what the hell he was talking about, but when Leonard told him it cost $26,000, Bobby laughed. Then Maggie had Trevor, her stepfather, buy it for Bobby as a birthday present.

Bobby did a fast sweep of the outside of his car. Within thirty seconds the Boomerang lit up like a slot machine hitting the jackpot. The tracking device was almost identical to the one Bobby had placed in Samantha Savage's car. Except this one was an even newer model, and Bobby knew from a PI convention at the Javits Center earlier in the year that these were the sophisticated little tracking devices used by the FBI and NYPD ever since September 11.

Bobby left it where it was for now. He didn't want whoever had planted it to know that he knew it was there. When you discover a bug, it becomes *your* bug. To misdirect the people who planted it.

Knowing he was on somebody's radar screen, Bobby headed back to the *Fifth Amendment.* He dialed Izzy's cell phone, which he'd told Izzy to lend to Herbie for the stakeout. The call went directly to voice mail.

"Herbie, Bobby here, call me with an update."

It was almost midnight by the time he reached the *Fifth Amendment.* He parked the car in the lot, palmed his gun as he walked through the underground garage, and made it on board. The boat was empty, bobbing on the rough tide.

He put away his pistol, opened the salon door, and realized he'd forgotten to set the alarm when he'd rushed out with Janis. He reached for the gun when the lights were flicked on and he squinted into the faces of two white men, who came to fuzzy focus as Noonan and Scarano.

A third guy, Eric, James Ford's muscle-bound driver, stepped out of the kitchenette and placed a pistol barrel at the base of Bobby's skull.

"No fucking around this time," said Eric.

"Is this where I say 'Take me to your leader'?" Bobby said.

"No, this is where you start saying your fucking prayers, asshole," Eric said.

Bobby felt a swell of water rock the boat as the three men formed a pocket around him and led him out onto the deck. Lightning pitchforked in the wet sky, and Bobby saw that a sixty-foot cabin cruiser had pulled alongside the *Fifth Amendment* and lowered a gangplank. The men led Bobby aboard. As he walked, he gazed up at the rotunda overlooking the Boat Basin. The black Navigator sat there like a waiting hearse.

He thought of diving into the water, shouting for help, or fighting these guys. But with three guns in three separate hands, he knew if he resisted, he was a dead man. Besides the water was choppy, with a snotty tide ripping downriver like a mean streak in a giant.

On board, Bobby was led into a salon that looked like a four-star-hotel suite with a sectional white leather couch, matching overstuffed armchairs and leather recliner, marble-topped coffee table, and matching end tables. Velour drapes smothered wooden blinds on the large windows. The big-screen TV set dominated a fully equipped entertainment center. Eric sat on a stool at the full-service mahogany bar near the door. Noonan and Scarano sat on the couch. Scarano lifted a heavy mallet with which he crunched walnuts in a deep wooden tray on the coffee table, popping the crumbled contents into his mouth, chewing the nuts to a sticky paste.

James Ford rocked in an antique country rocker, swirling a glass of white wine, dressed in khaki shorts, a Hawaiian shirt, and Top-Siders with no socks.

"Have a seat, Bobby," Ford said, his voice low and sure.

"Actually, I'm not staying long, so . . ."

The cruiser's motor revved and the boat lurched swiftly downriver in the fast current, staggering Bobby sideways.

"Jeez, guys, no one told me I won a cruise," Bobby said.

"Could change the course of your life," Ford said, smiling, sipping the wine.

"What's the deal, Ford?"

"You're a good investigator."

"Wish I could say the same for you."

"Too good."

"Uh-oh, did we just hit the iceberg?" Bobby said.

Ford said, "Wisecracks won't help you here."

"Sorry. What will?

"Intelligence. We all know you're a tough guy. Now it's time to be smart instead of tough."

Scarano hammered another walnut, picked at the nutty bits amid the shells.

"Be specific."

"It was just a hit-and-run."

"Right," Bobby said. "A hit-and-run murder."

"Get off it," Ford said.

"Then let's see Noonan's and Scarano's tape of the hit-and-run."

Scarano smashed the next walnut so hard it scattered out of the wooden tray onto the carpet. Ford looked at the scattered shells and pointed at them.

"The maid," Scarano said.

Ford continued to point.

"I got a broken toe, Mr. Ford," Scarano said.

Ford kept pointing at his floor. "How many times do I have to tell you to clean up after yourself?"

Scarano got up and began collecting the shell bits from the floor, placing them in the wooden tray with the other walnuts.

"That's a good girl," Bobby said.

Scarano glared up at Bobby. "I'm gonna kill this motherfucker."

Ford continued to point at the floor. "Under the coffee table, too."

"And then go fetch your leash and I'll take you for walkies," Bobby said.

Noonan looked at Ford and said, "I told you not to try talking to this asshole."

"Quiet," Ford said, and turned to Bobby. "What tape are you talking about, Emmet?"

"The one you saw them making of the Twoboro Social Club when the hit-and-run happened," Bobby said.

"Really? And how could I have seen that?"

"On the tapes you got from the Verrazano," Bobby said. "The ones Steve Greco busted your balls about. Before you had him killed. See, I think Noonan and Scarano were staking out Vito "Sleighride" Santa's club on an organized-crime detail. And by accident they got the hit-and-run on tape. Rather than blow their cover, they just kept filming. Then I think they tried to use their tape to blackmail whoever it was that was driving the yellow van. Except you got them on tape trying to blackmail someone. And you blackmailed the blackmailers, using the tapes against them. That's why they work for you like lapdogs. And together the three of you somehow or another are hooked up with Deity, who controls Lethal Injection Records. I have most of the dots connected."

Bobby watched Scarano look from Bobby to Noonan to Ford, who squirmed in his chair.

"You're making things up as you go along," Ford said, smiling.

Bobby checked his watch, yawned, and said, "Nah."

Ford said, "You're in over your head, Emmet."

"Maybe. You throwing me a line?"

Ford stood, walked to the bar, picked a bottle of wine from an ice bucket, poured himself another glass, and took a sip.

"I brought you aboard to see if you want to stay aboard."

"Sink-or-swim time? Explain."

"Work for me."

"Wow-wee kaz-ow-ee, is this my lucky day or what?"

"I checked into you. Aside from being a wiseass, you were a great cop. Worked big cases. Major collars. Gangsters, killers, dopers, crooked CEOs, pols, and judges. You even busted crooked cops in a three-quarters medical-pension scam. And they paid you back with frame-up, a murder rap, and a jail sentence. You're divorced from one of the richest women in New York. All of that and you waste your talents working for a sleazy ambulance chaser."

"Hey, I was innocent and he got me out of the joint."

"True, but look at what you've been doing since. Living on an old bathtub with a cat. A weekend father driving an eight-year-old Jeep. Scrounging out a living helping hip-hop skells stay out of the joint. A man of your talents deserves better, Robert Emmet. For God's sake, you're named for a great Irish patriot, a legend. You should live like one."

"I'm listening."

"Work for me, I'll make you rich."

Bobby pointed at Eric. "You mean, like Eric, here, who you sent to kill me in Lutheran Medical Center the other day and winds up shooting his crime partner?"

Bobby pointed at Noonan on the couch and Scarano on the floor. "Or do you mean I can get to kiss your ass like Special Agent in Charge Noonan over there? Or get down on my hands and knees like Agent Lassie and lick the soles of your shoes?"

Scarano smashed the hammer down on Bobby's right toe. Bobby howled, grabbed his foot, and hopped around the room.

"How's it feel, you cocksucker?" Scarano asked, hoisting himself up and limping after Bobby. "Hah, you broke my fucking toe, you douche bag. Now I broke yours. How's it feel?"

Bobby hopped across the salon, groaning, grimacing. Ford smacked Scarano on the back of the head.

"Moron," Ford said to Scarano, and turned to Bobby. "I apologize for that piece of stupidity."

"This how you treat a new partner?" Bobby asked.

Ford took a sip of the white wine. He looked at Bobby, who stood cranelike on one foot, clutching the hammered one with his other hand. He loosened his boot laces. Bobby glared at Scarano, who sat back down, a small smirk on his face. Noonan swiped the mallet from his hand.

"What do you say, Bobby?" Ford said.

"I can't think with my toe pounding. Plus I'm bursting for a leak."

Ford nodded toward the head. Bobby stepped inside. Lightning flashed outside the tiny porthole window, rain peppering the glass. He saw that they were passing the *Intrepid* aircraft-carrier naval museum at 45th Street as they moved downriver, where the now-defunct Concorde was lashed to the deck.

Bobby relieved himself and rummaged the medicine cabinet. There were the usual array of over-the-counter medicines and products—aspirin, Dristan, Midol, Alka-Seltzer, toothpaste, Band-Aids, eyeliner, Neutrogena pads, shaving cream, aftershave, disposable razors, antiwrinkle cream, a prescription bottle for Zyrtec.

He unscrewed the cap from a bottle of Compound W wart remover and shoved a plastic squeeze bottle of Bain de Soleil into his back pocket.

He took another prescription jar for antibiotics, dumped them into the bowl, and filled it with Obsession aftershave and put it into his shirt pocket, uncapped.

He was about to walk out again, then remembered to limp with the right toe. He wanted Ford and the Feds to think Scarano had broken his toe. But the angry Fed had smashed his mallet down onto the tip of his steel-plated construction boot, specially designed for construction workers to protect their toes from falling tools, bricks, and debris on building sites.

He left the laces untied.

He limped into the salon and Ford now sat on a stool at the bar.

"Some leak," Ford said.

"A real pisser," Bobby said.

Ford laughed. "So, what do you think of my proposal?"

"I'm in."

"Just like that?"

"Just like that, yeah. I'm tired of scrounging. I want mine."

"That's what I thought you'd say," Ford said. "No negotiation. No questions. No numbers crunching. No percentages. No dollar amounts. No risk factors. No curiosity beyond just getting safely off this boat tonight."

"I figure you'll pay well for my silence and cooperation. What am I supposed to do? Contact my accountant? Ask my lawyer to draw up a legal contract for an illegal operation?"

Ford laughed. "At heart, you're still just a cop with no imagination. Cursed with a civil service mentality. Survival instinct instead of a businessman's wary options. If you'd have given me an argument, made me talk you into it, asked me to explain why Cookie Calhoun was dead and why Steve Greco had to die and how many others will also have to go, I might have believed you were actually interested in my proposal. But, no, instead, in a panic, you use the john. You realize there's no escape. Your only move is survival."

"What, I can't just be a greedy, corrupt fuck like you guys?"

"If I wanted another yes-man I'd hire Marv Albert. What I needed was your skills, Bobby. Your talent. Instead you *yes* me. And that's why I'm sorry I have to say *good-bye*."

"You're crazy," Bobby said. "I want in. Talk to me. Before other people who know what I know talk to me about you."

Ford didn't listen, just nodded to Eric and the Feds. "He fell off his own boat."

Ford turned to walk into his main bunk room as the three men surrounded Bobby.

"I know who Deity is," Bobby said.

Ford froze, stood mannequin still. He turned and Bobby saw a splinter of concern in his eyes. "You're bluffing."

"I've told certain people."

Bobby saw Noonan lick his lips. "Mr. Ford, maybe we—"

Ford walked to Bobby, smacked his face. "Who's Deity?"

"We both know who he is."

Ford stared into Bobby's eyes and grinned. "I don't believe you."

"You should. Your life depends on it."

Ford said, "No blood on my boat."

Bobby stomped the arch of Ford's foot, ground his heel into the ligaments. Without looking Bobby reached into his shirt pocket, snatched the prescription jar filled with aftershave, tossed it into Eric's eyes. He yowled. Ford fell. Noonan and Scarano were on their feet with guns drawn. Bobby tossed the Compound W into Scarano's eyes, and he screamed like a man in boiling water. He squirted the suntan oil in Noonan's eyes and used him as a human shield as he backed toward the rear of the boat.

Bobby kicked a beer cooler overboard and watched it spin in the wake of *The Highwayman.*

The two blinded Feds staggered out of the salon, aiming their guns.

Bobby leapt into the black river.

TWENTY-FIVE

Rain gunned out of the wet-wool sky as Bobby was swept into the foaming wake of *The Highwayman*. Then his heavy boots pulled him under. When he fought his way to the surface, lightning illuminated the Empire State Building. He could also see the Thermos beer cooler floating some fifty yards away, bobbing red and white on the inky river.

Before he could do anything, Bobby had to get the steel-toed boots off his feet, or the same boots that had saved his life inside the boat would take him down for good. He'd anticipated that he would wind up in the water, so he'd left the boots untied. He kicked one boot off with the help of the other. Then had a harder time pushing the second one off with his socked foot.

As the storm raged, he felt the boot sucking him down. He tried to keep his eye on the cooler. It was getting away from him in the current. Ford's boat slowed and made a wide U-turn in the river, coming back for Bobby.

Bobby went under. All he could see was a bile green mass as he held his breath and grasped at his boot with both hands. But with no leverage in the river, he spun head over feet several times, pinwheeling downstream. He broke water, exploding his breath and sucking fresh air. He swallowed water. It tasted of oil and sludge and rat shit and death.

He went under again, and as he wrestled with his boot, he felt the vibrations of *The Highwayman* groaning back toward him, the propeller motor churning water, the sound chilling his bones. Then the current sucked him toward the whirring blades.

Bobby paddled. He enlisted every fiber of muscle he'd earned in jail and in all the daily workouts since. His big thoroughbred shoulders pushed him back up for air. He exhaled dirty air and gulped lungfuls of new air and dove deep, under the pull of the propeller, as he breaststroked past the Chelsea Piers at Twenty-third Street. He surfaced briefly and tried swimming for the lighted piers, but the current was too strong. And here came Ford's boat. Again. Cleaving the water like the snout of a monster, aiming to cut him in half.

Bobby arrowed his arms down and as bullets spit into the water around him. He went down, deeper, and deeper, until only a salty, liquid blackness was in front of his eyes.

He held his breath and thought of no one but Maggie. *I will live for you, kid, I will live for you . . .*

Down low, beneath the storm, below the boat, below his city, he glanced upward, and as lightning scribbled in the sky, the cooler bobbed into vague view on the surface current. In the afterglow he could make out Ford's boat some thirty yards to the left of the cooler. Bobby frog-paddled in the direction of the cooler. His lungs ready to burst, his muscles burning, bubbles leaking from his nose, he finally touched it before he broke water. Grabbed a handle. Then he twisted himself onto his back, keeping his body submerged and shielding his face against the far side of the cooler, not visible to the searchlight splaying from *The Highwayman*.

Bobby took slow, measured breaths and pedaled his feet below the water as the current swept the cooler downriver, with Bobby gripping the handle for dear life. Lying on his back he saw lightning sizzle in the sky. Rain stitched his face. As he passed the old Fourteenth Street meat markets, he heard *The Highwayman* rumbling downriver, still beaming the light. Bobby was amazed that no police boats or Coast Guard cutters were patrolling. It was one of the great myths of the war on terrorism. Even after 9/11 the city of New York was wide open to attack from the waterways.

"Did you get the son of a bitch?" he heard Ford shout as the boat passed, beaming the light.

"Gotta be dead," said Noonan.

"Fuckin' dolphin would drown in that storm," said Scarano.

Their voices seemed unreal, like faraway tape recordings, in the wet wind. Lightning scorched the sky. Thunder rumbled across New York, then clapped like the report of a thousand cannons as the current quickened, rushing the cooler and Bobby farther downriver.

After living on the water for several years now, Bobby knew every marina in the New York archipelago. He knew that the North Cove Yacht Harbor, nestled at the base of where the Twin Towers once rose into the Manhattan sky, was back in service after being closed after 9/11. It was the last marina before he would be jettisoned into the busy harbor, where he could easily be killed by ferries, tankers, and tug traffic. Bobby knew that if he was going to make it out of the river alive in this tempest, he needed to make it into the North Cove inlet. Which meant he would have to ford the current and steer the blessed cooler inland.

He waited until *The Highwayman* passed, then he swung himself up onto the cooler, bear-hugged it with one arm, swam against the current with his free arm, kicking his powerful legs across the might of the ancient, unforgiving river.

Every time he seemed to make three feet of progress, Bobby was pushed back two. Paul Simon's "Slip Slidin' Away" played in his head like a death dirge. But he paddled and pedaled on. The muscles in his arms and legs scorching. His hip locked and seared. His right shoulder went numb from overuse.

I'm going to die, he thought.

But then he saw it. Saw the inlet. Saw the dim lights of North Cove Yacht Harbor flickering like dying embers in the downpour. He swam harder. His legs were hollow and limp. He swallowed more foul water. "... the nearer your destination, the more you're slip slidin' away ..." The current was so strong he could not lift his right arm anymore. It was a useless appendage, a doll's arm. Then his legs just stopped moving. And he felt himself being sucked back out into the current, slip slidin' away ...

Then he thought of *Maggie.* Her crumpled face. At his funeral.

And Bobby managed to slap the right arm over the cooler. He swam with the fresh and rested left arm. He swung it until it hit the water like a lone blade of a broken windmill, around and around and around and around. Like a runaway machine. Fierce and determined and very much alive.

And then, all at once, like a free-falling elevator hitting a cushion of air, he felt the current ease. And Bobby spun in a small whirlpool, then felt himself spooling into miraculous still water.

Thirty seconds later Bobby paddled the cooler to the algae-covered stone seawall of North Cove Yacht Harbor. He probed the wall until he found a slick rung of a rusted steel ladder. He could still not use the right arm. Could not feel his feet in the rungs of the ladder. He felt paralyzed from the right arm across and down his torso. He used his left arm to hoist himself up one rung at a time.

And then Bobby Emmet plunked himself onto the granite ledge of Manhattan Island, the most precious rock on planet Earth. He pulled the cooler that had saved his life up on the shore with him. As he lay on his side, panting, rain needling his face, for the first time he noticed a hand-lettered word on the cooler in pink paint—*SO*.

He thought it might mean something, but as he lay there in the falling rain, with lightning splintering the pitiless sky, the only two things he could focus on were his next glorious breath and Maggie. Who'd made him find the reserve he needed to save his life.

After several panting minutes Bobby sat up, back propped against a concrete fence railing. In front of him was the muddy hole of Ground Zero.

Bobby Emmet felt like the luckiest man in New York.

TWENTY-SIX

Wednesday, June 22

The next morning Bobby rented a gray Ford Taurus, as nondescript as a tail car can be, packed a tub of Pampers baby wipes, a few changes of clothes for disguises, two wigs, several hats, three pairs of tinted shades, and sneakers and shoes. He grabbed his spare photo cell phone and left an outgoing message on his river-ruined phone to call his new number. He shoved a pair of what the Snoop Shop called "rearview" sunglasses in his shirt pocket, which were ordinary dark shades except that a half inch of the outer rims of each lens were mirrors, like side mirrors on a car, which allowed you to spy people behind you.

He installed his tracking computer receiver and drove out to Bayside, Queens, by 6 a.m. He sat outside the Bay Vista condominiums where Samatha Savage lived overlooking the Cross Island Parkway and the sun-sparkling sapphire of Little Neck Bay under a rain-scrubbed sky.

It was going to be a long day. He had apples, bananas, sharp cheddar cheese, pumpernickel bread, and a gallon of spring water in the car. He never forgot his half-gallon pee-bottle on a stakeout.

He was convinced that Samantha Savage had placed a bug in his Jeep and followed him to the hospital the night before, then back to the boat basin, and alerted the Feds that he was on the way. Even crazy old Angelina Donatella said Savage had gleaned from her as much as she could about the Cookie Calhoun murder. And Bobby was now certain that Ford was behind Cookie's murder. He also suspected that Savage was in cahoots with Ford. Maybe even Ford's secret lover. The same Ford who'd tried to kill him the night before. But he needed proof. Before he went after Ford, he thought he could get to him through Savage.

He needed to know more about her. Bobby believed that almost everyone had a secret life. Secret alkies, kleptos, chocoholics, sex fiends, abandoned children, people with a buried criminal past. He'd even investigated a gay man once who turned out to be a closet heterosexual. And used his gay pose to conceal his life as a serial rapist of women.

All you needed to find a person's dark secrets was to become his or her shadow.

And from his vantage on Eighteenth Avenue in Bayside, Bobby had a clear view of Samantha Savage's front door and parking lot. He used a pair of binoculars to scope each resident that left. His body was still aching from the ferocious river ride the night before. But he had no real damage. Just a ruined cell phone and sore muscles. Even a man who worked out like Bobby discovered muscles he didn't know he had when confronted with drowning.

He told Patrick about what had happened to him the night before. But they both agreed that the abduction and attempted murder were not provable. Ford, Noonan, and Scarano would simply deny the allegations. Ford would have wiped off any of Bobby's prints on his boat by now. Even the ones in the medicine chest, because they'd know he'd rummaged in there after throwing the aftershave and sunscreen in their faces. The cooler was useless as a piece of evidence. Even if Ford's prints were inside, all he'd have to say was he lost his cooler weeks ago. You can't arrest someone on a coincidence.

Bobby wasn't beat-up or shot. It would be his word against that of two Feds and a decorated retired cop. A waste of time.

Besides, right now Ford and the Feds didn't even know if Bobby was dead or alive. He was best served proving they were responsible for Cookie Calhoun's murder and maybe even Stephen Greco's. Patrick also told him he had still been trying to get his hands on the video footage Noonan and Scarano had shot of the hit-and-run ten years ago. But it was still a federal tape and still considered classified, and unless Patrick requested it as part of a specific investigation, the Feds would not release it. And Patrick wasn't a cold-case cop.

"I do have a few people inside, though," he told Bobby. "They're gonna try to burn a copy off for me. Might take a few more days."

"My mark just showed."

"Later."

Bobby slumped lower in his seat as Savage walked from the front door and along a walkway to the parking lot, dressed in jeans and sandals and a sporty summer top. He followed her as she strode to her black Navigator, clicked the remote, and climbed in. She didn't even look at herself in the rearview mirror the way 98.6 percent of hot women do before starting the car and peeling out.

She drove out of the lot and passed him right by as she headed up to Bell Boulevard and drove through a to-go and ordered a large coffee. Bobby watched from across the street, then dogged her onto the Cross Island Parkway.

Bobby stayed about fifteen car lengths behind, driving in the right-hand lane, as the tracking device in her car made an orange blip on his computer terminal that displayed a digital map of the tristate area. He expected Savage to head off toward the Grand Central Parkway to the Brooklyn-Queens Expressway to Brooklyn, or Staten Island, maybe even to the Midtown Tunnel to Manhattan.

He was surprised to see her take the Whitestone Bridge toward the Bronx. He watched the blip and was more surprised when she merged into the Hutchinson River Parkway north toward upstate New York.

He followed at a discreet distance until he saw Savage get off at the Saw Mill to Route 117.

"Where the hell is she going?" he said aloud, eating a banana, as "Hey Jude" played on the car radio.

Then the blip on the screen made a sharp left onto something called Harris Road and proceeded at a slow pace for a half mile. Then the blip on his screen went still, pulsing. Meaning Samantha Savage had parked.

The whole trip had taken about thirty-six minutes in light traffic.

By the time Bobby drove to within visibility of the black Navigator, he saw that it was parked in the visitors' lot of the Bedford Hills Correctional Facility—a maximum-security female prison housing some twenty-eight hundred inmates accused of murder, bank robbery, kidnapping, drug trafficking, gangbanging, child abuse, extortion, even rape. This was where the notorious 1960s radical Kathy Boudin did her twenty-two years for the death of two cops in the infamous Brinks armored-car robbery.

Bobby dialed his brother Patrick again and asked him to see if he could request which prisoner a suspended NYPD Member of Service named Samantha Savage had visited at Bedford Hills.

"That could take a full day, because it'll have to go through channels," Patrick said. "I'll have to explain why I'm requesting it. Since nine-eleven, every single request on the NYPD computer has to have a cop's name and tax ID number attached. And it's all monitored in fear of terrorist infiltration."

"She is suspended and under investigation," Bobby said. "You're in the Intel Division, for chrissakes, little bro. Just say you want to know which known felons she's visiting, because this can't be an official visit while she's suspended. And if she's saying it is, she's in deeper."

"That'll work."

Bobby drove to a McDonald's, ordered two garden salads, a large orange juice, a cup of tea with milk, and six oatmeal cookies, and sat eating, drinking, and listening to talk shows for the next two hours. He peed, washed his hands with a baby wipe, and punched on the oldies station. After ninety-nine minutes, he saw Samantha Savage leave the all-women's prison, wiping her eyes with a tissue and blowing her nose.

Spying her through the binoculars, he could see that her strong, pretty face was crumpled with grief. This time when she climbed into the Navigator, she sat for several minutes, slumped over the steering wheel crying, wiping her eyes. Then she put eyedrops in her eyes, applied fresh eye makeup, fixed up her hair, and drove off toward the city.

Bobby stayed on her tail, a mile back, following the electronic blip.

Savage returned to Bayside, proceeded to the Bay Terrace shopping mall, which was essentially a huge parking lot surrounded by stores. She stopped in Boston Market for lunch. Bobby sat in the parking lot and killed another hour, watching her through the big window.

Then Savage shopped in the Gap and Express, for another hour. Bought new sneakers in Foot Locker, and then he saw her enter Victoria's Secret, which ate up yet another hour. Bobby put on a blond wig, rose-tinted aviator shades, a Mets hat, and got out and peered in at her shopping in the underwear section. She fingered thong panties and a lace teddy. Bobby imagined her in the frilly undies, and the images got jumbled up with a reverie of Cookie McNulty on that rainy day, and the sultry smile of Scarlett Butler bathed in the magenta light of sunset.

He was growing aroused. He doused his urges with thoughts of his dinner with Dianne Rattigan, who he suspected was somehow in bed with James Ford.

Broads are nuts, Bobby thought. *From a state pen to a panty rack.*

Bobby watched her pile all the new clothes into her Navigator and then go into Waldbaum's to do a food shop. Bobby strolled around the Bay Terrace shopping mall, checking out the new books in the window of Barnes & Noble.

In the reflection of the bookstore window he saw Savage push her shopping cart to the Navigator and load in the groceries.

Bobby followed her back to her condo complex and watched the doorman help her unload all her shopping into the lobby before parking the car.

Bobby kept sitting on her, staking out the condo complex.

He was convinced that eventually she would hook up with someone that would reveal something to him. There was a secret in her life. Maybe it was up in Bedford Hills. Maybe it was upstairs in her apartment. But she was hiding something.

Two hours later Savage emerged from her condo in jogging gear and new sneakers. Bobby was wearing sneakers and put the wig back on and pulled on a hoodie and trotted behind her down to the two-and-a-half-mile walkway along Little Neck Bay.

Bobby put on the "rearview" shades.

He jogged a hundred yards behind Savage, admiring the way her ham muscles bunched into hard, round cantaloupes in her spandex shorts. Several men and a few women turned their heads when they passed Samantha Savage, headphones plugging her ears. She was in phenomenal shape, jogging at brisk seven-minute miles from one end to the other, passing Bobby once on the return trip, but not recognizing him as he bowed his head in his hoodie, wig, and rearview shades.

Dozens of other joggers, power walkers, in-line skaters, dog walkers, and couples treaded the esplanade as the magenta sun set on magic hour, passing the quaint Bayside Marina, which Bobby had docked at a few times over the years.

Then Bobby watched her make a detour down the marina pier that fingered out into Little Neck Bay. At the end of the pier was a small concession stand that sold soft drinks and burgers and fries and fish, tackle and bait. People rented boats from a second concession. About two hundred boats were docked at the marina and the outlying mooring fields. Men and women and teenage boys fished for eel and red snapper off the end of the pier.

Bobby watched Savage buy a sixteen-ounce bottle of Poland Spring water and guzzle it in two long gulps. She paid the counterman, asked him for a pad and pencil, scribbled something onto the paper, and walked to the end of the pier. Bobby watched her twirl the note into a tight cylinder, shake the remaining drops from the plastic bottle, and stuff the note inside. She screwed the cap on the bottle.

A note in a bottle, Bobby thought. *Is this chick gonna ice herself?*

Bobby saw her check her watch, then look around, checking to see if she was being followed. Bobby cheered on a kid yanking a wiggling snapper from the bay.

Then in the rearview glasses he saw Savage toss the Poland Spring bottle off the pier into the placid waters. A thirty-foot Stingray swooped out of the southern expanse of the bay, and Bobby saw it head straight toward the bottle. He watched Savage rush off and turn her head once, in the direction of the boat, then resume jogging. The Stingray approached and slowed and half-circled the bottle. A man with a long-handled fishing net scooped the bottle into his netting. Bobby turned and saw that it was the same man who caught the pigeons for Iglew's tiger. The engine revved. And then the Stingray roared off, speeding toward the Whitestone Bridge. Bobby pulled the small spyglasses from his hoodie pocket and focused on the name on the disappearing boat: *TB II.*

"Son of a bitch," he mumbled.

Bobby raced to keep Savage in sight as she jogged back home.

He went back to his rental car, stripped to the waist, and cleaned himself with baby wipes, knowing Savage was upstairs in a nice hot shower. Maybe not alone. He remembered that Scarlett had told him that Ford had a secret girlfriend that no one knew about somewhere in the city. He wondered if Savage was that woman. Maybe that's why Ford was in the courtroom that day at Tu Bitz's trial. And why she'd crumpled so badly under cross-examination. And why Noonan and Scarano were also there.

They'd gotten to her.

Or she'd become Ford's woman. And then they'd double-crossed her. He was trying to make all the threads stitch together. No matter which way he weaved them, they formed a noose, form-fitted for Samantha Savage's neck.

Bobby sprayed on underarm deodorant, put on a clean shirt. Forty minutes later Savage emerged from her lobby dressed in skintight, white clam diggers and sandals and a black belly shirt and drove to the Loews Bay Terrace movie theater. She bought herself a ticket. Bobby counted to ten-Mississippi, then went to the cashier and said he was late, that his girlfriend had just bought a ticket. He couldn't remember the name of the flick. He described Samantha Savage to the ticket girl.

"Lucky you," she said, smiling, punching out a ticket to the latest Julia Roberts movie. "Lucky her, too."

Bobby paid for the ticket, searched for and found Dianne Rattigan's phone number, called her, and told her he was running late and might not be able to make dinner until ten o'clock. She said that would be fine; she'd start cooking at nine.

"I've been thinking about what you asked me," she said. "I wrote down what Cookie Calhoun told me that day in my logbook. I gave it to Detective Ford. But I made a Xerox. I always do in case of a lawsuit. I dug it out and have it stashed in a safe place. I'm afraid of sharing it with you. You have to talk me into it. It depends on how many wines you force on me. But I'm kind of afraid. I want to help that family, Bobby. I don't want that poor kid to hurt himself. But I want you to reassure me I'm going to be safe. Especially from that cop."

"I won't let anything happen to you," Bobby said.

"I need you to convince me when you get here."

Bobby said he would and hung up.

Ugh, he thought. *I'm leading this poor woman down the garden path.*

When he entered the theater lobby, Samantha Savage stood at the concession counter. Bobby walked past her, wearing his disguise, and into the theater showing the Julia Roberts chick flick and took an aisle seat on the left-hand side of the theater. Women always sat in the center rows.

Bobby sat through the coming attractions and slumped in his seat when he saw Savage enter with a small bag of popcorn and a small soda. *Why do chicks always eat a small bag?* Bobby wondered. *One kernel at a time?*

She took an aisle seat in the second row of the center section.

The theater was half full. Then as the credits for the main attraction began to roll, a black man entered the theater alone in a flap of lobby light and took the aisle seat directly behind Samantha Savage. When the music swelled over a loud opening sequence, the black man leaned on the back of Savage's chair and whispered in her ear. Bobby couldn't hear what he said. But he saw Savage nod. Her shoulders rigid. Her hand frozen in the popcorn bag. The black man reached around her and put his hand in the popcorn bag, dropping a note. Then he grabbed a handful of the popcorn from the bag. He ate the popcorn and whispered some more in Savage's ear as she stuffed what he'd given her down her bra.

The black man glanced over at Bobby, who sat wearing the Yankees hat and the Woody Allen glasses and the long, hippie-style blond wig.

"Fuck you lookin' at, Frosty?" Iglew asked, chomping popcorn.

Bobby turned away, hunched his shoulders, and slumped lower in his seat like an intimidated nerd.

Then Iglew whispered in Savage's ear again, grabbed and ate more popcorn, massaged her neck, then stood, shot his cuffs, traced the backs of his fingers over her high cheekbones, and kissed the top of her head. He glared at Bobby, who cowered in his seat. Then Ignatius "Iglew" Lewis strutted out the back door of the theater.

Bobby sat watching for another ten minutes as Savage placed her popcorn on the floor and lifted her small soda to her lips with two trembling hands. He figured she'd put her note, possibly from the inmate she'd visited upstate, in the plastic bottle. Threw that in the bay. Where it was picked up by a boat named after Tu Bitz. Who probably gave the information to Iglew to meet her here, in the dark, unnoticed. Where he passed her his response.

Too weird, he thought.

They didn't want to be seen together or use phones to communicate. And now Iglew had given Savage some new information that had her rattled, trembling, unable to eat even a small bag of popcorn, which a good-size gerbil could devour during the first ten minutes of a Julia Roberts flick, which was made for popcorn lovers.

Bobby watched Savage check her watch several times. Iglew had probably instructed her to stay for at least ten minutes so that they would not be seen in the same borough together.

Then Samantha Savage got up to leave. She paused in the dark and whispered to Bobby.

"Sir, I want to say I am so sorry he spoke to you that way," she whispered. "Really I am."

Bobby grunted and waved her off, head bowed.

She left in a wash of lobby light as the door opened and closed. Then Bobby counted to fifteen-Mississippi, took off the Yankees hat, turned his reversible jacket from the blue side to red, pulled on a white, nylon mesh hat with a Mets insignia, a pair of small oval shades, and followed.

Halfway across the darkened parking lot Bobby saw the unmistakable tight white pants approaching Savage's black Navigator. She pulled jangling keys from her clutch purse. Then Bobby's pace quickened with the speed of his heart when he saw another black Navigator slither from a spot at the far end of the lot. With its lights off. Windows as black as the eyes of a shark. Bobby's skin prickled, hairs rising on the backs of his hands.

He wrapped his right fist around his .38 caliber revolver and started to run. Savage looked at the ground as she approached her car, the headlights flickering and alarm disengaging with a beep as she hit the remote. In the flicker of her black Navigator's headlights Bobby saw a kiss-shaped dent near the left rear bumper of the second black Navigator. Then he saw the tinted passenger window of the moving Navigator power down. Four inches. Just enough for the long barrel of a silencer to emerge.

"Sammy!" Bobby shouted at full sprint.

Savage spun. She was so startled she almost fell over her own feet. Just as the muzzle flash lit up the night. Bullets stitched the driver's door of her car. Her side window shattered into cubed diamonds.

The tires of the second black Navigator squealed a U-turn. Bobby ripped off several shots in midair as he dove at Savage. He smashed into her at fierce force, wrapping his arms around her, knocking the wind out of her lungs. Smothering her body with his, he dragged her close to the first black Navigator. A second eruption of muffled bullets sizzled from the second black Navigator, perforating Savage's vehicle and sparking as they skipped off the tarmac of the lot.

Savage felt toned but soft in all the right places beneath him, trembling as the shooting continued. He looked down at her. She gaped into his eyes. Terrified. "Don't let me die, Bobby," she said.

As bullets skipped around them he kissed her lips. He didn't mean to. It was an impulse. Then Bobby rose to a kneeling position, fired three more shots, puncturing the back window of the fleeing second Navigator. The getaway Navigator swerved down Twenty-first Avenue, making a mad right through a red light and careening toward the Clearview Expressway. He could not make out the license plate number in the dark.

"Hold me," Savage said, trembling on the concrete ground. "Hold me, Bobby. Please hold me."

TWENTY-SEVEN

He continued to hold her long after they were finished making love in her king-size bed in the condo overlooking Little Neck Bay, and then in the shower where they lathered each other with soap and shampoo.

"Hold me," she said again.

He stood her under the nozzle, letting the water run down her smooth, tight back, and stared her in her beautiful but still-frightened eyes. He flattened the palm of his large hand against the small of her back.

"No more room for lies," he said.

"The truth can get you killed, too. I can't."

"Let that be my problem. Who'd you visit in Bedford Hills?"

"You followed me there?"

His hand on her back moved lower. She moaned. "You left sobbing."

She made an indignant move for the shower door. He slammed it closed, pinched an erect nipple between his thumb and forefinger, and held her in place.

"This is the place to come clean. Who'd you visit?"

"I can't tell you that. It could get *her* killed."

"Why'd you toss the note in the bottle into Bayside Marina?"

"You son of a bitch . . . I can't tell you that either."

He squeezed her nipples harder. "Tu Bitz picked it up. The guy you *busted*. The guy you testified against. Whatever was on the note brought Ignatius Lewis to the movie house to see you. What's up with that? You fucking *him,* too? One of his honey-dip sack chasers?"

"Never," she said, slapping his face.

234

He slid his hand down her back and crunched one cheek of her buttocks in his big paw.

"Oww."

"You carry a signed picture in your wallet. 'Love, always. Iggy.' "

"I posed as a fan."

"Backstage groupie. What they call a heave-ho?"

She dug an elbow into his ribs. He squeezed her harder. She yelped.

He said, "You on his payroll?"

"Negative!"

"You rent your tin?"

"Absolutely not!"

He spun her around, grabbed her second nipple, leaned forward to her face under the hot spray and kissed her. She bit his lower lip. He became aroused again.

"Tell me," he said, his lips circling her lip on the letter *m,* then spinning her around. "You're standing here naked. You just made love to me in every conceivable way imaginable."

"You saved my life," she said as he entered her from behind. She made a soft mewl, then arched her back and backed into him slowly.

"Tell me," he said as he thrust into her.

"Oh, *God* . . . But please don't make me regret it."

"Tell me why Iglew came to see you, what he said, before he tried to have you killed back there."

"He would never try to have me killed."

She grabbed the overhead nozzle pipe with one hand, pulled him deeper into her with the other. He grabbed a handful of her sudsy nappy hair as she thrust backward into him, water running off her flawless skin.

"Who was in that other Navigator?"

"Oh, baby . . . I don't know."

"Iglew arranged it."

"No!"

"How can you be so sure he didn't try to kill you?"

"Oh . . . my . . . God . . . shut up talking."

"How do you *fucking* know?"

"Because Ignatius loves me!"

And he plunged deeper and she panted and growled and let out a war whoop as she bucked and writhed and streaked her hands down the wet, soapy wall until she grabbed her ankles and Bobby also erupted.

She turned and looked into his eyes, dreamy with orgasm, her face shrouded in steam and suds, smelling of apricot soap and herbal shampoo. She kissed his lips and sucked his tongue into her mouth.

"That . . . was . . . amazing," she said, looping her arms around his neck.

"Is it this good with James Ford?" Bobby asked, reaching behind her and turning the faucet joystick all the way to cold.

In those brief three seconds it took for the hot water to empty from the pipe before turning icy cold, she said, *"What?"*

Then he hugged his arms around her wasp-thin waist and blocked the shower door with his bulk, as the freezing water blasted her back. She screamed.

She unhooked her arms from his neck, wrestling to get free. But Bobby held her in place, under the freezing shower.

"You fuck!" she shouted.

"So do you. Anyone who can get you ahead! Me. Iglew . . ."

"I never slept with him."

"But James Ford is your secret lover."

"The only thing I'd touch Ford with is a bullet," she said, shivering, fighting to free herself from Bobby's atomic grip in the freezing shower.

He held her under the spray as she shivered, dark nipples hardening, shoulders narrowing and shrinking into herself.

"Bobby . . . I . . . wish . . . I could tell you . . . everything," she said, teeth chattering and lips blueing.

"You're not getting out of here until you do."

"Oh . . . my . . . God. I'm not that weak! Go ahead. Give me pneumonia. I am not now nor have I ever been Iglew's or James Ford's lover. That I can tell you. I despise Ford. He . . ."

"He what?"

"I can't tell you."

"Then don't ask for my help."

"I *need* your help," she said, looking into his eyes, shivering. "I need you."

"Showering with you is making me feel dirty."

He let go of her, stepped out of the stall, toweled off, sprayed on deodorant, and dressed in clean clothes he'd brought up from his rental car.

He looked at her. She shivered, her teeth chattered, and she wrapped her arms around herself.

"You say such hurtful things," she said. "I made love to you."

"You used me," Bobby said, dressing. "Where I come from, that's called getting fucked."

"I need your help. Please don't leave me. Where are you going?"

"Actually, honey, I have a date with an older woman," he said, hoping that might stir up a new activity that would cause someone to make a mistake.

"You're a bastard."

"When you climb to that status, give me a call," Bobby said, tying his shoes and walking out the door.

TWENTY-EIGHT

Bobby carried the bouquet of daisies and the two bottles of chardonnay down Bay Ridge Parkway, checking the addresses. He'd bought two bottles of wine because he was going to get Dianne Rattigan stewed if that's what it took to get her to tell him what Cookie Calhoun had told her in the ambulance before she died a decade ago. It had taken Bobby over fifteen minutes to find even an illegal spot for the rental car in Bay Ridge.

Dianne Rattigan lived about a mile from Janis McNulty, who had left several messages for him. But first he had to go through the cautious motions with Dianne Rattigan, who knew something about that long-ago hit-and-run. He had to be cagey. This could be a trap. He had his 9mm automatic in his belt and a .25 in his front pants pocket. At the least he expected there to be cameras or tape recorders going. So he'd also brought his portable pen-shaped bug sweeper from the Snoop Shop. The pen had a sensor that picked up any microwave or radio-frequency waves between 100 hertz and 1.5 gigahertz. It worked on the same principle as his Boomerang Non-Linear Junction Detector and would vibrate in his shirt pocket if any recording devices were in operation in Rattigan's room.

He didn't know if this money-conscious middle-aged woman had been bribed or threatened or both, but Rattigan knew something she wasn't telling him. He'd already made love to one woman he didn't trust. He couldn't stomach another. But he was determined to get the information out of her whether it took wine, charm, or a few threats of his own.

He found the building, pulled open the heavy street door, and entered the vestibule. He rang the bell for apartment 2C. He waited a minute. No

238

answer. He rang again. Waited. Then he heard the sound of a trash can rattling outside and turned and looked through the street door. He saw a janitor in a Mets cap and wearing work gloves drag a garbage can out of the downstairs alley where the building's trash cans were stored and leave it at the curb. Then he noticed the janitor stroll to a dark vehicle parked at a hydrant about twenty-five yards up the block from the building, with its engine idling.

Bobby was angry with himself for not spotting the idling vehicle when he'd walked in. He was too busy searching address numbers. Bobby stepped down the two steps from the doorbell panel, placed the flowers and wine parcel on the marble floor, and peered out from a better angle. The janitor in the Mets cap took his hands out of his pockets. He was still wearing gloves. In June. The janitor climbed into the vehicle.

An SUV, he thought, getting a better look. *Christ, no . . .*

The SUV lurched from the hydrant spot, and as it pulled into the glow of a lamppost, he saw that the back window of the black Navigator had bullet holes in it. His heart thudded. He'd made those bullet holes in a parking lot in Queens a few hours before.

Bobby yanked open the street door, pulled out his 9mm, and ran after the black Navigator that rocketed up Bay Ridge Parkway. The chase was futile. He ran instead to the building where Dianne Rattigan lived. He didn't bother ringing her bell again. He shouldered the door that was secured with a flimsy bell-and-buzzer catch lock and ran to the second floor to apartment 2C. He didn't need to jimmy this door. It was unlocked. "Lying Eyes" by the Eagles blared from inside.

Bobby entered and walked across the gleaming parquet floors of the foyer and onto the soft deep pile of a Persian rug in the dining room. He held the bug sweeping pen aloft to see if he was being taped or bugged. The pen remained still. It didn't vibrate. He switched it to the light mode and the red light didn't light up either. The room was bug-free.

The outside of a cube-jammed silver ice bucket drooled cold sweat. On a side serving table, carved wooden salad spoons with Celtic engravings stood erect in a matching engraved wooden bowl of arugula mixed with red grapes, crumbled feta cheese, and thin slices of red peppers. Fresh bakery Italian bread lay cut in an Irish-linen-lined wicker basket. The smell of salmon and garlic wafted in from an adjoining kitchenette. Two candles waited to be lit in Waterford crystal candleholders on the table that was draped with a white-on-white Irish linen tablecloth with matching folded napkins and set for two with blue delft plates with Celtic designs and sparkling Waterford wineglasses and sterling silverware.

Bobby feared there was one setting too many.

He was right.

The Eagles kept singing about the cheating side of town when Bobby entered the bathroom where Dianne Rattigan's body hung from the polished-brass shower-curtain rod, secured by a pair of black panty hose that had been garroted about her soft neck. She wore a brand-new Lord & Taylor skirt suit with a string of expensive imitation pearls and matching earrings. Her hair had been freshly cut, styled, colored, and blown out, and her nails on the strong hands that had saved thousands of human lives were neatly manicured and painted a soft sunset pink. A string of rosary beads with a Celtic cross hung from her right hand. Her portable Bible and black high heels, three feet apart, lay on the bathroom floor in a pool of her own urine that had formed inches below her bare feet.

Bobby figured Dianne had clutched her rosary and Bible for solace and pitiful protection in the final moments before her death that she knew was coming. The smooth black soles of the high heels told him they'd never been worn outside her condo door and had been bought for her dream date with Bobby Emmet, whom she called Samse. But who Bobby knew was just another rotten prick of a man bent on exploiting her, before someone else robbed her of her life.

If she'd never met me, he thought, *she'd still be alive. Like Steve Greco.*

Bobby hadn't cried in a long, long time. But at this moment he felt like letting the rapids flow. He didn't. He didn't want the release. He wanted to store the anger, guilt, and anguish until it built into a monstrous killing rage. He wanted to keep that rage roaring like a furnace inside so that if and when he killed the person who'd done this to this kind and lonely woman, he would have not one gram of guilt at leaving that scumbag in a pool of his own postmortem piss.

He thought of cutting her down but didn't. Instead he called his brother Patrick on his cell phone, told him as much as he could fit into one minute, and asked for another ten minutes to look around before Patrick relayed it as an anonymous tip to the local precinct.

"You gotta bring this to a head, bro, before they kill or frame you," Patrick said.

"Been there, done that."

Bobby entered the bedroom and saw that the drawers had been rifled.

Bedding disturbed. Closets rummaged. The killer had been searching for something, then fled when he heard Bobby ring the doorbell.

He used a paper towel to poke around, certain not to leave any fingerprints. The Eagles greatest-hits album cross-faded into "Take It Easy" as Bobby searched countertops, wondering where she might keep something she'd written down a long time ago. He sifted through junk drawers, a rolltop desk, bookcases, and an old shoe box in the bedroom closet filled with mortgage papers, old tax records, divorce papers, and legal documents. Someone had already been through everything that Bobby checked. He glanced at the wall clock. The cops would probably be here in another four or five minutes.

He checked the oven, microwave, dishwasher, the freezer, the kitchen cabinets. He lifted the Persian rug in the dining room and glanced behind framed museum-exhibit posters of impressionist artists, probably bought on afternoons when she'd wandered the great galleries alone. He searched through her pocketbook, but there was nothing of interest. There were no photos in her wallet—no nieces or nephews, no children of her own.

He placed his piece of salmon, his baked potato, and his ear of corn into a Ziploc bag and carried it with him so that the police would not think there was a dinner companion. He put away his table setting—silverware, plate, napkin, wineglass, candle, and candleholder—in their appointed places in the china cabinet.

He looked at the clock again and was about to leave when he saw a holy water font under a crucifix by the front door. An old-fashioned Catholic, Dianne obviously blessed herself every day before she left to deal with the dead and dying. And on her way home she stopped and lit candles for them in hospital chapels, taking the names of the people she'd promised to pray for from behind the flap of the portable Bible. . . .

He froze. Removed his paper-towel-covered hand from the doorknob and hurried back into the bathroom. He lifted the Bible that lay in the urine between the high heels on the floor. He rinsed it under the cold-water tap that he turned with the paper towel. Then shut off the water.

He dried the Bible cover and looked behind the book jacket flap. It was jammed with note papers. He didn't have time to go through it now. He walked back toward the front door. He paused at the holy water font and walked back to the table. He lifted the book of matches from the table, lit the one remaining candle, and although he was what he liked to call a retired Catholic, he dipped his right hand into the water and blessed himself in honor of a good woman who did not to deserve to die that way.

". . . take it ea-sy, take it ea-sy . . ."

He left with the Bible just as the elevator approached the second floor.

Bobby hurried to the stairs and went up one flight, listening to the cops stepping off the elevator on the second floor. He pressed the elevator button on the third floor.

"First let's see if it's real before we call the squad," he heard one cop say. Then he heard what sounded like a nightstick rapping on a heavy door. "Miss Rattigan, it's the police, you in there, hon?"

The cops rang her doorbell and banged the door again. This time a female cop called, "Ms. Rattigan, it's the police. Open the door please. Or we're coming in."

The elevator opened on the third floor. Bobby stepped on and pressed the lobby button. As the elevator descended he peered out the wired, circular window as it passed the second floor. He caught a glimpse of two uniformed cops entering Dianne Rattigan's apartment, pistols at their sides.

Bobby stepped off the elevator in the lobby, walked to the vestibule, collected the daisies, and put the Ziploc bag with the dinner Dianne Rattigan had made him in the wine bag, saw the police patrol car double-parked out front, and hurried down the street to his illegally parked rental car.

He clutched Dianne Rattigan's Bible in his fist.

TWENTY-NINE

Bobby drove the rented Taurus up Bay Ridge Parkway to Fort Hamilton Parkway as another police cruiser and a detective car pulled up in front of Dianne Rattigan's building and made a right on Seventh Avenue. He wound through the night streets of Bay Ridge, checking his rear- and side-view mirrors to be certain he wasn't being tailed. He wasn't.

He made a left onto Ninetieth Street and parked in a pool of shadows on the tree-darkened street. He killed the headlights and sat in gloomy silence for several minutes, gun in his fist, checking his mirrors, listening, watching, to be sure that he had not been followed. Not one car drove past in three minutes.

He lifted the Bible and opened the flap and clicked on his penlight, which could not be seen from outside. He'd removed evidence from the scene of a crime, which was a crime. But he'd done it in hopes of solving an old murder that he was certain was at the root of Dianne Rattigan's. Eventually homicide detectives might be able to connect the dots. But not in time to save Brian Calhoun from himself. Plus he didn't think the Bible would mean much to anyone else. Except those responsible for killing her. The janitor wearing the Mets cap he'd seen leaving Dianne Rattigan's condo building wore gloves in June, which was what had made Bobby suspicious to begin with. Whoever killed her had gone there with that intention and wouldn't have left prints.

But they might have left something better. A clue to Cookie Calhoun's murder.

He opened the Bible and took the note papers from under the flap. He looked at the names of the maimed, the sick, and the dead that Dianne Rattigan had stored there. They were people she'd attended to that day and maybe the day before. One was a knifing victim in Lutheran ICU, another an auto accident DOA, one was a baby who had fallen down a flight of stairs and fractured its skull.

Then he found one that was folded into one of Dianne Rattigan's obsessive little squares, with gorgeous parochial-school handwriting on the outside of the fold: *For Samson's eyes only. Ha ha. CC's last words.*

A chill shivered across Bobby's shoulders as if Dianne Rattigan had just shaken him like a patient who was losing consciousness. She'd made a clandestine joke out of the note containing Cookie Calhouns final words, saying they were for Bobby's eyes only. She probably planned on teasing him with the note. Bobby figured she'd probably planned on playing a little cat-and-mouse parlor or bedroom game with Bobby after too much wine with that dinner that no one ever got to eat.

Bobby took a deep breath, thinking, as his lungs filled, that Dianne Rattigan would never get to take another one. Never find her second act in life that she'd been searching for amid the damaged and the dead of Brooklyn. Then Bobby opened the Xerox of a page from an old logbook. He read her notes:

> Hit&run vic, Carla Calhoun, delirious, mumbling. Vic appears to have broken pelvis, spine injury, collapsed lungs, arms and legs broken. Massive internal inj. & bleeding. Last words: "She's doing Rodney's time . . . she's doing Rodney's time . . . and now they're gonna kill me because I know who Deity is . . . don't tell her . . . don't tell her . . . don't tell her . . . Rodney knows I know who Deity is . . . don't tell her . . .don't tell her . . . don't tell her . . . She's doing Rodney's time . . ."

The rest of it was filled with medical jargon about the nature of Cookie Calhoun's injuries and the medications and emergency medical procedures performed in the ambulance on the way to the hospital.

Bobby was frustrated. *Don't tell her? Don't tell who, what?*

And who was the woman doing Rodney's time?

The only female prisoner Bobby had come across since working the Cookie Calhoun case was the one Samantha Savage had visited in Bedford Hills that morning. The identity of whom he wouldn't have until Patrick got back to him tomorrow.

For knowing this vague bit of disjointed information they killed Dianne Rattigan? Bobby thought. But why now? Ten years later? There could only be one reason. Because they knew that Dianne knew that Cookie knew Deity's identity. *And she was going to tell me about it,* Bobby thought.

And Bobby could think of only person who might have known Bobby was going to visit Dianne Rattigan. *I told Savage I had a date with an older woman,* Bobby thought.

He had told Savage that just to wound her for being evasive with him. To knock her and all her treacherous beauty down a peg. But Bobby feared she might have figured out who it was. He'd seen a black Navigator leaving Lutheran Medical Center right after he'd first spoken with Dianne Ratti-gan. And so after Bobby had left her naked and shivering in the shower stall, she could have climbed out, dressed in a fury, and sped to see Dianne first. While he was shopping for flowers and wine and searching for a legal parking spot. But the black Navigator on Dianne Rattigan's block was the one with the bullet holes in the rear window. The one from which someone had shot at Samantha Savage in the movie-house parking lot. He blinked into the darkness, his mind a maze of what-ifs.

What if somewhere along the way today she realized I was following her. Maybe in the movie house, when she looked straight at me and apologized for Iglew's nasty remark, he thought. *And then what if she had Iglew stage the attempted hit on her. And then bedded me. A little too easily. To figure out what I knew, and my next move, and guessed right that it was to get Dianne Rattigan to tell me Cookie Calhoun's dying words.*

And then, he figured, Savage might've called Iglew and told him to go and have Dianne whacked to keep what she knew about Deity's identity secret.

He banged the steering wheel, guilt and rage and betrayal boiling in his guts.

Nothing is too paranoid, he thought. *Think outside of the box in these paranoid times and you are trapped in a bigger box, like a series of ever-larger Chinese boxes.*

He needed to narrow it down, magnify it all by ten, needed to know who Savage had visited in prison. Whoever it was might be the one whom Cookie Calhoun said was doing Rodney Calhoun's time.

He searched through the rest of the bits of paper, but nothing else meant anything to Bobby. He started the car. And drove like a homing pigeon toward the night lights of the Verrazano Bridge. Rodney Calhoun was in a bed in a nursing home on the other side. When Bobby came to the corner of Ninety-second Street and Fort Hamilton Parkway, he stopped for a red light. And realized he was sitting across the street from Twoboro Social Club and Janis McNulty's building. Idling in the very intersection where Cookie Calhoun had been murdered. He leaned across the seat and gazed out the passenger window at the tenement building, which was owned by Exit 82C Inc., James Ford's dummy corporation with a Cayman Islands address. Angelina Donatella's windows were darkened, an aging, frightened goom sitting in the gloom. The lights were on in the McNultys' apartment. Dull light leaked from under the door of the social club.

He thought he saw a sliver of light as a curtain moved on one of Angelina Donatella's windows, but the motorist behind him beeped his horn the microsecond that the light changed from red to green. Bobby made the left onto Ninety-second Street, then drove a half block and made the fast right where the yellow van that had killed Cookie Calhoun had made its decade-old getaway.

Before him the Verrazano glowed against the dark, sleeping mammoth of Staten Island, and Bobby imagined it as the on-ramp to purgatory.

He also imagined the driver of the yellow van speeding along the extended bridge approach, merging with the other endless traffic from the Belt Parkway, then crossing the big span. And then he imagined the yellow van vanishing into the murky netherworld of Staten Island that was held together with backroom political deals, the greedy whims of overfed gangsters, and at least one crooked cop who ruled the roads of the forgotten borough like some feared and fabled highwayman. In some ways Staten Island was more like a corrupt Southern town run like a fiefdom, by a power broker like Vito "Sleighride" Santa and a corrupt sheriff like James Ford.

Bobby paid the toll in cash so that there would be no record on his E-ZPass that he was ever here and drove straight to the Narrows View Nursing Home.

THIRTY

Through the black hood of his sweatshirt, Bobby felt the barrel of the gun at the base of his skull as he peeked in the front window of the Mustang.

"If your name ends in a vowel and I owe you money, this is the time to say bye-bye, Mamma mia," Herbie said, cocking his .357 Magnum, which fit his immense hand like a derringer.

"Christ, I owe *you* money, Herbie," Bobby said. "I thought you might be sleeping."

Bobby turned around outside the gates of the Narrows View Nursing Home where Herbie had been on stakeout, watching for signs of Rodney Calhoun for a day. The nursing home sat on the shadowy rise overlooking the Narrows, a way station for eternity, the last stop for the old-timers with Alzheimer's before the graveyard and anything that might lie beyond.

"Herbie Rabinowitz never sleeps on the job. Especially when I got dagos dunning me."

"I thought you joined Gamblers Anonymous, Herb."

"I did, but I got thrown out for running a Super Bowl pool. I mean, Jesus Christ, but these people are fucking sticklers. Anyone who don't bet on the Super Bowl should be indicted under the Patriot Act, no?"

"What are the odds that Rodney Calhoun isn't in his bed?"

"I wouldn't take your money. He's in there, enough space between his ears for a three-bedroom condo, drooling enough to fill an Olympic-size pool. I've been sitting here a day, popping Hydroxycuts like Tic Tacs, the old ones with the ephedrine, doing push-ups, sit-ups, working with my dumbbells, watching that shvarzter's window with the binocs, and the only thing I seen move in and out are the Rasta piss-pan brigade. I thought the

Hasids were moon shots with the curlicue lice ladders and the Grizzly Adams beards and the fur hats in July, but the Rastas with their dreads and their Jiffy Pop hats and their all-day ganja-for-God routine run a close second on the loony-tunes scale. Fact, I've been up all day, doing a lot of thinkin', and if heaven's gonna be filled with Rastas, Hasids, nuns, boy-buggering priests, suicide-bomber-blessing imams, and born-again generals and congressmen, I'm seriously considering giving up my Orthodox ways, gobbling a coupla BLTs in a Russkie massage parlor on the Sabbath, and reserving a place at the big green table at the great crap game in the subcellar of oblivion. Whadda you think, Bobb-o?"

Herbie couldn't stand still, arms and legs moving like Michael Jackson onstage, the .357 dangling from his right fist, eyes popped like Ping-Pong balls, his tongue a pasty white, and his yarmulke bobby-pinned on the side of his head the way the hip-hop crowd wore their baseball hats.

"If you showed up in heaven looking like that, you'd have it to yourself, Herbie."

"I'm serious, Bobb-o."

"I'd suggest you sleep on it."

"How can I sleep knowing that Brian Calhoun kid might off himself because he blames himself for his mother dying?" Herbie asked, popping two more Hydroxycuts and gulping them down with a bottle of Jolt, a triple-caffeine-fueled cola. "So I ain't sleeping till we figure this one out."

Bobby knew gym rats who used the legal, over-the-health-food-store-counter, ephedrine-laced Hydroxycuts for rapid weight loss, but they made you wired. Intense. Impulsive. They also made pleasant people short-tempered and watchdog mean, snapping at family, friends, and foes for the smallest of reasons.

"Easy on those Hydroxycuts, Herbie," Bobby said. "They could make an Amish elder do a skyjacking."

"They don't do shit to me," Herbie said, popping another pill. "Fact, I'm gonna go back and tighten that health-food-store yuppie's neck like a window shade. I think he sold me the ephedrine-free pills."

Herbie was a nut bag after one coffee. Sleepless for a day on Hydroxycuts and packing a .357, he was a tabloid headline waiting for the presses. Bobby didn't like drugs, but these were legal, and after what Ford, Iglew, and their goons had tried to do to him and what they succeeded in doing to Steve Greco and Dianne Rattigan, Bobby wasn't sorry that Herbie was juiced on gorilla biscuits.

"Come on, take my back."

Bobby had dressed in black sneakers, black pants, and black hoodie. He took a black gym mat from the trunk of Herbie's car, draped it over the razor wire at the top of the Hurricane fence surrounding the nursing home, and he and Herbie scaled the fence and slinked along the parking lot to the laundry building annex.

The hum of washers and dryers spinning from inside the one-story annex covered their footfalls. A sprinkle of stars and a half-moon peeked out of a partly cloudy sky. Bobby tossed a grappling hook attached to a nylon rope up to the roof, lassoed a galvanized-steel steam-chimney pipe, and climbed, his muscles still smarting from the Hudson River gauntlet the night before.

Herbie kept watch, shielded by a large outdoor generator. Bobby scurried across the roof and peered in Rodney Calhoun's window. Heavy night drapes blocked his view. Bobby tried opening the window. It was locked. He took out his Swiss Army knife and tried jimmying the lock. After three minutes of trying, Herbie appeared behind Bobby.

"Trouble?"

"Yeah."

"Want me to do it?"

"You know how?"

"Does a rabbi take his tax exemption?"

"Okay, give it a try."

Herbie pointed the .357 and fired before Bobby could yell, *"No!"*

The sound was deafening. Bobby's ears rang. He couldn't even hear himself say, "You asshole!"

He also didn't hear Herbie shout, "What?"

Bobby pushed aside the drapes and peered in.

Rodney Calhoun's bed was empty.

The bedding was pulled as tight as a snare drum in neat little hospital corners. Herbie's bullet had perforated the center of the down pillow, a blizzard of down feathers floating in midair as a panicked nurse entered. She screamed when she saw Bobby and bug-eyed Herbie, scratching his scalp with the muzzle of the smoking .357.

"Am I a great shot or what?" he said. "Wouldda went right through his eye."

Bobby pushed Herbie toward the rope. He shimmied down. Herbie jumped, landing in a tumbling roll. A security guard raced out the front door of the nursing home, raising a pistol. Herbie approached him. The panicked guard assumed a shooter's stance.

"You got a problem, asshole," Herbie said.

"Stop! I'm warning you!"

Bobby yelled, "Herbie, stop!"

"Fuck this guy."

Herbie rushed the guard. The guard fired. Dead center. Herbie fell. Bobby's heart sank as adrenaline burst in him like a splatter, inflaming his chest and flushing his face.

"He wouldn't stop," the guard said. "He wouldn't stop . . . I tried to warn him."

But Bobby was too shocked by seeing Herbie get up off the tarmac and starch the guard with a single right hand. And as Herbie bent to pick the guard off the floor, a black Navigator with its lights out raced out the front gates.

"I always wear a vest when I owe money to the wops," Herbie said.

"We gotta go, Herbie," Bobby said, rushing for the fence.

They scaled it, Bobby told Herbie to meet him in the parking lot of a McDonald's near the entrance of the bridge on Hylan Boulevard, and they both took off from the nursing home as cop cars with lights and sirens going approached the front gates.

THIRTY-ONE

By the time Bobby got to the McDonald's parking lot, Herbie was already sipping a large coffee. He handed Bobby a container.

"You've been sitting on that nursing home for a day and you never saw Rodney Calhoun leave?" Bobby said.

"No."

"Did many cars come and go?"

"Nah. I mean, funeral parlor collects dead old-timers like a garbage pickup every day. Then new people are delivered in ambulettes. Sick old whiners are taken to the hospital, most of them old Yids with gas complaining of coronaries, my guess, trying to milk Medicaid for every last shekel before they put pennies on their eyes. I know my tribe."

"Did you check them out?"

"How am I gonna toss every hearse and ambulance and stay undercover?"

"What about that black Navigator?"

"That comes and goes."

"How often?"

"Twice a day . . . like that."

"How do you know Rodney wasn't in it?"

"Because, I cut in front of it once. Made the driver stop short."

"Did he get out?"

"No. She didn't get out."

"A woman was driving it?"

"Yeah."

"What did she look like?"

251

"Ya know, like a broad."

Bobby sipped the coffee. It wasn't bad. "What color was her hair?"

"I dunno, she wore a hood, dark shades."

"Young, old, decrepit? What?"

"Maybe twenny, twenny-five, thirty or thirty-five, forty, like that."

"Great. White, black?"

"That's a really good question."

"You don't know what color she was?"

"It was dark. She didn't get out. She wore a hood, gloves, and shades at night. Whadda I look like, some kinda racist to you? I'm still grappling with worldwide anti-Semitism; being a mockie ain't easy in the terror age. You think the dune coons picked New York to bomb because there's so many wops and micks? So I have no idea if she was white, Porto, light-skinned shvartzer, a high yalla, sand monkey, or a wahoo. She wasn't a Chink, that I can almost swear to. I was kinda busy checking out the inside of the Navigator, making sure Rodney wasn't in there, which is my j-o-b, no?"

"You sure he wasn't?"

"Positive."

"Who else was in the van?"

"A white guy."

"How can you be so sure?"

"He had hair like one of the Beach Boys."

James Ford, Bobby thought.

"He gets out, mouthing off, flashing a badge, saying he could have me locked up," Herbie said, reenacting the scene. "I told him I'd ram his badge so far up his ass he could wear it as braces. He reached behind him like he was going for a gun. I grabbed his hand and yanked his thumb backwards until he yelped like a kicked poodle. The chick kept hitting the horn, yellin' for him to get back in the car, that they had a piece of work to do. I told him that would be a good idea before I ripped off his balls and roofed them. Finally he did. And they raced away and that was the end of that dance."

Bobby's phone began to ring.

"Did the Navigator have bullet holes in it then?" Bobby glanced at the window of his cell phone and saw Izzy's number and answered it. "Hold on, Iz, I'm with your lunatic cousin. . . . Urgent . . . so's this, hold on, I said."

Izzy kept yelling as Bobby flattened the phone to his chest.

"I didn't see any bullet holes when they left," Herbie said. "But I went back to my stakeout perch and they came back later. That time they did."

"Who else left the nursing home?"

"Night workers. Women mostly. A few jabbering Guadaricans, a few urine-colored doctors who drove Jap cars, a small herd of Rastas passing blunts. This is what we got to look forward to in old age, Bobb-o, being a ninety-year-old monkey in the middle of the League of Third World Nations until one of 'em gets tired of wiping your ass and they put the pillow over your bony puss and—"

"These Rastas, couldn't Rodney Calhoun have been one of them?"

"He's a zombie and he doesn't have dreads."

"Faking the Alzheimer's, wearing a wig?"

Herbie drained his coffee. "I never thought of that. That's why you're the boss."

Bobby looked at the stars, then at the Verrazano, then off toward Jersey. Stuck between heaven, hell, and Herbie, he thought. "Where would a degenerate gambler who doesn't want anyone to recognize him go?"

"Speaking from experience, definitely not AC or Vegas because they have cameras everywhere," Herbie said. "He'd look for a down-low game."

"Not in Manhattan, either, right?"

"Maybe Harlem, but they might know him there, too. Certainly not here on Staten Island, either. My bet is a Chinaman, a game in Queens or Brooklyn. Gimme five hundred felt gelt and lemme try and find him."

"You already lost him once," Bobby said, counting out five hundred-dollar bills and handing them to Herbie.

"I'm gonna make him pay for that," Herbie said, and jumped back into the Mustang and roared off toward the Verrazano.

Bobby lifted the phone to his ear and said, "What's so urgent, Izzy?"

"Someone tried to stab Golden in the joint tonight," Izzy said. "His bodyguard took the blade. The guards stepped in. They got Golden into solitary."

"Did he call you?"

"Yeah, he's ready to pull the trigger. He's terrified. He wants to get out. He's ready to play."

"When will he be out?"

"I was at the Brooklyn courthouse earlier where Golden's papers have been sitting for six months. He's not a bad jailhouse lawyer, this scheming fuck. But I rewrote them anyway, cited four different appealable issues, including prosecutorial suppression of exculpatory evidence, a Fourth Amendment issue, an incompetent defense, at least three questionable rulings, and a whisper to the Brooklyn DA that Golden might be able to shed light on an old murder."

"How soon, Iz?"

"I'm getting to that. First, can't I demonstrate how fucking brilliant I am? The first thing I learned on Brooklyn's Court Street was Boss Tweed's old saw that 'it's better to know the judge than the law.' If you know both, you're God's caddy. Not only do I know Judge Arthur Cranberry, I used to clerk for this horny WASP fuck when he was old, before he got ancient, and I used to call up the escort services for him and have them come to chambers. He paid them with judicial credit cards. And this was in pre-Viagra days when he needed a string attached to a helium balloon to get it up. He never wore pants under his robes, used to play with his balls while handing down decisions. I can't tell you how many good-looking female defendants walked at bench trials in Judge Cranberry's court and then literally got down on their knees to thank him in chambers."

"A new low for Lady Justice."

"I gave Cranberry his first box of Viagra ten Christmases ago. Now there's this new pill, Cialis, better than Viagra, that gives you a boner on demand for two days in a row without the stuffy nose and the flushed face. I brought him a six-month supply from the dirty Paki online pharmacist I'm defending, and I told him I'd bring him someone to demonstrate how good it works at court tomorrow, and so Cranberry is ready to spring—get it?—Golden in the a.m., setting aside the verdict and inking a new trial date. Which means Golden'll break-dance out the door. Is that a great fucking piece of work or what?"

"Literally."

"Meet me at the Brooklyn courthouse at nine a.m. I don't want anything to happen to this poor son of bitch on the way home," Izzy said.

"That's not gonna be his first stop anyway."

THIRTY-TWO

Thursday, June 23

As rain pecked at the big courtroom windows, Izzy made his formal motions in front of Judge Arthur Cranberry, and with the reluctant blessing of the State Attorney General's Office, Sid Golden's verdict was set aside. It took just shy of ninety minutes to clerk Golden out of the system, and Izzy kept pacing the hallways, checking his watch. Then the elevator opened and Izzy said, "Here she is now."

Just then Bobby finally saw the court officers lead Sid Golden out of the side courtroom door. Bobby steered him straight to the stairway. He didn't want to get on an elevator with anybody who might try to whack him in the tight space. Bobby had used his ID card showing that he was a retired cop to avoid going through the metal detector at State Supreme Court in Brooklyn. He had his 9mm jammed into his waistband, covered by a Hawaiian shirt. He carried a folded copy of the *Daily News*.

Izzy paused in the hallway and shook hands with a gorgeous brunette woman in her midthirties with big dark eyes, cheekbones like a pair of Alps, and a mouth that made Angelina Jolie look thin-lipped. Her short white skirt was offset by red high heels.

"Room 401J," Izzy said. "Give him the GFE experience, Francisca, and keep the heels on. Talk dirty to him in Spanish, capice? Always call him Your Honor. His favorite line is 'I throw myself on the mercy of the court, Your Honor.' After that he loves his taint munched when you go snorkeling under the robes. Got all that?"

"No prublum, Issy."

"And don't expect a tip. Because besides being as tight as a Korean tick's ass, we might need him on your appeal if we go down at trial."

"I understand, Issy."

Izzy followed Bobby into the stairwell as Francisca went in search of Judge Cranberry's chambers, clacking her red heels on the municipal marble of Brooklyn past an alabaster statue of the Blind Lady of Justice.

"That's why they say the law is an ass," Izzy said, following Bobby and Golden down the stairs.

"In Brooklyn it's a piece of ass," Bobby said.

"So what do you think of her?"

"What're you gonna do if the judge finds out Francisca is Francisco?"

"Some guys like to do it in the keister for Easter, but Cranberry only likes a little Monica for Hanukkah."

"Gleason's Law 101."

"First, lemme tell you about Gleason's Law sixty-nine, as in juror number nine."

"I don't wanna know any more," Bobby said.

"What the hell are you guys talking about?" Golden said.

"You don't ask questions, humpo," Izzy said. "I just gave you back your shit life because you're gonna answer some questions. Like where're those cooked books?"

"Get me out of here safe and alive," Golden said.

As they reached the basement level, Bobby drew his weapon, covered it with his folded *Daily News,* and walked past the County Clerk's Office, where jury duty was handled, and various civil and criminal record rooms. Clerks pushed carts loaded with dockets and other blue-backed court papers. A janitor pushed a big broom across the shining floor. Bobby flashed his ID to a court officer at the side door and they exited into Borough Hall Park via a side entrance through which millions in municipal funds had gone missing over the decades.

Bobby stepped out first, surveying the soggy park, ghostly empty in the falling rain. Attorneys hurried from the subway, carrying briefcases and shielding themselves with umbrellas. A kebab guy stood idle under his colorful umbrella as smoke scattered in the wind around him. A Parks Department parkie bossed around two black guys wearing orange Community Service jackets and hoodies who had been ordered to clean the park as part of their alternative sentence of the court. Bobby thought it was great how justice worked in Brooklyn. Young black guys cleaned parks in the rain for misdemeanor offenses as a sitting judge was serviced by a kneeling transvestite con artist in his chambers in exchange for cutting loose a gold smuggler, who had been framed by a dirty cop for drug conspiracy under the Rockefeller laws, a cop who Bobby believed was responsible for Cookie Calhoun's murder.

It made some twisted sense, he thought. The law sucked.

Bobby waved Golden and Izzy out and directed them toward Adams Street where he had his Jeep parked.

Bobby scanned the street for black Navigators or anything else that looked suspicious. Nothing stood out.

"I'm getting soaked," Golden said.

"Freedom really sucks like that," Izzy said. "It rains on the outside."

Bobby looked back toward Borough Hall Park to see if anyone was following. No one was. Just two Community Service guys in orange vests raking the wet green lawn.

Bobby opened the Jeep, shoved Golden into the backseat, handing him a bulletproof vest. "Put this on, stay down on the floor, and keep this over you."

He laid a bulletproof blanket on top of Golden. Izzy looked at Bobby.

"What, I don't rate a lead blanket?" Izzy said.

Bobby grabbed a bulletproof vest from the backseat and dumped it on Izzy's lap.

"Got anything smaller, in gray, to match the suit?"

"Yeah, a bullet."

Izzy said, "You really think—"

"They tried to kill him inside. You don't think they're gonna try it out here?"

Golden spoke up from the backseat. "Nice. Now I'm free to die?"

Bobby pulled from the spot as Izzy donned his vest.

Izzy said, "Where we going, Sidney?"

"It's been eight years; I'm kind of foggy."

"Okay, get out," Izzy said.

"Take Flatbush Avenue," Golden said.

"Which way?" Bobby said,

"The Jew way," Izzy said. "Out."

"If Prospect Park is still there, at Grand Army Plaza, veer toward Eastern Parkway."

"We're going to Crown Heights?"

Golden said, "You expected the Golan Heights?"

Bobby kept watching his mirrors. He didn't see anyone unusual on his tail. He'd removed the bug from his Jeep, but in the rain he had failed to give it a quick sweep. But he didn't think he was being followed.

He took Eastern Parkway out to Crown Heights, where the Caribbeans and the Hasidic people had lived side by side in fragile peace since August of 1991 when a black child killed by a car driven by a Hasid triggered a riot that left a different young Hasidic young man stabbed to death.

Both populations had coexisted since then in the same neighborhood, without major incidents.

"I would give my right arm for a Kornblatt's knish," Golden said.

"Where do we turn?" Izzy said.

"Right on Utica, three blocks, make a left."

Bobby followed Golden's instructions and slowed on the side street.

"You got a broad stashed here?" Izzy asked. "If you do, take it from me, after eight years, she's either banging somebody else or she's so fat you'll hope she is."

"The synagogue," Golden said.

In the center of the street was the Young Israel of Crown Heights Jewish Center, a compact, little red building that looked as if it had once been a firehouse.

"You hid the cooked books in a Jew temple?" Izzy said.

Golden said, "You can think of a better place?"

"The rabbi probably threw them out," Bobby said.

"No way," said Golden.

"Was he in cahoots?" Izzy scratched under the bulletproof vest. "Taking a piece in the elbow to run interference with the law? Or was he smuggling gold, too?"

"No, no, no. It's a very poor temple. I just made Rabbi Yurick a gift."

"What kind of gift?" Bobby asked.

"Let's go in, and I'll show you," Golden said.

Bobby held the 9mm under the *Daily News* as he walked Golden down a flooded side alleyway alongside the temple. He rang a doorbell. They waited in the rain for a full minute.

"This Rebbe got West Indians as Shabbes goys here? Shabbos shvartzer or what? Forget CPT, whoever the fuck's inside is on Island time, which is about eight gears slower than homegrown Colored People Time. Ever order a tropical drink in the islands? By the time the Rastas ganja-mope your piña colada to you poolside, it's coconut soup. Like they shipped it down from their aunt's house here in Brooklyn on a Haitian raft. I'm convinced those people will discover how to reverse aging, mon, because they already discovered how to make time stand still—"

The door to the temple finally opened, revealing a wizened, white-bearded rabbi.

"Rabbi Yurick, it's me, Sid Golden?"

The rabbi cupped his ear and shouted, "Aaah?"

Izzy elbowed Bobby and said, "He's why they call it *Young* Israel. Dollars to doughnuts his grandmother's inside making soup."

"Sid Golden, Rabbi . . ."

Bobby kept looking down the alley, to make sure no one was following. Cars passed on the side street, tires whispering in the rain. No black Navigators passed. A cop car slithered by, followed by a few nondescript cars, a municipal green truck, a couple of yeshiva vans, and a series of yellow school buses. All of them inching slowly behind the prowling cop car, unwilling to honk their horns at the cops.

"Sid who?" The rabbi searched his pockets for his glasses, squinting into the rain.

Across the street a Hasidic man scattered grass seed on his newly turned front lawn. The leaves on the tree above him were still budding to life in the first week of summer. Something bothered Bobby about it. But as thunder barked from the brooding sky, Bobby couldn't put his finger on it.

"It's me, Sid Golden, Rabbi Yurick! I made you a gift of the golden Aron Hakodesh. The Holy Ark for the scrolls, a special gold ark for your Torah."

Izzy whispered to Bobby, "The ark is the abracadabra center of the synagogue. Just like if it ain't a Duncan, it ain't a yo-yo, without a permanent Holy Ark with at least one handwritten Torah scroll containing the Five Books of Moses, then it ain't a synagogue. This shitbird made the rabbi the ark to store the scrolls in, which for a rabbi is as important as my scrotum is to me. They also store other sacred objects in the ark like the megillah, which is the Scroll of Esther, that they read on Purim, or maybe your basic havdalah set, ya know, the candle and the spice box used for Shabbat, and maybe the shofar, the ram's horn that they blow on Rosh Hashanah. It ain't Louie Armstrong, but put two Jews under one roof and it's a given one a them is gonna toot his horn about his son's grades. Those are extras. The main thing is the Sefer Torah, scroll of Torah. Believe me, I had this shit beaten into my skull as a kid. This beard gotta love Sid Golden, because if you give him a gift like that, a golden ark, you're taking El Al first-class straight to heaven, all expenses paid."

The rabbi found his thick glasses, yanked them behind his ears, and narrowed his eyes as he peered at Golden.

"Sidney Golden?"

"Yes, Rabbi, I just got released and I need—"

Rabbi Yurick flung open the door and waved them in from the rain to the rear living quarters of the synagogue. It was stuffy without air-conditioning. Fans blew the humid air around. Izzy and Golden grabbed yarmulkes from a small table and placed them on their skulls. Izzy tossed one to Bobby. "Put on your Yid lid, goy boy."

"I have a bone to pick with you Sidney Golden, okay?" Rabbi Yurick said, slamming and triple-locking the heavy steel door.

"What, Rabbi?" Golden drifted into the temple area, moving toward the Holy Ark in the small chapel that could hold maybe two hundred people. The Ner Tamid, or Eternal Light, hung above the ark. Dull, rainy light shone through a floor-to-ceiling stained-glass window bearing a large leaded-glass Star of David.

"The colored boys broke in, okay? They tried to steal my ark, okay? I pulled out my pistol, okay?" The rabbi pulled a pistol from his pocket, waved it around.

"Shvarzter's with tigers," Izzy said. "Now rabbis with rods. While in Rome . . ."

Bobby lowered the rabbi's gun. "Easy, Rabbi. We're not here to steal anything."

"I fired a bullet over their heads," Rabbi Yurick said. "They dropped the ark."

Golden said, "Oh, shit."

The rabbi cupped his ear with his gun hand and said, "Aaah?"

"He said, 'Oh, shit!' " Izzy cleared his throat after shouting and mumbled, sotto voce, "You deaf fuck."

"That's what I said, too," Rabbi Yurick said. "After they left and I picked up the ark that this schmuck told me was solid gold. It chipped when it fell and I saw it wasn't solid gold at all. I said, 'Oh, shit!' Some gift! God will punish you, Sidney Golden!'"

Izzy looked from the rabbi to Golden and said, "Tell me you didn't make him a gold-plated lead ark, you cheap prick. You made steel-plated solid-gold football trophies for gangsters and a gold-plated lead Ark for your own rabbi? The Rockefeller laws are too good for you!"

"Look at it this way," Golden said, shoulders hunched, palms up. "If the colored kids got away with it, no great loss, right? Like built-in insurance."

"You're a disgrace, Golden!" Rabbi Yurick said. "You're nothing but a *cheap Jew!* A gank-ster! A cheap Jewish gank-ster that gives us a bad name with your gold-plated ark! I have my sacred Torah scrolls in a lead ark! You son of a bitch! I prayed you would *never* get out!"

But Golden was already at the ark, running his fingers down the smooth side, where he popped open a hidden panel. From inside the hollow bottom he removed an old ledger. As preserved as the day Golden went to jail.

He handed it to Izzy and rubbed his hands together in a mission-accomplished gesture, shooing them away. "Even Stevens."

"Aaah?" said Rabbi Yurick, cupping his ear.

Izzy said, *"He said, 'even Stevens.' "*

"Even Stevens my ass," Rabbi Yurick said. "You owe me a gold ark, Sidney Golden! Or I will spread the word in the community."

The word *community* lit up in Bobby's head like an orange flare. It clashed with the image of the guy laying grass seed across the street under a budding tree. What the hell was the Community Service worker outside the courthouse with the orange vest doing raking a lush green lawn in June? In the rain? Made no sense. It was the cover of a guy raised in a concrete jungle. Then he remembered the municipal green truck rumbling down the street outside the temple. Twice. *A Parks Department truck,* he thought

Bobby pulled his own gun. Thunder clapped across Brooklyn like a scolding from the heavens. And then the stained-glass window exploded in a storm of colored shards. A litter basket hurtled into the temple. All Bobby could see in the mayhem was two orange vests. Then Golden diving for cover, three bullets indenting his bulletproof vest. The gold merchant slid with a scream behind the altar pulpit. Izzy belly-surfed under a pew. And after his eyes adjusted to the blinding muzzle flashes, Bobby focused on the two orange vests again, the same ones worn by the Community Service workers downtown. Both of the guys wearing them fired automatic weapons, holding them sideways like in John Singleton movies.

Bobby shot one in the hip in midair, spinning him around in a crimson scream.

"Mama, I'm a die!" he howled.

The rabbi stood in front of the ark, bathed in the Eternal Light, and fired at the second guy, who fell into a mash of jagged glass. Face-first. He scrambled amid the razor shards. Pushed himself up. Wobbling. Gushing blood. The shattered glass opened deep slashes on his hands and face and he staggered through the shattered window frame into the street, helping his wounded pal, who screamed, "Mama, I'm a die! Mama, I'm a die!" Their orange vests were bulletproof, Bobby thought, drawing a bead on his head.

The rabbi fired at him first, blowing off a lump of his neck. But the man staggered through the empty window frame into the rain-swept street as a man dressed in a Parks Department uniform sprayed bullets into the synagogue with an Uzi.

Bobby had to tackle Rabbi Yurick, who would not move from in front of the ark.

"Gimme the ledger, nobody dies," the black man shouted.

Bobby fired at him. Now the rabbi aimed and fired, whizzing a shot right past the Uzi shooter, smashing the driver's window of the Parks Department truck.

"You Jew motherfuckers crazy!" the gunman shouted, backing away, firing.

"Le's book!" shouted the slashed and shot guy.

"Mama," screamed the other wounded one.

Bobby got up when the Uzi gunman dove into the rear bed of the Parks Department truck and the glass-slashed one fishtailed away from the curb.

Inside the rabbi approached Sid Golden. "You hid something dirty in the ark, in my house of God, you son of a bitch?" He still had the pistol in his hand. Bobby gripped his arm.

"I had no choice, Rabbi," Golden said. "I couldn't trust anybody, everyone turned against me."

Rabbi Yurick smacked Sid Golden's face. "Get out!"

"All of this will be paid for, Rabbi," Bobby said.

"All of you, get out!"

"The police will come," Bobby said.

"They come twice a month already," he said. "Leave them to me."

Bobby held the ledger in one hand and his pistol in the other as they stepped through the glass and the blood and out the window frame, back into the rain.

THIRTY-THREE

"He can't stay here," Izzy said, unlocking his office door, picking up an Express Mail envelope that had been shoved through his mail slot. "This is my office. This is where I do crucial private consultations with broads. Like juror number nine, who just sent me the signed papers and a little something extra, it looks like."

"It's the safest place in the world," Bobby said, leading Golden through room number B378 in the basement of the Empire State Building, the steel door emblazoned with the legend *Israel Gleason Esq. Attorney at Law.* "Look how long it took us to get in the building. You have NYPD, FBI, the Terrorist Task Force, Homeland Security, bomb-sniffing dogs, and private square badges and more security cameras and metal detectors than the White House here now."

Bobby flicked on the overhead fluorescent light, where one rod blinked and hummed like a dying lightning bug. Bobby showed Golden a double bed in a small conference room, and the bathroom with a sink, toilet, and shower stall. The main room had a desk, sofa, file cabinets, small TV, clock radio, fridge, microwave oven, and phone.

"I stayed here awhile when I first got out of the can," Bobby said. "Especially in the winter months, when the boat was cold. Good location. Safe. Never use the phone. You have to lay low for a few days."

Bobby plopped into the swivel desk chair and opened the ledger detailing Golden's old gold-smuggling rackets. "Decipher this chicken scratch," Bobby said.

"They teach you in yeshiva that the only way to protect yourself from lawyers is with the penmanship of a doctor," Izzy said, ripping open the

Express Mail envelope and removing the legal contracts, and a videotape. His eyes narrowed. "The fuck is this?"

"That's why the ledger reads like a prescription for arsenic?" Bobby said.

"We must have gone to the same school," Golden said.

"Find the June twenty-fifth entries," Bobby said.

Golden put on his thick, state-issue glasses and pulled the desk lamp closer and inched his nail-bitten right index finger down the fountain-pen-inked entries.

"Here it is," he said. "June twenty-fifth . . ."

Bobby looked at the entry as Izzy poured sugar-free cherry Kool-Aid into a bottle of Poland Spring and guzzled it and walked into the conference room with the videotape, in a panic as he read an accompanying note.

"All I see is numbers and initials," Bobby said.

"The numbers are kilos of gold minus the weight of the packaging and the steel casings," Golden said. "There were eight hundred and thirty kilos of gold wrapped in thirty-seven kilos of steel.

"Who drove the goddamned van that killed Cookie Calhoun?" Bobby said.

"QD," Golden said, jabbing his finger into the paper.

"Who the hell is QD?"

"We used the letter of the alphabet preceding the worker's real initial for the first name. And the letter following the real initial for the last name."

"Whadda we need here? A Hebrew Enigma machine? This ain't fucking Synagogue Scrabble, Sid. Tell us who QD is on the QT."

Izzy pushed the videotape into the VCR and hit play.

Bobby looked at the ceiling and said, "So QD is really . . ."

"RC," Golden said.

"So QD is really RC, and RC was who, Sidney?"

Golden looked at a code key on a separate page and glanced up at Bobby.

"Rodney Calhoun," Golden said.

"Oh, holy fuck," Izzy screamed from the conference room.

Bobby bent over the ledger papers, tracing his finger down the numbers and initials. "And who the hell is his helper? HM?"

Bobby started mumbling the alphabet to figure out the decoded letters.

Golden said, "You mean IL."

Bobby nodded. Golden searched his coded key and his list of scrambled names.

"Some kid he hired that he said he loved like a son," Golden said. "Iggy."

"Iggy?" Bobby said. "As in Ignatius Lewis?"

"Yes. Iggy Lewis."

"I'm fucking doomed," Izzy shouted from the conference room. "Bang goes my piece of the house! My license!"

Bobby ignored Izzy, leaned over Golden. "Iggy was driving?"

"No, he just helped him load the truck."

"Rodney drove that much money around on his own?"

Izzy's cell phone rang in the conference room. Bobby heard Izzy shout, "It's a bad connection, Herbie. You tracked who to where? Okay, I'll tell him, but I got bigger worries right now. I'm watching myself get fucked outta a million clams in living color."

"No," Golden said to Bobby. "The drivers never went alone. Never."

"A tail car?"

"Sleighride always sent someone to ride shotgun."

"You mean to ride behind him in case of a roust, or a hijack by rival skells?"

"Yeah. They'd pick them up a block or two away after they were sure they weren't being tailed by the police. No one ever knew any names. Sleighride sent his own people to watch his investment until it was safe on board a ship. According to my records, that day it was loaded onto a freighter in Port Richmond, Staten Island."

It all fit together for Bobby. The yellow van killed Cookie Calhoun, then sped over the Verrazano and delivered the cargo of golden football trophies on the James-Ford-protected highways of Staten Island and had them loaded onto a freighter in Port Richmond, bound for the Caymans.

"You know what the tail guy looked like?" Bobby asked.

"It was a woman."

"A woman? He sent a woman to babysit a couple of thousand pounds of gold? Brilliant idea. Who'd be looking for her?"

Thinking, *Don't tell her . . . Don't tell her . . . Don't tell her . . .*

"A police officer," Golden said. "On Sleighride's pad. A real honey, I heard."

Bobby thought about Samantha Savage, and how much of a honey she'd been covered in suds. She'd rented her tin to a mobster as a young cop. And all these years later she was probably still trying to get her piece of the action that she was screwed out of back in the day. Probably recruited by James Ford. *And the one who killed Dianne Rattigan,* he thought.

Bobby walked into the conference room where Izzy sat on the edge of the bed, despondent. Bobby closed the door.

"Rodney, Iglew, and Savage," Bobby said.

"Bobby, she fucked me," Izzy said.

"The key to it is Rodney."

"Herbie called and said he thinks he tracked Rodney down to a Chinese gambling den in Sunset Park. Goes from midnight to five a.m."

Bobby nodded. "I'll call him. What the hell are you so upset about?"

Izzy hit the play button with his remote, and Bobby saw Izzy having sex with juror number nine. "Oh, *Jesus,* turn it off," Bobby said, shielding his eyes.

Izzy hit the stop button. "Bitch has me live on hidden camera having sex with a client in exchange for handling her divorce," Izzy said. "I can be disbarred."

"What does she want? Is she blackmailing you?"

"She wants me to continue to represent her. Pro bono! Or else the DA and the ethics panel get the tape. Here I am thinking I'm fucking her and she's fucking me."

"As Dorothy Parker once said, 'Sometimes the fucking you're getting ain't worth the fucking you're getting.' What are you gonna do?"

"What can I do? I'll be on her retainer for life! This twat."

Bobby's cell phone rang again. This time it was his brother Patrick, telling him he needed to see him in person.

THIRTY-FOUR

At 3:43 p.m. Bobby bought a chicken kebab sandwich with lettuce, tomatoes, and tahini sauce, and Patrick ate the lamb, from the stand outside the Brooklyn Army Terminal where the NYPD Intelligence Division was located. Patrick had a file folder under his arm.

They carried the sandwiches and sodas to the hood of Bobby's Jeep and ate standing up.

"Six different cops had this poor Arab investigated," Patrick said. "Including me. Had the food tested for poisons. Had his vendor's application vetted. I just think he has big balls to open a kebab stand outside the NYPD Intelligence Division after nine-eleven."

"They didn't create civilization because they're stupid. He knows the squad has been tripled and that everybody's working OT, and that cops get paid shit and so they eat shit. Actually, this isn't bad."

"What I got for you is bad. Or good. Depends on how you look at it."

"What?"

"You doing this Samantha Savage babe?"

Bobby shrugged. "I think she did me. Why?"

"She tied into Dianne Rattigan's death? That's still listed a suicide."

"Maybe."

"That means you think Savage might've been involved in her death."

"Somehow, maybe. I'm working it."

"So far it has nothing to do with Intel, but if it does, I want it."

"Of course."

"Because it might be. Listen, Detective Samantha Savage was part of a task force. And she's suspended. And it all just doesn't look pretty for the PD."

"What doesn't?"

"You asked me to find out who she visited in Bedford Hills yesterday."

"Right.

"She visited Delilah Toole."

Bobby stopped in midchew, wiped his mouth with a napkin, took a slug of soda, and said, *"Who?"*

"She visited her mother. Delilah Toole, maiden name of a woman later known by the married name Delilah Savage. When she was arrested, she went by the last name of her common-law husband."

"Yeah, who? What name?"

"Calhoun."

Bobby dropped the sandwich onto the wax paper on the hood of his car and stared off at Lady Liberty and the skyline. His eyes followed a slow, stubborn tug that grunted a freighter out toward the Narrows. Beyond it laid the twisted heap of Staten Island.

"As in Rodney Calhoun?"

"Her arrest file says she claimed Rodney Calhoun and Delilah Toole, aka Delilah Savage, founded Lethal Injection Records in the mideighties. She was a Baruch College business grad. They used about ten grand of his seed money to start what is now a three-hundred-million-dollar company. Delilah had fifty-one percent. Rodney had forty-nine. He came up with the seed money. She wrote the business plan. She was smarter than him. Or at least she thought she was. She had two kids so she made sure she gave herself controlling interest. I don't think Rodney understood it at the time, but he signed the papers. He was a degenerate gambler, a druggie, thought of himself as a ladies' man."

"How do you know all this?"

"All in the file, the probation sentencing report. Looks like the record company got in trouble early on because Rodney put money up his nose and gambled like a fool."

"Who'd he owe?"

"Organized Crime Unit says he owed Vito 'Sleighride' Santa a bundle."

"And when Delilah found out, she probably went nuts, and so he went on the street to bail it out," Bobby said. "And got deeper into Sleighride."

"Probably. But the Staten Island DA said Delilah started moving drug weight."

"So she's doing time for drugs?"

"Yep."

"Under the Rockefeller laws."

"Twenty-five to life."

"Don't tell me, the arresting officer was . . ."

"James Ford."

Bobby thought of Cookie Calhoun's dying words to Dianne Rattigan: *She's doing Rodney's time, don't tell her, don't tell her, don't tell her . . .*

But why didn't Cookie want to tell her? Bobby wondered.

"This was how long ago?"

"Sixteen years."

"Her daughter Samantha was what, fourteen?"

"Thirteen, from a previous marriage. Samantha's biological father died of a heroin overdose when she was a kid. She was in a boarding school. She hated Rodney. Rodney didn't get along with her. Typical blended-family stuff. Delilah wanted nothing but the best for her. Proper schooling, a star athlete, Little Miss Proper. But it cost money to keep young Samantha in school. Her son with Rodney had just turned eleven. He was in a boarding school, too. She didn't want her kids raised the way she'd been, in a housing project. She started a rap label as a way of getting the money to raise her kids in a boarding school where everyone sounds like Donnie and Marie Osmond. And as a record mogul, Delilah Toole Savage Calhoun always put on a big antidrug front."

"She had an eleven-year-old son with Rodney Calhoun at the time?"

Patrick held up a finger as he chewed his bite of gyro, washed it down with a gulp of Mountain Dew. "Yeah, the courts gave him to an aunt, Delilah's sister, to raise."

"Where?"

"Richmond projects in Staten Island, where Delilah grew up."

"RIP? What was the aunt's name?"

"Lynette Toole Lewis."

"Was the kid's name Ignatius?"

Patrick nodded and said, "Iggy Lewis."

"That's why Iglew's hell-bent on changing these Rockefeller laws. He's been trying to get his own mother out of the can."

"Fat chance."

"*Phat* with a *ph,* which means *good,* if you give a *fat* with an *f* enough wad of money to the right gubernatorial candidate."

"Now that *is* Intel domain. Bribing a public official."

"Patrick, I think the only one in the way of Santa, Ford, and Deity getting control of Lethal Injection, which was a license to print legal money as rap took off in the eighties, was Rodney's common-law wife, Delilah. If they killed her, it would have raised all kinds of red flags. And so Rodney set her up, planting drugs in her car. No one was *not* going to believe a rap-label owner was into drugs."

"So she was set up by Rodney and arrested by James Ford?"

"Right."

"It says once she was busted, she signed over her piece of the floundering company to Rodney, so that he could try to raise money for a good defense lawyer."

"That gave Rodney controlling interest of Lethal Injection. And both Rodney Calhoun and James Ford were owned by Vito 'Sleighride' Santa and this Deity."

"Yeah, and Ford busted Delilah in Staten Island, where they owned the DA and the judges."

"Who was this hotshot lawyer they hired to defend her?"

Patrick thumbed through the file as Bobby took a bite of his kebab. "Guy's name was Brightman. Joe Brightman . . . hey, isn't he the governor's—"

"Yeah, same guy. He probably went in the tank to send this poor woman into deep freeze for life. And then Cookie found out that someone was doing Rodney's time."

"And learned that someone was Delilah," Patrick said.

"And the identity of this Deity character, and to shut Cookie up, Santa or Ford, or all of them, made Rodney marry her so she couldn't testify against him. And then they had him move upstairs from Sleighride's Twoboro Club, where they could keep an eye on him. He was the front for the company. But then Cookie started threatening to expose what she knew."

"And so they killed her."

"And they put Rodney into a nursing home. And made him put his son, Ignatius Lewis, who was a legit rapper, as the front man for the company. To hide their identities, they had to give Iglew power of attorney for all contracts, taxes, and formalities. But Sleighride and Deity are the real secret owners."

"You think this Iglew kid even knows his father set up his mother?"

"My guess is he thinks his father is a zucchini, vegetating in a nursing home. I don't even think the mother knows it. I think Samantha has been trying to find out how her mother wound up in jail ever since. And I'm sure her mother wants to keep a low profile because she doesn't want to embarrass her daughter on the PD. My bet she's also been threatened that she'll be killed inside if she makes waves."

Patrick said, "Kind of makes sense that young Samantha became a cop. Joined the Hip-Hop Task Force. Trying to find out who framed her mother. Sad, too."

"I wouldn't start feeling too sorry for Samantha, yet. Ten years ago a young female cop rode a tail car behind a shipment of Sleighride's smuggled gold being transported through Brooklyn in a yellow van. That van killed Cookie Calhoun."

"And you think that female cop was Samantha Savage? Renting her tin?"

"It's a possibility."

"But she arrested Tu Bitz, one of her brother's main guys."

"That might have been a diversion," Bobby said. "When Janis McNulty started making noise last year about reopening her mother's case after her kid brother's first suicide attempt, Samantha might have looked for a way to cover her ass."

"As a way of making her look like she was legit?" Patrick asked. "Making a bust that she knew couldn't stick to deflect blame from her? And Tu Bitz?"

"Maybe."

"But that would put her in bed with the very people who framed her mother."

"Maybe until she could find out which one was responsible. Or maybe out of greed. Or intoxication. Hey, when I worked in the DA's office, we had a cross-investigation going between the mob in Philadelphia and New York. And I'll never forget that there were two young Turks down there, brothers, who wanted so bad to be *gangsters* working for Little Nicky Scarpo, that even though they knew Scarpo had personally whacked their own father, they became loyal soldiers in his mob. Just to be *gangsters*. On the other hand maybe Samantha's after revenge. Or justice. I just can't be sure. I don't trust what I don't know. I'm only four days into this."

Bobby ate the last bite of his sandwich. "One thing I know for sure is that all of the answers lead to someone named Deity, who has something on all of them."

"Who the hell knows his identity?"

Bobby looked off toward Staten Island.

THIRTY-FIVE

Bobby drove straight up Sixty-ninth Street to Fort Hamilton Parkway, made a right, and told Janis McNulty he'd meet her in the pizzeria downstairs from her apartment.

As Janis entered, Bobby was already sitting at a table, with two slices and two Cokes on the tabletop. As Janis was about to take her seat, she was almost knocked down by a gang of kids who jostled a bedraggled older woman who came barreling from the direction of the ladies' room, dressed in rags and a head shawl, carrying two dirty shopping bags, mumbling to herself.

"Chill out, people," Janis shouted.

"Check out the MILF, yo," shouted one white kid.

"She the singer from Bigga Wiggaz, butt like J. Lo."

"I'll wash out your mouth with my fist," Janis said.

The jostled woman didn't say anything, just kept walking for the front door in a bull rush amid the teenagers, and scooting out the front door, where she jumped into a waiting car service.

"Assholes!" Janis shouted.

Bobby checked his watch. It was 6:05 p.m. He was going to meet Herbie at the Chinese gambling den in Sunset Park at 1 a.m. He had some time to kill.

"You see those punks? Hassling the poor bag lady. Hassling me."

"The poor bag lady hopped in a car service?" Bobby said, laughing.

"Another fake. Nobody's legit anymore, man."

"Relax. You're wound up. I need to ask you a few questions."

She sat and sprinkled salt, pepper, garlic powder, red pepper, and

274

oregano on her slice and took a crispy bite, washing it down with a sip of Coke.

"I'm sorry . . . Brian's got me crazy. I found a rap song he wrote today. It's all about 'break-dancing and cloud-prancing, hip-hopping and be-boppin' with Moms in heaven.' I'm losing it. The more I learn, the more I worry. Did you know that suicide is most prevalent in males of mixed races between ages fourteen and eighteen?"

"No, I didn't—"

"That thirty thousand people a year do themselves? More suicides than murders. Some years three to one. Most, Brian's age. Right now the new shrink says he's in a worse depression because his suicide failed. Sometimes failed suicide attempts are a cry for help. Sometimes they make kids more suicidal, because they think they're such losers that they can't even kill themselves right."

"Maybe he needs new medication."

"They have him on some shit called Depakote, which is supposed to be a mood stabilizer. I think it makes him worse. He sits around all day eating nothing but cans of whipped cream and straight Bosco out of the squeeze bottle. One bottle of Bosco and can of whipped cream after the other, spraying it in his mouth. He says the sound of the whipped cream coming out soothes him because the whipped cream reminds him of the clouds where he's gonna meet Mama. I might need some of his medicine soon."

"Did you know that Rodney had another son?"

"I heard that. I never met him. I think he had less to do with him than Brian."

"What if I were to tell you that his son was Iglew?"

Janis stared at Bobby for a long moment, took a sip of soda, and pushed the slice away. "I don't need you messing with my head."

"I'm serious."

"Oh, holy shit, you're telling me Iglew is Brian's brother? Half brother?"

"Ignatius Lewis's mother is named Delilah."

"I've heard that name. Mom and Rodney used to argue about someone named Delilah. I just thought it was an old flame of his."

"Delilah had a daughter, too. Named Samatha. Samantha Savage."

Janis narrowed her eyes. "Wasn't she the cop at the Tu Bitz trial?"

Bobby nodded.

Janis rubbed her temples. "I got a kid brother upstairs, ready to kill himself, who is the half-kid-brother of Ignatius 'Iglew' Lewis and a hip-hop task force cop chick?"

Bobby nodded.

"And this has something to do with my mother's hit-and-run?"

"Maybe."

"How?"

"I think your mom knew Delilah was set up for a major drug bust by Rodney so he could get control of Lethal Injection Records."

"Rodney had a piece of LI Records?"

"He owned it with Delilah, and your mother threatened to expose it. And there's something else you should know."

Bobby looked her in the eyes. She stared at him, swallowed, and said nothing.

"Rodney was driving the yellow van that day, Janis."

Her eyes shimmered with rage, betrayal, despair. "Rodney . . ."

"An attractive woman cop might've been riding shotgun, in a tail car."

"Attractive woman cop? You talking about Samantha Savage? His step-daughter? Brian's half sister?"

He nodded. "Maybe. But that's still a big maybe."

"And you're fucking this pig?"

"What?"

Janis stood, pushed her chair away from the table, and pointed a finger at Bobby.

"What part of the question don't you understand? The *fucking* or the *pig?"*

"I think you should sit down, be quiet, and listen."

She stormed out the door, with Bobby following onto the rainy side-walk, where the lights of the Verrazano reflected in the dirty puddles.

"Janis, wait."

She turned, pointed a finger in his face, talking in a low, tight seethe. "You're telling me an avalanche of shit here, Bobby." She held up ten fingers and folded them down one at a time as she made her points. "Lemme get it straight. Okay. So you're telling me that my whacked-out stepfather whacked my mother. And maybe with the help of his *black* stepdaughter. Who's a cop. Who is investigating the same murder. And who's the half sister of a guy who is my half brother's half brother. On my mother's killer's side?"

"It's New York, people get tangled up in knots—"

"And you call her *attractive?* Which to me means you're *doing* her. Which means you're doing my mother's stepdaughter, but you wouldn't sleep with me."

Bobby drubbed his lips and said, "That never even occurred to me."

"There! You just admitted it! Sherlock Holmes uses a magnifying glass and you use your *dick* to solve cases?"

How the Christ did I get this twisted up? Bobby wondered.

"I never said I was doing her."

"But you did, didn't you? Tell me the truth."

Bobby figured she wasn't ready for the *whole* truth and it was none of her business, and he was sure he was going to hell anyway, and so he said, "No."

She stared him dead in the eyes. "You lie."

"Suit yourself."

"I'm gonna go upstairs, grab a kitchen knife, and I'm gonna get a car service over to that nursing home in Staten Island and I am going to cut Rodney's heart in half."

"He's not there."

"I don't care if he's not all *there.* I'm gonna kill him anyway."

"No, he's not there, there. He's missing. But I'm gonna find him."

"You work for me and so you have to tell me everything I ask or else—"

"You fired me."

She looked tired and wounded, but still beautiful in the garish night neon and streetlamps mirroring in the wet Brooklyn streets, framed against the Verrazano.

"I fired you so you'd make love to me. You wouldn't. But now you're *fucking* me. *Nice.*"

"You have enough on your plate."

"I want Rodney's heart on a plate. And his pig of a stepdaughter's."

"You're jumping ahead of yourself. And keep quiet. I don't want Mrs. Donatella to hear you."

"Fuck her, too. I'm tired of her bull—"

"Go back up to Brian. I'm trying to work this thing. I'm close."

"How the hell do you think it's gonna play for him to learn that he isn't responsible for his mother's death because we just found out his father and his half brother's half sister did it?"

"If that's true, at least he'll know *he* didn't. But I wouldn't tell him anything until we know everything. This is still a work in progress. I want to bring the kid solid proof."

She took a deep breath, looked at the sky, rain speckling her high cheekbones, and nodded. "I know why you wouldn't make love to me."

"Forget it, Janis, it was just too much beer on a forgotten rainy day."

He thought of Scarlett, a law student, normal, low-maintenance. If he were looking for a "relationship," which he wasn't, she'd be the one. Not Janis, with her grief, her suicidal half brother, a second screwed-up brother. And Iglew and Samantha Savage tossed into the can of mixed family nuts. Plus he couldn't get involved with the big sister of a boy Maggie was crazy about.

"A forgotten rainy day, huh?"

"Some days are best forgotten."

"A forgotten rainy day like the one you had with my mother, Bobby?"

Bobby stood in the drizzle and swallowed. He was drowning in entanglements.

"What?" He didn't know what else to do but play dumb.

"She kept a diary. Stuff like that she wrote down."

"Oh. Well, but . . . um . . . so . . ." He choked on the word *so.*

"So, thanks for not making me part of some freaky mother/daughter act."

"Janis, your mother was very special, but that's all I'm gonna say about—"

"Me, too. Except this: Mama thought you were a great guy. I second that emotion. And that's the end of that track."

"Was there anything in the diaries about Rodney, Deity, anything like that?"

"She stopped keeping them when she met him. Or if she did, they're missing." Janis nodded at him. "Listen, I gotta go back up and keep my kid brother from killing himself because of a hit-and-run the world chose to forget."

"I haven't."

"Thanks, for that," she said, then kissed his cheek. "I really needed to hear someone say so."

"So . . ." There was that word again.

Janis faked a smile and walked into the tenement. But for some reason that he couldn't quite understand, the word *so* echoed in Bobby's head. Then he thought of the word or initials *SO* on the cooler he'd kicked off *The Highwayman* into the river.

THIRTY-SIX

And so . . . Bobby drove over the Verrazano, through Staten Island, and south into Jersey, paying cash tolls all the way to Surfside Heights. He called Maggie from the road.

"You okay, Mag?" he asked, passing the gruesome toxic landscape of industrial Jersey called cancer alley.

"Mom has me grounded. Won't let me out to visit Brian. She has guards outside all the doors. She checks on me every twenty minutes to make sure I haven't tied ninety-nine bedsheets together to climb down to Columbus Circle."

"Well, Brian's not in a good frame of mind, kiddo, and—"

"I know. He emails me. He's read *The Lovely Bones* three times and *Five People You Meet in Heaven* twice. He sent me a new song he wrote. It's about being with his mom up there. I write him back. Telling him to be good to himself down here, Dad. But he just blames himself. I wish there was something else I could do."

"Maybe there is."

"Name it."

"I'm a little haunted by the initials *SO,*" Bobby said. "Can you maybe check out a Suzy, possibly last name O'Hara? I don't know the Social Security number. But maybe originally from Paramus. See if there's a Scarlett Butler at Princeton. If not, then see if there's a Suzy O'Hara at Princeton Law. Maybe twenty-seven years old."

"Okay, any other databases?"

Bobby remembered that when Steve Greco showed him the NYPD requisition for the security tape from the Verrazano Bridge, it was signed

279

by P.O. S. O'Hara in the police commissioner's office. That was a long shot. It was probably a male cop. And you probably couldn't count the number of O'Haras in the NYPD. But it nagged him. Because he'd also seen those initials somewhere else, somewhere few people would ever see.

"What the hell, also run it through the NYPD database," Bobby said.

"No problem."

"And send me a photo over the phone if you get some kind of match."

"Done."

"And you hang in there, Mag. Brian's problems will be far from over even if we convince him he's not responsible for his mother's death. You understand that?"

"Yeah, I do. It's not like I'm thinking of getting married, Dad. I just care about him. You understand, don't you?"

Bobby thought of Janis. And Dianne Rattigan. And people he'd met and liked and cared about and said, "Absolutely."

Bobby hung up and by 7:32 p.m. he took Exit 82C and rolled down the beach road to the Starfish and parked on the side road across from the parking lot, partially obscured by wild reeds. Through the binoculars he saw James Ford greeting customers on the surfside patio, shaking hands with his left. His right hand was Ace-bandaged from Herbie yanking on his thumb.

Bobby's first impulse was to get out, walk to the bar, order a Bloody Mary, and accidentally on purpose spill it over Ford's white suit. Then break all the bones in his face.

But he knew Ford had his goons around. Bobby was certain at least a few maverick Surfside PD cops were on his pad, taking free meals and motel rooms for young babes snatched from the Urge and Surge parking lot on DWI busts, offering to cut them loose in exchange for sex.

It was Ford's town, the way Wyatt Earp had owned Tombstone. He was sure the local judge was also a Starfish customer and owed his gavel to Ford's campaign contributions. Ford had made Surfside a smaller version of Staten Island, where he was now the big fish in the small pond.

So he had to be careful down here. Bobby could be shot, buried, and never found in a place like Surfside.

So he decided to just watch. Scarlett Butler wasn't working the bar. He sat and watched for over two hours, as the sky swirled from pink to orange to black, his body aching from the wicked river, the gymnastic sex with Samatha Savage, and too much time in the small car.

He switched to the nightscope glasses and saw James Ford approach two women. He kissed the cheek of Agnes Hardy, who was accompanied by a slender, frosted-blond woman in her late fifties, wearing a floppy summer hat and tinted glasses. Bobby made her for a campaign adviser. Scarlett Butler had said Hardy had eaten there a few times. Bobby realized he'd seen the campaign aide dining the last time he was there. *Probably laying the foundation for the Ford connection,* Bobby thought. *Whatever the hell that was.*

Bobby watched Ford, Hardy, and the campaign adviser walk toward the parking lot. He was ready to spend some of his ride back to New York tailing Ford.

But then they all climbed into the back of a white stretch limo, the door held open by a chauffeur. But something was wrong with the picture. The chauffeur was a woman. That in itself wasn't so startling. A lot of women worked as chauffeurs. But this woman was different. Familiar. She walked with the carriage of a toned athlete, looking splendid in the formfitting uniform. When he adjusted the nightscope glasses, he could see that even with her hair piled under the chauffeur's hat and wearing rimless glasses, the driver was Scarlett Butler.

He checked his dashboard clock: 10:02. He was cattle-dog tired but on an impulse he tailed the limo south onto the Garden State for about thirty-five minutes, and then the Atlantic City Expressway to the new $1.2 billion Borgata Hotel Casino, the big building standing majestically on the marina in an ever-changing spectrum of colors against the darkened sea.

Scarlett pulled into the eight-lane drop-off area, parked with the motor running as bellhops and valet parkers jockeyed to attend to the low and high rollers who pulled up in limos and pickups. Scarlett opened the back door. Ford, Hardy, and the campaign aide stepped out. Ford exchanged a few words with Scarlett, then turned and followed the two women through the front door, which was held open by a uniformed doorman.

Waiting for them was Joe Brightman.

And then the four of them disappeared into the frantic jumble of the casino.

A valet approached Bobby, writing his plate number on a ticket. Bobby waved him off. He didn't want to park the car. Instead he watched the white limo pull away and followed. Not until he was leaving the Borgata round-about did Bobby notice a big billboard announcing *One Night Exclusive Engagement Featuring—IGLEW!*

Bobby slowed as he passed the giant billboard of Iglew sporting a Lethalwear hoodie, dark shades, and a toothpick in his lips, sneering out at the passing motorists.

He continued following Scarlett Butler north, back toward Surfside Heights. After a few miles he felt foolish. He'd wasted his time tailing a woman who was trying to put herself though college, slinging cocktails and driving a limo. The one woman he'd met in the past week who might even be girlfriend material.

He followed her into Surfside Heights, where he was going to pull abreast at the first light, honk, and ask her if he could buy her a nightcap somewhere.

But then he saw her stop at Highwayman Complete Auto Care a few blocks from the Garden State Parkway, where workers toiled into the night. Scarlett climbed out of the limo, sans hat, her hair now a wild lioness's mane and sexy spilling down the formfitting chauffeur's uniform, and approached a tired-looking man in soiled overalls. She took on a different demeanor. This time she was bossy, impatient, jabbing her designer watch with an index finger, flailing her arms. Then Bobby saw Scarlett walk back to the limo, point a finger at the grease monkey, jab her watch again, hop back in the limo, and race off.

Bobby pulled up in front of the auto shop and got out. The air was filled with the noxious smell of oil-based paint. He walked up to the same guy Scarlett had just talked to and pretended to be lost. He asked how he could get on the Garden State Parkway.

"Go two lights, hang a right, then a second set of lights, hang a left, and follow the signs," the guy said as Bobby peered past him into the shop where he saw two Hispanic workmen spray-painting an SUV forest green.

"Thanks," Bobby said. "You guys work all night, huh?"

"Pain-in-the-goddamn-ass rush job."

"Must be a good customer."

"Boss's babe, so whadda ya gonna do?"

Bobby just nodded. "When Jimmy Ford wants something done, you do it, right?"

"In this town, bet your ass," said the guy from Highwayman Complete Auto Care.

* * *

On the drive back to Brooklyn, Bobby called information and asked for the name of an old lawyer acquaintance from his DA days named Harry Childs, of Kormel, Childs and Mercer. He got a recording but listened to an emergency nighttime number for Childs. He dialed it and it rang five times before Harry Childs picked up.

"Yeah," said Childs, woolly with sleep.

Bobby told him who it was and said he was calling to give a reference for a young woman lawyer named Scarlett Butler who had gone up for an interview.

"Bobby Emmet?" Childs said. "Christ almighty, pal, I haven't heard from you in *what?* Five, six years? Since before you went to the can. And you think a call out of the blue at twelve thirty at night when I have a summation in the morning is gonna help get some babe you must be banging a job? I wish this was legit. Because I'd make sure we didn't hire her, if we were hiring, which we are not, because we have a fucking hiring freeze on and we just laid off three lawyers and—"

"You aren't doing job interviews?"

"No, but give me her name, Emmet, I'll spam a Do Not Hire email to every lawyer in town for waking me up before my summation in the mor—"

"Thanks, Harry, you're a samurai."

Bobby hung up. Two minutes later the phone rang.

"Dad, there's no Suzy O'Hara at Princeton," Maggie said. "But there was a Susanne O'Hara who graduated five years ago. She's a lawyer, not a law student, and she's thirty-two, not twenty-seven. Could it be the one?"

Bobby thought of Scarlett wearing the *Suzy* nameplate behind the bar and telling him it was to deceive pickup artists. "Where's she from?"

"Paramus. I'm trying to find a photo. And any NYPD info on her."

They exchanged I-love-yous, and Bobby hung up and continued driving north.

He followed the signs toward Staten Island and the Verrazano Bridge. He had an appointment with Herbie in Brooklyn.

He dialed Samantha Savage, who whispered, "Hello?"

"You want to know who's responsible for putting your mother in Bedford Hills?"

There was a long echoing pause from the other end of the line. "If you're trying to make me feel smaller than the way you left me, congratulations."

"I want you to meet me. Alone. I don't want your brother, Iggy, to chopper up from Atlantic City."

There was another long pause. "How do you know?"

He told her where and when to meet him. Then he called Janis and told her the same.

THIRTY-SEVEN

The basement of The Great Wall Fish Co. at 4888A Eighth Avenue in Sunset Park, Brooklyn, stank of flounder, shrimp, octopus, cigarette smoke, beer, whiskey, perfume, and money.

The Chinese had settled Eighth Avenue in Sunset Park because the number 8 was considered the luckiest number in Chinese culture. So the address, that included four eights, made it the most popular gambling den in Brooklyn's Chinatown, where at all times at least eight games were running.

Gorgeous Asian women wearing micromini silk skirts and high heels sashayed through the room serving cigars, cigarettes, and drinks. The law banning smoking didn't affect underground Asian gambling dens. Young, pretty Asian hookers sat at tables waiting to be hired for good luck at the tables and sex for the winners. Six one-hundred-gallon tanks filled with exotic Cambodian arowana fish that sold for as much as $15,000 a head bathed the room in an aquatic hue.

Herbie stood at the craps table shaking a pair of red dice in his big hand, glaring at the Rasta with long dreadlocks and dark shades who stood at the end of the table smoking a Kool 100, sipping a Scotch and milk on the rocks, with a beautiful Chinese woman at each elbow.

"Come on you blood clots, mon, bring me some luck," the Rasta shouted to the women. "Make this big boy roll the snake eyes, mon. Kiss them monies for your boss man my little blood clots, mon."

The women kissed his fistful of money, leaving little lipstick stains before the Rasta dropped the cash on the green felt. The house croupier watched Herbie shake the dice, shouting at the players in Chinese to get their bets down. The rest of the Chinese men at the table threw down their money in a commotion of shouting and smoke.

Men stood at other tables playing craps, blackjack, roulette, and mah-jongg. Rock and roll blared from invisible speakers. Two hard-looking Chinese bouncers stood by the front door leading to the street, wearing 9mm automatics in their waistbands.

Herbie rolled the dice, a three and a four, and crapped out. He heard the Rasta whoop. Watched him collect his money and pinch each Asian hooker on her behind.

"Too bad, big boy, mon. Kill yourself. Better luck next life, mon."

Herbie looked at the Rasta, nodded, and checked his watch. It was 1 a.m. He walked to the exit to leave. One of the two bouncers opened the door. The other chatted with a hooker, shifting his weight from side to side like a little hard guy.

Herbie said, "Sayonara, amigos."

"We no hablo no Jap, Jewboy," said the little hard guy, turning to the hooker.

Herbie pushed the door open wide, then grabbed the bouncer by the nape of his neck with his right hand and clutched the second bouncer by his long hair with his left. He clashed their heads together like human cymbals. The hooker screamed. The bouncers fell, one out cold, the second little hard guy moaning, eyes rolling in his head.

Herbie said, "That's Brooklynese for night-night."

Bobby walked in and said, "Jesus Christ, I told you to just compromise them."

"Call it a rest stop on the road map to peace," Herbie said.

Bobby removed a 9mm automatic from one bouncer while Herbie disarmed the second one. The bartender raced through the crowd and leapt into the air, sailing at Bobby with a flying kick like a stunt out of a Hong Kong flick. Bobby stepped aside, threw a six-inch right-hand punch into his Adam's apple in midflight, and the bartender fell, clutching his throat like a boa swallowing a cow. Bobby frisked him. He was clean.

Panic shook the room. Hookers screamed. Men shouted. Some dove under tables.

Herbie shouted, "This is *not* a stickup. This is an ass-kicking. Everybody put their hands flat on the tables in front of them."

Bobby watched Herbie grab the little hard-guy bouncer and tell him to translate. "I don't know any fucking Chinese, man," the bouncer said. "I'm third-generation."

Herbie pointed to a hooker standing next to the startled Rasta, shoved a few hundred of the Rasta's money down her blouse, and told her to translate. She did, and all the people in the room placed their hands on the gaming tables.

Bobby noticed that the shaken Rasta was furtively dialing a cell phone. He nudged Herbie, who snatched the Rasta's phone and wedged it under his heel and ground it to an electronic mash.

"Hands on the table, *mon,*" Herbie said.

The Rasta complied.

Bobby checked his watch and opened the street door again. Janis McNulty entered. She and Samantha Savage eyed each other like a couple of attack dogs.

"The hell she doing here?" Janis asked.

"You rushed out without your blackface, Sistah Wannabe?" Savage said.

"You're whiter than Martha Stewart."

Bobby looked at them—one was a white rapper and the other was a buppie.

"Easy on the bitch bash, ladies, there's someone here you both have in common."

Bobby walked to the nervous, fidgety Rasta.

"Choo wan, mon? I just play some crap."

Bobby pulled the dreadlock wig off his head and the dark shades off his face, revealing a middle-aged, bald Rodney Calhoun.

"Choo doon, mon?" Rodney said, frightened.

"Ladies, say hello to your stepfather," Bobby said.

Janis and Samantha looked from each other to Rodney Calhoun. Each had lost a mother to Rodney Calhoun. One to a jail cage. The other to the grave.

Bobby said, "Samantha, say hi to your long-lost stepfather, the sweetheart who helped set up your mother for the drug bust that got her twenty-five to life. And got him control of LI Records. Janis, as you already know, the yellow van that killed your mother was driven that day by your stepfather, Rodney, here."

Rodney flailed his hands in front of him, his body spastic like a man being electrocuted. "No! He's wrong, girls! I swear to you. I'm a victim here, too. Like you two. It wasn't like that. Wasn't like that at all."

"Never seen two broads kill a guy before," Herbie said. "I could charge money."

Neither woman said a word. They just stared. Janis moved toward him first, the click of her high heel on the cement floor like a nail going into a coffin.

"Rodney, if you don't tell us the truth, I'm gonna go to plan B," Bobby said.

Herbie counted out what he'd lost from Calhoun's winnings, stuffed the money in his pocket, and gave the rest to the two hookers who'd brought him table luck.

One hooker translated in rapid Chinese to the cement-faced gamblers.

"I swear. I never set up your mom, Samantha. Never. I loved Delilah. And Jan, you have to believe me, I would never hurt Cookie. She was the mother of my son. I could never—"

"*Son?*" Janis said, her second high heel stabbing into the stone floor. "You haven't seen your *son* in years. Your *son* has tried to kill himself because he thinks he's responsible for what *you* did to his mother . . . my mother."

"It wasn't me, Jan! I swear!"

Bobby said, "Okay, then, Rodney. Who? Tell us, loud and clear, who did what to whom and why and for how much and when and all of that."

"I . . . I can't . . . you don't understand. You don't want to know."

"Okay," Bobby said. "Plan B for revenge of the babes it is."

Bobby reached into his back pockets and took out two handguns. He gave Janis a .38 Smith & Wesson and gave Samantha a Glock 9mm.

"He's all yours, girls," Bobby said, and started walking toward the door.

Rodney's eyes bulged. The Chinese dove for cover as Samantha and Janis approached Rodney with guns raised, outstretched.

Rodney backed away. "No! Stop them," he said, backing all the way to a stone, whitewashed wall, and sinking to a catcher's crouch, covering his head with his arms as his stepdaughters aimed their guns at him.

"Strip," Janis said.

Samantha looked at Janis in astonishment.

"Say what?" Rodney Calhoun said.

Janis looked at her watch on her left wrist as she pointed the gun with her right. "I'm gonna count down from ten, and if you aren't balls-ass naked, I'm gonna shoot you in each foot. Ten . . . nine . . ."

Rodney yanked off his shirt, kicked off his shoes, and unbuckled his pants.

". . . six . . . five . . ."

Rodney stood in his underwear, a middle-aged man with a sizable paunch. "Okay?"

"Balls, ass, asshole," Janis said, staring at her watch. "Three . . . two . . ."

Rodney pulled off his underpants and stood completely naked in the room full of people, his toneless body shivering in the air-conditioning, his privates shriveled at the point of two pistols.

"You must be the exception to the mool rule," Herbie said.

"What did my mother ever see in you?" Janis asked.

"You framed my mother?" Samantha said, shielding her eyes from Rodney's nakedness. "You put her in a cage. Stole her away from me! Ruined her life! My life. You sniveling, puny coward."

"No! That was all Ford's idea. Ford, and his squeeze, and Deity."

"Who the hell is Deity?" Samantha asked, yanking the slide on her 9mm.

"You don't wanna know, but all Deity's orders came through the chick."

"What chick?" Janis said, ramming her gun into Rodney's testicles. He howled.

"The same one who drove the yellow van," Rodney said.

Samantha put the barrel of her pistol into Rodney's right ear, mashing his face against the stone wall. He sobbed, his body racking with fear.

"Don't you dare try that pussy act with me," Janis said, grinding the gun into his privates.

"I beg your pardon," Samantha said, glaring at Janis.

"Fuck you, too," Janis said.

"I'll deal with you later, toilet mouth," Samantha said, pressing the gun barrel harder into Rodney's head. "I want a name, Rodney."

Rodney said, "Ford's girlfriend."

Samantha and Janis looked at Bobby, who stood blinking.

"The name, asshole." Janis cocked the hammer of the .38.

"I don't know her whole name. I think she was a cop. She tailed me in the car that day. They wanted me to kill Cookie. I couldn't do it. I drove the car home. I wanted to warn her. But all the kids were home. I was scared. I didn't know what to do. I tried to make her take the day off. Told her to clean the house. When I left the apartment, I got in the yellow van. I was gonna just go drop off the gold football trophies. And run. Run away. Keep running. But the chick cop in the tail car, I think she was Ford's bitch, she was there. Wearing a hoodie, big dark glasses, and a scarf around her face. Slick. She told me to drive. I refused. She made me get in the driver's seat. She put the gun to my motherfuckin' head. I could never kill Cookie. They wanted me to kill Delilah, too. I couldn't do that either, man. I'm not a killer. But when we turned the corner, here was Cookie crossing the street and I tried to take my foot off the gas to hit the brake, but the crazy bitch stomped her foot on my foot and held it down with the gun to my belly, and then she grabbed the wheel with her free hand and aimed the van right at Cookie, and then the van hit Cookie and I'll never forget Cookie's face or the sickening sound or the blood, and we just kept going across the Verrazano and my mind went blank and I had a nervous breakdown, and they really did put me in the hospital for a long, long time, all drugged up, and made me sign over the company to Iggy but with Deity as a silent partner and—"

"What the fuck was her name?" Janis said. "The one who killed my moms?"

"Believe me, Jan, you don't wanna know all of this. All you wanna do is go home and have a life and be good to my little Brian like you always been good to him and leave alla this shit alone, because it's bigger than me and you and everybody in this room and even bigger than you can imagine and, Samantha, I swear to you, the only way to keep your mother alive all these years was for me to make sure she never rocked the boat or they would have killed her inside and they still might now if—"

Janis said, "Her name, Rodney, or I swear on my dead mother I'll blow those balls right off."

"Suzy! That's all I know. Suzy. And she took orders from Ford and Deity."

Bobby walked across the room, was about to show him a photo that Maggie had emailed him to his photo phone. Before Bobby could ask, the door to the gambling den burst open. Two men in suits and wearing hoods stood in the doorframe firing automatic weapons. The room exploded into pandemonium. Chinese men and women stampeded for the fire exits, overturning tables, money and drinks and ashtrays scattering.

Bobby and Herbie fired back at the two men, who took dead aim at Rodney Calhoun. Samantha also crouched to a firing stance and attempted to fire. But there were no bullets in her pistol.

Janis turned to Rodney, aiming her gun, but before she could decide to fire, a round, red polka dot appeared in the center of Rodney's forehead, the flesh beveled inward on the wound, his head whipping into a grotesque crooked-mouthed angle like someone frozen by an eternal g-force.

Janis aimed in the direction of the bullet that had ended Rodney's life but clicked an empty pistol. Herbie marched right at the shooters, firing two pistols. He was spun around and dropped when his bulletproof vest took two slugs.

As fast as the two men appeared at the door, they were gone, one of them limping badly, slamming the cellar door behind them. Bobby made the limper for Scarano, and the second guy for Eric.

Bobby ushered Herbie and the two women out after them.

By the time Bobby reached the top step, he figured out that Rodney hadn't made a phone call at all. Bobby wondered who'd sent them. Rodney'd obviously sent Ford a text message from his cell phone as to his whereabouts. And Ford had sent his two goons with the sole mission of silencing Calhoun.

Mission accomplished, Bobby thought.

But Rodney Calhoun had told him who had driven the yellow van that day ten years ago that killed Cookie Calhoun.

And Suzy O'Hara, who went by the name of Scarlett Butler, mixing and matching the names of the heroine of *Gone with the Wind,* was going to give him Deity.

THIRTY-EIGHT

Bobby saw the Bridge Boro Ambulance parked outside as they approached Janis's apartment building. Georgie Gorgeous and a few wiseguys from Twoboro Social Club watched the commotion from the sidewalk, whispering amongst themselves as it neared 3 a.m., probably disrupted from their own all-night card game.

"Oh my God!" Janis yanked open the door before Bobby even stopped the car.

"Calm down!"

Bobby skidded to a stop, threw the car in park, left the motor running, and burst from the car and raced after Janis, who ran into the tenement, fully expecting to see a sheet-covered Brian being carried down by the paramedics.

Instead Janis froze in the lobby, hands to her mouth, sobbing as she saw the EMTs carrying Angelina Donatella down the stairs, an oxygen mask over her mouth, her gray hair frazzled, and eyes open and stunned and skittery. When she saw Bobby, she outstretched her hand and grasped Bobby's hand in her firm grip, her diamond ring digging into his flesh. As she grabbed him, her pocketbook tilted sideways on the gurney, and Bobby saw two passports visible. "Killing . . . me." Her moan was muffled by the mask.

"Please stand clear," the EMT shouted.

Bobby asked the driver, whom he recognized as Dianne Rattigan's partner, Paul, what was wrong with her.

"Heart," Paul said, rushing her down the stairs on a stretcher that they placed on a gurney. "She dialed nine one one . . . chest pains, trouble breathing."

Bobby nodded. He glanced at the passports again and figured the scared old goom was probably thinking of lamming when her heart exploded from excitement.

Bobby watched Georgie Gorgeous and his crew whispering as the EMTs placed Angelina Donatella into the back of the bus and slammed the doors. Then Paul hurried to the front of the ambulance.

Janis stood in the lobby, her back against the wall, regaining her composure.

"I'll be next," she said.

"Poor old dame is under a lot of pressure."

"I shed no tears for her."

"Someday I'll explain."

"Don't bother."

Bobby shrugged.

"I wanted that son of a bitch Rodney alive," Janis said. "So that he could tell his son that his mother was murdered. That it wasn't Brian's fault. Now what am I supposed to do? This kid can't catch a break."

Bobby watched the ambulance pull away, lights and siren going, and noticed that it was a different ambulance company from Dianne Rattigan's.

"You know who this chick Rodney was talking about is?" Janis asked.

"Not sure."

"Where you going now?"

"I was going to get some sleep, like the rest of the human race."

Bobby drove like a homing pigeon in the direction of the Gowanus Expressway toward the Brooklyn Battery Tunnel. He called Herbie, made him promise to get some kind of sleep, and told him to be available tomorrow because he thought this whole thing was coming to a head. Herbie said he'd be at the *Fifth Amendment* by dawn. Bobby dialed Patrick, unloaded everything he knew, and said he might need him the next day, too.

"When it becomes official, I'll be there," Patrick said. "By the way, I haven't forgotten about that second surveillance tape, the one Noonan and Scarano shot the day Cookie Calhoun died. But I keep getting queries as to why I want it if I'm not working that case. My bluffs and fakes aren't working. Either I go on the record officially or I have to withdraw the request."

"Damn. I wanted to see that tape to be sure."

"It's not a simple request for NYPD to ask the FBI for a ten-year-old surveillance tape on an organized-crime stakeout. It gets strangled up in ego, jurisdictional turf. But I do have a guy from Homeland Security who confirmed off the record for me that the two agents in the surveillance car with plate number US28K1 the day Carla Calhoun died were Tom Noonan and Lou Scarano. I'm horse-trading with him for a copy of my file on a Bay Ridge mosque for a copy of the tape. I might have the tape by the weekend."

"It could be too late. But I'd sure like this kid Brian to see it if it proves in any kinda visible way that his mother was murdered and that this wasn't an accident. I think I'm close to cracking this sucker. Once we got the yellow van, the rest'll fall in place. But I need something to *show* this kid, to keep him from killing himself."

"So who gets the reward money?"

"Well, I don't know yet."

"I guess don't a tell her, huh?"

Bobby was weary, his shoulders aching, his brain a little numb and fuzzy. "Don't tell her what?" Bobby asked, yawning. "Who?"

Patrick laughed. "I didn't say 'don't tell her,' dummy. I said dough-na-tella."

"What's this, an Abbott and Costello 'Who's on first?' routine?"

"You need sleep, bro. I was just asking if that crazy Italian woman is gonna get the reward. The one you had call-forwarded to me so I could descramble her blocked number."

"You mean Angelina Don—"

"Yeah, Dough-na-tella, Angelina Dough-na-tella. Did she get the reward money already? For telling you how to find the yellow van?"

Bobby stopped in midyawn, veered the Jeep toward the right lane for the Thirty-ninth Street exit off the Gowanus. He held his phone at arm's length, clicked the photo icon, navigated through the stored photos, and selected one of a woman in silhouette peering down from a window.

"Ho-ly shit," Bobby said.

THIRTY-NINE

Bobby exited the Gowanus, made a U-turn, and sped back toward the Verrazano and drove straight across the empty span to the Narrows View Nursing Home. He parked in the same spot where Herbie had done his stakeout.

He sat for almost two hours, nodding a few times as the overture of dawn whispered across Staten Island. He rolled up the windows, switched the music and the air conditioner on high to keep from slumbering, and spied the lobby through the nightscope glasses.

Then he saw three people appear in the lobby. A man and two women. One of the women pushed a wheelchair. Sitting in the wheelchair was a fourth person, a teenage girl who sat in a hospital gown, clutching a Raggedy Ann doll, her head drooped to the side. Bobby dialed the focus finder and saw that the man had his arm draped over the shoulder of the other woman. The girl in the wheelchair had the distinct Mongoloid features of a child with Down syndrome.

The trio stood talking animatedly in the lobby of the nursing home, but his view was partially blocked by an ambulance parked at a small emergency port.

Bobby needed to get closer, get a better angle and sharper focus. He slinked out of the Jeep, taking his 9mm, a pair of regular binoculars, and his nightscope glasses with him, and scurried along the Hurricane fence encircling the nursing home. He shut off his phone and settled for a vantage amid some scrub pines and rosebush hedges looking straight into the fluorescent-lit lobby.

He used regular binoculars this time, which eliminated the green hue of the nightscope. He dialed the focus finder again, and now he could see the man in the trio standing with his arm around the shapely younger woman as they spoke to the older woman who stood behind the wheelchair.

Bobby was certain she was the frosted-haired woman Bobby had seen at Starfish restaurant in Surfside. The one whom Scarlett Butler had chauffeured to the Borgata Hotel where Iglew just happened to be playing an exclusive engagement. She wore what designers called a power suit, and as she stood behind the wheelchair, she jabbed a finger toward the man and woman who had their backs to Bobby, her mouth gnashing words through scarlet lips.

The other two seemed to take the tongue-lashing like schoolchildren, heads slightly bowed—silent, still, abashed.

The woman made a grand gesture to the kid in the wheelchair, flailed her arms, gathered the fingers of both hands together, Italian style, and shook them at the couple in front of her. She then shoved the wheelchair halfway across the lobby in a fit of anger, and in the same motion she smacked the man standing in front of her across the face.

Two nurses ran after the runaway wheelchair and caught it as it spun in a circle, the teen half-sliding out of it. The girl in the wheelchair was crying now. Bobby watched the drama unfold as the woman raised her hand again, as if ready to backhand the younger woman. The younger woman backed away and was shielded by the man.

When they both turned away from the older woman, Bobby could see James Ford protecting a terrified Scarlett Butler.

"Jesus Christ," Bobby said aloud.

Now he tilted the glasses down the frosted-haired woman's pantsuit and saw the spaghetti-strapped, high-heeled sandals. He looked at the cellphone photo of the woman in silhouette peering down from the window of James Ford's Rumson house the night that Joe Brightman had brought Agnes Hardy there for a secret visit.

"Deity," he said, the word lost on the night wind that blew toward the Verrazano.

FORTY

It took Bobby less than fifteen minutes to drive across the Verrazano into Bay Ridge. On the way, he turned up the volume of his phone, heard the beep indicating he had a message, and saw there was a call from Maggie. He dialed her back.

"Dad?"

"What the hell are you doing up this late?"

"Late? It's morning. Up most of the night. Heard from Brian. He's totally depressed. Talking about the music he wants at his funeral. How he wants to be buried next to his mom. Heartbreaking. Scary. So I've been up all night, in case he needed to talk, and I dug up that stuff for you."

Fatigue blanked his mind. "What stuff?"

"You asked me to find out about people with the initials *SO* in NYPD."

"Oh, right, of course."

"We talking early-onset, here, old man?"

"What?"

"Forget it. Wait, that was a bad pun, forget that, too."

"Okay, get to the point."

"Does a Police Officer Susanne O'Hara fit the bill? I think she's the same as the lawyer I told you about earlier. She's from Paramus."

He felt himself rocketing through midair with a gorgeous blonde clutching his bulging biceps, looking out over the magic-hour sunset of Surfside Heights.

"You sure?"

"Yes. She went on NYPD at twenty, stayed on for two years before she got a three-quarters medical pension. Her police car got in an accident in Staten Island."

"She worked in Staten Island?"

"Yeah, this is where it gets good, Dad. Her training officer was that other guy you asked me about."

"James Ford?"

"Yep."

"While she was waiting for her medical pension, she was assigned to desk duty in the commissioner's office at One Police Plaza."

Bobby remembered seeing the signature for the tape requisitioned by Steve Greco. It had been signed by P.O. S. O'Hara from the police commissioner's office.

"So I did a more advanced background search of this James Ford," Maggie said. "I'd only done a business and employment search before. And I accessed several databases including Nexis-Lexis. But they had nothing. Until I accessed the *Staten Island Advance* archives and learned Ford was born and raised in Staten Island. Ford's father was a cop who ran for state assemblyman over there. He was humiliated by his opponent in the campaign and was eventually caught in a campaign-finance scam. It caused a big scandal that was reported only in the *Staten Island Advance*. He was facing jail time. He was so distraught that he killed himself with his own gun."

"Who ran against him?"

"Luke Patterson."

"Oh, God . . ."

"Patterson won. He became a big state assemblyman for like sixteen years. Four years ago, as we all know, he got elected governor."

"And Ford has been planning his revenge since. What happened to the widow, Ford's mother?"

"She was so upset by the whole scandal that she moved back to Brooklyn, went back to her maiden name."

"Donatella?"

"How'd you know? And isn't that the same name as the crazy woman that lives downstairs from Brian?"

"First name, Angelina?"

"That's her."

"Thanks, Maggie. Don't mention a word of this to anyone, especially Brian or Janis or Jimi Jim. They might do something stupid. Meanwhile, one of us better get some sleep. And it's not gonna be me. Love ya, kiddo."

"Ditto. Later, old man."

Bobby parked for the red light on Ninety-second and Fort Hamilton and saw Georgie Gorgeous and a few of his wiseguy underlings still hanging outside Twoboro Social Club, sipping coffees, looking weary, as if they'd been up all night. Gorgeous leaned on a new Cadillac, arms folded across his chest, staring up at Angelina Donatella's window, whispering to a fat, sweaty guy in a black knit shirt. The fat guy kept nodding. Bobby imagined them arranging Angelina's funeral the moment news of Sleighride's death reached Brooklyn.

Bobby parked around the corner from the McNulty/Donatella tenement, took his lockpick, gun, and a pinch bar with him, and entered a pre–World War II tenement on Ninety-first Street. He jimmied past the inside hallway door, climbed four flights to the roof, and crossed over three roofs to the McNulty/Donatella rooftop. He pinched open the tin-covered roof door and descended past the McNulty/Calhoun door, pausing to hear a drunken Jimi Jim say, "There's gotta be more to life than worrying whether that little fuck kills himself, Jan."

"Shut your filthy mouth," Janis screamed.

Bobby went down another creaky flight to Angelina Donatella's apartment. Her front door had a Medeco cylinder, which made it unpickable. He walked to her back door and had no problem picking the Yale lock. He entered and walked straight for the sliding-mirror doors of her bedroom closet. He slid one door open, and inside the shallow closet he saw a rack of Kmart housedresses, frumpy old-lady pantsuits, a couple of wool coats, and four pairs of Payless shoes. He stepped back and eyeballed the depth of space between the closet and the wall. He knew it had once been deeper.

Bobby pushed the old-lady garments aside and roamed his hands over the wall behind them. He found a flat 0-ring that melded into the pressed board. He snared the ring and it popped out and the false inside wall slid open. Bobby entered the eight-foot-deep walk-in closet, fingering racks of Versace, Armani, Donna Karan, and Valentino power suits. He bent and examined scores of pairs of shoes by Fendi, Anne Klein, Bruno Magli, and Stacia DKNY.

He took out a familiar-looking pin-striped power suit that the frosted-blond, middle-aged woman in Starfish had worn earlier in the night, when Suzy O'Hara was her chauffeur, the only one she could trust with knowledge of her movements, when she drove frosted-haired Angela Donatella, Agnes Hardy, and James Ford to the Borgata Hotel, where Joe Brightman greeted them at the entrance. In the hotel where Iglew was staging an exclusive one-night concert.

Bobby then saw a row of dummy heads bearing expensive wigs. Some dark, some redhead, and several frosted-blond ones in different styles she wore when she was out. He also found a matted-hair one like the one the "shopping bag lady" had worn in the pizzeria the day before.

On the next rack he found what looked like body armor, but realized that it was a "fat suit," which the Hollywood makeup people used to make skinny girls like Gwyneth Paltrow look obese in a movie like *Shallow Hal.* On a small vanity dressing table Bobby saw the prosthetic noses, the heavy eyebrows, even a dark latex mole she wore on her chin.

Bobby had read a column in the *Daily News* once about a makeup artist who said the easiest way to alter your identity was with fat padding, a large prosthetic nose, heavy brows, and glasses.

Angelina Donatella wore her hair gray and scraggy and a fat suit in the apartment, leaning from the window, cursing at people who dared to pass her window. That was her identity as a goomara put to pasture.

But when she went out, she took off the fat suit, the fake nose, the phony chin mole, and put on a frosted-hair wig, a $2,500 Versace suit, tinted Gucci glasses, and a pair of Fendi sandals.

Bobby found photographs of Angelina Donatella, some with Vito "Sleighride" Santa at Gurney's Inn in Montauk and down on the Jersey Shore, and others shot in Key West and Fort Lauderdale and Boca Raton. In these shots she had a small button nose, normal eyebrows, frosted-blond hair, and a slender figure. She was an attractive woman.

She was also the goomar of one of the most powerful La Cosa Nostra bosses in Brooklyn.

And yet she was even more than that.

Bobby found photos of Angelina Donatella and Sleighride at Disney World, Universal, and Great Adventure. In all of them they had a Mongoloid child with them. Bobby began connecting dots and figured that when Vito Santa made her pregnant and she gave birth to a Down-syndrome-afflicted child, Angelina Donatella set out to secure a worry-free future for herself and her daughter. Remembering that her own husband had been destroyed by secret tape recordings—which led to his political ruin, public scandal, and death by his own hand—when Angelina Donatella became Vito Santa's mistress, she also began secretly taping his private meetings. Vito Santa used Angelina's apartment to avoid being taped by the Feds. And was taped by his goomar instead.

Using the tapes and the secret child, whom the old gangster adored, Angelina Donatella compromised Vito Santa. She became more than some piece of "side ass." She became the most powerful goomata in New York. Enlisting her police officer son into the grand plan, and wielding those tapes and exploiting her handicapped child as leverage, Angelina Donatella vowed silence in exchange for control of a small, upstart record label that Sleighride had appropriated, as payment for a gambling debt, that she thought had potential.

She became Deity, a neo-mythical hip-hop alias, the secret owner of Lethal Injection Records. And if it took a little more blackmail and murder to keep it afloat and profitable, she had no problem doing both. She could always make it look like the normal workaday antics of that violent subculture. But when Cookie Calhoun accidentally learned that Angelina Donatella was the secret owner, that she was the mysterious Deity, Angelina ordered Rodney Calhoun, Cookie's own husband, to kill her.

When Rodney Calhoun balked at that mission, James's girlfriend, Susanne O'Hara, made sure that it happened. The woman who called herself Scarlett was equally determined not to wind up like her mother in Paramus, scrounging through life.

Bobby scoured the apartment, rooting for evidence that Angelina Donatella was Deity. The fat suit and the wigs and the fake nose added up to nothing more than a costume. The accoutrements of a schizophrenic. But they didn't spell murder or blackmail or conspiracy. Other than a collection of rap records, many by Iglew himself, nothing here linked Angelina Donatella to Lethal Injection Records or Cookie Calhoun's murder. Nothing here incriminated Angelina Donatella in any crime. All Bobby found was evidence that she lived a triple life, as a wacky neighborhood racist grouch, as a gangster's goomara, and a woman who liked to dress up in rags and designer clothes and slip out of her apartment through the trapdoor in the pizzeria below, as she had the other day, almost bumping into Janis McNulty on the way out the door, amid a swarm of nutty teenagers.

As Bobby searched through a bureau drawer, his phone vibrated. He looked at the number. It was Max Roth from the *Daily News*. He said hello in a soft voice.

"Remember you asked me to find out about that palimony lawsuit against Luke Patterson a long time ago?" Roth asked.

"Yeah?"

"I found something that was sealed about twenty-five years ago. Got it from a *Bergen Record* reporter who got it from a clerk down at the Paramus Courthouse. I mean, there's nothing terrible here. No physical abuse. No police reports. Patterson had a relationship with a chick, and when he took a mope on her, she filed a suit. It should stay sealed. Piece of shit. Except there's a campaign going on and—"

"Paramus? The case was brought in Paramus?"

"Yeah, by a woman, a single mother with a kid. Patterson was a young lawyer then. The woman claimed he said he would help her get her unfavorable divorce settlement reopened. Her husband was a lawyer, politically connected, and he basically took a cakewalk for a younger dame. The new guy, Patterson, promised to reopen the case, but never took a retainer or anything. He just gave her guidance. Young, single lawyer with a woody in his pants. What else is new? At best it might have been a borderline ethics violation. He was single. She was divorced. One thing led to another, the guy moved in for a while, shacked up with her. He never did get her divorce settlement reopened."

"What was the woman's name, Max?"

"Butler. Her ex-husband's name was—"

"O'Hara."

"You knew?"

"Makes sense."

"Patterson settled with her. The little kid was like eight. A girl. She called Patterson 'Daddy,' for chrissakes. The O'Hara woman had affidavits from schoolteachers saying Patterson came to school calling himself the kid's father. In the end he paid her like fifty grand to make it go away. The woman felt used and dumped. The same way her lawyer husband had used and dumped her. Then Patterson moved to Staten Island, hung a shingle with Joe Brightman, got involved in a local political club, ran for the City Council, then the Assembly, against some cop who killed himself. You know the rest."

"I know that little girl never forgave him," Bobby said.

"I hate dirty-laundry stories, but I might want to use some of this, ya know. If I don't, the *Post* will. What else should I know?"

"I'll give you tons more so long as you don't print anything until I give the green light, our usual deal, okay?"

"Deal," Roth said.

Bobby told Roth he'd call him the next day and left the way he came, so that he would not be seen in the street.

By a little past 9 a.m., on the drive back to the Seventy-ninth Street Boat Basin, it all started to make sense.

Both James Ford and Suzy O'Hara had something in common—both had parents who were hurt by Luke Patterson when he was an ambitious young man. Both wanted revenge. Bobby's guess was that after James Ford investigated Patterson's past he discovered the old paternity lawsuit. Bobby figured Ford tracked down Suzy, who went by the alias Scarlett, down in Jersey where she was a struggling young woman, slinging cocktails through college. One look at her and Ford was swept off his feet, as Bobby had been.

He probably urged her to join NYPD, where together he had a plan to use his police power to undermine the man they both hated. Ford was already working with his mother, the mistress of a big gangster, to gain control of a fledgling record company in Staten Island that had real potential.

If they got enough money and influence together, they could work not only to politically embarrass Luke Patterson but to entrap him in a campaign-finance bribery rap that could send him to jail.

Bobby couldn't think anymore. He needed sleep in a day that would not end.

FORTY-ONE

When Bobby arrived back at the *Fifth Amendment,* Ignatius Lewis was sitting in a deck chair facing his half sister, Samantha Savage.

"Let me guess," Bobby said, 9mm at his side. "You were out taking your tiger for his nightly walk and you just happened to drop by."

Iglew said, "My mother's in the can, my sister tells me my father took a bullet tonight, like I give a shit, and maybe this is no time for joking."

"Okay," Bobby said, still holding the gun, looking around to make sure none of Iglew's homeys were with him. "What can I do for you?"

"You got a DVD player or you still dinosauring with VHS?"

"My daughter made me get one."

"Good, 'cause I want to hire you and you need to see why."

"I'm not for hire."

"He's being blackmailed," Samatha said. "I told him you'd at least hear him out." She looked at him, lashes batting. "For me."

"All right."

"Can we take the boat out, I'm feeling kind of paranoid," Iglew said.

Samantha gave Bobby a pleading look. He nodded, untied the boat from the dock, climbed to the fly deck, put the key in the ignition, pushed in the buttons of the two parallel start switches, and brought the twin diesel engines to life. Bobby grabbed the helm and backed out of the dock and pointed south on the river.

He steered toward the harbor, where he cut the engines by the light of Lady Liberty's torch.

Still carrying his 9mm, Bobby walked down to the salon door, unlocked it, deprogrammed the alarm, and led Samantha and Ignatius inside. Ignatius handed Bobby a DVD, which Bobby clicked into the machine, and in seconds the TV screen ignited with a digitally recorded scene on a familiar-looking boat between Ignatius Lewis and Governor Luke Patterson.

"That's James Ford's boat."

"How you know that?"

"He took me on a cruise to nowhere once."

On the TV, Iglew plopped a briefcase on a coffee table. He opened it. It was filled with cash. It looked like a Hollywood remake of an old Abscam tape or the one that entrapped auto mogul John DeLorean. Only these were shot on high-definition digital and the picture and sound were perfect.

"Who set this up?" Bobby asked, hitting the pause button on his remote clicker.

"The Feds who worked with my sister," Iglew said. "They work for Ford."

"Noonan and Scarano?"

"Yeah. They told me if I made a contribution to his campaign, all legal, it would help make him do the right thing about the goddamned Rockefeller laws. Bad enough I'm up against Roc-A-fella Records and Rocawear. The Rockefeller laws got my moms in a cage."

Bobby hit the play button again. On the TV screen Iglew pushed the briefcase toward Luke Patterson as they spoke.

Iglew: All I want is for you to sign a law repealing the Rockefeller laws when it passes your desk.

Luke Patterson: I can't accept money to sign a bill like that. For any bill or anything.

Iglew: You can't use the money?

Luke Patterson: I can certainly use the money. Especially running against Agnes "Hard Cash" Hardy. But I can't take it in a lump sum in a suitcase. If you want to contribute this much money to my campaign, you'll have to do it legitimately. By check or money order. It has to be registered, and accounted for.

Iglew: I want you to take this money as a legitimate contribution.

Luke Patterson: I appreciate that.

Iglew: In exchange for a repeal of the Rockefeller laws.

Luke Patterson: I can't accept that. That I won't do.

Iglew: Then how about you take it and just give my moms one of your executive holiday pardons?

Luke Patterson: I might consider doing that but not for money. On the merits.

Iglew: I was told you needed money.

Luke Patterson: I need lots of money. But in this state the most I can accept is three thousand five hundred dollars from any individual. If I intend to ask for matching funds, and even then all they'll match is four dollars for every dollar on the first two hundred and fifty. So that a two-hundred-and-fifty-dollar contribution becomes a thousand with matching funds.

Iglew: I could get every nigger in RIP to contribute two fifty each.

Luke Patterson: That could be helpful, but it has to be done legitimately. It's very tricky. A councilman named Leveler in Queens went to jail for this sort of thing. Each contributor must fill out a separate card, name, address, and signature. If you give them all two hundred and fifty bucks each and suggest that they send it to my campaign, it will be kosher.

Iglew: That's a pain in the ass. I can't just give you that kind of loot?

Luke Patterson: No. But your company can give me a personal loan. If it's large enough, I could forgo matching funds.

Iglew: How much you need to not have to go along with these campaign contribution laws?

Luke Patterson: I need a war chest of fifty million to compete with Agnes Hardy.

Iglew: What if I come up with that?

Luke Patterson: I can accept that as a personal loan, as long as there is no guarantees that it's in exchange for votes or a pardon.

Iglew: I can do that. Here's the first ten mil—

The DVD ran out at this point.

"They have you trying to bribe the governor of New York," Bobby said.

"Is it enough?"

"Yes."

"What about the governor? They got enough on him?"

"Maybe. Even if it doesn't hold up in court, it could wreck him politically to show this is how he does business. Talking million-dollar cash payments with a hip-hop star. It certainly wouldn't win him any votes upstate or in the white burbs."

Samantha said, "That's what I told him."

Bobby walked back outside and Samantha and Iglew followed him up to the fly deck, where he restarted the boat and set sail past Red Hook and Shore Road for the Narrows.

"Who set this whole thing up?" Bobby asked.

"Brightman," said Iglew.

"And Ford," Samantha said. "They've been secretly running Lethal Injection all along. They don't own it. Deity owns it."

"I'm just the HNIC," Iglew said.

"That means 'head negro in charge,' " Samantha said. "It wouldn't look good for the company for people to know that a white politico and a white cop were actually running it, with a white attorney named Brightman."

"Now they want to liquidate the company because they all want out?" Bobby said.

"That's right. But I have the power of attorney. They need my signature. Three other labels have made low-ass bids for it. Two hundred mil and under. I don't want that to happen. I helped build this from a chump Staten Island label to a powerhouse. I threatened to go public and say I don't own the controlling interest in the goddamned company."

"He threatened to reveal dangerous stuff," Savage said. "That some phantom he never met named Deity owns it. That half the money can't be accounted for."

"That's right," said Iglew. "So Ford and Brightman asked me if getting my mother out of jail might make me change my tune about going along with a smooth transition. I said it would. I'd do anything to get my mother out the joint. So they set up the meet earlier tonight with the governor on a boat docked at the marina across from the Borgata Hotel. But unbeknownst to me, they taped it. As soon as the governor left, I went back to my hotel room. And a bellhop delivered this disc to my room. I watched it in the room. And then I got the phone call saying I either sign the sale papers for the company or they'll send the tape to the DA. They're blackmailing me. So I finally said, fuck it. I called Samantha. She took me to see you."

"Why didn't the two of you just make a public effort to get your mother a new trial a long time ago?" Bobby asked, guiding the *Fifth Amendment* under the Verrazano, gazing up at the immense span that had taken on a new meaning for him.

"She was already turned down on two appeals when we were kids," Iglew said. "Now she asks us not to work for an appeal. She says no politician would want to publicly associate himself with the drug-dealing mother of a rap star. But I know she was afraid that bringing a spotlight on her case might get us killed."

"She was afraid it would hurt me on the police department," Samantha said. "It certainly would've gotten me kicked off the hip-hop task force. I even lied on my NYPD application about whether any of my family were convicted felons. I said no. I wanted to work this job to find out on the inside who framed my mother and how. So I could expose it."

Bobby steered the *Fifth Amendment* toward Staten Island, circling toward Princes Bay.

Iglew leaned closer and said, "She was afraid of us getting killed. And it was made crystal clear to me through guys with no necks, Vito Santa's guys, that if I ever tried to publicly reopen my mother's case, she'd never make it out the jailhouse door alive."

"They knew any kind of scrutiny of Lethal Injection would lead to Rodney Calhoun, Vito Santa, and Deity," Samantha said. "Now that Sleighride is ready to die, and you're digging up the Cookie Calhoun thing, they want to unload the company. Cash out. Hit the road, have the money transferred to a numbered Cayman Islands account, where it will be transferred to a Swiss numbered account, and then get their own behinds out of the country."

"Who did they decide to sell it to?" Bobby asked, steering the *Fifth Amendment* toward the dense, darkened forest of Wolfe's Pond Park.

"To a Christian gospel label called Celestial Blue Records," Iglew said. "They want to turn LI into a 'clean rap' label. And they are willing to spend three hundred and fifty million for it. A cash bank transfer. Tomorrow."

Bobby paced the salon, weary and angry. "Who the hell owns Celestial Records that they can afford that kind of cash?"

"Agnes Hardy," Samantha said.

"Perfect," Bobby said.

"Legally, all she did was keep her options open," Savage said. "Brightman wanted to make sure he stayed in power one way or the other. So he had secret meetings with Hardy and Ford. Brightman assured Hardy that her mere presence in the race would put Patterson at a severe financial disadvantage. Make him desperate for cash. They thought that if they could have Iggy approach Patterson with a cash offer to support a certain piece of legislation, or a pardon, they could compromise him. On videotape. Which could force him to withdraw from the race. Which would mean she'd be the next governor. In exchange they wanted certain assurances from her."

"Like what?"

"That our mother would *never* get a pardon," Iglew said. "That the state would do everything to make sure my sister would go to jail."

"That Brightman would get some kind of appointment to a job with a lot of patronage," Samantha said. "Like running the state health and hospitals system. Or the jails. And Ford wanted to be appointed head of the State Highway Patrol. Do you know what this guy who parlayed a highway job in Staten Island could do if he ruled all the state roads of New York? He would turn that job into the Yellow Brick Road."

Bobby nodded. "They could put you in the can on the perjury rap. And hold the tape over Iggy's head."

"That tape is supposed to make me sign on the dotted line to unload the company," Iglew said.

"When's the signing supposed to take place?"

"This afternoon."

"And what do you want me to do?"

"They've been using me as their house nigger for the last ten years. Tonight for the first time my sister tells me Ford is the dude who set up my moms. They're setting my sister up. And now he's setting me up."

"You also have a half brother," Bobby said. "Named Brian Calhoun, who wants to kill himself because he blames himself for his mother's death."

"I want you to help me stop these motherfuckers," Iglew said. "Now, I could round up some homeys and go on a rampage. Have my boys shoot all their asses dead. But at the end, my moms is still in jail. My sister might still go to the joint. And now me, too. And this kid I didn't even know was my little brother, trying to waste himself. I want you to get the rest of these tapes back. I want you to help prove my moms and my sister were set up. All that."

"All that's probably impossible. No way to get all the tapes you made with Luke Patterson back."

"Okay, so I do some time. What's bribery gonna buy me?"

"First offense?"

"Yeah."

"Three years, maybe. Unless you become a cooperating witness against the rest of them."

"Asking me to be a rat?"

"Helping to put away the people who put your mother in the can isn't being a rat. It's being a son."

Iglew said, "I heah that. These people had it all sewed up. They had it all."

"Until that white-trash girl in Brooklyn hired you to look into her mother's old hit-and-run," Samantha said. "You pulled a loose thread and the whole thing started to unwind."

"Don't call her white trash," Iglew said. "I feel bad she lost her moms in all this. She raised my kid bro. And the girl can sing, yo."

Samantha said, "I guess I give her credit for never giving up."

Bobby asked, "You think Deity will show up at the signing?"

"My guess, yeah," Iglew said. "It's the score of a lifetime. You wanna see where every dime's going, every *i* dotted, every *t* crossed."

Bobby steered the boat toward the biggest compound on the Tottenville shore, where Iglew's yacht was moored at his dock.

"How many babes you got living in there with you, like little slave girls?"

"Bobby, maybe I should answer that for you."

"Let him answer," Bobby said.

"That's all part of the *act,* caveboy," Iglew said. "Nothing is what it seems. I never did time. I'm no Five Percenter. It's part of the image, the street credibility. All the homeys back home thought I was away in prison when I was in boarding school. Where in addition to a first-class education, I found out who and what I was, Brother Emmet."

"What's that supposed to mean?" Bobby said.

"What it means is that my brother—"

"Let him answer," Bobby said.

"Thinks you're cute," Iglew said.

"Cute?"

"We have the same taste in men," Samantha said. "Maybe it runs in the family."

Bobby said, "The honeydips in the pool . . ."

"Beards."

Bobby steered the boat toward the dock and looked at Samantha.

"You knew he was gay all along?" Bobby asked.

"What difference does it make?"

"Well, to start with, it makes me like him a whole lot better," Bobby said.

"How should I interpret that?" Iglew said.

Samantha said, "No, how should *I?*"

Bobby smiled, shook his head, and eased the *Fifth Amendment* against the dock.

"But just because he's gay doesn't mean he didn't send people to try to kill me. Black dudes wearing his clothes line, in Lutheran Medical Center. On my boat. At the bowling alley in Bay Ridge. In a Jewish temple in Crown Heights."

"Not me, man," Iglew said.

Bobby looked at Samantha. "Ford."

"I never killed anyone before in my life," Iglew said. "That doesn't mean I'm not ready now."

"Okay, at the contract signing, I'll take your back," Bobby said. "But I have priorities. Number one, keeping a kid who happens to be your half brother from killing himself. To do that I have to get proof he isn't responsible for his mother's death. Two, prove that Samantha was set up by these very bad people. Then I have to prove that your mother was framed. Saving you, Iggy, is last on my list."

"Cool," Iglew said. "How do you intend to do all that?"

"I need to sleep on it," Bobby said. "And we'll talk later. But I need you to promise that you'll do it my way. And that you don't tell another soul that I'm involved, or what our plan is. No matter how much you think you can trust them. Give me your word on that or I'm out."

Iglew looked at Samantha. She nodded.

"Word is bond," Iglew said.

Iglew nodded, rose, and walked out onto the deck toward the exit gate. Samantha paused near the fly-deck stairs.

"Thanks," she said.

"I haven't done anything yet."

"Yes, you have. You finally believed me."

"Yeah, well . . ."

"Care for some company?"

"If you stayed, I wouldn't sleep."

"Not a wink," she said, cinching the tip of his chin. "Some other time, maybe?"

"Some other time, positively. Right now I need two hours of shut-eye."

She kissed him and he watched her join her brother and walk off into his mansion on the bay.

A little past 10 a.m., the sky a riot of squawking gulls, Bobby steered the *Fifth Amendment* out to deep sea, where he could be totally alone. He dropped anchor. He thumped into the salon, locked the door, set the alarm, placed his 9mm on the night table, and fell face forward into bed and let the ocean rock him to sleep.

FORTY-TWO

Friday, June 24

The phone awakened Bobby at 1:13 p.m. The sky shook big fists of dark clouds, all the gulls screeching inland before the storm.

"Hello."

"Dad, I'm scared. He will do it this time."

"Calm down. What—"

"Brian is missing."

"Oh, Jesus."

"He called me."

Bobby sat up, his eyes still shut, his voice lumpy with sleep. "From where, Mag?"

"Wouldn't say. Said he wanted to say good-bye. I wouldn't let him."

"What's today?"

"June twenty-fourth. Tenth anniversary of his mother's death."

"Where would he go, Mag?"

"I dunno. I hung up on him. I know it'll make him call me back. He'll want me to say good-bye to him."

"How do you think he'll do it?"

"He tried cutting his wrists, tried drugs; I think he'll try something more certain."

"He have access to a gun?"

"Not sure, Dad. I'm scared."

Bobby's phone beeped with a call interrupt.

"Hang in there, kiddo. When he calls again, tell him that I have solid

313

proof that his mother was *murdered*. And that I can prove who did it and why."

"Do you?"

"Tell him what I said, Maggie. Keep me posted. Love, ya."

Bobby switched over to the other line and said hello as he saw storm clouds moving in from the blue yonder like the dust from an advancing army. Bobby hurried out of the cabin, into the afternoon, and up the ladder to the fly deck.

Janis said, "I know Brian finally did it."

Bobby assured Janis that Brian was still alive and would be calling Maggie back.

He started the engines as winds began to mount.

"Bobby, what am I gonna do?"

"You're gonna sit tight and wait for his call. This thing is ready to pop. I'm gonna put people in a room and get them talking. I'll get the proof we need that your mother was targeted for murder."

"I gotta be there with you."

"No way. It could get hairy."

"But you'll let Samantha Savage go."

"I didn't say that. But at least she can handle a gun. If the gun were loaded when I let you confront Rodney, you would have murdered him."

"I gotta be there."

"You have to wait for Brian to call."

"Don't play me, Bobby. I hired you, remember that—"

"I'll call you when I have the proof in my hands."

FORTY-THREE

Ford arrived first.

The dashboard clock said 4 p.m. He sat in the backseat, with Noonan fidgeting beside him, briefcase on his lap. Scarano slouched in the front passenger seat, and Suzy "Scarlett" O'Hara drove the green Navigator, windshield wipers flapping in the afternoon rain, passing through the twelve-foot security gates and up the circular path to Iglew's mansion overlooking Princes Bay. Gulls stood on the soggy beach in hunched, glum cliques, like day laborers waiting for work. The American flag billowed in the rainy wind.

Iglew and Ford and Brightman had argued all morning about where the secret signing away of the record company would take place. Ford wanted to do it aboard his yacht. The night before Bobby had nixed that idea and told Iglew that he had to control the environment. Iglew wanted them to come to his mother's apartment in the RIP projects. Ford laughed that away, saying Deity wouldn't be caught dead in a place like that, and suggested his estate in Rumson.

Iglew said no way and suggested the meeting take place at his seaside mansion in Staten Island. Ford told him he'd have to discuss it with Deity. Ford called back an hour later to say that would be okay.

And now Suzy O'Hara drove past the gazebo and the six-car garage.

Visibility was less than an eighth of a mile into the gray mouth of the sea. Tugs grumped and tankers groaned in the dense fog. The Navigator circled past the tennis courts and the full-court basketball court, and the aviary, and pulled up in front of the mansion that faced the sea.

Iglew stood between the two Corinthian columns with Tu Bitz and the bald bodyguard.

O'Hara parked the Navigator at the bottom of the steps.

All four doors opened. Ford stepped out, carrying a briefcase. Scarano and Noonan circled to the rear of the car, opened the hatchback door, and each removed duffel bags that they draped over their shoulders.

O'Hara joined Ford and climbed the wide steps to the mansion, followed by the two Feds.

"This ho can't be Deity," Iglew said.

"I'll slap your face, boy, you call me a ho again," said O'Hara.

Tu Bitz laughed. "Oh, shit, bitch be dissin' you, man."

"Can we go inside?" Ford said.

They walked through the marble foyer, passing the living room, music room, and kitchen, and into the Florida room, overlooking the sprawling back deck that interlocked with the in-ground swimming pool, hot tub, and boat dock, offering a gateway to the Atlantic.

Noonan and Scarano dropped their duffel bags, grasped their weapons, and checked the kitchen that lay beyond a pair of swinging doors and a bathroom diagonally across the room. The bald bodyguard shadowed the Feds, also gripping an automatic pistol.

"Now what do you want me to sign?" Iglew said.

Ford placed the briefcase on the table, opened it, and removed a sheaf of papers.

"Look them over, then we're going to need your signature," Ford said, handing Iglew a Montblanc pen. "In those bags you'll find thirty million dollars in cash, all in one-hundred-dollar bills. Plus a letter from Governor Patterson, pardoning your mother. "

Iglew said, "How did you get that?"

"With the same videotape," Ford said.

"First you framed my mother for drugs that weren't even hers," Iglew said, "then you compromise me and the governor on tape and offer me her freedom in exchange for the record label."

Ford looked around the room. "If you're taping this, well, it's just a push, isn't it?"

"I'm not signing anything until I talk to Deity," Iglew said, tossing the Montblanc pen on top of the contracts.

"Who the fuck do you think you're fucking with?" O'Hara said. "We have a videotape that will make you a jailhouse pen pal with your mother."

Ford held up a hand to O'Hara, telling her to ease up. "Why do you need to speak to Deity?" he asked Iglew.

"Because, I wanna look into the eyes of the person who's walking off with my label."

"It was never yours to begin with," Ford said. "You were a face."

"A black face."

"That's right. This company made you famous. Before you came here, you were loading trucks and doing rap battles."

"On the contrary, my own talent and the talent I attracted made me famous and the label a success and everybody in this room rich."

"If you didn't have a label, you wouldn't have been shit."

"I want more," Iglew said.

"What more?"

"I wanna *know* some things. And I want to hear it from the horse's mouth."

"The horse's mouth doesn't speak to the horse's ass," O'Hara said.

"Just for the record, Ford, this little ho can't keep her legs or her mouth shut," Iglew said.

"Your lyrics are barely literate," O'Hara said. "And you've made tens of millions while Ph. D.s walk around panhandling carfare, and you have the fucking balls to ask for more?"

Iglew looked at Ford and pointed at O'Hara. "I don't let the help—anybody's help—talk to me like that. Last time I saw this bitch, she was in heat, kneeling in front of Bobby Emmet. Not in prayer, I might add."

"That's a fucking lie," O'Hara said.

Ford looked at her, blinking.

"You don't believe this black bag of shit, do you?" O'Hara asked.

Iglew smiled, cleared his throat, and said, "Thou doth protest too much."

"If you sign the transfer," Ford said, "I can notarize it myself and then I can get these to our attorney and complete the sale and get your mother out before the election—"

"I'm not signing anything until I speak to Deity," Iglew said.

Ford said, "Why are you making this difficult?"

"I'm making it a mandatory requirement. I want to look Deity in the eye before I sign away the most promising rap label in the world to anybody. If Deity really owns it, make him show on the set."

O'Hara pulled out her own pistol and pointed it at Iglew, "Sign the fucking papers, pal. All of a sudden you speak like James Earl Jones and you're making demands?"

The black bodyguard and Tu Bitz drew their weapons. Now the two Feds brandished their guns.

Ford reached over and took O'Hara's pistol from her. He looked in her eyes, without uttering a word, and turned back to Iglew. "Sorry for that bit of stupidity. Sometimes I find it hard to believe I trained her. Or trusted her."

"What the hell's that supposed to mean?" O'Hara said.

Ford took out his cell phone, used the walkie-talkie feature to talk to someone using the same cell phone system, and said, "He's insisting on meeting Deity."

Ford glared at O'Hara. She shook her head no. "I swear, James, I never—"

"Don't let her jive ya, man," Iglew said. "She rode Bobby Emmet like a prize bull on his boat. I was following Emmet, seeing what he was up to. Saw it with my own eyes. She wore pink thong panties. But not for long. Bobby Emmet's a good-lookin' dude. Irish like her, all them hard-ass muscles like you used to have, Ford. You might have sent her to pick his brains for you. But she picked more than that."

"Don't listen to this cretin," O'Hara said.

Ford smiled, checked his watch, and then the sound of a motorboat rose from outside the window. The dinghy became visible about a hundred yards offshore.

The dinghy docked and Eric, Ford's muscle-bound bodyguard, stepped off first, offering a hand to Angelina Donatella, who stepped onto the dock dressed in a black rain slicker.

Eric led her through the rain, past the bubbling hot tub and the dimpled swimming pool, where Styrofoam chairs and inner tubes floated on the surface. They entered the Florida room of the main house.

Donatella stepped into the room.

"Who, pray tell, are you?" Iglew said.

"I am Deity."

Iglew cracked up laughing. "Expect me to fall for this stunt?"

"This isn't meant to be amusing," Donatella said. "I'm in a rush. Sign the paper."

"I ain't signing shit till I get some answers," Iglew said.

"Okay, ask the questions," Donatella said, waving her hands toward herself.

"Did you set up my mother to do time so you could get the record company?"

"Yes, of course," Donatella said, touching Ford's face and smiling. "My beautiful son and I did that."

"*Yes? Of course?*" Iglew said. "You admit it? You planted drugs, set up my mother to do twenty-five to life under the Rockefeller laws, and you have the audacity to admit that to my face?'"

"Um . . . yeah, that's correct." Donatella shrugged and smiled. "Now, anything else?"

Iglew looked at her, blinking, astonished. "You robbed me of my *mother*."

"I can empathize. But it was *business,* fella. And she'll be out *some*day. Someone else deprived my son of his father and me of a husband. *Forever*. So I more than know how it feels. But look at all you got in return. We're even giving you your mommy back."

"You didn't stop there, did you?" Iglew said. "You also manipulated and blackmailed my father. You tried to make him kill his new wife, the Calhoun lady."

"What can I tell you," Donatella said. "He was sloppy. He revealed my identity. She had to go. He couldn't stand her anyway. They fought like cat and dog; you don't know the half of it. But when push came to shove, he didn't have the balls for the job."

"He was such a loser that *I* had to wind up doing it," O'Hara said.

"Anything else?" Donatella said, checking her watch. "I really am in a hurry . . ."

"You left another kid, a half brother of mine, without a mother or father."

"He had a big sister," Donatella said. "And, hey, now he has *you*. And you have thirty mil and—"

"The kid is suicidal," Iglew said.

"We all have our crosses to bear. You get him the best shrinks your money can buy. Sign the paper, take the money, and go save him, save the world. Me, I have a million things to do. Three hundred million, in fact. I have lawyers to meet. Money to transfer, a plane to catch. I'm getting impatient. Sign the paper, Ignatius."

"I'm not signing shit, you raving sociopath," Iglew said.

Deity nodded to Tu Bitz, who stood behind Iglew. He placed a pistol at the base of Iglew's head.

"Sign it, Ig."

"*Et tu,* Tu?" Iglew said.

Tu Bitz said, "Ate two what?"

Ford and Donatella laughed. "Come on, sign the paper, Ignatius," Donatella said.

"No."

Now the bald bodyguard also leveled his pistol at Iglew.

"You bought my own friends," Iglew said.

"You have to learn never to trust anyone," Donatella said.

Iglew said, "I'm not signing."

Donatella smiled, walked behind Tu Bitz and Iglew, in long, deliberate strides.

"Oh, yes, you will."

"What makes you so cocksure?" Iglew asked.

Donatella lifted her arm from under the rain slicker and pointed her gun right at the back of Iglew's head and cocked the hammer.

"They'll find you here in a burning mansion and assume you are just one more crazy rapper killed in a hip-hop beef," Donatella said. "There will be nothing left but ashes. First we'll find your video system, take the tapes, then torch the place, and your mother will never get out of jail."

"You're gonna have to forge my signature," Iglew said.

"Nah, you're gonna sign," Donatella said.

"No, I—"

Donatella whipped her pistol four inches to the right and blew off the top of Tu Bitz's head in a deafening strawberry fog.

Iglew grabbed both ears, stamped his feet, let out a scream as he looked down at his lifeless comrade.

"Because I'll blow off the top of your head next," she said, her voice a whisper. "He betrayed you anyway. You should thank me for killing him."

Trembling, Iglew grasped for the pen amid the gun smoke and the pink mist.

"Atta boy," Donatella said, aiming the gun at him as he prepared to sign.

Then Herbie rose from the hot tub outside the bay window, tossed aside his snorkel, and burst through the bay window dressed from head to foot in Kevlar body armor, which Bobby had purchased from the Snoop Shop. The black bodyguard shot at him, the bullets thudding like spitballs and clacking to the floor. Herbie shot him as a muffled wail escaped from inside his armor.

Ford scrambled toward the swinging kitchen doors.

Bobby Emmett now appeared from the pool house firing his own 9mm automatic. Eric opened fire on him. Herbie dropped Eric with three fast shots. Then Scarano shot at Herbie, toppling him with a barrage of automatic fire. Herbie got up and marched after Scarano, who retreated up the marble stairs as he reloaded a new clip. He aimed again. Herbie shot him and Scarano slid down the white marble steps, leaving a crimson runner.

Noonan crouched low, snuck up on Herbie, trying to get a clear shot into the open eye slot of his body armor.

"Noonan," Bobby yelled.

The Fed turned, fired at Bobby. It missed. Bobby's bullet hit Noonan dead center in his chest. He went down. Bobby ran outside after Ford.

Iglew picked up Tu Bitz's gun and joined the chase after the fleeing Ford, banging through the kitchen doors.

Noonan rose, adjusted his bulletproof vest, and grabbed the legal papers off the desk, fired at Iglew, hitting him in his left butt cheek, flipping him onto the Mexican tiles in front of the door leading to the basement.

Iglew reached up for the doorknob, Noonan's bullets stitching a backward letter *S* on the wooden door. Iglew pulled the door open, taking another bullet in the wrist, and scrambled through it to the basement stairs, slamming the door closed behind him.

"You are going to sign the fucking papers," Noonan shouted. "I waited ten fucking years for this."

Bobby walked across the music room, aiming his gun. "Forget it, Noonan."

Noonan fired in Bobby's direction, the bullet smashing a Ming vase, and then he turned and yanked open the door to the basement stairs. To go after Iglew. With the papers. Bobby raised his pistol. He never fired.

Instead he watched the giant striped paw with the ferocious claws reach out and hook Noonan's neck, under the right jawbone. The 450-pound Bengal tiger lifted Noonan off his feet, like a carcass on a butcher's hook, and sunk his teeth into Noonan's rib cage. Bobby heard the bones crunching in the tiger's massive jaws as Noonan screamed. And then Noonan didn't scream anymore as the monster dragged him down the cellar stairs, his shoes banging on each step.

Bobby slammed the door.

Bobby rushed through the house after Ford, O'Hara, and Donatella. He searched each room as he heard Herbie stomping behind him.

He didn't see anyone. He told Herbie to search the attic. Bobby ran downstairs.

Outside, rain pelted the paving stones of the circular drive as Bobby rolled out the door. Bullets skipped past him on the wet stone stoop. Through the rain he saw Donatella running for the dinghy. To head back to *The Highwayman.*

Ford and O'Hara ran for the green Navigator.

It wasn't there.

Bobby shouted, "It's over Ford. I have everything all of you just said on videotape. Don't make me kill you in front of your mother."

Ford fired at him, the bullet gouging a chunk of marble from a Corinthian column. Bobby rose to fire back. His automatic jammed. Ford grinned, walked toward him. O'Hara yanked on his sleeve.

"Let me, James!"

Bobby pulled the pink thong panties she'd tossed him on the boat, hand-embroidered with the initials *SO.*

"You might want these back, honey buns," Bobby said.

Ford looked at the panties, "I gave you those—"

"James . . . baby . . . it was part of a *game* . . . I never fucked him . . . it was just—"

"A whole lot of fun," Bobby said.

"You *fucked* him," Ford screamed.

"Nooooo," she said. "I did everything you asked. I killed for you. I killed the Calhoun woman, that bigmouthed Dianne Rattigan hag, but I never fucked him, baby."

Ford shot her in the open mouth. "Yes, you *did.*"

"Actually, just for the record, no, she *didn't,*" Bobby said. "Baby . . ."

Ford looked down at her, then up at him, aimed his gun. "You fuuuck!"

Samantha Savage appeared from behind the gazebo, aiming her gun at Ford's head. "Drop the gun, Ford."

Startled, he spun toward her. Aiming his gun. She killed him. Fast. One shot in the heart. She looked down at him. Blinked. Then she emptied her gun into him in one long automatic barrage.

Angelina Donatella was almost in the dinghy. She froze as she watched her son die, her eyes filling with horror. She stalked out of the water toward Samantha. Her gun raised in the rain as she splashed up the driveway. "You killed my boy."

Bobby shouted, "Sammy! Watch—"

Savage spun. Tried to fire at Donatella. But her gun was empty. As Donatella took dead aim at her, a pair of headlights switched on behind her, igniting the long silver needles of rain. The green Navigator hurtled at Angelina Donatella, picking up more speed with every split second.

Angelina Donatella lived only long enough to see Janis McNulty's face behind the wheel as she splattered Donatella's life across the windshield.

Rain fell and a minute passed as slowly as had the last ten awful years.

"How the hell did she get here?" Bobby asked Samantha, nodding to Janis.

"She called me," Samatha said. "She insisted. What the hell, I mean, we're almost, sort of, kind of like *sisters*. So I told her to come and stay out of the way."

Bobby's cell phone rang as he sat on the stoop in the falling rain waiting for his brother Patrick to come and clerk the mayhem.

"Hey, Mag."

"Dad, Brian called me to say good-bye."

"Where is he?"

"He called me from the Verrazano Bridge. He was gonna jump. I told him you had the proof that his mother's death wasn't his fault. I hope you're telling the truth. I told him to meet us at his place. He said he was going home."

EPILOGUE

Before leaving Ignatius Lewis's house, Bobby removed the secretly recorded videotapes from the Florida room on which James Ford, Susanne O'Hara, and Angelina Donatella admitted that they had planned and carried out the murder of Cookie Calhoun.

Patrick Emmet had also finally got his hands on the ten-year-old FBI surveillance tape shot by Noonan and Scarano that showed Susanne O'Hara steering the yellow van directly at Cookie Calhoun in what was an obvious and intentional murder.

Patrick was also investigating Joe Brightman's political chicanery in the gubernatorial race. But on face value, Patrick didn't know if a case could be made against Brightman. There was probably going to be a federal and NYPD turf war over the case. One way or the other, Patrick was going to make points and probably get a promotion.

But Bobby was not going to offer up the tape of Iglew trying to bribe Governor Patterson. The letter of pardon that Ford had tried to use to entice Iglew to sign the Lethal Injection sale was bogus.

Agnes Hardy had not done anything illegal in trying to purchase a record label. Anyone who might have implicated her in anything else illegal was now dead.

Later that night, Bobby and Janis McNulty played all the tapes for Brian Calhoun in the kid's living room in Bay Ridge. Brian watched, rolling the John F. Kennedy half-dollar through the fingers of his right hand until he got to the part where Susanne O'Hara admitted she'd killed Brian's mother. Maggie squeezed Brian's left hand as he flipped the half-dollar out the window of his apartment, into the street where his mother had been murdered.

325

Traffic buzzed along, heading for the Verrazano Bridge.

His half brother Iglew called from the hospital to say he wanted to discuss signing Bigga Wiggaz to a three-record deal.

"Tell that asshole we already have a contract," Jimi Jim said.

"He's my brother," Brian said.

"Tell him we'll have our people contact his people," Janis said.

Two days later, Izzy Gleason made a motion in front of Judge Cranberry to set aside the conviction of Delilah Toole. Cranberry called Izzy to the bench.

"Where is Francisca," the judge asked. "She's the absolute best I ever—"

"She told me she'll be throwing herself on the mercy of the court this afternoon."

Izzy walked back to the defense table where Delilah Toole sat in nervous anxiety. Izzy winked at Bobby and Samantha Savage, who fidgeted in the mostly empty courtroom. Iglew sat in the same row, dressed in a Brooks Brothers suit. Judge Cranberry then declared the conviction of Delilah Toole vacated.

Samantha Savage and Ignatius Lewis then leapt to their feet and embraced their mother.

On July 1, Bobby Emmet sat at the helm of the fly deck of the *Fifth Amendment,* revving the twin diesel engines, ready to set sail with Maggie to visit his mother in Marco Island, Florida. Patrick would be flying down to meet him. As Bobby walked down to disengage the rope from the dock cleat, he saw Brian and Janis McNulty and Samantha Savage standing on the planks of slip 99A.

"You mind if we say good-bye to Maggie?" Brian asked.

"Sure, she's inside," Bobby said.

"Hi, Bobby," Samantha said as she followed Brian on board.

"Hey, Sammy," Bobby said, watching her walk in her little white shorts and sandals into the salon.

Bobby and Janis were now alone on deck.

"Thanks for everything," Janis said. "The whole family, me, Brian, Jimi Jim, Samantha, Iggy . . ."

"I did it for Cookie."

"You were right, of course, you and me could never . . ."

"My friendships usually last longer than my romances anyway."

"But, on the other hand, you and Samantha . . ."

"I treated that lady badly."

"She digs you."

"She shouldn't."

"She knows you did what you thought was right at the time. The DA said they might drop her charges if she resigns from NYPD and forfeits her pension. She'll probably take the dealio and run security for her brother."

"Too bad. She was a good cop until she crossed the line."

"I won't play cupid, Bobby. I just wanted to let you know where her head's at. She's too uptight and formal to let you know herself."

Bobby nodded.

Maggie, Brian, and Samantha walked out of the salon with a blast of Eminem at their backs. They all kissed good-bye. As she was leaving the boat, Samantha Savage stopped in front of Bobby.

"Thanks for giving me back my mother. For helping my brother. For every—"

"Can I call you when I get back? Dinner or something?"

Samantha glared at Janis, then smiled at Bobby. "Aff—that'd be cool."

She kissed him. He flattened his palm against her lower back and kissed her.

"Check yuse out, yo," Maggie said with a war whoop, and she and Brian laughed.

Samantha climbed off the boat onto the dock, abashed.

Eminem thumped as Bobby tossed the rope onto the dock and shoved the boat away with a long pole.

He waved. They waved back. Then Bobby climbed to the fly deck and backed out into the river.

"She's a ha-ha-hottie, old man," Maggie said.

"Shut up, squirt. And turn down that goddamned music, will ya."

Then Bobby steered the boat downriver, out into the glittering harbor, and in twenty-odd minutes he was passing through the Narrows, under the magnificent Verrazano Bridge, and off into the wild blue yonder.

ACKNOWLEDGMENTS

I am indebted to Alonzo Westbrook's *HipHoptionary*, a vital guidebook to modern urban slang. Thanks to my daughters Katie and Nell, who helped give this manuscript its Bay Ridge white-chick street cred. And to Mitchell Ivers, my editor, for his always excellent ideas and notes. And as always to my agent Esther Newberg, whose word is bond.